JENNIFER ESTEP

Poison
PROMISE

AN ELEMENTAL ASSASSIN BOOK

POCKET BOOKS

New York   London   Toronto   Sydney   New Delhi

Pocket Books
A Division of Simon & Schuster, Inc.
1230 Avenue of the Americas
New York, NY 10020

This book is a work of fiction. Any references to historical events, real people, or real places are used fictitiously. Other names, characters, places, and events are products of the author's imagination, and any resemblance to actual events or places or persons, living or dead, is entirely coincidental.

First Pocket Books paperback edition August 2014

POCKET and colophon are registered trademarks of Simon & Schuster, Inc.

For information about special discounts for bulk purchases, please contact Simon & Schuster Special Sales at 1-866-506-1949 or business@simonandschuster.com.

The Simon & Schuster Speakers Bureau can bring authors to your live event. For more information or to book an event, contact the Simon & Schuster Speakers Bureau at 1-866-248-3049 or visit our website at www.simonspeakers.com.

Manufactured in the United States of America

10 9 8 7 6 5 4 3 2 1

ISBN 978-1-4767-7150-2
ISBN 978-1-4767-7152-6 (ebook)

Praise for Jennifer Estep's thrilling Elemental Assassin series

"Watch out, world, here comes Gin Blanco. Funny, smart, and dead sexy."

—Lilith Saintcrow, *New York Times* bestselling author

"A raw, gritty, and compelling walk on the wild side."

—Nalini Singh, *New York Times* bestselling author

"This series kicked off with a bang, and the action hasn't let up since."

—*Fresh Fiction*

"Jennifer Estep is a dark, lyrical, and fresh voice in urban fantasy. . . . Gin is an assassin to die for."

—Adrian Phoenix, author of *On Midnight Wings*

"Man, I love this series."

—*Yummy Men & Kick Ass Chicks*

THE SPIDER

"The 10th Elemental Assassin novel is actually a prequel: The ever excellent Estep takes readers back in time to a significant assignment that helped mold Gin Blanco into the deadly assassin known as the Spider. This origin story is tough and compelling, dramatically showcasing the consequences of the choices Gin makes."

—*RT Book Reviews* (Top Pick!)

HEART OF VENOM

A Goodreads and *RT Book Reviews* nominee

"Amazing series. . . . Estep is one of those rare authors who excels at both action set pieces and layered character development."

—*RT Book Reviews* (Top Pick!)

"Wonderfully intense and graphic fight scenes, a plot that doesn't slow down, and bad guys that bring new meaning to the word *sadistic*. . . . Continues the Elemental Assassin series tradition of high-octane, heart-pounding action with an expert assassin who will go above and beyond to protect those she loves."

—*All Things Urban Fantasy*

DEADLY STING

"Classic Estep with breathtaking thrills, coolly executed fights, and a punch of humor."

—*RT Book Reviews* (Top Pick!)

"This book is brimming with suspense and fast-paced action. There's never a dull moment!"

—*Under the Covers Book Blog*

WIDOW'S WEB

"Estep has found the perfect recipe for combining kick-butt action and high-stakes danger with emotional resonance."

—*RT Book Reviews* (Top Pick!)

"Filled with such emotional and physical intensity that it leaves you happily exhausted by the end."

—*All Things Urban Fantasy*

BY A THREAD

A Goodreads and *RT Book Reviews* nominee

"Filled with butt-kicking action, insidious danger, and a heroine with her own unique moral code, this thrilling story is top-notch. Brava!"

—*RT Book Reviews* (Top Pick!)

"Gin is stronger than ever, and this series shows no signs of losing steam."

—*Fiction Vixen*

SPIDER'S REVENGE

A RITA nominee and an *RT Book Reviews* Editor's Choice Pick

"Explosive . . . outstanding. . . . Hang on, this is one smackdown you won't want to miss!"

—*RT Book Reviews* (Top Pick!)

"A whirlwind of tension, intrigue, and mind-blowing action that leaves your heart pounding."

—*Smexy Books*

TANGLED THREADS

"Interesting storylines, alluring world, and fascinating characters. That is what I've come to expect from Estep's series."

—*Yummy Men & Kick Ass Chicks*

"The story had me whooping with joy and screaming in outrage, just as all really good books always do."

—*Literary Escapism*

VENOM

"Estep has really hit her stride with this gritty and compelling series. . . . Brisk pacing and knife-edged danger make this an exciting page-turner."

—*RT Book Reviews* (Top Pick!)

"Since the first book in the series, I have been entranced by Gin. . . . Every book has been jam-packed with action and mystery, and once I think it can't get any better, *Venom* comes along and proves me completely wrong."

—*Literary Escapism*

WEB OF LIES

"Hard-edged and compelling. . . . Gin Blanco is a fascinatingly pragmatic character, whose intricate layers are just beginning to unravel."

—*RT Book Reviews*

"One of the best urban fantasy series I've ever read. The action is off the charts, the passion is hot, and her cast of secondary characters is stellar."

—*The Romance Dish*

SPIDER'S BITE

"The fast pace, clever dialogue, and intriguing heroine help make this new series launch one to watch."

—*Library Journal*

"Bodies litter the pages of this first entry in Estep's engrossing urban fantasy series. . . . Fans will love it."

—*Publishers Weekly*

To my mom, my grandma, and Andre—
for your love, patience, and everything else you've
given to me over the years.

To my papaw—you will be missed.

ACKNOWLEDGMENTS

Once again, my heartfelt thanks go out to all the folks who help turn my words into a book.

Thanks go to my agent, Annelise Robey, and editors, Adam Wilson and Lauren McKenna, for all their helpful advice, support, and encouragement. Thanks also to Trey Bidinger.

Thanks to Tony Mauro for designing another terrific cover, and thanks to Louise Burke, Lisa Litwack, and everyone else at Pocket Books and Simon & Schuster for their work on the cover, the book, and the series.

And finally, a big thanks to all the readers. Knowing that folks read and enjoy my books is truly humbling, and I'm glad that you are all enjoying Gin and her adventures.

I appreciate you all more than you will ever know.

Happy reading!

✻ 1 ✻

"Someone has a birthday coming up."

The voice in my ear rumbled in a low, slow way that was as sexy as all get-out, but I still grimaced at his words.

"Don't remind me," I grumbled. "I've been trying to forget about *that* particular date on the calendar for weeks now."

Holding a backpack in one hand and my phone in the other, I stopped inside the doorway, letting the college students stream out of the classroom and move into the corridor. They hurried toward the exit, along with the professor, all eager to get away from the hallowed halls of learning as quickly as they could, but I stayed where I was until the sounds of their cheerful chatter had faded away and I could resume my own conversation.

"What's so bad about turning thirty-one?" Owen asked.

Even though he couldn't see me, since we were talking on the phone, I still shrugged as I stepped out of the classroom and ambled toward the doors at the end of the corridor.

"Nothing, on the face of it. It's just another day and just another number. I won't feel any different before, during, or after that day than I do on any other. But this time of year . . . bad things always seem to happen around my birthday."

"Oh." My lover's voice slipped from sexy and teasing to quiet and serious in a heartbeat. He didn't say anything else. He knew exactly what *bad things* I was referring to. My mother and my older sister being murdered. Thinking that Bria, my baby sister, had also been killed. Fletcher Lane, my mentor, being tortured to death.

"I just . . . don't want to jinx things by talking about my birthday," I said. "And I don't even want to *think* about the surprise party Finn is planning."

Silence.

"What party?" Owen finally asked, three seconds too late to be believable.

"The always party."

"What?" he asked again, genuinely confused this time.

"The always party. The party that Finn *always* plans for me. The one I *always* tell him I would rather do without. The one the sneaky bastard *always* manages to surprise me with anyway, just when I think that I'm finally safe from him and his shenanigans."

Finnegan Lane, my foster brother, thought that birthdays were a time of great celebration, jubilation, and excitement and should *always* be marked with cake, presents, and people hiding in a dark room waiting to jump out and scream at you the second you turned on the lights. I was fine with the cake and the presents, but people jumping and screaming in my direction always made me reach for one of my silverstone knives.

Such were the instincts of an assassin.

"He always manages to surprise you with a party?" Owen asked. "Every single year? I find that hard to believe."

"Yeah, well, I am no match for the mercurial wiles of Finnegan Lane. Three years ago, he threw the party a week before my birthday. Two years ago, he waited until three weeks after my birthday."

Last year had been the only one in the last ten that Finn hadn't thrown me a party, since Fletcher had been murdered right around that time. Neither one of us had felt like celebrating anything then.

I skirted around a janitor who was mopping the linoleum floor. The sun slanting in through the windows made the smooth surface gleam like a new penny, but the longer I stared at the drying streaks of water, the darker they became, turning a dull, rusty red and morphing into another liquid. Blood. Fletcher's blood, oozing all over the blue and pink pig tracks on the floor of the Pork Pit—

"Gin?" Owen asked. "Are you still there?"

I shook my head to get rid of the unwanted memories. "Sorry, I'm still in one of the buildings. The reception is terrible in here. Hang on a second, and let me go outside."

I reached the end of the corridor and pushed through the doors, stepping out onto one of the quads at Ashland Community College. Stone buildings ringed the open grassy space, and a couple of maples towered up out of the ground, their red- and orange-streaked leaves providing patches of dappled shade that danced over the lawn. After the intense air-conditioning inside the building, the humid heat of the September evening felt like a warm, welcome blanket wrapping around my body. I tilted my face up to the sun, enjoying the sensation, before it turned into the inevitable, muggy, stifling burn.

Students moved back and forth across the quad, staring at their phones as they headed to other buildings or stepped onto the cobblestone paths that wound through campus and over to the parking lots. It was after seven now, and this was the last class period of the day, so everyone was ready to go somewhere else for the night, whether it was to the library to study, home to Mom and Dad's to do laundry, or to a nearby bar to soak their overworked brain cells in enough alcohol to make them forget everything they'd learned today.

I stopped long enough to heft my backpack, with its pens, notebook, and copy of *You Only Live Twice* by Ian Fleming, a little higher on my shoulder. The book was for the spy-literature course I was taking. I liked learning new things, so I was something of a perpetual student at the college, always signing up for a class or two every semester. When I was younger, the classes had helped kill the time between my assignments as the assassin the Spider. Now the classes helped kill the time between people trying to murder me because I was the Spider. Funny how much my life had changed in the last year.

"Gin?" Owen asked again. "Are you still there?"

I meandered toward the parking lot where my car was. "Anyway, as I was saying, every year, I beg and plead for

Finn to forget about throwing me any sort of party, and he always pays absolutely no attention to me whatsoever."

"Do you want me to talk to him?"

I snorted. "You can try, but he won't listen."

Owen laughed. "Yeah, probably not."

"Just try to rein him in a little bit, okay? I don't need some enormous party with streamers and balloons and stuff. A nice, quiet dinner with you, Finn, and Bria would be great."

"Streamers and balloons? Sounds like he really goes all out," Owen teased.

"You have no idea," I grumbled again. "Those parties?"

"Yeah . . ."

"One of them featured a petting zoo. Finn rented a bouncy house for the other one. Set it up on the lawn outside Fletcher's house. I went over there after work one day, and *surprise!*"

Owen laughed again at my snarky tone. "I'll see what I can do."

We started chatting about other things, and I let his voice wash over me, enjoying the deep, familiar rumble of his words. All the while, though, I focused on my surroundings, scanning the quads, peering into doorways, and easing around corners in case anyone was lying in wait for me. A vampire baring his fangs in anticipation of sinking his incisors into me. A giant flexing her hands, eager to wrap them around my throat and strangle me. A dwarf rolling his shoulders, ready to tackle me and beat my head against the ground. A Fire elemental cupping flames in the palm of her hand, preparing to roast me with her magic.

Just because no one had attempted to kill me at the community college yet didn't mean that some enterprising fool wouldn't have the bright idea to try. They'd certainly made the effort pretty much everywhere else I went. So many people had tried to murder me at my barbecue restaurant, the Pork Pit, that I'd lost count of how many of them I'd offed instead.

People had been trying to take me out ever since I killed Mab Monroe, the head of the Ashland underworld, back in the winter. With Mab gone, there was an opening for a new king or queen of crime in the city, and many folks saw my murder, the Spider's murder, as a stepping-stone to the throne.

Me? Well, at first, I'd just been trying to fly under the radar and survive all of the assassination attempts. But now people were really starting to piss me off. You'd think that I had killed enough lowlifes for all the others to get the message to leave me the fuck alone already, but apparently, brains were not in abundance in Ashland. Shocking, I know.

But I made it over to the parking lot without anyone jumping out of the shadows, shouting, screaming, and trying to shoot, stab, bludgeon, or magic me to death. Still, I remained vigilant as I approached my car, since this area was close to Southtown, the dangerous part of Ashland, home to gangbangers, hookers, their pimps, and down-on-their-luck homeless bums. And those were some of the nicer folks around here. They wouldn't care about murdering me because I was the Spider. They'd be more than happy to kill me for my phone, my car keys, and what might be in my wallet.

I stopped at the end of the path and scanned the lot in front of me. Like most places this close to Southtown, the area was a bit worse for wear. Jagged cracks zigzagged across the pavement, before collapsing into wide potholes, while the white paint that marked the parking spaces was so faded that you could barely make out the lines. Fast-food bags, crushed cigarettes, and jumbo-size soda cups overflowed out of the trash cans, and the steady breeze sent them gusting along the blacktop, along with the *tinkle-tinkle-tinkle* of glass from broken beer bottles.

A variety of gang runes and graffiti tags had been spray-painted onto the concrete barriers that cordoned off the lot from the construction site next door. The words *Vaughn Construction* were embossed on a metal sign hanging on the chain-link fence that ran behind the barriers, although the *V* in *Vaughn* had been turned into a giant red heart, thanks to some tagger's artistic talents. I made a mental note to get Finn to find out what Charlotte Vaughn was building here. Or perhaps I'd pay Charlotte a visit one night and ask her myself.

I didn't see anyone, but instead of moving forward, I held my position and reached out with my magic. People's feelings, actions, and intentions sink into whatever stone is around them, and as a Stone elemental, I can hear and interpret all of those emotional vibrations. Like, say, if someone was lurking behind one of those concrete barriers, a gun in his hand, ready to rise up and shoot me the second I was in range, then the barriers would mutter to me, the same way a man might mutter under his breath as he impatiently waited for me to hurry up and get here, already.

But the concrete and the pavement only grumbled

with displeasure about all of the spray paint, cracks, and potholes that marred their surfaces. No one was here to try to kill me. Good. Perhaps I would actually get through one day without having to fight for my life.

I strolled through the lot, listening to Owen and still looking for any signs of trouble, but my silver Aston Martin was right where I'd left it. I'd bought the car a few weeks ago at Finn's insistence. He had demanded that I have my own Aston, since I had a bad habit of getting his keyed, beaten, dented, bloodied, and generally destroyed.

I glanced around a final time, still half-expecting some idiot to pop up from between two cars, yell, and charge at me with a weapon, but I was the only one here, so I focused on my conversation with Owen again.

"So what's on tap for tonight?" I asked.

"Well," he said, "I thought we would stay in and have a quiet evening. You, me, a nice dinner, perhaps some quality time watching TV in my bedroom."

"Watching TV? Really?"

"Well, if you absolutely insist, we can skip the TV-viewing portion of the evening," Owen suggested in a husky tone.

Even though he couldn't see me, I still smiled. "Let's."

He laughed, and we kept chatting as I pulled my keys out of my jeans pocket and unlocked the car door—

"Where do you think you're going?"

The harsh words and the smug tone that went with them made me stop and look over my shoulder. While I'd been talking to Owen, three twenty-something guys had entered the parking lot, all of them wearing jeans, polo shirts, and sneakers. A girl the same age hurried along in front of them, her arms crossed over her chest and her head down, her speed increasing with every step as she tried to get clear of the guys.

The girl's backpack bounced on her right shoulder, and a large pin shaped like a pig holding a plate of food, all done in blue and pink crystals, winked at me. I frowned. I knew that pin. It was a rough approximation of the neon sign that hung outside the Pork Pit. Sophia Deveraux, the head cook, had ordered a whole box of the pig pins and given them to the restaurant's waitstaff to wear.

I focused on the girl and realized that I knew her too. Long, wavy black hair, hazel eyes, bronze skin, pretty features. Catalina Vasquez. She worked as a waitress at the Pit and took classes at the college, just like I did.

And it looked like she was in trouble, just like I was most days.

Catalina scurried forward, moving as fast as she could without actually running, but the guys weren't going to let her get away that easy. One reached forward and grabbed her backpack, jerking it off her shoulder and making it fall to the ground. Books, notepads, pens, and more tumbled out of the bag. Catalina scowled, but she didn't make a move to bend down and pick up her stuff. Instead, she stood her ground, her hands clenched into tight fists, as though she wanted to throw herself at the guys and give them a good pounding.

I leaned against the side of my car, watching the situation unfold.

"Listen, Troy, I've told you before. I'm not into drugs. I don't use them, I don't buy them, I don't sell them, and I sure as hell don't date guys who do," Catalina said.

Troy, the guy who'd grabbed the backpack, stepped forward. He was around six feet tall, with dirty-blond hair, brown eyes, a beefy build, and a mean smile. My own lips curved in response in a smile that was far meaner than his.

"Ah, come on, Cat," Troy purred, stepping closer to her. "Don't be like that. We used to be friends. We used to be a lot more. I remember how good we were together, don't you?"

Troy reached out, as if he were going to curl a lock of Catalina's hair around his finger, but she slapped his hand away before he could touch her.

"That was a long time ago," she snapped. "Before I knew better."

Troy's eyes narrowed. "You know, given our history, I was going to be nice about this. Not anymore."

He snapped his fingers. One of the other guys stepped forward, unzipped the black backpack he was holding, and pulled out a fistful of plastic bags, all filled with pills. He handed the bags to Troy, who held them up so that Catalina could see them.

"All you gotta do is take these pills over to that barbecue restaurant where you work and pass them out to the waiters and the customers," Troy said. "Give them out here on campus too. Think of them as free samples."

He snickered, and so did the other two guys.

Catalina's jaw clenched tight, and she glared at Troy, her hazel eyes almost black with anger. "I'm not pushing your pills. Forget it. Find someone else to sell that poison for you."

Troy reached toward her a second time, but Catalina slapped his hand away again. Troy surged forward, and the other two guys stepped up behind him, the three of them crowding Catalina and forcing her to back up against the chain-link fence on that side of the lot. Troy's two minions were actually older guys—vampires, given the glint of the fangs in their mouths as they leered at Catalina.

"You move out of the neighborhood, and you suddenly think you're better than everyone else. Well, not so high and mighty now, are you?" Troy sneered. "Not when there are three of us and one of you."

She coldly looked from one guy to the next, not a flicker of fear showing in her face. Impressive. Catalina was tougher than she'd ever let on at the restaurant.

"Actually, I'd say that there are just two of you," Catalina said, jerking her head at the vampires. "From what I remember, you don't like to get your hands dirty, Troy."

A flush crept up Troy's neck, spreading into his cheeks. "Well, you'd know all about being dirty, wouldn't you? Since all you do is clean up other people's shit all day long."

Catalina stiffened, but she didn't respond.

"You know, if you won't play ball, then you aren't leaving me a lot of options," Troy said. "I can't have you going around school after turning me down. That would send the wrong message to a lot of people. Last chance, Cat. Take the pills—or else."

The two vampires crept a little closer to her, smiling even wider and showing off even more of their fangs. Troy's meaning was clear: get with the pill-pushing program or get drained.

Catalina lifted her chin and glared at Troy. She wasn't backing down, no matter what. I admired her for it, really,

I did, but it was also stupid of her. She should have just accepted the pills and flushed them later. Oh, I knew that Catalina didn't want to take the pills and get sucked in with Troy and his thugs, but it was too late for that. This was about to get very ugly for someone.

Good thing ugly was what I specialized in.

"Gin?" Owen asked.

I realized that he had asked me a question, probably more than once, and I focused on his voice again. "Sorry, babe. I've gotta go."

"Is something wrong?" he asked.

"Nah. I just see a bit of trash that needs to be taken care of. I'll be there soon."

Owen and I hung up, and I slid my phone into my jeans pocket, before opening the car door and throwing my backpack into the passenger's seat. Then I slammed the door shut.

The sharp *crack* reverberated through the parking lot, and the three guys turned to stare at me. Catalina tried to edge away, but the two vamps spotted her furtive movements and flanked her, keeping her pinned against the fence. I pushed away from my car, stuck my hands into my pockets, and strolled in their direction.

Catalina recognized me, her boss, at once. She let out a small gasp, her face paled, and she started shaking her head *no-no-no*, although I couldn't tell if she was trying to warn me off or worried about what I was going to do to the three guys hassling her.

But Troy didn't see her reaction. Instead, his gaze slid past me to my car. When he realized that I was driving an Aston Martin, a greedy smirk slashed across his face.

"Hey, hey, foxy lady," he called out. "You lookin' for some action? You lookin' to score a little sumthin' sumthin'?"

I smiled back at him, showing almost as many teeth as the two vampires were. "Sumthin' like that."

Behind Troy, Catalina kept shaking her head *no-no-no*. She opened her lips, but one of the vamps rattled the fence beside her, a clear sign for her to keep her mouth shut. But there was no need for her to waste any more of her breath on these fools, especially not to try to tell them who they were messing with. Besides, Troy wouldn't have heeded any warning. He was completely focused on me, a potential customer, and I could almost see the dollar signs churning in his head as he calculated how much he could take me for.

"Well, you are in the right spot, baby. Because I have got just the thing for you."

He held out one of the bags, and I took it from him. A single pill lay inside the plastic, its deep, dark red color making it look like a drop of congealed blood. I flipped the bag over and realized that a rune had been etched into the surface of the pill: a crown with a single flame arching up out of the center of it, the symbol for raw, destructive power.

Still, despite the bloody color and the symbol, the pill looked more like a kids' vitamin than a dangerous drug, but I knew all too well how deceiving looks could be. Most people didn't think that I seemed anything like a dangerous assassin—until my knife was cutting into their guts.

"What's this?" I asked.

Troy's smirk widened. "It's the latest, greatest thing on

the market, baby. It will rock your world. Nah, scratch that. It'll just burn it down instead."

The two vamps snickered at his cheesy lines. Catalina rolled her eyes. Yeah, that's what I wanted to do too, but I decided to let things play out.

I tucked the pill into my jeans pocket. Not because I had any intention of taking it but because Bria would no doubt be interested in it. Detective Bria Coolidge, one of Ashland's few good cops, actually cared about things like trying to keep drugs off the streets. I tried to help her out whenever I could, despite my own life of killing and crime.

"Now that you've seen the goods, let's talk about payment, baby," Troy crooned. "Normally, a hit like that is fifty a pop."

My eyebrows shot up in my face. "Fifty bucks for one pill? That must be quite a joyride."

"Oh, it is," Troy said. "Believe me, it is. But if you don't have that much cash on you, don't sweat it. I'm sure we can work out some other form of payment."

His brown eyes tracked up and down my body, taking in my black boots and dark blue jeans and the tight green tank top I had on under my black leather jacket. Behind him, the two vampires did the same thing, licking their lips like I was a bottle of booze they were going to pass around. Oh, everybody was going to get a taste of Gin Blanco, all right, just not the kind they expected.

I bared my teeth, all pretense of a sweet smile long gone. "You call me *baby* one more time, and you'll be eating through a straw for the next six months."

Catalina sucked in a breath, but confusion filled Troy's

beefy face. When he finally realized that I'd threatened him, his brown eyes narrowed to slits.

"Those are big words coming from a little lady," he snapped. "You should be more respectful. Think about who you're talking to."

"Oh? And who would that be?"

His chest puffed up with self-importance. "Troy Mannis, that's who."

"Never heard of you."

He blinked, and his shoulders slouched. I couldn't have deflated his ego any faster if it was a balloon I'd popped with a pin. But anger rose up to fill the empty space inside him. "Well, you should," he said, his voice dropping to a low growl. "Because I run this campus, and if you're looking to score here, then you have to go through *me*. You don't have a choice. Nobody here does."

"Oh, there's always a choice," I drawled. "Like me going through *you* and leaving nothing behind but bloody little smears on the pavement."

Troy threw back his head and laughed. So did the two vampires, who had moved away from the fence and were now flanking him. Behind them, Catalina eyed me with a wary gaze. She'd heard the rumors about me being the Spider, just like everyone else who worked at the Pork Pit. Well, she was about to see how true they were.

"You must be on something already, flying high, to say something like that," Troy said. "Maybe you don't know who I am, *baby*, but you don't want to piss off the people I work for."

This time, my smile was a little more genuine. "Actually, I *love* pissing people off. Important people, rich people, dangerous people. I'm an equal-opportunity pisser-offer. You know why?"

"Why?" He asked the inevitable question.

"Because the bigger and tougher they think they are, the more they bleed. Just like you will."

Troy opened his mouth, but I was tired of talking, so I didn't give him a chance to insult me again. Instead, I snapped my fist up and sucker-punched him in the throat.

Troy's eyes bulged in surprise, even as he choked and gasped for air. The bags of pills fluttered out of his hand, and he stabbed his finger at me over and over again, in a clear kill-that-bitch-right-now gesture to his friends. The vampires charged at me, but I was ready for them.

The vamp on my right was quicker, and he reached for my neck, probably so he could snap my head to one side and bury his fangs deep in my throat. But I darted forward, turned my body into his, grabbed his right arm, and flipped him over my shoulder. His head cracked against the pavement, and he moaned with pain. He rolled over onto his side, and I kicked him in the ribs. The vampire started dry-heaving. He wouldn't be getting up anytime soon.

A hand wrapped around my waist from behind as the second vampire yanked me back up against his body. I let him pull me toward him, using his own momentum to help me drive my elbow deep into his stomach. While he gasped for air, I slammed my boot onto the top of his foot, then grabbed his arm and flipped him over my shoulder too. The vamp landed on top of his buddy, making the other man's head crack against the pavement again. I lashed out and kicked the second man in the ribs too, just so he could have the same stomachache as his friend.

While the two of them were coughing and wheezing, I turned back to Troy. He'd managed to suck enough air back into his lungs to do something supremely stupid: pull a switchblade out of his pants pocket.

I laughed. "A switchblade? Really? Doesn't your boss have enough money to buy you a gun?"

Troy growled and slashed at me with the weapon. I let him swing at me, easily sidestepping his wild blows.

"Hold still, you bitch!" he screamed.

I grinned again. "Why, all you had to do was ask, sugar."

I stopped. Troy came at me again, and this time, I knocked the blade out of his hand, then tossed him over my shoulder the same way I had his two friends. And for the third time, I followed it up with a hard kick to the stomach. By the time I finished, the three guys were a moaning, groaning pile on the pavement.

I circled around them, debating whether to keep kicking them, but Catalina stepped forward and held up a hand.

"Gin," she said. "Don't. Please."

I looked at her, then at Troy and his friends. Considering.

If these punks had jumped me in the alley behind the Pork Pit, I would have pulled out one of my knives and finished the job. But I was out in the open in broad daylight, with Catalina here to witness any slicing and dicing that I might do. I tried to avoid traumatizing innocent folks whenever possible. Besides, Troy and his loser drug-dealing friends weren't worth getting blood on my clothes.

So I gave her a sharp nod. Catalina let out a relieved sigh.

Troy groaned again and rolled off his two friends. He started to get up, but I put my boot against his neck, not hard enough to crush his windpipe but with more than enough pressure to get his attention. Eyes wide, he stared up at me, pain and rage darkening his brown gaze.

"I think we've established that you are not, in fact, the prince of this particular kingdom," I said. "But I am certainly the queen bitch around here. And if I ever see you selling drugs or hassling anybody—anybody at all—then what I did to you today will feel like a foot massage. Are we clear?"

"Whoever the hell you are, you're going to pay for this," Troy snarled, his angry gaze cutting to Catalina. "And you too, Cat. I promise you both that."

Catalina let out another sigh, although this one sounded more sad than relieved.

I removed my boot from Troy's neck and leaned down so he could see that my gray eyes were even colder and harder than the pavement around us. "My name is Gin," I growled. "Like the liquor. I'm sure you can figure out the rest. You think you're such a tough guy? Well, come look me up, and we'll find out."

He snarled and grabbed at my ankle, so I kicked him again, even harder than before. After that, the only thing Troy was capable of was wheezing, kissing the asphalt, and desperately trying not to throw up.

I grinned, knowing that my work here was done.

✳ 2 ✳

I saw a flash of movement out of the corner of my eye, reminding me that I wasn't alone with my attackers.

I cautiously approached Catalina, who had stepped away from the chain-link fence and was staring down at Troy. Emotions flashed in her hazel eyes, and her lips were pinched tight in what almost looked like regret, although I had no idea why she would feel that way about Troy.

"You okay?" I asked.

Instead of answering, Catalina edged past me and scurried over to where her backpack lay on the cracked asphalt. She scooped the wayward pens, books, and other items back into her bag as fast as she could. Couldn't blame her for that. I'd want to get away from me too, if I was in her position. Her sharp, hurried motions made the Pork Pit pig pin on the side of her backpack sparkle, like a cartoon character that was laughing maniacally at me.

She was so busy grabbing her stuff that she didn't

realize that her wallet had also fallen out of the bag. I crouched down, plucked the leather off the pavement, and flipped it open.

Catalina Vasquez. Twenty-one. Five foot four. Lived in an apartment at 1369 Lighting Bug Lane.

I let out a low whistle. "Lightning Bug Lane? That's a nice part of town. Especially for a college student."

Catalina snatched her wallet out of my hand and shoved it into her backpack. "Just forget it, okay? Forget you saw me, forget about Troy, and I will forget all about *this.*"

She gestured at the three guys, all of whom were still groaning on the pavement.

Catalina slung her backpack onto her shoulder and surged to her feet. I did the same and stuck my hands into my jacket pockets, trying to look as nonthreatening as possible for someone who had just taken out three bigger, stronger guys without breaking a sweat.

"I didn't need your help, Gin. I was handling things fine on my own."

"Yeah," I agreed. "For someone about to get the stuffing beat out of her by some lowlife drug dealer and his friends."

Anger flared in her hazel eyes. "I could have handled Troy. I always have before."

"So you know him, then."

She gave a sharp jerk of her head.

"Look, if you're in some sort of trouble—"

"Forget it," Catalina snapped. "I'm not in trouble, I'm not one of your charity cases, and I don't need your help, Gin."

I arched an eyebrow at her vehement tone. At the Pork Pit, Catalina was always positive, calm, cheerful, and upbeat. In all the months she'd worked for me, I'd never heard her so much as raise her voice before, not even when a customer complained, a kid spilled a drink all over the floor, or someone left her a lousy tip. But now she was glaring at me like I was the one who'd threatened her, instead of Troy and his friends.

Catalina must have seen the questions in my face, because she pinched the bridge of her nose before dropping her hand. "Look, I'm sorry I yelled at you. Thanks for helping me out. I appreciate it. Really, I do. But this is nothing. Okay? I'll see you at work tomorrow."

"Sure."

Catalina tried to smile at me, but it was a miserable attempt. She tightened her grip on her backpack, spun around, and marched across the lot. At first, I thought she was getting into a rusted, rattletrap truck that had seen better days, but Catalina moved past the truck and popped open the door on a very nice late-model Mercedes-Benz, a car that was a little too nice for someone who worked as a waitress.

I paid my folks good wages but not *that* good. And that street where she lived was in one of the city's nicest suburbs, close to Northtown, the part of Ashland where the rich, social, powerful, and magical elite lived. So what was she doing being harassed by some drug dealer? Especially one who knew her? Because there had been nothing casual or random about the way Troy had spoken to Catalina. From what he had said, they used to be friends—and more.

I'd never paid much attention to Catalina before. I'd had too many other things to think about these past few months, too many folks trying to kill me, and too many new enemies to face down to give her much thought. She was just a girl who worked for me, although she was an excellent employee and had lasted longer than most of my other waitresses. But I was very interested in her now. Because if Troy wanted her to push drugs, then she was already in way over her head. And if he or whoever he worked for thought that I was letting anyone deal any-thing in my restaurant, well, I'd be happy to show them how wrong they were—and how I handled threats to my gin joint.

Catalina threw her car into reverse, backed out of the space, and peeled out of the parking lot as fast as she could without blowing out her tires on the cracks and potholes. I made note of her license-plate number so I could pass it on to Finn later.

I didn't know what was going on with Catalina Vasquez, but I was going to find out.

I got into my own car, cranked the engine, and left Troy and his two still whimpering friends behind. I steered out of the lot and cruised the streets around the college, mak-ing random turns and keeping an eye on the rearview mirror. Just because I hadn't seen anyone else with Troy didn't mean that more of his friends hadn't been hidden in the shadows, and I didn't want anyone following me to my destination.

But no one was tailing me, so I made a final turn out of the downtown loop and headed for the much nicer, though no less dangerous, confines of Northtown. My Aston Martin might have been a snazzy set of wheels at the college, but up here, my ride was downright shabby compared with some of the Audis, BMWs, and Bentleys that whizzed by. And the estates that the cars turned into were even more impressive, with massive mansions, pristine pools, and landscaped lawns stretching as far as the eye could see.

I drove through an open iron gate and parked in front of one of the smaller, more modest and tasteful mansions in this particular neighborhood. A scan of the yard satisfied me that no one was skulking around, so I got out of my car and used my key to let myself into the mansion.

Thick rugs covered the hardwood floors and metal sculptures perched in the corners, giving the spacious home plenty of cozy personality. Noise and flickering lights drifted out of one of the downstairs living rooms, so I headed in that direction.

Two college-age girls wearing yoga pants and T-shirts sprawled across a sofa, sharing a tub of cheesy popcorn, watching some rom-com on the flat-screen TV mounted to the wall. One girl was quite beautiful, with blue-black hair, blue eyes, and a lithe figure. The other was also striking, with frizzy blond hair, dark eyes, and burnished brown skin that hinted at her Cherokee heritage.

Eva Grayson was Owen's baby sister, and Violet Fox was her best friend. The two girls could be found hanging out together more often than not, and it looked like they were settled in for a movie night, given the buckets of popcorns, open bags of M&M's, and stacks of DVDs that covered the coffee table in front of the sofa.

"So has someone loved and lost yet?" I drawled, leaning against the open doorway.

"Nah," Eva said, still staring at the screen. "We're still at the I-hate-you-but-I'm-strangely-attracted-to-you-anyway stage."

"Ah," I said. "That's my favorite part."

The floor creaked behind me, and a pair of warm, strong arms wrapped around my waist. "Mine too," a husky voice murmured in my ear.

Owen pressed a soft kiss to the side of my neck. I leaned back against his body and breathed in, his rich, faintly metallic scent filling my nose. He kissed the other side of my neck, making me shiver, and I turned around and stared up into his violet eyes. Despite his slightly crooked nose and the faint white scar that slashed across his chin, I thought that Owen Grayson was the most handsome man I'd ever seen. I smoothed back a lock of black hair that had fallen over his forehead, then stood on my tiptoes and returned his soft kisses with a much more direct and steamier one of my own.

Eva rolled her eyes. "Ugh. Take it to the bedroom, folks. We have enough fireworks to watch on the screen."

She tossed a handful of popcorn at us, and so did a snickering Violet. Owen and I both laughed as we broke apart.

"Don't worry," Owen said, leaning over the side of the couch and mussing his sister's hair. "We won't make you witness any more horrible public displays of affection. Although didn't someone tell me that she had a chemistry test tomorrow?"

Eva swatted his hand away, wrinkled her nose, and shot

an evil glare at a thick book peeking out from underneath one of the bags of M&M's. "Maybe. This is why Violet and I are having a movie night. So we can relax before we study."

"Right." Owen drawled out the word. "Let me know how well that works out."

He ruffled Eva's hair a final time before giving me a slow, suggestive wink. He crooked his finger at me and started walking backward down the hallway toward his bedroom. I grinned and had started to follow him when a thought occurred to me.

I turned back to the girls. "Y'all know Catalina from the restaurant, right? She takes classes at the college too."

Eva shrugged, but Violet nodded.

"Yeah, I know Catalina," Violet said. "She's my partner in English lit. We're working on a research paper about mythology."

"Has she ever said anything to you about a guy named Troy?"

"Troy?" Violet asked. "Do you mean Troy Mannis?"

I nodded.

"Yeah. He's her ex. The two of them used to go out, back before Catalina's mom died."

I frowned. "Her mom died?"

Violet pushed her black glasses up on her nose. "Yeah, maybe sometime last year? I think it was before she started working at the Pork Pit. Her mom was hit and killed by a drunk driver. That's all I really know. Catalina doesn't talk about herself much."

Well, that was more than I'd known about Catalina. I'd get Finn to dig deeper and fill in the rest of the blanks for me.

"Why are you asking?" Violet asked, her face scrunching up with worry. "Is she in some kind of trouble?"

Eva stared at me too, that same worry flashing in her blue eyes as she chewed on her lip. Even though Owen and I tried to shield them from the worst of it, both girls knew exactly what I did as the Spider and all the problems I was having with Ashland's underworld bosses. Still, there was no reason to ruin their evening with what had happened at the college.

"Nah," I said, waving my hand. "Catalina helped me out with something, so I thought I'd return the favor and give her an extra day off with pay or something."

Both of the girls relaxed at my lie. On the TV screen, the rom-com couple murmured flirty insults to each other in some fancy restaurant.

"Well, I'll let you get back to your movie," I said, waggling my eyebrows in the direction Owen had gone. "Especially since I have my own hot date tonight."

Eva and Violet both laughed and threw more popcorn at me, chasing me out of the living room.

I headed down the hall, past Owen's office with its rows of weapons mounted on the walls, and over to his bedroom. I opened the door, stepped inside, and let out a surprised gasp.

Warm golden light enveloped the area, as flames danced on the tops of dozens of lit candles. The slender white tapers covered every available surface, from the dresser to the nightstand to the desk in the corner, and still more candles flickered in the attached bathroom, as though they were peering at their own reflections in the mirrors there. Their vanilla scent tickled my nose in a pleasant way. Moonlight beamed in through the open curtains, adding to the soft, muted, romantic atmosphere. So did the silver platter of chocolates and the champagne chilling in a bucket of ice sitting next to the bed. Music hummed in the background, a soft jazz tune.

It took a lot to surprise me, but Owen always managed to do it. He stepped forward out of the shadows along the wall and held out his hand. I took it, enjoying the feel of his warm fingers wrapping around mine, and let him lead me deeper into the room.

I gestured at the candles, chocolates, and champagne. "This is a little more than just dinner and watching TV."

He grinned and pulled me into his arms, his violet eyes glinting with a mischievous light. "I know, but I wanted to do something special tonight. Just because. Although you can think of it as part of your birthday surprise if you want, even though it's a few days early."

I gasped, clutched my hands to my heart, and looked around in mock horror. "Please, please tell me that Finn is *not* hiding in your walk-in closet, waiting to jump out and scream at me."

Owen laughed, the deep sound rumbling like thunder out of his chest. "Trust me. Finn isn't here. Tonight it's just you and me."

I wrapped my arms around his neck. "And that's just the way I like it."

"Me too," he whispered back.

Owen's lips met mine, and I forgot about everything else except him.

* 3 *

We spent a very pleasurable night together, before I left the next morning to go open the Pork Pit for the day's cooking and customers.

The lunch rush passed by in the usual hurried fashion, and I managed to hold on to my mellow mood all the way until three o'clock, when some idiot tried to crack open my skull with a baseball bat as I was taking out the trash in the alley behind the restaurant. It was hardly a surprise, since that's how a lot of my midafternoon trash runs ended these days. At least the bags of garbage helped hide all the bodies that I littered the pavement with.

I opened the door and stepped into the back of the Pork Pit. Sophia Deveraux, the head cook, was standing by one of the freezers, tying on a black apron embossed with tiny grinning hot pink skulls. The apron matched the rest of Sophia's Goth clothes—black boots, black jeans, and a black T-shirt with a single large pink skull on it.

Bright pink gloss covered her lips, and silver streaks glittered in her black hair. A black ribbon ringed her throat, a pink cameo dangling off the end. The delicate necklace looked a little odd with her T-shirt and skull apron, but I wouldn't dare tell Sophia that. I had no desire to hurt her feelings or get knocked into next week by her dwarven strength.

Besides, I wasn't exactly presentable right now, given the blood that coated my hands. So I went over to one of the sinks, turned on the tap, and started washing my hands. Sophia's black eyes fixed on the pale pink stains that swirled down the drain.

"Problem?" she rasped in her eerie, broken voice.

I shrugged. "No more so than usual. Just be careful where you step. There's another pool of blood right outside the door. And we have another visitor sleeping under some garbage bags who needs to be put on ice. Regular size. Nothing special."

Sophia nodded, understanding my cryptic words, since she disposed of many of the bodies that I left behind as the Spider. On her break, she'd haul the dead guy over to the refrigerated cooler that she kept in the next alley over for these situations. Yep, just the usual routine around here these days.

"Who was he?" she rasped.

I shrugged again. "Just some guy. No obvious runes on him, but then again, I didn't look too hard."

I'd been too busy slicing his guts open with one of my knives to pay much attention to what he looked like. Then again, I never did that. Not anymore. Not these days, when pretty much everyone in the underworld wanted me dead. I was mildly surprised that Troy and his friends hadn't yet made an appearance at the restaurant to get revenge on me for kicking their asses last night.

Then again, the day was still young.

When I'd washed away the blood, I dried off my hands, put on a clean blue work apron over my own dark jeans and long-sleeved black T-shirt, and stepped through the double doors into the front of the restaurant.

The Pork Pit was something of a dive, the sort of place that outsiders would turn their noses up at, but the locals flocked to it because they knew we served up the best barbecue in Ashland. Blue and pink vinyl booths squatted next to the windows, while more tables and chairs crouched in the center of the storefront. Matching fading, peeling blue and pink pig tracks curved over to the men's and women's restrooms, while a long counter close to the back wall featured padded stools.

It was too early for the dinner rush, so only a few folks were currently eating. My gaze roamed over the customers, but they were all engrossed in their barbecue sandwiches, burgers, fries, and other fixings, along with their sweet iced teas, fruity lemonades, and cold sodas. No one paid me any attention as I went over to one of the tables, grabbed a plate with a fresh grilled cheese sandwich and an untouched mound of onion rings, snatched a parfait glass that held a triple chocolate milkshake, and took everything back over to the counter.

"Well, that took *forever*," a snide voice chirped as I rounded the end of the counter. "What did you do? Kill somebody while you were gone?"

The voice and the attitude belonged to a guy sitting

on the stool closest to the cash register. With his expensive suit, chiseled features, and perfectly cut and styled walnut-colored hair, most women would have considered him exceptionally handsome. Me too, if I didn't also know how totally annoying he could be. I stopped and shot a cold, withering look at Finnegan Lane, not that the expression bothered my foster brother at all.

"Ah," he said in a sly, knowing tone. "You did."

His green eyes locked onto the food in my hands, and he perked up, like an eager puppy about to get a treat. "Hey, are you going to eat that?"

I rolled my eyes, but I set the plate and the milkshake down on the counter in front of him. Finn shrugged out of his gray suit jacket, tucked a white paper napkin in at his chin to protect his gray silk shirt and tie, and enthusiastically dug in. Chowing down on a dead man's food didn't faze him in the slightest. Few things did.

"As I was saying before you so rudely left to take out the trash," Finn said, once he'd slurped down half the milkshake in a long swallow, "I really think I've outdone myself when it comes to your birthday this year."

I sighed. "And I've told you, *repeatedly*, that I don't want, need, or desire some stupid surprise party. We go through this same song-and-dance every single year."

Finn grinned. "Exactly! Why, you might say that it's our own little tradition. One that I am more than happy to uphold."

I groaned.

"I will let you pick out the flavor of the cake, if that makes you feel better."

"How very gracious of you."

He beamed. "Isn't it?"

I sighed again, but Finn started talking about cakes versus cupcakes, vanilla versus chocolate, buttercream versus cream-cheese icing. After a few seconds, my eyes glazed over, and I was in serious danger of falling off my stool from the sheer boredom of his ramblings.

Catalina Vasquez stepped out of the restroom and started to walk over to the table I'd cleared. She stopped when she realized that the food and the guy were gone, then headed over to me.

"Gin?" she asked. "Is something wrong? Why did that guy leave? I just served him."

"Apparently, he had an appointment that just wouldn't wait."

Finn snickered at my deadpan drawl, but I ignored him.

"Go ahead and wipe down that table, please," I said. "Trust me. That guy isn't coming back."

That table belonged to the idiot with the baseball bat who'd jumped me in the alley. He wasn't going to do much of anything now, except rot out in the heat.

Catalina nodded, either not hearing or choosing to ignore the sarcasm in my words. "Sure thing. I'll get right on it."

I nodded and grabbed my book, as though I were going to read a few pages, but I kept my gaze on Catalina the whole time. When she'd shown up a few hours ago to work her shift, she'd murmured a polite hello to me, tied on an apron, and gotten to work. She hadn't said anything about me saving her last night, and I hadn't brought it up, but she'd gone out of her way to stay on the opposite side of the restaurant from me all day. I didn't know if it was because of the beat-down I'd given Troy or because she didn't want me asking her any more questions. Didn't much matter. I was getting to the bottom of things one way or another.

Finn waited until he'd plowed through half of his food and Catalina had moved over to serve another customer before he looked at me. "This is what's so urgent? Me tracking down info on one of your waitresses? This is what I canceled my afternoon nap for?"

I arched an eyebrow. "I didn't know they let you take naps at the bank."

In addition to helping me whenever the Spider needed a bit of backup, Finn also ostensibly worked as an investment banker, although *shameless, greedy money launderer* would have been a far more accurate description of his job.

He waved his hand. "*Let* is such a narrow word. The higher-ups at the bank want all their employees to be well rested. Sometimes I happen to take that rest on the couch in my office in the middle of the afternoon."

"Next thing you know, you'll be demanding milk and cookies afterward," I muttered.

Finn eyed the almond-flavored sugar cookies in the cake stand on the counter with hungry interest. "I should get *something* for schlepping all the way over here on a moment's notice. You can give me, say, a dozen of those cookies. After I finish my milkshake, of course."

I snorted.

While Finn kept eating, I filled him in about my run-in with Troy and his goons, in addition to Catalina's nice car and her even nicer address. I also told him the tidbit Violet had mentioned about Catalina's mother passing away.

"I've never heard of the guy, but if her mom died, she could be living off some sort of insurance settlement," Finn suggested, polishing off the rest of the dead man's grilled cheese. "That might explain the car and the apartment."

"Maybe," I murmured, watching Catalina seat a couple, hand them menus, and take their drink orders. "Either way, I want to know everything there is to know about her. And Troy Mannis too. He doesn't strike me as the type of guy who takes the word *no* very well, much less the ass-kicking that I gave him and his friends."

"Consider it done."

Finn pushed his empty plate away and slurped down the dregs of his milkshake. But instead of untucking the napkin at his chin, getting to his feet, and leaving, he crossed his arms over his chest and gave me an expectant look.

"What?" I growled.

"You know what," he replied in an annoying, sing-song voice. "You're the one who brought it up in the first place."

I sighed, grabbed the glass cake stand, and pushed it over to him. Finn cackled with glee as he removed the top and started cramming cookies into his mouth.

"Now that we've taken care of business, let's get back to what's really important: your birthday party," he mumbled between bites.

I groaned.

"Mark my words," Finn crowed. "By the time I get done, you're going to have the best birthday *ever*."

I closed my eyes as he started chattering on about my party again. I would have laid my head down on the counter and cried, but there were too many witnesses for that.

After he got his sugar fix, Finn left the restaurant. In between torturing me with what he might cook up for my not-so-surprise party, he did also promise to dig to the very depths of Catalina, Troy, and anyone and everyone they might know. That was comforting, even if all the birthday talk wasn't.

I kept one eye on Catalina as she worked her shift, but the rest of the day passed by quietly, and no one else came into the restaurant with the sole intention of killing me. In fact, nothing particularly noteworthy happened at all, and I was starting to think that I would get through unscathed.

Until two women strolled through the front door.

One of them was a giant, seven feet tall, with a short, sleek bob of golden hair, hazel eyes, and milky skin covered with a smattering of pale freckles. The other woman was my size, about five-seven or so, with a beautiful mane of wavy hair that flowed past her slender shoulders. At first, her hair seemed to be a rich sable brown, but then she stepped into a patch of sunlight, and I realized that it was actually an intense auburn, with coppery streaks woven in among her lustrous locks, almost like her hair was glowing with some sort of inner fire. Both of them wore expensive pantsuits, black for the giant and a cool white for the other woman.

Catalina directed them over to a booth that was right across from my position at the cash register, and the two women sat down.

The giant glanced around, her cold gaze taking in everyone, from the other customers to the waitstaff to the people passing by on the sidewalk outside. I recognized the hard stare and the mental calculations. So she was a bodyguard, then, one who seemed to be exceptionally protective of her client, judging by the way she sized up every person who walked by in terms of how much of a potential threat they might be and how fast she could take them down. And I was willing to bet that it was *fast*. Her body wasn't as heavily muscled as that of other giants, but her tall figure hinted at a lean, coiled strength that would crack out at you like a whip—fast, stinging, and merciless.

In contrast, the second, shorter woman seemed completely unconcerned by her surroundings. Then again, why should she be worried when she had a seven-foot-tall meat shield watching over her?

The auburn-haired woman took the menu that Catalina offered her, then glanced around the storefront. Her face was neutral, but I got the feeling that she was analyzing every single thing in the restaurant, albeit in a different way from how the giant had.

Finally, her gaze met mine.

Sculpted eyebrows, high cheekbones, heart-shaped mouth. Her features were flawless in their symmetrical beauty, and her creamy skin had a faint pink undertone to it, which made her look even more vibrant and alive. Her eyes were a vivid green, the intense color standing out against the black of her large pupils.

She realized that I was staring at her, and a small smile split her crimson lips, revealing her perfect white teeth. She returned my stare with one of her own, seeming deep in thought, before nodding at me. Then she turned back to the giant, leaned forward, and murmured something to her friend. The giant's flat gaze flicked to me for a few seconds before she too leaned forward. Soon the two women were engrossed in their conversation and not paying any attention to me at all.

That should have reassured me, but it didn't.

I frowned. Something about the woman's soft smile and thoughtful expression nagged at me, making me think maybe I'd seen her somewhere before, somewhere important, somewhere that I should remember—

"Problem?" Sophia rasped.

The Goth dwarf was standing off to my right and stirring the pot of Fletcher's secret barbecue sauce that was bubbling away on one of the stoves, flavoring the air with its rich, smoky mix of cumin, black pepper, and other spices. Sophia had noticed my keen interest in our new customers.

I kept staring at the two women. They both ignored me completely, which made more and more alarm bells start going off in my head. The only people who did that to me in my own restaurant were the ones who had some sort of sinister and dastardly plans for my demise.

By this point, the two mystery women had given Catalina their order of cheeseburgers, sweet-potato fries, and macaroni salad and were talking softly to each other in between checking their phones. Neither one of them so much as glanced in my direction, but I felt like they were aware of me all the same.

I hopped off my stool, went over to the counter close to where Sophia was standing by the stoves, and started slicing veggies for the rest of the day's sandwiches. As I whacked my way through a red onion, I subtly tilted my head in the direction of the two women.

"You ever see them in here before?"

Sophia matched my casual cool move for move, reaching over and grabbing a ladle for the barbecue sauce as though she weren't really eyeing the women.

"No," she replied, sticking the ladle in the sauce. "Giant looks strong, though."

"Do me a favor. See if you can snap a photo of them before they leave, and send it to Finn. Maybe he knows who they are."

Sophia grunted her agreement, and we both went back to work.

An hour later, the two women had finally finished their meal and pushed their plates away. Sophia chose that moment to stroll back to the restrooms, tapping her fingers on her phone as though she were texting. She discreetly angled the phone at the women as she passed them, then finished her text and slid the device into the back pocket of her jeans before disappearing into the bathroom. She didn't give me a thumbs-up, but I knew she'd gotten shots of them.

The two women slid out of the booth. I thought that they might come over to the cash register to pay for their food and make some not-so-veiled threats about ending my existence. But instead, the giant threw several bills down onto the table, then opened the front door for the other woman.

The two of them strolled outside. A black Audi with tinted windows pulled up to the curb, and the giant opened the back door for the auburn-haired woman. A few seconds later, they were both inside the vehicle and cruising away to parts unknown.

Even though they had left and nothing had happened, the strange tension I'd felt ever since they'd stepped into the restaurant didn't ease. I went over to their booth and peered out the windows, but the car and the women were long gone. Maybe they'd just wanted a hot meal and nothing else. Maybe they hadn't had any hidden agenda for eating in my restaurant. Maybe I was just being overly paranoid—even for me.

I sighed and grabbed the plate that the auburn-haired woman had been using, along with her silverware.

The second my hand closed around her fork, a burning sensation shot through my skin, as though the silverware were red-hot.

I was so surprised that I dropped the utensil. It clattered to the floor with a loud, reverberating *bang*, almost as if someone had fired a gun inside the restaurant. Everyone turned to look at me—the other customers, Catalina, even Sophia, who had stepped out of the restroom. But I ignored their curious gazes and focused on the fork, expecting to see some sort of elemental Fire rune flare to life on the handle and wondering if I could reach for my Stone magic, use it to harden my skin, and throw myself down on top of it in time to protect everyone else from the upcoming blast of magic—

But nothing happened.

No runes, no Fire, no magic, no explosions, nothing

that would indicate that the fork was anything other than a fork.

Catalina stopped her wipe-down of the next table over. "Gin?" she asked in the same cautious voice she'd been using with me all day. "Is something wrong?"

I shook my head. "Nah. It's nothing. Just a case of butterfingers."

Catalina gave me a strange look, like she didn't believe me, but she finished wiping down the table, then moved over to the next one. The customers went back to their food and conversations, and Sophia returned to the stoves, although she raised her black eyebrows at me as she passed. I shook my head at her, then crouched down on the floor, still staring at the fork.

Folks had left me all sorts of nasty surprises in and around the Pork Pit these past few months. Everything from saw-shaped runes frosted into the doors that would spew out razor-sharp needles of elemental Ice when someone tried to open them, to trip-wires strung across the alley floor that would trigger a double-gauge shotgun, to good old-fashioned ticking time bombs hidden in the backs of the restroom toilets. No one had tried to booby-trap the silverware yet, although I supposed it was only a matter of time before someone thought of it.

But I wasn't going to find out what was wrong by just staring at the fork, so I drew in a breath, reached out, and carefully picked it up again. Once more, it burned my hand, although the sensation was much fainter now. Whatever had made the metal feel like it was scorching my skin was slowly fading away, like warmth quickly seeping from a pan that had been taken out of a hot oven, but I'd been right about what had caused the sensation.

Magic—elemental magic.

I wrapped my hand around the metal and concentrated, trying to identify what kind of magic it was, but it didn't feel like the Fire power that I'd expected it to be. Otherwise, hot, invisible pins and needles would have been stabbing into my skin, and I would have experienced a similar sensation if it had been Air magic. The faint, steady burn wasn't cold or hard, so it wasn't Ice or Stone magic either, the two areas I was gifted in, and it didn't feel like some offshoot power like water or electricity.

I frowned. The auburn-haired woman was definitely an elemental, and her power—whatever it was—must have somehow soaked into the fork while she'd been eating. That was the only explanation that made sense, since some elementals constantly gave off invisible waves of magic, even when they weren't actively using their power. But whatever her magic was, it was something I'd never felt before.

And that worried me more than anything else.

4

A few more customers came into the restaurant, but it looked like it was going to be a slow night, so I decided to close early.

Besides, I wanted to go home and go through Fletcher's files to see if there was any mention of the auburn-haired woman and her giant friend. The two of them hadn't said a single word to me, but I couldn't help but think that they were a dangerous threat all the same. Folks always said that animals could sniff out evil, and I'd gotten pretty good at it myself these past few months. I'd had to, in order to survive.

Catalina was the last of the waitstaff to leave. She pushed through the double doors and stepped into the storefront, her backpack dangling from her hand. She called out a soft good night to Sophia, who grunted in response, and rounded the end of the counter.

Catalina stopped in front of me. "Good night, Gin,"

she said, even though her gaze skittered away from mine just like it had all day long.

"Night."

Catalina gave me a tight, awkward smile, still not really looking at me, then headed for the front door, opened it, and stepped outside. She stood on the sidewalk and hooked her backpack over her shoulder, the sunlight making the pig pin on the side of her bag sparkle with an evil light. Catalina pulled her phone out of her jeans pocket and started checking her messages as she strolled down the street and out of sight.

I stopped wiping down the counter and watched her go, wondering if Finn had found out anything yet about her, where her money was coming from, or her boy Troy—

Think of the devil, and he shall appear.

Troy Mannis stepped into view right outside of the windows. He stared in the direction Catalina had gone, then turned and said something to someone behind him. A second later, the same two vamps who'd been with him at the community college joined him. Together, the three of them headed after Catalina.

I'd been so sure that Troy would come after *me* for kicking his ass that it had never occurred to me that he might take his anger out on Catalina instead. But I didn't need an Air elemental's precognition to know what he and his friends would do to her the second they got her alone.

"Where does Catalina usually park her car?" I asked Sophia, throwing down my towel.

"Garage on Broad Street. Why?" the dwarf rasped.

"Her little problem from last night has reappeared."

I had told Sophia what had happened to Catalina at the college when the dwarf had helped me open the restaurant this morning. Her black eyes sharpened. "Need some help?"

I shook my head. "Nah. Stay here and close down the Pit, please. Besides, it's been a slow day. I could use the exercise. If I need you, I'll call for pickup and disposal afterward. Okay?"

Sophia's grin matched the ones of the hot pink skulls on her apron. "It's a date."

I pulled open the front door of the restaurant and stepped outside. It was still muggy out, although the heat wasn't as oppressive as it had been earlier in the day, and the faintest note of fall whispered in the air, one that said that the warm day would soon give way to a deliciously cool night.

I scanned the pedestrians and spotted Troy about a block ahead of me. Despite the heat, he wore a black leather jacket, and so did the two vamps who were with him. You didn't wear something like that in this weather unless you had something to hide. Like, say, a gun or some other weapon.

I needed to get to Catalina before Troy and his friends did, so I jogged across the street and cut through an alley on the far side. But the narrow passage wasn't deserted— far from it.

Several hookers leaned against the Dumpsters that lined the walls, wearing sky-high stilettos, sequined tube tops, and leather miniskirts that were barely bigger than the towels that I used to wipe down tables. The women had been chatting and laughing before they started plying their wares for the night, but their easy camaraderie and chuckles faded the second I entered the alley.

One of them shot me an angry glare for daring to wander into their territory. "Get lost, honey. This ain't no amateur hour around here."

Another hooker grabbed her arm. "Shh! Don't you know who that is?"

She whispered something in her friend's ear that made the other woman's mouth gape open and her knees knock together. My assassin moniker, most likely. The hookers who worked the streets around the restaurant had heard the rumors about who I really was, and they were smart enough to believe them. The first woman ducked her head to me in a silent apology, but I was in too much of a hurry to care.

Most of the women gave me sharp, respectful nods as I passed, even going so far as to step back so I could jog by them more easily. Others actually moved all the way behind the Dumpsters, plastering themselves up against the alley walls as flat and as fast as they could. None of them actually spoke to me, but they knew that I was even more dangerous than their pimps lounging in the cars parked on the surrounding streets, and they didn't want to do anything to attract my attention.

I reached the end of that alley and cut through two more before I ended up on Broad Street. Since it wasn't one of the main drags, this area was mostly deserted, except for the few commuters who hadn't left downtown already and were rushing to their cars in the hopes of getting home in time for dinner and to tuck their kids into bed.

I looked left and right, but I didn't see Catalina anywhere. She must be in the garage already. If I was lucky, she was alone, and Troy and his friends hadn't gotten here yet. If I wasn't lucky, well, Sophia would come and help me clean up the mess, like she'd promised. So I palmed one of the silverstone knives hidden up my sleeves, hopped over the metal pole that barred the exit, and entered the garage.

The stones started murmuring the second I stepped into the structure.

Naturally.

The cold, graffiti-tagged concrete bellowed like a chorus of bullfrogs—low, dark, and sinister. I tightened my grip on my knife and slid into the nearest shadow, scanning the rows of vehicles, wondering if Troy and his friends were already here. But the stone continued to rumble at a steady level, and I realized that it was only reflecting back the paranoia of all the folks who'd scurried to their cars, worried that they were going to be mugged, and especially of the ones who'd had their fears realized and their heads dashed against the pillars while some lowlife rifled through their pockets.

Satisfied that I was alone, I moved deeper into the garage. My boots scuffed on the concrete, while the smells of gas, oil, and exhaust hung in the air. I didn't spot Catalina on this level, so I crept up the stairs to the second story. I paused in the open doorway, listening. Footsteps echoed on this level, the steady beat almost drowning out the soft tune she was humming, one I recognized from all her hours at the Pork Pit. I shook my head. If Troy didn't hurt Catalina, someone else lurking here surely would. She was practically painting a target on herself, making that much cheerful noise in a place as dark and dangerous as this.

I left the doorway behind and headed into the main part of the garage. Several cars squatted in their spaces, waiting for their owners to come claim them for the night. Catalina was walking down the center of concrete, not even bothering to glance around to see if anyone was following her. I shook my head again. It was a wonder she hadn't been mugged in here before now.

Catalina spun her key ring around and around on her index finger as she approached her car, the same very nice Benz that she'd been driving at the college. She stopped by the driver's door.

"Hello, Catalina," I called out.

She shrieked and whirled around, her keys flying off her finger and clattering to the concrete. Her eyes bulged even more when she realized that it was me calling out her name, but her expression quickly turned wary, and she couldn't hide the fear that flickered in her gaze—fear of me.

My heart clenched at the sight, at the knowledge that she was scared of me, or at least scared of my supposed reputation as the Spider. I would never intentionally hurt an innocent person, but she had no way of knowing that.

"Gin?" Catalina asked, her hand latching onto the door handle, even though the car was still locked. "What are you doing here?"

"Saving you."

She frowned. "From what?"

"Your ex-boyfriend. The oh-so-lovely gentleman who was hassling you last night."

Her frown deepened. "Troy? What's he got to do with this?"

"Everything. When you left the Pork Pit, he and his friends were right behind you. Call me crazy, but I doubt that they just want to talk."

I crossed my arms over my chest. Carrying my knives was second nature to me, and I didn't even realize that I was still holding one of them until Catalina's gaze locked onto the blade glinting in my right hand. She eased to the side, putting a little more distance between us.

"Troy wouldn't hurt me," she said, her voice cracking on the last two words. "Not really. He's a hothead with a big mouth, that's all."

"And what about his friends?" I countered. "They're not going to be too happy about the beat-down I gave them. Neither will whoever they work for—trust me. Troy and his friends aren't on their way here to offer you a heartfelt apology."

Catalina opened her mouth, but the heavy smack of footsteps cut her off.

"C'mon." Troy's voice drifted over to us from a distance. "The bitch has got to be up here."

Catalina sucked in a surprised breath, but I was already moving forward, grabbing her hand and pulling her around to the opposite side of her car. I made her crouch down beside me in the shadows.

"You stay here," I ordered. "Out of the way. I'll deal with Troy and his friends—"

This time, I was the one who got cut off by the squeal of tires and the rumble of several engines.

I scooted forward and peered around the back of Catalina's car. Troy and his two friends had gotten here faster than I'd expected, because they now stood in the middle of this section of the garage. But Troy was as surprised as I was by the noise, and he turned to look behind him.

Two black Cadillac Escalades zoomed up onto this level, one going right and the other turning left, both of them stopping just before they hit the concrete walls. A few seconds later, a third car sedately drove up and parked in the middle of the metal V that the other two vehicles had created.

Unlike the other dark, anonymous cars, the third vehicle was completely memorable—an old-fashioned baby-blue Bentley that was chromed, waxed, and polished to perfection. It was the sort of fancy, high-end car that Finn always drooled over, one that was known throughout Ashland but especially over in Southtown, where its owner lived.

Now I knew exactly who Troy dealt for. Things had just gone from bad to worse. Story of my life.

Catalina crept up beside me, peering around my shoulder. She sucked in a breath when she spotted the blue car. "Oh, no," she whispered.

Yeah. That about summed things up.

"Stay still, and be quiet," I murmured. "No matter what happens. And if I tell you to run, then you *run*, and you don't look back."

Catalina nodded, too frightened to do anything else.

Men poured out of the two black Escalades, six of them total, all wearing dark suits and sporting wing tips that were as clean and shiny as their cars. They were all smiling, showing off a set of perfect, polished fangs in each and every one of their mouths. I'd heard that their boss was big on his men always looking their best, right down to their pearly-whites.

I looked past the enforcers to the man who got out of the driver's seat of the Bentley. He was short and lean, and everything about him was a soft gray, from his suit and shirt to his hair and eyes. Silvio Sanchez. I'd never had the misfortune of meeting him, although I knew him by reputation. Smart. Ruthless. Vicious. The sort of sneaky, underhanded, backstabbing vampire you did not want to mess with.

Silvio being here was bad enough, but he opened the back door of the Bentley so that another man could get out—one who was a hundred times more dangerous than Silvio had ever dreamed of being.

Truth be told, the other man wasn't an impressive figure. Oh, he was around six feet tall, but his arms and legs seemed almost too long for the rest of him, as though he were a gangly teenager who hadn't grown into his own body yet. He had a string-bean physique and not much in the way of muscles, a fact that his clothes emphasized. His white pants almost completely covered up his white sneakers, while his long-sleeved button-up shirt was about two sizes too big, although the baby-blue fabric perfectly matched the paint on his Bentley. A white bow tie patterned with baby-blue polka dots hung loose and limp around his neck.

His face looked young too, his skin pale, his cheeks rounded with a perpetual bit of baby fat, even though I knew he had to be at least forty, if not older. His black hair was slightly mussed, as if he ran his hands through it repeatedly and didn't care how it looked. Silver glasses perched on the end of his hawkish nose, making his pale blue eyes seem larger than they actually were.

All put together, he looked like a calm, quiet, geeky kind of guy, a fact that the pens and notepad sticking out of the plastic pocket protector on the front of his shirt only reinforced. But he was anything but the mild-mannered fellow he appeared to be. I knew him by reputation too.

Beauregard Benson, the drug-dealing vampire king of Southtown.

✻ 5 ✻

While Benson studied Troy, I studied Benson.

Even among the underworld bosses, Beauregard Benson was someone everyone talked about in hushed whispers. Unlike some of the other crime lords and ladies, Benson didn't bother with selling blood, running hookers, or bankrolling bookies. Drugs were his forte. Uppers, downers, pot, heroin, crack, meth, oxy. If it could get you higher than a kite, then Benson was the one you were paying for the ride up into the wild blue yonder—and the piranha that was waiting to chew you up and spit you out on the way down.

Benson finished his perusal of Troy before turning to Silvio. "Is this the one?" he asked in a high, nasal voice that perfectly matched his geeky wardrobe.

"Yes, sir," Silvio replied in a soft, bland tone.

Benson nodded, then pointed at the two vampires standing with Troy, snapped his fingers, and jerked his thumb over his shoulder. "Gentlemen, you may leave now."

"Sorry, Troy," one of the vamps muttered.

The two vamps skirted past Benson and Silvio and hurried out of the garage as fast as they could. Meanwhile, the six men who'd been in the Escalades closed ranks, forming a circle around Troy. And I realized exactly what this was: an execution.

Troy had come here to hurt Catalina, but he was the one who wouldn't be leaving.

Troy frowned, not comprehending that he was a dead man standing. "Mr. Benson? What's going on? Why are you here?"

Benson plucked his glasses off his nose. He held out a hand, and Silvio stepped forward and passed him a white silk handkerchief, which Benson used to clean the lenses.

"I'm here because apparently, you can't handle having your own territory," Benson said, focusing on his glasses. "Did you think that I wouldn't find out what happened?"

"If this is about last night, I can explain—"

"Of course this is about last night," he said, tucking the silk into his pocket before sliding his glasses back onto his nose and peering through the lenses at Troy. "You and your friends went to one of our Air healers to get patched up. Your friends were smart enough to contact Silvio immediately afterward and confess their incompetence. Yet you did not. Do you want to tell me why?"

"It was nothing," Troy insisted. "Somebody got lucky and got the drop on me. I was going to take care of it. Tonight."

"Hmm." Benson cocked his head to the side, as

though Troy were some curious specimen he was examining. "And yet here you are, all alone, in an empty garage. That doesn't give me a great deal of confidence in you, Mr. Mannis."

Troy's eyes flicked from the face of one vampire to the next. For the first time, he seemed to realize that his boss and his entourage hadn't dropped by for a polite chat. He swallowed and rubbed his hands on his jeans to wipe the nervous sweat off his palms.

"I can explain, Mr. Benson—"

"Explain what?" Benson cut him off again. "How someone threatened, embarrassed, and beat up you and two other members of my organization, the men I specifically gave to you to help with the new distribution at the college? What *do* you have to say about that?"

"I—I—I—" Troy sputtered, but he couldn't get the words out.

They wouldn't have saved him anyway.

"Don't you know that your embarrassment is *my* embarrassment?" Benson said. "You know that I don't tolerate mistakes or people hiding things from me. And I *especially* don't like my employees talking about my business interests to outsiders."

I frowned. It sounded like Troy had been blabbing. But about what? And to whom?

"But you've done all of those," Benson continued, "with your worst offense being running your mouth when you should have known to keep it shut. And now I'm afraid that you have to suffer the consequences of your actions, all your actions, Mr. Mannis."

Troy bolted.

He knew what was coming, and he wanted no part of it. Couldn't blame him for that. But the two vampires at the front blocked his exit and pushed him back into the waiting arms of the four men behind him. Two grabbed Troy's left arm, while the other two held tight to his right side, immobilizing him.

Beside me, Catalina let out a soft gasp, her right hand fisting in the fabric of my T-shirt sleeve, even as she clamped her left hand over her mouth to muffle the noise she'd made. Lucky for us, everyone was focused on Troy and his frantic attempts to buck, thrash, and kick free.

Everyone except Silvio.

The vamp frowned, his gray gaze scanning the garage before latching onto Catalina's car. His frown deepened, his brow furrowed, and his eyes narrowed. I tensed, wondering if Silvio might ask one of the men to make sure that the garage was empty and how many of the vamps I could cut down before they surrounded me. But after a few seconds, Silvio fixed his attention on Troy again.

By this point, Troy's struggles had dwindled down to tremors that racked his body from head to toe. "Please, Mr. Benson," he begged. "*Please*. I'll do better. You know I can do better."

"I'm afraid that it's too late for apologies, pleas, and promises, Mr. Mannis," Benson said, his voice calm, if still very nasal. "You are only as strong as you appear to be, and I can't have any weak links in my organization. Especially not now, when I'm rolling out a new product."

New product? I wondered if he meant the red pill Troy had given me at the college.

Benson snapped his fingers. Silvio reached into the

Bentley and drew out a long white coat, the sort that a scientist might wear in a lab. Benson held out first one arm, then the other, and Silvio carefully helped his boss into the garment, smoothing the fabric down over his arms and back the way a valet might. Silvio even did up the buttons on the front, so that the white coat covered Benson's clothes.

Troy shuddered, as if he knew what was coming next. So did the vamps holding on to him.

Benson smiled, his fangs glinting like pointed diamonds in his mouth, the sharp tips ready to cut through flesh and bone—Troy's. He strolled toward his minion, his stride smooth and steady, and snapped his fingers again. At the command, the four vamps holding Troy let go and stepped back. If I was the kid, I would have been hightailing it out of here, but he didn't move at all. Instead, he stood absolutely still, as if he was frozen in place by the Medusa gleam of Benson's glasses.

I thought that Benson would grab Troy, snap his neck to the side, and bury his fangs in the kid's throat, but to my surprise, Benson clapped a hand on the younger man's shoulder, as if to let him know that there was no real harm done. Troy sagged in relief.

And that's when Benson made his move.

His hand darted over and wrapped around Troy's throat. Benson lifted the other man up as easily as he had snapped his fingers, then pivoted and slammed Troy down onto the ground, hard enough to crack the concrete. It was an impressive display of strength, even for a vampire.

Troy must have had some giant blood in his family

tree to survive that kind of blow to the body, because all it seemed to do was daze him for a few seconds, before he started gasping, choking, and clawing at Benson's hand around his throat.

Instead of tightening his grip, Benson actually let go of his dealer. He crouched over the terrified man and started stroking his hand down Troy's cheek, as soft and easy as you please.

"There, there," he cooed. "Don't be frightened. It'll only hurt for a minute."

Benson's crooning only made Troy panic more. He heaved and kicked and flailed, but it was as if all the strength had suddenly left his body, because he didn't actually go anywhere, and his struggles were the weak, pitiful thrashes of a dying animal.

Silvio and the other vamps stood by, still and silent, in a ring around the two men. Everyone but Silvio averted his eyes.

A strange blue glow began to emanate from Benson's hand, so pale at first that I thought it was just a trick of the fluorescent lights overhead. But the glow grew and grew, and Benson's eyes took on the same eerie tint, magnified by his glasses.

But the strange thing was that the glow seemed to be moving *from* Troy and *into* Benson. Every time the vampire stroked his hand down Troy's cheek, the blue light intensified, like Troy was some sort of human cigarette that Benson had taken a quick hit off of.

The normal thing, the expected outcome, the logical action, would be for Benson to plunge his fangs deep into Troy's neck. All vamps needed blood to live, since all those frosty pints of O-negative contained essential vita-mins they required, just like other folks needed solid food to maintain a healthy playing weight. And depending on whose blood they were swilling down, vamps could get more than minerals from it. Regular human blood was enough to give most vamps enhanced senses, along with extra speed and strength. But if they drank from giants, dwarves, or elementals, vamps could absorb the traits of those races—a giant's strength, a dwarf's durability, an elemental's magic.

But Benson didn't go for Troy's throat. Didn't bare his fangs. Didn't seem at all interested in all of that sweet, sweet blood pumping through him. Instead, Benson kept stroking his hand down Troy's cheek, as if it was enough for him just to smell the salty sweat streaming down Troy's face; hear his small, weak, incoherent cries; and see the pain, panic, and fear twisting his whole body.

Maybe that *was* enough for Benson.

Maybe . . . maybe Benson wasn't feasting on the drug dealer's blood because he was dining on something else instead: Troy's emotions.

Some vamps could do that, could tear all of the pain, fear, anger, and love out of a person as easily as they could rip open someone's throat with their fangs. I'd never seen that sort of vampire in action before, though.

And I wished that I hadn't now.

Even as the blue glow intensified on Benson's hand, Troy seemed to deflate, like a cake that was caving in on itself. His beefy body grew thinner and thinner, his skin and cheekbones sinking in on themselves, as though he were the victim of some sort of sudden, extreme starvation. His dirty-blond hair fell out in clumps, and his breath came in a gasping, choking death rattle I knew all too well.

Even as Troy withered, Benson seemed to grow and grow, his chest expanding, his body lengthening, his arms and legs bulging until his white lab coat and pants barely contained them. One second, he was a thin, awkward, stringy puppet of a man. The next, he'd swelled up like a bodybuilder on steroids who looked like he would pop if he sneezed too hard. Troy's emotions must be giving the vampire power, strength, and energy, the same way someone's blood might. It looked like Benson had the odd bonus of getting actual, physical muscle mass from them too.

But the most disconcerting thing was that I could actually *feel* Benson pulling the pain, panic, and fear out of Troy, along with his life. Invisible sandpaper scraped at my skin, rubbing it raw. I could only imagine the excruciating pain Troy must be experiencing, being the focus of that sandpaper as it dug down deeper and deeper into him. But the sandpaper didn't just wear down Troy. It also pulled out bits and pieces of his feelings along the way and then somehow transferred all his emotions, all his energy, all his life, into Benson, as though the vamp were a scarecrow being stuffed with straw.

Perhaps it was a by-product of the vamp's ability, but fear blasted over me like heat from a sauna. Oh, yes. I could feel every single scrap of Troy's hot, sweaty fear, like burrs desperately sticking to my own skin, before Benson pulled them away and swallowed them whole.

"No," Catalina whispered. "He doesn't deserve that. We have to save him."

She started forward, but I clamped my hand over her mouth and dragged her back against me, making sure that we were both still hidden behind her car.

"It's too late for him," I muttered in her ear. "And us too if you don't be still and keep quiet."

Catalina struggled for a moment before slumping against me in defeat. She knew as well as I did that Troy was already dead.

Poor bastard. I almost felt sorry for him.

It took Benson less than two minutes to suck out all of Troy's emotions. And when it was done, and Troy's now bald, skeletal head lolled to the side in death, the vamp let out a long, loud, satisfied sigh, as though he'd just enjoyed the finest gourmet meal. I half-expected him to belch, but apparently, he was too dignified for that.

Benson got to his feet. His eyes burned an electric blue from Troy's pain and fear, the orbs brighter than all the lights in the garage combined. He smiled at no one in particular, and the glow from his eyes painted his fangs the same disturbing shade. None of the other vamps dared to meet his gaze, except for Silvio, who stood by patiently, no emotion at all showing on his face.

"Well," Benson crooned. "That was a nice snack. I hadn't realized how hungry I was."

Even his voice was larger now, bolder, stronger, and more nasal than ever before. The sound reverberated through the garage, making Catalina shiver beside me and the concrete wail and whimper with the last dregs of Troy's fear.

With Troy dead, I expected Benson to get into his car and leave, but instead, he reached inside his coat and pulled a small notepad out of his shirt pocket, along with a pen. The *click* of him snapping his thumb down on top of the pen boomed as loudly as a gong in the absolute quiet of the garage.

He crouched over Troy's body, examining it from all angles, and started scribbling on his pad. I grimaced. Benson was actually taking *notes* about what he'd done to the drug dealer, as though it were an innocent science experiment, instead of a brutal execution. Not only did he take notes, but he actually pulled out his phone, snapped several photos, and then held the device up to his lips and started murmuring his observations into it. I wondered if he had some sort of sadistic memory book of all the people he'd killed. It wouldn't surprise me.

Silvio remained still and quiet behind Benson, although the other vamps shifted on their feet, staring at the oil stains on the floor instead of at their boss. Nobody wanted to think that they might be in Troy's position one day—dead, drained, and deconstructed.

"We're done here," Benson finally called out, getting to his feet and putting away his phone, pen, and pad.

Benson snapped his fingers, and one of the vamps hurried to open the rear door of the Bentley. The others got back into the Escalades, but Silvio walked over to Troy, bent down, and started rifling through his pockets, taking Troy's wallet, phone, and the bags of pills he had stuffed in his jacket.

Oh, no. Couldn't leave those behind when another one of Benson's dealers could sell them.

Silvio started to rise, but his gaze caught on something glinting off to the left: Catalina's keys.

She'd dropped them when I'd startled her earlier, and they lay about five feet away from her car, in the middle of the floor, right out in the open. I tilted my head and ground my teeth together to hold back a curse. I was still peering around the back of the car, and the faint motion caught his attention. His gray gaze locked with my wintry one. Even worse, he spotted Catalina too, since I was still holding on to her.

Silvio's eyes widened, and his lips puckered. Another second, two tops, and he would open his mouth and yell at the other vamps to drag us out from behind the car. Then his boss would either feast on our emotions or give us to his men to play with. Neither option was pleasant to contemplate. Oh, I could kill some of the men but probably not all of them. Not before they got hold of Catalina, and especially not with Benson looking like some roid-rage wrestler spoiling for a fight. Our best chance of surviving this was to hotfoot it out of here as fast as we could.

"Something wrong, Silvio?" Benson called out to his second-in-command from the back of the Bentley.

"Get ready to run," I muttered in Catalina's ear.

Silvio stared at me for another heartbeat before dropping his hand down beside Troy's body and then smoothly rising to his feet. "Of course not. Just making sure I got everything."

He pivoted on his wing tip, strode back over to the car, and slid in behind the wheel, as if nothing had happened. But he'd seen us. I *knew* that he had. So why the hell wasn't he screaming about our presence to Benson and the other vamps?

I thought it must be some sort of trick, some ruse to get me to lower my guard and lose any chance I had of sprinting deeper into the garage and getting Catalina to safety. But Silvio cranked the engine, turned the car around, and steered it down the ramp. The two SUVs followed him.

A minute later, we were alone, and the only sound in the garage was the dark muttering of the stone around us.

✵ 6 ✵

As soon as Benson and his vamps were out of sight, I got to my feet.

"Come on," I told Catalina. "We need to leave. In case they decide to come back."

Catalina continued to slump next to the rear tire. Instead of standing, she curled in on herself. A sob escaped her lips, and she just crumpled. She buried her face in her hands, making her long, wavy black hair spill over her shoulders, then pulled her knees up to her chest and started rocking back and forth on the dirty concrete as she cried.

I left her to her tears. For now. My knife still in my hand, I went over to Troy—or what was left of him.

It wasn't pretty.

I'd once seen a water elemental pull all the moisture out of a giant's body, leaving nothing behind but a wet deck and a sloppy pile of skin and bones. This reminded me of that—except it was *worse*.

It wasn't that Troy looked particularly gruesome in death. Given his now hairless head and thin figure, he resembled a cancer patient more than anything else. And his bulging eyes and scream-frozen mouth didn't bother me in the slightest, not given all the times I'd put that same shocked and horrified expression on someone's face. But there was an . . . emptiness in his still body, as though he were nothing more than a brittle, hollow shell, like an egg without a yolk inside. I supposed that was exactly what Troy was now, since Benson had scooped out everything inside him worth taking. Being bitten and drained of blood by a vampire was bad enough, but what Benson had done, well, it wasn't something I wanted a repeat viewing of—ever.

I slid my knife back up my sleeve, crouched down on my knees, and rifled through Troy's pockets, even though Silvio had already picked them clean. Sure enough, I came up empty. But my movements shifted Troy's body to the left, and a gleam of plastic on the concrete caught my eye. I reached down and pulled a bag out from beneath the folds of his jacket.

A single blood-red pill lay inside the plastic.

It was the same pill, stamped with the same crown-and-flame rune, that Troy had given to me at the college. I remembered how Silvio's hand had dropped down to Troy's side before he'd driven off with Benson. He'd deliberately left the pill behind. Why? He'd seen me and, no doubt, knew exactly who I was. So why hadn't he told his boss that I was here? And why leave one of the pills behind? Whatever Silvio Sanchez was up to, it didn't make any sense.

I got to my feet and held the pill up to the light, turning it this way and that, but there were no other runes or marks on it, and I certainly wasn't going to swallow it to see what it would do to me. Maybe Bria would find it useful.

I slid the pill into my jeans pocket, then stalked over, grabbed Catalina's keys from the floor, and rounded the side of the car. The sharp *jangle-jangle-jangle* of metal cut through her sobs, and she slowly lifted her head. This time, I didn't take no for an answer. I put my hand on her arm and gently helped her to her feet.

"Come on," I said, unlocking the car and opening the passenger's-side door. "We need to get out of here. I'll drive you home."

"You're not—you're not just going to *leave* him there, are you?" Catalina croaked out.

She moved away from the car and headed in Troy's direction.

"You don't want to look at that," I called out.

But it was already too late. Catalina's face paled at the sight of her ex-boyfriend lying on the cold concrete and the horrible way he'd died. She clamped her hand to her mouth, staggered away a few feet, and threw up.

I sighed and leaned against the side of the car. When she finished, Catalina straightened up, pulled a tissue out of her jeans pocket, and used it to wipe off her mouth. I hoped that she would hurry over to the car and that would be the end of things, but instead, she went right back over to Troy's body, with disgust, guilt, and grief tightening her pretty features as she stared down at him.

"We need to call somebody . . ." Her voice trailed off.

"And tell them what?" I asked, my voice more sarcastic than it should have been. "That we witnessed Beauregard Benson, one of the most dangerous men in Ashland, kill one of his own dealers? It's not exactly a news flash. What we need to do is get out of here and forget this ever happened."

Catalina whipped around, her hair flying around her shoulders, her hands balling into fists. "I'm not leaving him!" she screamed.

The concrete around her let out a single sharp wail that melted into low, gravelly mutters of determination. The sound matched the mulish expression on Catalina's face. I thought about knocking her out, shoving her into her own car, and driving away with her. But I had the feeling that if I took so much as one step toward her, she would start screaming again—or, worse, bolt out of the garage.

If she did that, someone was sure to see her, and word would get out about Catalina running away from the scene of a gruesome murder with me chasing her. Then we'd both be in more trouble than we already were. Maybe I should have been more sympathetic to the trauma Catalina had witnessed, but I had enough problems already without attracting the attention of Beauregard Benson.

Since I couldn't get Catalina to leave and I didn't want Benson and his men to come back and find us, that left me with only one option.

"Okay, okay," I said. "I'll call someone. Look, I'm doing it right now, see?"

Catalina stared at me, still angry and suspicious, so I

pulled my phone out of my jeans pocket and hit a number in the speed dial. Three rings later, she picked up.

"Coolidge."

"Hey, baby sister."

"Hey, Gin." Bria paused. "What's up?"

"Why ever would you think that something's up?" I said in my best, most innocent, I-haven't-killed-anybody-in-hours voice.

"Because you never call me at work unless your work has somehow become *my* work," she said, a teasing note creeping into her voice. "So who is it this time, and how many bodies are there?"

The fact that she could joke about it was something of a miracle. Detective Bria Coolidge was a good cop, and my being the Spider was something that didn't exactly sit well with her at times. But we'd slowly come to an agreement ever since she'd returned to Ashland. Bria would never like my being an assassin, but she understood why I did it, the same way that I understood her being a cop and wanting to help people, even if the law was a running joke in our city and the only justice most folks got was what they made for themselves.

"Just one," I said, answering her question about bodies. "And it isn't even one of mine."

"What?" she asked, her voice still light. "Did Finn kill someone instead? I bet he just *loved* getting his new Fiona Fine suit dirty."

"No. It wasn't Finn. It was Beauregard Benson."

I expected another teasing comment, but Bria went immediately completely quiet, so quiet that I could hear the faint hum of her phone.

"Where are you?" she growled.

I frowned at the odd, intense tone in her voice, but I told her about the parking garage.

"I'll be there in ten," she snapped, every word sharper and louder than the last. "Don't move, don't let anyone see the body, and don't touch anything."

"What—"

I started to ask her what was going on, but she'd already hung up on me.

I stared at my phone, wondering at Bria's unexpected angry reaction. My sister dealt with criminals on a daily basis, some of whom wore badges and called themselves cops. But the mere mention of Benson's name had made her go from carefree to nuclear in five seconds flat. What could possibly be going on with Bria and Benson—

"Who was that?" Catalina asked, seeming a little calmer than before.

"Bria. My sister, the cop. You've seen her at the restaurant."

She nodded. "She's nice. Polite. A good tipper. Pretty too."

"She'll be here soon. Probably with Xavier," I said, referring to Bria's partner on the force.

Catalina nodded again and looked at Troy. She hesitated, then let out a breath and slowly sank down onto the floor next to his body, not caring about the dirt, oil, and other grime she was smearing all over her jeans. She reached out, as if to touch his withered hand, but thought better of it and ended up resting her palm on the concrete next to his.

"I don't expect you to understand," she said. "But I can't leave him."

"I know he was your ex, but he was trying to force you to deal drugs, and he followed you here tonight. He was going to hurt you bad, Catalina. Maybe even kill you."

She sighed, her face suddenly decades older than her twenty-one years. "I know. But he was still my friend. From before my mom died."

She looked at the back wall of the garage, but her gaze was even more distant. Jo-Jo sometimes got that same look, whenever she was peering into the future and hearing whispers about it. But Catalina wasn't an Air elemental, so the only thing she was seeing was the memories of her own past with Troy.

I lowered myself to the floor on the other side of his body. "Your mom died last year, right? Killed by a drunk driver?"

"Yeah," Catalina said, her tone flat. "In the spring. The drunk guy died too, so I didn't even have anyone to be angry at, you know?"

Yeah, I knew all about the anger that came with losing a loved one, especially so suddenly, so senselessly.

She drew in a breath. "My dad split when I was a kid. I never knew him. But my mom was great. Before she died and I . . . moved, we lived in Southtown. On Undertow Avenue."

I let out a low whistle. Undertow Avenue was one of the roughest streets in all of Southtown, the kind of place the cops wouldn't even go, unless there were at least a dozen of them and it was broad daylight. Even then, they'd still be outnumbered by the gangbangers, dealers, and other violent folks. Undertow Avenue also happened to be in the heart of Benson's territory. No wonder Catalina had known who he was. She'd spent her life living in his shadow.

"Troy lived in the house next door to ours," Catalina said. "His dad was a mean drunk who beat him and his mom, so he would always come over to my house to hide out. My mom would feed him cookies. Troy loved her chocolate-chip cookies so much."

She smiled, but tears streaked down her face. "Troy watched out for me, you know? Even when we were little, he'd walk me to school and keep the other kids from hassling me. When we got older, we were more than friends. I loved him. At least until . . ." Her voice trailed off.

"Until he started dealing drugs for Benson," I finished.

She shrugged. "I can't really blame him for it. In our neighborhood, that's what a lot of people did to make money. It was just another job to them, and him too."

"So what happened?"

Instead of looking at me, she traced her fingers over a black skid mark next to Troy's hand. "Being part of Benson's crew, there was always pressure to meet his weekly quotas. Troy was always stressing and scrambling to keep up. One day, we were arguing. He wanted me to start selling to help him out, but I didn't want to. He hit me."

Her hand rose to her left cheek, as if she could still feel the sting of that long-ago blow. Maybe she could, deep down in her heart.

"He said it would never happen again, but I'd seen that story too many times before, so I broke up with him. A month later, my mom died, and I . . . had the chance to get away, from the neighborhood, from Troy, from all the memories of my mom, so I took it. Maybe that was weak of me, but I took it, and I haven't looked back since."

I wondered what she wasn't saying, like exactly where she had gotten the money to escape from all the haints that haunted her in Southtown. But I stayed quiet, wanting to hear the rest of her story.

Catalina's hand fell back down to the concrete. "Everything was fine until the fall term started a few weeks ago. That's when I saw Troy again. He'd started dealing on campus, and I ran into him on one of the quads. He begged me to give him a second chance. I told him the only way I'd do that was if he quit working for Benson and got a regular job."

She shook her head. "He didn't like that at all. He said that I was a traitor, that I'd moved away and didn't remember what life was like in our neighborhood. I told him that there were lots of good, honest, decent, hardworking folks where we came from. I told him that my mom had never dealt drugs to make money. He said that I didn't have any loyalty to him, to everything we'd been through together, to how he'd protected me all those years."

Her gaze flicked to his bald head and sunken features. She shuddered and looked away. "I told him to leave me alone, but he kept following me around campus, trying to get me to go out with him. I could tell he was getting angrier and angrier, but I never thought that he'd actually hurt me. Last night, when he had those two vamps with him . . . that's the first time he ever really scared me. And now he's dead," she finished in a faint, tired tone.

"It's not your fault. The choices Troy made, the path he followed, he did all of that himself. And you are certainly not responsible for his death."

"Well, it feels like I'm responsible," Catalina whispered. "For everything. Maybe if I'd been more understanding, maybe if I hadn't demanded that he quit dealing, maybe if I'd just given him another chance, I wouldn't be sitting next to his body right now."

"Maybe," I replied. "Or maybe he'd be sitting next to yours if you had made him angry again."

She finally raised her gaze to mine, with guilt, grief, and memories swimming in her teary hazel eyes. "I know that he wasn't the same guy I grew up with, but I still cared about him, you know? He didn't deserve what Benson did to him."

"No," I replied. "The Troy you knew didn't deserve this."

Catalina fell silent, lost in her memories, her hand finally creeping over to touch Troy's. We sat like that, lost in our own thoughts, each of us haunted by the dead man between us.

❖ 7 ❖

Ten minutes later, I heard the distant rumble of an engine, growing louder and louder as it spiraled up to this level of the garage. I recognized the sound.

I finished my text to Sophia, telling her that I was fine and to go on home for the night, and hit send. Then I looked at Catalina.

"The cops are here," I said, getting to my feet.

Catalina nodded, but she stayed where she was on the floor by Troy's side.

A large, anonymous sedan rounded the corner, catching me in its headlights. The vehicle slowed, then stopped, and the doors opened, revealing two familiar figures. The driver was a woman with shaggy blond hair and bright blue eyes, beautiful enough to be a model, despite the no-nonsense black boots, dark jeans, and dark blue button-up shirt she wore. A gold badge glimmered on her black leather belt, next to her holstered gun. A giant with a shaved head, ebony skin, and dark eyes maneuvered his tall, muscled frame out of the passenger's side. Despite the late hour, a pair of aviator sunglasses were hooked into the neck of his white polo shirt.

Detective Bria Coolidge and Xavier headed in my direction. Xavier stopped by my side. I opened my mouth to call out a greeting to Bria, but she didn't even look at me as she stalked by. Power walkers didn't move that fast.

I frowned. Did my sister just blow me off for a dead body?

Bria's quick steps slowed when she spotted Catalina sitting on the concrete, but her presence didn't stop my sister from hurrying over, bending down, and studying Troy's body with a cold, critical eye, much the same way that Benson had done earlier.

"Yeah, that's good ole Beau's handiwork, all right," Bria said, disgust dripping from each and every one of her words.

Her voice might have been venomous, but her eyes were dark, her mouth was set in a hard line, and her hands were clenched into tight fists. For a second, Bria looked exactly like Catalina had right before she'd thrown up—sick, wounded, and vulnerable.

Bria eyed Catalina. A bit of sympathy flashed in my sister's eyes, momentarily softening them, but the expression was quickly snuffed out, and her features hardened again.

Bria surged to her feet and stalked back over to me, her movements even quicker than before. "Tell me what happened."

I stared at her, wondering what had her so riled up. "Aren't you even going to ask if I'm okay?"

"What? Why? You're fine. You're always fine." Bria waved her hand. "Tell me what happened, Gin. Now."

I frowned at her dismissive attitude and abrupt tone, but Bria just sighed, rolled her eyes, and crossed her arms over her chest, as though I were the one being curt and childish. So I gave in and filled her and Xavier in on everything from Catalina's run-in with Troy last night, to him following her to the garage, to Benson showing up and killing Troy.

The only thing I didn't mention was Silvio Sanchez seeing Catalina and me, and then apparently leaving a Burn pill behind for me to find. Maybe Silvio thought he could squeeze me for some money to keep his mouth shut. Maybe that's why he hadn't told Benson we were here. Either way, I wanted some time to puzzle out the vampire's motives. And Bria's too, since she was acting so strangely.

Bria's speculative gaze zoomed back over to Catalina. "She's one of your waitresses, right? Does she work for Benson too?"

I frowned again, wondering why she was so focused on Benson. "No, but she grew up with Troy."

I told them a condensed version of what Catalina had revealed to me about her past. Xavier shot Catalina a sympathetic look, but Bria started tapping her foot, the toe of her boot *snap-snap-snapp*ing against the concrete, racing along with her thoughts.

"What about that pill you found?" Bria asked.

I pulled the plastic bag with its blood-red pill out of my pocket, and she snatched it out of my hand. For a second, I thought about snatching it back from her. Bria's lack of manners was starting to get on my nerves.

"You know what it is?" I asked.

Her tense expression grew even grimmer. "It's called Burn. It's the latest designer drug on the streets, courtesy of Benson."

"Burn? Why that name?"

"Because it's supposed to make you feel like you are a mile high and like your veins are on fire at the same time," Xavier rumbled in his low, deep voice.

"Well, I suppose that explains the rune stamped on it," I murmured. "That crown-and-flame design represents raw, destructive power. But that's not Benson's rune, is it?"

"No," Bria said, still staring at the pill. "His is the letter B with two fangs sticking out."

"Supposedly, just one of those little babies will take you on the ride of your life," Xavier chimed in. "Human, vampire, giant, dwarf. It'll knock you on your ass no matter how big and strong you are, make you see things that aren't there, and generally screw with your head, according to the reports and what we've seen. It's supposed to be a real trip."

"Elementals too?" I asked.

He and Bria exchanged a glance.

"We've actually heard that it's even more potent for elementals," she said. "And it doesn't seem to matter how strong or weak their magic is or what element or offshoot they're gifted in. It really packs a punch with them. Nobody knows why, though."

"But haven't you guys analyzed the pills to figure out what's in them?"

She shook her head. "We've tried, but the lab folks

haven't been able to figure out all the ingredients. They've told me that there's something that gives the pills their zing, but that they haven't been able to pinpoint it yet."

Her words made me think back to the fork I'd touched in the Pork Pit. The utensil had had plenty of *zing*, so much so that it had practically sizzled with the auburn-haired woman's magic, whatever it was, before the sensation had slowly started to dissipate. And now here was something else that was unknown, dangerous, and deadly.

I didn't believe in coincidences. I never had, and all the close calls, deadly schemes, and tangled webs I'd navigated through ever since I'd killed Mab Monroe had made me more suspicious and paranoid than ever before. So I couldn't help but wonder if the woman at the Pork Pit could somehow be connected to Benson and his drugs. But I didn't see how. The auburn-haired woman had magic, and Burn was just a pill, just a chemical compound. Maybe they had nothing to do with each other. Maybe the woman had just come into the restaurant for a good meal. Maybe she meant me no harm. Maybe . . .

I rubbed my throbbing temples. *Maybes* always made for one hell of a headache.

"Anyway," Bria said, sliding the plastic bag with the pill into her pocket. "I'll call the lab and see if anyone is working tonight. Maybe it's not too late to get this one analyzed."

She pulled her phone out of her jeans pocket, hit a button, and held the device up to her ear. "Hey, it's Coolidge. I need to talk to whoever's left in the lab . . ."

She started pacing back and forth, her boots *crack-*

*crack-crack*ing against the concrete again. The longer Bria talked, the higher and faster her voice got, and she kept throwing one hand up into the air, punctuating all of her sentences, even though the person on the other end of the phone couldn't even see her.

"What is up with Bria?" I asked Xavier. "She's usually not this . . ."

"Forceful? Gung-ho? Eager to nail a bad guy's ass to the wall?" he said.

"I was going to say cold, rude, and dismissive. But yeah. All that too. I mean, she's always happy to throw drug dealers and other criminals in jail, but this seems . . ."

"Personal," Xavier finished.

"Yeah."

He looked at Bria, but she was still talking on her phone. Xavier nodded his head at me, and we stepped a few feet away from her. Catalina continued her silent vigil by Troy's body.

"Look, Bria asked me not to say anything," he began. "But with what happened tonight, I figure that you deserve a heads-up."

"About what?" I asked.

He glanced over to make sure that Bria wasn't listening to us before turning back to me. "Bria and I have been working on taking down all the dealers who sell Burn for a couple of months now, ever since it started showing up in Ashland over the summer. It makes people crazier than anything else I've ever seen, so crazy that they'll claw their own skin off because they think it's on fire or melting or something like that."

"Okay . . ."

"At first, it was just a routine assignment, you know?"

"Until . . ."

Xavier drew in a breath. "Until one of Bria's informants got caught up in the middle of it. Max Young, he was one of her snitches, eighteen years old, even younger than that dead kid over there. Typical story. Never knew his dad, mom died when he was ten, bounced around from foster home to foster home until he aged out of the system at eighteen. One of those guys who's always on the fringes, you know? Not really in a gang but staying on the edges in order to have the protection they offer in Southtown. Doing odd jobs for the real gang members to scrape together enough money for food and a lousy apartment every month. A nice kid, a likable guy, doing the best he could to survive."

"So how did he meet Bria?"

Xavier shrugged. "He was about to get the shit beat out of him by a couple of guys outside a Southtown bar. We were on patrol, and Bria jumped in and saved Max from them."

I knew my sister, so I could guess what had happened next. "And she took him under her wing."

"Yep," Xavier said. "Gave him some money, got him into a better, cleaner apartment building, even tried to get him to think about going back to school. In return, Max would feed Bria info about dealers, pimps who liked to beat the folks who work for them, gangbangers who were going to get a little trigger-happy with their rivals. Things like that."

My gaze cut to Catalina, who was still holding Troy's hand. She'd tried so hard to get away from Troy and the memories she had of growing up in Southtown, but here she was, another witness to the violence all the same.

"That sounds like low-level stuff," I asked. "So what happened to Max?"

Xavier glanced at Bria again. "Max calls Bria last week, all excited and bursting with pride. Says that he finally has some high-level intel for her—info that will blow her Burn case wide open. Says that Benson is the one distributing it. We knew that, of course, but we couldn't prove it, because—"

"No one talks in Southtown," I murmured, finishing his sentence, which was a common saying around Ashland.

"Exactly." Xavier nodded. "But Max says he can prove that it's Benson who's running the drug. Says he heard about a big shipment of Burn coming in from a dealer he knows. A kid selling at the community college, flashing a lot of cash and bragging about how much more he was going to make when the drugs came in."

My eyes narrowed. "That sounds like our dead friend there."

And if it was true, then Troy Mannis had been a marked man before I'd ever met him. Benson hadn't held on to his empire this long by letting his dealers blab about drugs coming into town. Most of the cops might take bribes and look the other way, but there were a few honest ones like Bria who could cause trouble for the vamp, especially if they got a tip that panned out. At the very least, the drugs could have been seized by the cops or jacked by a rival crew, and Benson would have been out hundreds of thousands of dollars, if not more.

I thought about what Benson had said to Troy about

paying for his actions, all his actions. He must have been talking about Troy's loose lips. Well, he'd certainly silenced them tonight.

"Yeah, that's what I thought too," Xavier said. "So anyway, Max sets up a meet with Bria. She goes to the location. Max is already there—dead. But that wasn't the worst part."

"And what would the worst part be?"

"The way Benson killed him." Xavier jerked his head at Troy. "It was just like that."

We both fell silent. I glanced at Bria, who was still talking on the phone. The death of any informant would be hard, but losing a kid like that—a kid she'd been trying to help—that would cut her deep.

"Max's death was also a message," Xavier said in a much softer voice. "To Bria."

"Why do you say that?"

"Because Benson stuffed a dead rat into the kid's mouth—and inked Bria's rune on Max's forehead."

I thought of all the pens I'd seen in Benson's shirt pocket. My gaze shot over to Bria and the silverstone pendant glimmering around her neck. A primrose. The symbol for beauty. Her personal rune.

"Has Benson made any threats against Bria?" My hands curled into fists at the thought.

Xavier shook his head. "No, nothing like that. But no one's giving her information anymore either. None of her snitches will return her calls about anything, even if it's not related to Benson. Nobody wants to end up like Max. So Bria's been on a tear to take down anyone and everyone associated with Benson and Burn."

"Why didn't she tell me?"

"She tried to talk to you about Benson once, when you were having that girls' day at Jo-Jo's salon. But she didn't get the chance—"

"Because that's the day Sophia was kidnapped," I finished. "But why didn't she try again? Especially after Max was murdered?"

Xavier gave me a pointed look. "And what would you have done if she had?"

I opened my mouth, ready to tell him that I would have supported my sister and let Bria handle things the best way she saw fit, but that would have been a lie.

I sighed. "I would have paid Benson a quiet visit on the sly. Or at the very least, some of his men, enough of them to send him a message not to mess with my sister."

"And we have bingo," Xavier said. "I know you, Gin. If there is the slightest risk to anyone you care about, then you will eliminate that risk. And we all know how you do that."

"By carving people up like Christmas hams," I finished.

"Exactly."

I shrugged. "Bria's hands are dirty enough just being related to me. Just acknowledging that I exist and that we have a relationship, that she cares about me. She doesn't need to sink down any deeper in the muck with me."

"And you need to realize that Bria is her own person, especially when it comes to being a cop," Xavier replied. "She likes to do things herself, in her own way and time. Just like you do. She really liked Max. We both did. She feels like Max's death is on her, and she wants to be the one to bring down Benson. You should understand that better than anyone else."

I scuffed my boot over a skid mark on the concrete. "Oh, I understand it, but that doesn't mean I like it."

After Bria finished her conversation, she slid her phone into her pocket and came back over to Xavier and me. "Cassie is in the lab. It took some convincing, but she agreed to stay and analyze the pill tonight."

Bria's convincing had sounded more like badgering, but I decided not to mention that. Xavier nodded, and my sister turned her gaze to me.

"And I'm going to need you to come downtown and make a statement about what you saw. About Benson killing that dealer."

My eyebrows zoomed up into my forehead. "You want me to what?"

"Make a formal statement," Bria replied, as if it were the most natural thing in the world. "To be a witness and help me build my case against Benson."

My mouth dropped open. Between it and my eyebrows, no doubt I looked like some cartoon character whose face was stretched out to comical proportions. The next thing you knew, my eyes would pop out of my head and roll away in surprise. "You can't be serious."

"Why not?"

"Because I'm an assassin, Bria," I snapped. "I kill people. The only testifying I do is with my knives."

She waved her hand, as though my dark occupation and all the blood on my hands were of no concern. "We can work around that."

I stared at Bria. Normally, she tried to keep our professional lives, so to speak, as separate as possible, although I knew that she would always have my back if I ever really needed her. But right now, she seemed perfectly willing to shine the uncomfortably bright spotlight of law and order squarely on me. It wasn't like her at all.

Xavier shrugged his broad, muscled shoulders at me, as if to say *I told you so*. Max's death must have hit Bria harder than even she realized, if she was willing to shove me in front of everyone just to get Benson. Surprise sparked in my chest, along with a little hurt that she wanted to use me this way. But she was hurting too, so I tried to reason with her.

"Really?" I asked. "And how are you going to work around the fact that I've killed just as many people as Benson has? Maybe more?"

Bria's hands dropped to her hips, and she tapped her fingers against her gold detective's badge. "I'll think of something."

"And what do you think will happen if you arrest Benson and your case actually goes to court?" I snapped. "Any halfway-decent lawyer has heard more than enough rumors and innuendos to totally discredit me. Assassins don't exactly make the best witnesses. I bet Jonah McAllister would pay Benson to be his attorney just for the pleasure of cross-examining me."

McAllister had been Mab's lawyer before I'd killed her, and he'd tried to have me murdered multiple times since her death. Back in the summer, I'd finally taken a bit of revenge on McAllister, putting him on the hot seat with the underworld bosses by revealing his involvement in a plot to rob them at the Briartop art museum. Ever since then, he had been staying out of sight and stewing in his Northtown mansion, but I had no doubt that he'd spent many long hours trying to figure out how to turn things back around on me. And something like this would be a golden opportunity.

Bria's hand slid from her badge over to her gun, her fingers instinctively curling around the weapon. "You don't understand, Gin. I have to get Benson. I *have* to. And you're my best shot at that."

For the first time, I noticed how tired my sister looked, the purple smudges under her eyes, the rigid set of her slender shoulders, the harsh slant of her mouth, as though she were disgusted with herself. Her blue eyes locked with mine, and I could see the pain shimmering in her gaze— along with the guilt.

"Look, if you want Benson taken out, just say the word, and I'll start working on it," I said, trying to find some way to help her and still keep what was left of my anonymity intact.

I knew that Bria wanted to do this herself, in her own way, within the black-and-white confines of the law, but Xavier was right. I'd do anything to protect the people I loved, and if I could help Bria by killing Benson, then I was more than happy to do it for her.

Especially since the vamp might decide to turn his attention to my sister if she kept pursuing him.

I drew in a breath. "It won't be easy, and it may take me a few weeks, but I'll figure out a way to get to him—"

"No." She shook her head, her blond hair snapping around her shoulders before settling back down into place. "*No.* I'm not going to ask you to do that. I'm not going to stoop to Benson's level."

"We're talking about *my* level right now." My voice was as cold as hers was hot. "And I can tell *exactly* what you think of that."

Bria ground her teeth together, but she didn't deny or contradict my words. Her silence shouldn't have hurt me, but it did. I might not have a badge, but I fought for justice in my own way, and I helped people when I could. I thought that Bria understood that—that she realized that we were the same that way.

Apparently not.

"I'll do it."

We all turned to stare at Catalina. She'd been so quiet since Bria and Xavier had arrived that I'd largely forgotten about her. Catalina let go of Troy's hand, got to her feet, and slowly walked over to us.

"I'll do it," she repeated in a stronger voice. "I'll be your witness. I'll tell everyone who will listen exactly what Benson did to Troy."

* 8 *

"No," I said, shaking my head. "No. You have no idea what you're getting yourself into."

Catalina's gaze cut to Troy's body again. Her face hardened, and her hazel eyes sparked with anger. "I know what I'm doing, and I know what I saw."

I moved closer to her. "You don't owe Troy anything. No sort of loyalty whatsoever. Not after what he did to you last night. Not after what he was most likely going to do to you here tonight."

Her fierce expression melted into a more melancholy one. "You're wrong. I do owe him. He took care of me all those years ago. This is the last way that I can take care of him. I want to do this, Gin. I want to testify. I *have* to do it. So please don't make this any harder than it already is. Okay?"

I could tell by the grim set of her lips that nothing I could say would change her mind, but I still felt compelled to try—

"If you want, we can take your statement right now," Bria said, and stepped up beside us before I could protest. "Save you the hassle of going down to the station."

My mouth dropped open, and I once again felt like a cartoon character whose face was stretched out to impossible proportions. Two minutes ago, she'd wanted me to march into the police station, right past all her fellow boys in blue, and now she was giving Catalina a free pass on that? Anger flooded my heart, replacing my earlier hurt.

"Excuse us, Catalina." I ground out the words. "I need to speak to my sister, the detective."

I grabbed Bria's arm and pulled her away. Xavier stayed behind with Catalina, talking to her in a low, soothing voice. I marched Bria over to the far side of Catalina's car, out of earshot of the others, then whirled around to face her.

"You have no idea what you're doing," I hissed. "You're going to get that girl killed. And for what? Just so you can collar Benson? Even if you arrest him, the chances of him spending any time in jail are slim to none. He has too much money, too much power, and too many connections for that."

"It'll be fine," Bria insisted in a stubborn tone. "Xavier and I can protect Catalina."

"From Benson? And the dozens of vampires who work for him? I doubt that. The second Benson hears that there's a witness to Troy's murder, he will do everything in his power to find and kill Catalina—and anyone else who gets in his way. That includes you."

Bria crossed her arms over her chest. "I'm a cop, Gin. I can take care of myself."

"Yeah, you can, but you're being awfully cavalier with Catalina's life. Xavier's too."

Her eyes narrowed. "I don't tell you how to kill people, so why don't you give me the same courtesy and quit telling me how to do my job?"

My whole body stiffened, and I had to work very hard to keep my face blank, as though her verbal knives had slid right off my skin, instead of burying themselves deep in my heart.

Bria winced, and she opened her mouth, almost like she was going to apologize. But then her gaze flicked to Troy's body, a shadow passed over her face, and her lips mashed down into a hard, flat line. She wasn't going to back down, so I decided to try another approach.

"Look, Xavier told me about your informant, Max," I said, trying to rein in my own temper and ignore the hurt I felt.

Her angry gaze shot over to the giant. "He had no right to do that—no right *at all*."

"I know you feel responsible for what happened to Max."

"I *am* responsible." Guilt and bitterness roughened her voice. "*I'm* the one who wanted info on Burn. *I'm* the one who pushed him to get in deeper with Benson's crew. Max did exactly what *I* wanted, and now he's dead. And *I'm* the reason why."

"Bringing down Benson won't change what happened to Max."

"No," Bria agreed, rubbing her thumb over her detective's badge. "But at least I'll know that the bastard will never do that to anyone else."

"Except Catalina, when he finds out about her."

Bria stiffened, and her hands balled into fists. Yeah, it was a low blow on my part, but that didn't make it any less true.

"If you'll excuse me, I need to take my witness's statement," she snapped. "I'm also going to call in the scene. Since you're so worried about being identified, it's probably better if you're not around when everyone else shows up."

Bria pushed past me and went back over to Catalina and Xavier. She gently put her hand on Catalina's arm, escorted her over to the sedan, drew a notepad and a pen out of the back pocket of her jeans, and started writing down Catalina's statement. Xavier gave me another troubled look, then went to stand next to Bria. He didn't like it either, but it was his job to back her up, and he'd do it, just like always.

Catalina started talking. I didn't hear her words, but I didn't need to. I'd seen the whole thing for myself. Instead, I watched Bria. The longer Catalina spoke, the more eager my baby sister's expression became, and a twinkle shone in her eyes, almost as if she was enjoying hearing about a young man's murder.

But the thing that bothered me the most was Bria's smile—a cold, cruel, satisfied expression I'd never seen her wear before.

But one that I'd sported all too often as the Spider.

Even though Bria had made it abundantly clear that I wasn't welcome here anymore, I stayed in the garage until she finished taking Catalina's statement. Bria moved off and started talking on her phone, notifying the rest of the po-po about the murder. Catalina drifted back over to Troy's body, saying her good-byes, while Xavier walked over to me.

"I'm going to follow Catalina home, then come back and help Bria," he said. "Bria's agreed to keep Catalina's identity under wraps for as long as possible. She's not going to tell anyone who Catalina is until she absolutely has to. Neither will I."

"Benson will still find out. You know he will."

Xavier shrugged. He couldn't deny it. He reached out, squeezed my arm, then went over and got into the sedan. Catalina bent down over Troy's body and touched his hand a final time before straightening back up. She wiped a few tears away and came over to where I was leaning against her car.

"Thank you for being here tonight," she said. "For saving me."

My heart twisted. I hadn't saved her so much as I had signed her death warrant. I should have found some way to sneak her out of the garage instead of letting her witness Troy's murder. Now Benson was going to kill her as soon as he found out that she'd seen what he'd done.

"See you at work tomorrow?" she asked.

"Sure."

I handed over her keys. Catalina gave me a shaky smile, more tears pooling in her eyes, then slid into her car and cranked the engine. She backed up and followed Xavier in the sedan out of the garage.

Bria was still talking on the phone, pointedly not looking in my direction. Maybe I should have tried to make nice with her, but right now, I was too angry and disgusted to bother.

So I went over to the stairs and plodded down them to the first level, my soft footsteps like a steady heartbeat against the dirty concrete. I stood in the shadows by the entrance, staring out at the street. The lights spaced along the sidewalks continually flickered, the weak, worn-out bulbs humming in warning that they could go dark at any second. The sputtering glows made it seem as though the graffiti runes spray-painted everywhere were moving, like roaches skittering along the street and up and down the building walls. Most of the cars that had been parked here earlier were gone, and I didn't see anyone schlepping down the sidewalks, not even a couple of hookers trolling for clients.

I sighed. It didn't matter if anyone was watching or not. The cops would be here soon enough, their blue and white lights flashing and drawing everyone's attention to the garage. And when word got out about exactly how gruesome Troy's murder had been and that there had been a witness to the crime, well, that would only make folks more interested in things, especially Benson in finding and eliminating Catalina.

But Catalina had made her choice to testify, and there was nothing I could do to stop her, even if doing the right thing would probably end up getting her killed. I sighed again, a little louder and deeper this time, stuck my hands into my jeans pockets, and ambled down the street.

I'd only gone half a block when a pair of headlights popped on behind me.

I palmed a knife and whirled around, thinking that

maybe Benson had already heard something on the police scanner and had come back with his vamps to investigate.

But the lights weren't from a car cruising down the street. They were on one already parked at the curb close to the garage entrance—a black Audi with tinted windows.

The Audi's engine churned steadily, sounding as smooth and silky as a cat's satisfied purr. I squinted against the glare of the headlights, but I couldn't make out who was sitting inside through the tinted windows. I doubted it was just a wayward commuter, though, hiding in his car until the scary woman with the knife decided to leave. Oh, no. If whoever was inside was an innocent bystander, he would be calling the cops and racing down the street as fast as he could, instead of sitting there playing a game of chicken with me. Maybe Benson had left some vamps behind to watch the garage for whatever reason. Either way, I wanted to know who was in that car and why.

So I sprinted toward the Audi, coming at the car from an angle, in case the driver decided to floor it, zoom up onto the sidewalk, and try to turn me into a bloody pancake against the side of the garage. I was a hundred feet away from the car and closing fast. Seventy-five . . . sixty . . . fifty . . . thirty . . .

The driver finally did floor it, and I tensed, ready to throw myself out of the way of the sleek hood and churning wheels. But I didn't have to. The driver turned the wheel sharply to the left . . . and zoomed away from the curb and down the street.

I cursed, whipped around, and ran after the car, even though there was no way I could possibly catch up with it. The Audi rounded the corner. A few seconds later, so did I, but the car was already two blocks away and picking up speed. I cursed even louder as I finally stopped. I hadn't even gotten the license plate to give to Finn.

It wasn't until the car had zipped around another corner, completely disappearing from sight, that I realized that the black Audi was an exact match to the vehicle the two mystery women had gotten into when they'd left the Pork Pit earlier this evening.

❊ 9 ❊

I frowned into the darkness, my mind racing through all the implications.

There was no way that the auburn-haired woman and her giant bodyguard could have followed me here from the Pork Pit. They'd left the restaurant before I did, and I'd cut through too many alleys for them to track me easily. But here they'd been all the same. Why had they been parked outside the garage? How long had they been there? And what had they been waiting for?

If they'd wanted to assassinate me, then one of the women should have rolled down her window, stuck a gun through the opening, and sprayed the sidewalk with bullets—at the very *least*. Tossed some grenades at me, run me over, pinned me against the garage wall and put a clip full of bullets in my chest. Oh, yes. They could have done any one of those things.

In addition to looking out for would-be assailants, I

also spent a fair amount of time imagining exactly how they might murder me. I supposed that it was my professional mind at work, so to speak, since I'd dispatched so many folks myself in such varying ways. I'd pictured all those scenarios before, along with dozens more. But instead of attacking me, the people in the car had just driven off, and I didn't think it was because I'd spooked them with my killer smile and my gleaming knife.

More theories swirled through my mind, each one darker and more violent than the last, but none of them answered my questions. I had a sinking feeling that there were some new players in Ashland—ones who seemed to know a lot more about me than I did about them.

But there was nothing I could do to confirm my suspicions about the women who may or may not have been in the Audi. Besides, Bria was right. The cops would be here any minute, and it would be better if I was gone.

So I slid my knife back up my sleeve, stepped into the shadows, and disappeared into the darkness.

Still keeping an eye out for the mystery car, I headed back to the Pork Pit. I took a few minutes to check the restaurant, but the lights were off, the doors were locked, and no one was hanging out in the alley, waiting to murder me. Everything was quiet, so I walked three blocks east to the side street where I'd parked my own car.

After I'd checked my vehicle for bombs and rune traps, I got inside and circled the downtown loop a few times, looking for the black Audi, but I didn't spot it. Whoever was inside had probably hightailed it up into Northtown by now. Still, I had a feeling that I'd see the Audi—and the two women—again.

When I was certain that no one was following me, I left downtown behind and headed out into the suburbs that flanked Ashland. Twenty minutes later, I steered my car up a steep driveway, gravel spewing out in every direction, before the vehicle crested the top of the hill.

Fletcher's house—my house now—came into view. Shadows cloaked the ramshackle structure, softening the harsh edges, odd angles, and obvious seams between the mismatched sections of white clapboard, brown brick, and gray stone.

Engine running, I sat in my car, scanning the entire area from the woods to the left, across the yard, and over to the steep, rocky ridge that dropped away from the front of the house. Just in case whoever had been in the Audi knew where I lived, in addition to where I worked.

But no one was hiding inside the tree line or crouched down beside the house, and the only movements were the breeze gusting through the trees and a few fireflies flitting across the yard, desperately flashing their fluorescent lights before the growing cold killed them. Satisfied that I was alone, I killed the engine, got out, and went inside.

If the outside of the house was a sprawling beast, then the inside was the creature's clogged heart, only with rooms, hallways, and staircases that curled, snaked, and zigzagged every which way, instead of veins, valves, and arteries. I headed upstairs, took a shower, and threw on some pajamas before padding back downstairs to the kitchen.

I poured myself some milk to wash the bitter taste

of car exhaust and questions out of my mouth, then wrapped my hand around the glass and reached for my magic—my Ice magic this time. I was the rare elemental who was gifted in not one but two areas—Ice and Stone, in my case. A silver light flared to life in my hand, centered on my spider rune scar, and cold Ice crystals quickly spread over the entire glass, frosting it and further chilling the milk inside.

When that was done, I grabbed a piece of pumpkin cheesecake studded with chunks of golden apples out of the fridge, topped it with some fresh whipped cream, and sprinkled everything with a bit of cinnamon. I opened a kitchen drawer and started to reach for a fork, but the memory of the burning silverware at the Pork Pit made me hesitate. I didn't even know the mystery woman's name, but she was already getting inside my head.

I grumbled at myself for my own paranoid foolishness, then grabbed a fork, some napkins, my plate, and my milk and headed into the den to relax on the blue plaid sofa. I forced all thoughts of the mystery women, Benson, Bria, and Catalina out of my mind as I concentrated on my snack. The rich, thick pumpkin filling, the faint crunch of the apples, the warmth of the cinnamon, and the light, airy cream made for a delectable dessert— so delectable that I went back for another piece. I deserved it after everything that had happened tonight.

While I ate my second piece of cheesecake, I called Finn and told him what had gone down at the garage. Finn was, well, *Finn*, especially when I told him what I wanted him to do.

"Do you know how many Richie Rich types in Ashland have black Audis?" he whined in my ear. "I have two myself. It'll take *forever* to find the one you're looking for."

"Just track down the car. Please? It's important. I know it is."

"Fine, fine," he grumbled. "I'm on it. Sophia sent me the pictures of the two women you saw at the Pork Pit too."

"Yeah, she copied me on that." I scrolled through the photos on my phone as I took another bite of cheesecake. "You ever seen them before?"

"Nope, but the brunette is something else. Yowza. Trust me. I *definitely* would have remembered her."

Even though he couldn't see me, I still rolled my eyes. "You mean you would have *definitely* remembered hitting on someone like her."

Finn might be involved with Bria, but that didn't keep him from being an incorrigible flirt. If someone was female, then Finn felt it was his duty to charm the socks off her, no matter her age, attractiveness, or availability. And he was amazingly good at it too. Finn could flirt his way into or out of almost any sticky situation, including those involving irate husbands and jealous boyfriends.

"I might not know who they are, but I can find out easily enough," he murmured. "At least when it comes to the giant."

"Really? How?"

"See that watch on her wrist? It's an expensive bauble. Shouldn't be too hard to track down who it belongs to, especially since there's only one store in Ashland that sells that particular brand of bling—and the Posh manager happens to owe me a favor."

I squinted at the screen, but it just looked like a watch to me. "Everyone in this town owes you some sort of favor."

"It does help to be popular." Finn's voice was smug in my ear. "Although technically, I suppose that it's *your* favor, since you were the one who actually saved her and her assistant from that dwarven robber."

"Nice to know how you're cashing in *my* favors."

"Always," he chirped, not the least bit ashamed.

We hung up, with Finn promising to roust some unsuspecting manager on my behalf. I dialed Owen next. He was understanding and sympathetic as always, the calm sounding board I needed him to be, especially when it came to the sudden tension between Bria and me.

"Siblings fight," Owen said. "You know that. Eva and I have had some doozies over the years. We always manage to find a way to get past it. You and Bria will too."

I sighed and snuggled down deeper into the couch cushions. "I do know that, all of that. But you should have seen Bria tonight. She was practically foaming at the mouth at the thought of using Catalina's testimony against Benson. It reminded me of . . ."

"Yourself?"

Owen's voice was gentle, but I still winced all the same. "Yeah."

"Bria's a cop," he said. "She's just as tough and strong as you are, and when she has a job to do, she doesn't let anything get in her way. The two of you are eerily similar that way. Must be a Snow family trait."

His teasing tone brought a ghost of a smile to my face, but it fled all too quickly, and my gray gaze drifted up to the fireplace mantel, where a series of framed drawings perched.

The runes of my family, dead and otherwise.

My mother Eira Snow's snowflake, for icy calm. My older sister Annabella's ivy vine, representing elegance. Their matching silverstone pendants draped over their respective drawings. The neon pig sign outside the Pork Pit that I'd drawn in honor of Fletcher. Owen's hammer for strength, perseverance, and hard work. And finally, Bria's primrose, symbolizing beauty.

"She's always going to be my baby sister," I replied, staring at the primrose drawing. "The one whose hair I used to brush while she drank invisible tea and chattered nonsense to her dolls."

"I know," Owen said. "But you can't protect her forever, Gin. At some point, you have to let go."

I didn't *want* to let go. Because every time I did, I lost someone else I cared about. I'd watched my mom disappear in a ball of Mab's elemental Fire. I'd let Annabella pound down the stairs at our house, and she'd been burned to ash by Mab too. I'd left Fletcher to go do a job as the Spider, which turned out to be a trap, and he'd been tortured to death in his own restaurant. So no, I wasn't letting go. I wasn't losing Bria too because I'd stood by and failed to act. Even if I was still angry and hurt by all of her harsh words and actions tonight.

"Gin?" Owen asked.

"Yeah, you're right," I said, lying through my teeth. "I should let Bria handle this one."

We talked for a few more minutes. Owen promised to come by the Pork Pit for lunch tomorrow, and I told him how much I appreciated him letting me vent. Then we hung up.

I tossed my phone down onto the coffee table, making the fork rattle on my empty plate. I stared at the fork, then at the runes on the mantel, then back at the fork.

What the hell. I went and got a third piece of cheesecake.

Sometime between polishing off my latest round of dessert and watching some mindless TV, I fell asleep on the couch.

The dreams started soon after that.

My dreams were more than weird, random images strung together—they were memories of all the bad things I'd seen, done, and survived. Most nights, I dreamed of the jobs I'd gone on as the Spider, the people who'd tried to murder me, and all the ones I'd killed in return. But tonight was a real blast from my past, back before I'd met Fletcher, back when I'd just started living on the streets and didn't know how I was going to make it from one day to the next . . .

I was so hungry.

Hungrier than I'd ever been before in my entire life. *So hungry that I was actually considering eating the withered brown apple I'd plucked out of the Dumpster behind this dive bar in Southtown. I didn't know why there was an apple in the trash outside a gin joint, but it was the only thing I'd been able to find today that was even remotely edible.*

Despite the constant grumbles in my stomach urging me on, I still held the apple out with two fingers, as if it might bite me like the rats that lived in the alleys sometimes did.

I turned the fruit this way and that, carefully scrutinizing every single part of it.

It only had two bites taken out of it. Most of it was still good. That's what I told myself. And really, I was too hungry to care how long it had been rotting in the Dumpster, what kind of germs it had on it, or how sick it might make me. Most nights, I just wanted to go to sleep in some dark alley and never wake up. If the apple killed me, well, maybe that would be for the best.

So I sank my teeth deep into the fruit, trying to tell myself that the bitter, sour taste was normal—natural, even. But it didn't stop me from devouring the whole thing. All too soon, the apple was gone, and I was left with nothing but a rotten core.

And I was still hungry.

Sighing, I tossed the core behind some trash cans for the rats to fight over, then turned back to the Dumpster and stood on my tiptoes so I could peer over the side and see if there was anything else lurking in the dark, damp corners that I'd missed. And not just food. Even though it was September, the nights were getting colder and colder, and I'd quickly learned that wrapping a few newspapers around your body was better than letting the wind whistle down the alleys and sink into your clothes. But I'd lost my stash of papers to a bum a few alleys over. Apparently, I'd been sleeping in his spot, over this sewer grate that blew up warm air, and he didn't like it. My ribs still ached from where he'd kicked me awake this morning, and I could still feel his dirty hands and sharp nails ripping the papers off my body so he could clutch them to his own sunken, shriveled chest.

After that, I'd started running, and I hadn't stopped until

I couldn't run anymore, which was how I'd wound up in this alley, scrounging for food yet again—

"What do you mean, you're finished?" an angry male voice called out.

"I mean I'm finished. You got what you paid for. You want something else, you pay for it up front. Those are the rules, pal," a younger, feminine voice snarked back.

I hunkered down beside the Dumpster and peered around the side. Two people stalked into the alley. One was a middle-aged man wearing a cheap suit, with a bad comb-over and a big, round belly that made it look like he'd swallowed a basketball. The other was a thin girl with teased bright crimson hair, a silver sequined tank top, and silver shorts that were way too short and tight, given the cool fall breeze. The girl wasn't that much older than me, maybe fifteen or sixteen, despite the heavy makeup that rimmed her brown eyes.

"I told you that I'm good for the money," the guy pleaded, scurrying along beside the girl, who was walking fast, despite the strappy silver stilettos on her feet.

"Sure you are, hon," she snarked again. "Just like all my other special friends."

"Well, if you won't give it to me, then I'll just take what I want," he snarled.

He reached out and shoved her up against the wall.

"Hey!" the girl shouted, slapping her hands across his face and chest. "Let go, loser!"

But he was stronger than she was, and I knew what was going to happen next. I'd seen it happen before to other girls in other alleys. Guys too. I should have slipped away while I could, before the man spotted me, but I couldn't ignore the way his hands tore at her skimpy clothes like the bum's had *done to mine this morning. And suddenly, I was more angry than scared.*

Before I even really knew what I was doing, I grabbed an empty beer bottle from beside the Dumpster, darted across the alley, and smashed it down on top of the guy's head. He growled as the glass shattered and sliced into his skull, but he whirled around to face me.

"You little bitch!" he yelled. "You'll pay for that!"

He reached for me, but I lashed out with the broken end of the bottle. It was a wild swing, but I got lucky, and the glass cut through his jacket and shirt and sliced a jagged gash all the way up his forearm. Blood spewed everywhere, the coppery scent overpowering the stench of garbage in the alley, but strangely, I wasn't afraid. It actually felt . . . good to do something other than run away.

"You little bitch!" the man hissed. "You cut me!"

He staggered forward, but the other girl stuck her foot out, tripping him, and he fell onto his hands and knees.

"Run!" the girl yelled, grabbing my hand and pulling me along behind her. "Run!"

So we ran and ran and ran, ending up in another alley four blocks over before we collapsed on top of the steps that led up to the bright, glossy, crimson-painted back door of a ratty-looking apartment building. I put my hands on my knees, sucking down giant gulps of air, but the girl started pacing around me, grinning from ear to ear.

She laughed and threw her hands out wide. "That was awesome! I loved the look on that guy's face when you cut him. Son of a bitch wasn't even going to pay for it. He deserved that—and more."

She spat onto the cracked asphalt before facing me again.

"*You know, you were pretty good with that bottle. You done that before?*"

I glanced down and realized that I was still clutching the neck of the broken beer bottle—and that the man's blood was all over my hand. I dropped the glass and kicked it away, sending it skittering down the alley. I grabbed the end of the red-and-black plaid flannel shirt I'd swiped off a Southtown clothesline a few days ago and used it to wipe the blood off my hand, wincing as I rubbed the raw, red skin of my palm.

The girl frowned. "*What's wrong with your hand? What's that mark on it?*"

My fingers curled into a fist, hiding the silverstone spider rune that had been branded into my palm. "*Nothing. I just burned myself a while back.*"

"*Oh, okay. Well, I'm Coral,*" she said. "*What's your name?*"

I shrugged, instead of answering her. I knew better than to tell anyone that my name was Genevieve Snow. If the Fire elemental who'd murdered my family ever found out that I was still alive, she'd come and kill me too. I just knew she would.

Coral eyed me, taking in the long floppy shirt that covered the three mismatched T-shirts I had on underneath, the gray cargo pants I'd tied around my waist with string from a kid's discarded kite, and the tattered too-big sneakers I'd stolen from a yard-sale table when no one was looking. The dirt and grime of living on the streets were smeared all over my face and hands, with even more matted in my dark brown hair. I hadn't had a shower in more than a week, and I smelled even worse than I looked.

Still, Coral's gaze took on an almost speculative look, as

if she could see through the layers of grungy clothes and filth to the person I used to be. The nice, quiet girl with plenty of food and clothes and a family that loved her.

"You hungry?" she asked. "You want some food?"

She said the magic word, and a loud, demanding rumble erupted from my stomach, answering her question.

Coral laughed. "Come on, kid. Let's get you a hot meal and get you cleaned up."

She drew a key out of the pocket of her silver short-shorts, slid it into the crimson door, and opened it. Coral crooked her finger at me. I bit my lip, hesitating, knowing that it was dangerous going anywhere with a stranger, no matter how nice she seemed. But I didn't have anywhere else to go, and I had absolutely nothing to eat, so I followed her inside, into the shadows, letting the door bang shut behind me . . .

I woke up with a gasp, the sound of that long-ago door slamming rousing me out of my dream. For once, I didn't sit bolt upright or thrash around. Instead, I lay there on the couch, my head twisted at an awkward angle, staring at the rune drawings on the fireplace mantel. I sighed, and some of the tension left me, even if the memories didn't.

They would never, ever do that.

I untwisted my neck and swung my feet over the side of the couch, sitting upright. I scrubbed my hands over my face, then stared down at the scars branded into my palms. A small circle surrounded by eight thin rays. My spider rune. The symbol for patience.

Something I had run out of a long time ago when it came to my memories. But ever since Fletcher had been murdered, they'd just kept coming and coming, reminding me of so many things in my past that I would rather forget. But the nightmares had been getting worse, the dreams more frequent, violent, and vivid, the closer it got to my birthday. They were so bad that I would sometimes have odd little daydreams about them, flashing back to whatever bad thing was buried in my subconscious at any given moment, even when I was wide awake. Like seeing Fletcher's blood on the floor of the college yesterday.

Like I'd told Owen, this wasn't my favorite time of year. Not by a long shot. But I'd get through it, the way I had everything else.

So I sighed again, turned off the TV, and went upstairs to bed, even if I knew that sleep would be a long, long time coming tonight.

✳ 10 ✳

The next morning, I got up, drove downtown, and opened up the Pork Pit right on schedule, as though it were just another day and nothing noteworthy at all had happened last night.

And Catalina did the same.

She showed up a few minutes before eleven to work her shift, just as she'd told me she would. She gave me a grim smile when she stepped inside the restaurant, before quickly lowering her eyes, pushing through the double doors, and heading into the back. Several minutes later, she reappeared, wearing a blue work apron over her jeans and long-sleeved white T-shirt. She stopped at the opposite end of the counter from me and started rolling silverware and straws into napkins.

It was the same thing she always did when she first started her shift, but her movements were slow and clumsy today, her fingers fumbling with the napkins like they were made out of butter, instead of paper. Her shoulders slumped forward, and her soft, subtle makeup couldn't hide the tired slant of her mouth and the faint pallor that dulled her bronze skin. Looked like I wasn't the only one who hadn't gotten much sleep last night.

A fork slipped out of her hand and clattered to the floor, breaking the quiet. Catalina let out a soft curse, stooped to pick it up, and tossed it into one of the plastic gray tubs we used for dirty dishes. Normally, she would glance in my direction, smile, and make some joke, but instead, she concentrated on the silverware and napkins again, hunching over the counter so that her black hair hung over her face like a curtain, hiding her tense, exhausted features from my sight.

In between us, Sophia stood at the counter, mixing up some macaroni salad. The silverstone hearts dangling off the purple collar around the Goth dwarf's neck tinkled together like wind chimes as she stirred the pasta, carrots, and other veggies together.

Sophia looked at Catalina, then at me, raising her black eyebrows in a silent question. I'd filled Sophia in on everything that had happened, so she knew why the waitress was strangely silent. I shrugged back. I wasn't going to push Catalina to talk about what had happened to Troy. I knew better than anyone else that there were some things you simply couldn't talk about, no matter how much they haunted your soul.

Instead, I hopped off my stool, strolled over to the front door, and flipped the sign hanging on it over to *Open*. A few minutes later, the first customer walked inside, and

Sophia, Catalina, and I started cooking and serving, with a few more of the waitstaff coming in to help out.

The lunch rush came and went with no problems. Still, in between cooking, wiping down tables, and cashing out customers, I kept one eye on the front door, waiting for Benson to send some of his men to try to eliminate Catalina.

Troy's murder was all over the news, with Bria being quoted as saying that the po-po were pursuing all available leads. She didn't mention having a witness, but sooner or later, she would have to tell one of the higher-ups in the police department about Catalina. Then it would be open season on the waitress, as far as Benson was concerned. I was glad Catalina had shown up for her shift, even if she didn't want to talk to me. At least while she was at the restaurant, I could protect her.

But the minutes slipped by and turned into hours, and nothing happened.

No vamps, no threats, no action of any kind. No one even tried to murder me when I took the trash out back after the lunch rush. That only made me more suspicious that something sinister was brewing. Whether it was related to me or Catalina, well, only time would tell.

But the most troubling thing was the fact that I didn't hear from Bria. Not so much as a text. No doubt, she was completely wrapped up in Troy's murder and tightening a noose around Benson's neck. At least that's what I kept telling myself, instead of dwelling on the fact that Bria's need for revenge was consuming her, the way it had consumed me in the past. Either way, her radio silence shouldn't have bothered me, but it did.

Especially since she called Catalina instead.

I went into the back to get a jug of ketchup to refill the bottles on the tables and found Catalina standing beside one of the industrial-size refrigerators, clutching her phone to her ear. Startled, she sucked in a breath and froze, the proverbial deer-in-the-headlights look on her face. When she realized it was me, she relaxed—but only a little.

A low murmur echoed out of her phone, as though someone were asking her a question.

"I'm okay," Catalina replied. "Someone just surprised me."

She listened for a few seconds. "Yeah, she's here right now. Do you want to talk to her?"

That's when I knew that Bria was on the other end. So I stopped and waited.

Silence. Then another low murmur sounded.

"Oh, okay." Catalina gave me an apologetic look and tiptoed a little closer to the back door, turning away from me. "So what's the next step, then?"

Disgusted, I grabbed the ketchup off a metal rack, shoved one of the doors open, and stormed back out into the storefront.

Catalina eased into the front of the restaurant a few minutes later, tucking her phone back into her jeans pocket. She looked at me, then bit her lip, grabbed a pitcher of sweet iced tea, and started refilling glasses.

I stood at a cooking station along the back wall, chopping up carrots and celery for another batch of macaroni salad and being far more vicious and violent than I needed to be with the defenseless veggies. A few feet away, Sophia hefted a vat of Fletcher's barbecue sauce off the hot burner and onto several oven mitts so it could cool down, the thick muscles in her arms rolling with the motion. She glanced at Catalina, then at me.

"Not her fault," Sophia rasped, picking up on my anger and frustration. "Innocent."

"I know," I muttered, slicing my knife into another carrot. "And that is what makes this whole thing all the more tragic and ironic. But whose fault is it going to be when Benson kills her for trying to do the right thing?"

Sophia didn't have an answer for that, and neither did I.

Thirty more minutes passed, and a few more customers came and went. I had just finished slicing the last of the celery when my own phone rang. I wiped my hands off, then pulled the device out of my pocket and stared at the number on the screen, hoping that it was Bria, finally checking in with me, finally letting me in, finally asking me to help her with this.

But it wasn't.

Disappointment surged through me, but I recognized the number, so I took the call.

"Gin?" Roslyn Phillips's low, sultry voice filled my ear.

"Hey, Roslyn. What's going on? Kind of early for you to be calling."

It was three in the afternoon, and Roslyn was something of a night owl, since she operated Northern Aggression, Ashland's most decadent after-hours club. Most nights, the drinking and debauchery at the club didn't kick into high gear until well past midnight.

"Oh, I came in early to do some inventory. It never ends." She let out a laugh that sounded more brittle than genuine. "Anyway, that's what I wanted to talk to you about."

I frowned. Roslyn had never once talked to me about inventory in all the years I'd known her. "What's up?"

"I finally have that special bottle of gin you asked me to order for you."

My hand tightened around the phone, and my danger radar pinged up into red-alert territory. I'd never asked Roslyn to order any booze for me. Something was wrong. Someone was there with her. Someone was using her to get to me.

"How many bottles are there?" I asked in a casual voice, in case anyone was listening on her end of the line. "I hope you got me more than just one. You know how much I love that stuff."

"Oh, yeah," Roslyn said, not missing a beat. "You're right. I forgot that you had ordered three bottles."

She knew what I was really asking: how many people were there with her. Three was more than manageable, and the idiots who'd strong-armed her into doing this were going to realize what a fatal mistake they'd made as soon as I got over there.

"Anyway, I thought that you might want to come and pick up the bottles this afternoon," Roslyn chirped, her voice going a bit higher, as though someone was telling her to hurry up. "Before the club opens up for the night."

My mind raced, trying to come up with a way to buy myself—and Roslyn—some more time. My gaze landed on the plastic tub full of dirty dishes that Catalina had set on the counter. I reached over, grabbed a fork out of the tub, and started scraping it against a plate that was sitting inside.

"Well, we're a little slammed, as you can probably hear. I've got about ten customers waiting for food right now. But I can probably be there in an hour, ninety minutes tops. Okay? Or will that be too late for you?"

Roslyn let out a relieved breath. "Sure, an hour or so will be fine. See you then."

"Oh, you can count on it."

✷ 11 ✷

I ended the call, slid my phone back into my pocket, and dropped the fork into the tub. My gaze cut left and right, scanning over the customers, but they'd all been here for at least fifteen minutes now, and I didn't see anyone obviously studying me to see how I reacted to Roslyn's call.

When I was sure that no one was watching me, I grabbed a newspaper from beside the cash register, then strolled toward the double doors at the far end of the counter, untying my blue work apron and hanging it on a hook on the wall as I went. I kept my movements easy and casual, as though I were just taking a break, but Sophia noticed the cold fury in my eyes and the hard set of my mouth as I stopped next to her.

"Gin?" Sophia asked. "What's wrong?"

"Nothing much," I drawled, plastering a pleasant smile on my face. "I just need to run over to Northern

Aggression. Roslyn has a rat problem that she needs some help with."

The dwarf frowned. "Rats? Roslyn never has—" She stopped, her black eyes narrowing. "Oh. Rats."

"Yeah. Rats. Care to help me find the poison for them?"

She nodded, pulled open one of the oven doors, and slid a tray of sourdough buns inside to bake. I headed through the swinging doors and into the back.

Since the restaurant was packed, all of the waitstaff were out front, seeing to the customers, so there was no one around to watch me toss the newspaper aside, march over to one of the freezers, and drag a black duffel bag out from behind it. I straightened up, put the bag on a nearby table, unzipped the top, and did a quick inventory of all the items inside. Money, fake IDs, tins of Jo-Jo's healing ointment, anonymous black clothes, and enough guns, ammo, and knives to start a small war. Satisfied, I zipped the bag back up and slung it over my shoulder.

The doors opened behind me, and Sophia appeared. Her gaze locked onto the bag in my hand. She knew exactly what was inside, because she had a similar bag, one with a grinning figure of Death holding a scythe printed on the side, hidden behind another freezer.

"Problem?" she rasped.

"Someone's decided to use Roslyn as leverage," I replied, and told her about Roslyn's call.

"Go with?" Sophia asked when I finished.

I shook my head. "Thanks, but no. I'll call Finn and Owen on the way over there. Bria too."

I went back over to the doors and looked through the round glass in the top at Catalina, who was passing out plates of food to a table full of customers. I turned back to Sophia.

"Stay here and keep an eye on Catalina for me. Okay?"

She nodded. "I'll call Jo-Jo too."

I knew what she really meant. That she'd let Jo-Jo know what was going on in case I needed the dwarven Air elemental to heal Roslyn or myself.

"Thanks. Roslyn sounded okay on the phone, but I have no idea if she'll stay that way."

Sophia nodded again, then reached out and took hold of my arm, giving it a gentle squeeze. "Be careful."

I grinned back at her. "Always."

Sophia went back out front to watch over Catalina in case Benson sent some of his vamps to the Pork Pit in search of her. Bria probably hadn't told anyone Catalina's name yet, but knowing that Sophia would look after the waitress let me focus on what I had to do now: get to Roslyn.

So I palmed a knife, opened the back door, and stepped out into the alley behind the restaurant, my head swiveling left and right, looking for anyone hunkered down beside one of the Dumpsters, leaning against the walls, or even stationed at either end of the corridor. If the person holding Roslyn hostage was smart, he or she would have someone watching the restaurant to tell them when I left so they could get ready for my arrival at Northern Aggression.

But the alley was empty.

No lurkers, no watchers, no assailants of any sort haunted the area, and the only sound was the *skitter-skitter* of a crumpled-up white paper bag bearing the Pork

Pit's pig logo that was being pushed across the cracked asphalt by the steady breeze. Well, just because no one was waiting in the alley didn't mean that there weren't watchers around somewhere.

Still being cautious, I walked to the end of the alley and fell into the flow of foot traffic on the sidewalk. I kept to the side streets as much as possible, quickly making my way over to my car, which I'd parked four blocks from the Pork Pit.

No one was following me, but I rounded the corner just in time to see someone snap a photo of my car, lean his ass against the hood, and start texting on his phone. No doubt, he was sharing the vehicle's location with his boss. So whoever had Roslyn had had his or her men stake out my car instead of the restaurant. Smart. Just not smart enough.

Apparently, Roslyn's captors had believed my lie about not being able to leave right away. Otherwise, the guy would have been skulking in one of the nearby alleys, instead of being out in the open right next to my car. Still, even if he wasn't expecting me for a while, it was sloppy of him to be so brazen, and I planned to use his carelessness to my advantage.

I glanced behind me, but this was a narrow street, with only a few cars parked on one side, and most of the store-fronts were boarded up. I was the only one on this par-ticular block, besides the guy at my car. Good.

I hoisted my duffel bag a little higher on my shoulder and started whistling a soft, cheery tune that Sophia had taught me. The guy looked up from his phone. He started to go back to his text, but his brain finally kicked into gear, and he recognized me. He froze, his thumbs jamming into his phone's keypad and making it beep at him.

Instead of going over and confronting him, I gave the watcher a pleasant smile and walked right on by my car, as though the vehicle weren't mine at all. I kept my steps slow and steady, as though I were in no particular hurry. After about thirty seconds, shoes slapped on the sidewalk behind me. A glance at my reflection in the dirty windows of a defunct Italian restaurant confirmed that the watcher was scurrying after me, his phone dangling from his hand.

I grinned.

My casual walk continued until I reached the end of the block. As soon as I stepped around the corner, I dropped my duffel bag and pressed myself up against the side of the building, scanning the area. The block off to my left was deserted, and an alcove was set into the wall two feet past my right elbow, leading to a battered metal door, although whatever business had been behind it was long closed. To my right, at the far end of this block, a bum wearing layers of tattered rags dug through a plastic bag of garbage someone had tossed onto the sidewalk, searching for tin cans to add to the load already in his shopping cart.

Normally, I would have kept going until I could lure my watcher into a completely deserted area, but the bum was focused on his recycling, and I wanted to get to Roslyn as quickly as possible.

Besides, I was good at killing people quietly.

So I stood against the building, knife in my hand, tuning out the usual humming and honking of cars and horns on the neighboring streets, and concentrating on the *smack-smack-smack* of the watcher's footsteps. He was a minute out and closing fast. I counted off the seconds in my head. Sixty . . . forty-five . . . thirty . . . twenty . . . ten . . .

The guy careened around the corner, his phone still in his hand, desperately trying to catch up with me before I disappeared completely. I grabbed the back of his suit jacket, spun him around, shoved him through the alcove, and slammed him into the door.

Crunch.

The sound of his nose breaking against the door was even louder than his hurried footsteps had been. The guy yelped and whirled around, blood dribbling down his face and murder in his eyes.

"Don't be an idiot," I warned.

Too late. He dropped his phone, his right hand darting toward the gun clipped to his belt, but I didn't give him the chance to use it. I surged forward, clamped my hand over his mouth, and cut his throat with the knife still in my other hand. He died with a choking, bloody gurgle.

The guy pitched forward onto me, but my clothes were dark enough to hide the worst of the bloodstains. I lowered him to the ground and propped him up against the battered door, with his legs sticking out of the alcove and his feet falling away from each other on the sidewalk, as though he were a drunk sleeping off a bender.

Tink-tink-tink.

My head snapped to the left at the sounds, but it was just the bum still picking through the garbage. Even as my attacker bled out, the bum hooted with glee, apparently having found the mother lode. He started tossing can after can into his shopping cart like a basketball player swishing free throws. Dude had some game.

I waited a few seconds, but the bum kept adding to his aluminum haul. He was either too preoccupied by his search to notice me, or he was smart enough to pretend that I hadn't just murdered a man a hundred feet away from him. Didn't much matter to me which one.

Since the bum was seemingly fascinated with his discovery, I focused my attention back on the dead watcher. I didn't recognize his face, but a pair of fangs gleamed in his mouth, which was frozen open in surprise at the brutal bit of death I'd just dealt him.

The man could have worked for anyone, but I couldn't help but think of Benson and his army of vamps. Could Benson be behind Roslyn's call? If so, I hoped that he was one of the three folks waiting for me at Northern Aggression. It was about time we had a face-to-face chat.

I started to get up, retrieve my bag from the sidewalk, and be on my way, when something let out a soft *beep*.

I went back down on one knee, keeping clear of the growing pool of blood forming around the vamp's body, and fished his phone out from underneath his leg. A message from an unknown caller lit up the screen.

Has she left yet?

I sent whoever was on the other end a text.

No. Still watching for her.

I waited a few more seconds, but apparently, the person on the other end was content to wait for the vamp to respond when he spotted me leaving. I slipped the device into the back pocket of my jeans, then pulled out my own phone and sent a text to Sophia.

Watcher in doorway on Dalton Street. Leave as is, or dispose of at your leisure. Your choice. G.

A few seconds later, Sophia hit me back with a smiley face: ☺

I grinned, put my phone away, and grabbed my duffel bag. I also took a moment to fish the dead guy's wallet out of his suit jacket and swipe the cash inside before wiping off my prints and leaving the empty leather on the pavement beside his body so it would look like just another robbery gone wrong. Then I got to my feet and headed toward the bum, who was sorting through the cans in his shopping cart.

He finally looked up when my shadow fell over him. His eyes narrowed, and he grabbed the handle of his cart, holding on tight with both hands, lest I try to wrest it away from him. But all I did was toss the crumpled bills I'd taken off the dead watcher on top of the sticky mound of cans.

"For helping to keep the streets clean," I said.

The bum gave me a suspicious look, but he snatched the money off the aluminum and tucked it into one of his pockets.

I winked at him, then turned and headed back toward my car, whistling all the while.

No one else was lurking at or around my vehicle, and no one had planted any bombs on it, so I was able to slide inside and zoom away without any more problems or delays.

While I drove, I pulled out my phone and called Bria, to let her know what was going on. But instead of picking up, my call went straight to her voice mail. *Hi, you've reached Detective Bria Coolidge with the Ashland Police Department . . .*

I growled in frustration, but I didn't leave her a message. The way things had gone between us last night, she was probably screening my calls, so I doubted that she'd listen to any voice mail I left her right now.

I tried Xavier next, since Roslyn was his main squeeze, but he didn't answer either. He was probably busy working with Bria on the best way to use Catalina's testimony against Benson. I dialed Owen too but struck out for a third time. Then I remembered that he had some big business meeting planned for this afternoon, so he was probably tied up with that.

But there was one person I called who actually picked up his phone.

"You have reached the always awesome, ever charming, and obscenely handsome Finnegan Lane," he chirped in my ear. "How may I be of service to you today?"

"Where are you?"

"Work. At the bank. Why?" His voice sharpened with every word.

I filled him in on Roslyn's call and her request for me to come over to Northern Aggression to pick up my nonexistent bottles of gin. Finn was silent for a moment, then let loose with a string of curses.

"You want me to come help you?" he said. "I can grab my guns out of the safety-deposit boxes in the vault and be right over."

"No. Roslyn said that there were only three of them. I should be able to handle that. See if you can track down Bria and Xavier. I've called them both, but their phones go straight to voice mail."

"I'll round them up and bring them over to the club as soon as possible," he promised. "Watch your back."

"You know I will."

I hung up and tossed my phone into the passenger's seat.

I drove fast and reached Northern Aggression in record time. I'd told Roslyn that I wouldn't be here for at least an hour, but I had no intention of sticking to that timeline. The element of surprise could help me rescue my friend, and I intended to exploit it to the fullest.

But instead of zooming into Northern Aggression's main lot and screeching to a stop in front of the entrance, I parked my car two streets over in an alley where no one would notice it. I glanced at my duffel bag on the passenger seat, debating whether I wanted to dig a gun, some ammo, and a silencer out of the dark depths. But I decided not to, since I was carrying my usual arsenal of five silverstone knives—one up either sleeve, one tucked against the small of my back, and one in the side of either boot.

My knives were my best weapons, especially in a situation like this that called for quick, quiet action. So I grabbed my phone, got out of the car, and tucked the device into my pocket. I also checked the dead vamp's phone, but there were no more messages, so I slid it back into my pocket as well and headed for the club.

I leapfrogged from one alley and side street to the next, until I ended up crouching behind a weeping willow at the far end of the parking lot in front of the club. I peered through the swaying screen of long green tendrils.

From the outside, Northern Aggression looked like an office building, plain and featureless, except for the sign mounted over the entrance—a heart with an arrow through it. Roslyn's rune for her club. Since it was mid-afternoon, the neon sign was dark, but when the crowds came out tonight, it would glow a bright red, then orange, then yellow, as though the pierced heart were a living, beating thing, pulsing in agony from the wound it had received.

A guy was standing by the entrance, his arms crossed over his chest and his eyes sweeping from left to right and back again. I didn't recognize him as one of the bouncers, and he wasn't wearing a gold heart-and-arrow rune necklace that would mark him as one of the hookers, bartenders, or other club workers. He shifted on his feet, his unbuttoned black suit jacket flapping around enough for me to get a glimpse of the gun holstered on his belt. Well, that certainly clued me in to the fact that he was up to no good. I grinned. Me too.

But I left the guy alone, since there was no way I could sneak up on him without him seeing me coming, given the open, empty pavement that stretched between us. Instead, I darted from tree to tree, skirting around the edges of the parking lot until I had worked my way over to the back of the building.

Another man was stationed at this entrance, a younger guy who had his head down and his eyes glued to his phone instead of keeping a watch out for me. Careless fool.

Lucky for me, a line of Dumpsters stretched from my position all the way up to the back door where the guy was standing, so I was able to use the containers as a screen between the two of us. It took me less than a minute to move from the edge of the lot to the Dumpster closest to him. But there was still about a twenty-foot gap between this container and his position at the door, which would give him more than enough time to let out one good, long, loud scream if he saw me coming.

So I reached down, picked up a loose bit of metal, and chucked it over his head. The metal hit the wall off to his right and then *tink-tink-tink*ed across the pavement, and the guy finally looked up from his phone. He cursed and swiveled in that direction, his free hand yanking the gun from the holster belted to his waist.

I skirted around the Dumpster and crept up behind him, moving fast. I was so focused on the guy that I didn't see the broken glass littering the pavement behind him until it was too late.

Crunch.

At the sound of my boots hitting the glass, the guy brought his gun up and pivoted toward me, but I was close enough to surge forward, dig my fingers into his hair, yank his head back, and cut his throat. His legs went out from under him, and he died with a raspy whisper, his phone and gun slipping out of his suddenly slack fingers and clattering across the pavement.

I moved over to the west corner of the building and pressed myself up against the wall, wondering if the noise of the phone and the gun tumbling end over end would carry all the way around to the front of the club and trying to guess which side the first man might approach from. But a minute passed, then another, and the other guard didn't come to investigate, so I figured that it was safe for me to slip inside the club.

I tried the back door, which was locked, so I reached for my magic and made a couple of Ice picks. Less than a minute later, the door *snick*ed open. I tossed the picks down onto the ground to melt away, eased inside the club, and closed the door behind me.

A long hallway stretched out in front out me, with rooms and corridors branching off on either side. I didn't know where in the club Roslyn and her captors might be, so I tiptoed down the hallway, peering into every room I passed, careful to keep up against the wall at all times, where it was less likely that the bamboo floor would creak and give away my position.

But no one haunted the back of the club. No hookers were in the locker room, putting on their makeup and heart-and-arrow necklaces and getting ready for another night of sin. No bouncers were carrying around cases of liquor to restock the elemental Ice bar out front. No one was waiting in Roslyn's office to talk to her. They must be out in the main part of the club, then.

I had started to slide down another hallway, to see if I could get a glimpse of what was going on out there through one of the many peepholes that were cut into the walls, when a toilet flushed in a men's room off to my left. I moved forward and stopped outside the door. A few seconds later, the door opened, and a familiar figure stepped out into the hallway: Silvio Sanchez.

He was once again wearing a gray suit, and he paused

long enough to straighten his matching tie, which gave me plenty of time to strike. But instead of cutting his throat like I had done to the other two men, I snaked my arm around his lean waist and pressed the point of my knife against his neck, right where his carotid artery was.

Silvio stiffened, but he did the smart thing and didn't try to fight back. If he had, I would have fileted him like a fish.

"Blanco?" he asked.

"Surprise, surprise," I hissed.

Silvio tried to step away from me, but the scrape of my knife against his throat persuaded him to stand still.

"Where's Roslyn? How many more men are in the club?"

"Just me and two more," he said. "That's everyone who's inside. I swear."

He didn't say anything about the men waiting outside, but I hadn't expected him to. Still, his head count lined up with what Roslyn had told me, so I decided to let Silvio keep breathing—for now.

"Where?"

"Out in the front part of the club. In the middle of the dance floor. He wanted to be able to see you coming."

I didn't have to ask who *he* was. "Well, that was smart of him. Otherwise, he'd probably be dead already."

"He hasn't hurt her, if that's what you're worried about," Silvio said, trying to save his own neck and his boss's too. "He just wanted to talk to you. There's no need for this to get violent."

"Oh, this has already gotten violent," I drawled. "Just ask the man you stationed by my car or the one at the back door here. Oh, wait. Silly me. You can't, because they are indisposed at the moment. Forever, actually."

Silvio swallowed, his Adam's apple bumping up against the edge of my knife, but he didn't respond to my taunt.

"While you're here, I am curious about one thing," I said.

"What's that?"

"I know you saw me and the girl in the parking garage. So why didn't you rat us out? Why leave that pill next to Troy's body and walk away like you hadn't seen anything at all? Did you think you could blackmail me? Get me to pay you to keep quiet?"

"I have my reasons."

I dug my blade into his neck, breaking the skin and drawing blood, to encourage him to start talking. Silvio stiffened even more, feeling more like a board pressed against my side than flesh and bone, but he remained silent. Whatever he was holding back, it would take more than a scratch from my knife to get him to spill his guts. I admired him for that—but only a little.

"Well, then, on to other matters. You and I are going to go out and do the whole meet-and-greet that your boss so desperately wants. Don't make any problems for me, and you might live through this."

"And if I do make problems?" he asked in a wry tone, even though he already knew the answer.

"Make so much as a whimper, and I will slit your throat," I hissed again.

Silvio nodded once. Smart man.

"Move," I ordered.

Silvio walked toward the door at the end of the hallway. I gripped his left shoulder with one hand and used the other to keep my knife at his throat, so our progress was slow but steady. We reached the door.

"Open it—slowly."

Silvio started to nod again but thought better of it, given the blade against his neck. He leaned forward enough to turn the knob and crack the door. The murmur of conversation drifted over to me.

". . . good to see that you've done so well for yourself, Roslyn," a familiar nasal voice said.

Silence.

"Thank you," Roslyn answered, her normally light voice tight with tension. "But I don't see the need for this."

A low laugh sounded. "Oh, I think we both know that I couldn't meet with your friend under any other circumstances. Not without killing her. And you wouldn't want that, now, would you?"

This time, Roslyn laughed. "You always were confident. In this case, too confident."

"We'll see."

Silvio slowly opened the door the rest of the way. I leaned to one side so that I could see over his right shoulder.

"Walk," I ordered him.

Silvio moved forward, his steps slow, careful, and steady. He didn't want to get sliced open. We would see if the same could be said for his boss.

We stepped through the door and into the main part of the club. The inside of Northern Aggression was all opulent glamour, from the springy bamboo floor to the red crushed-velvet drapes cloaking the walls to the glittering elemental Ice bar off to my left. The air was cool, bordering on frosty, to keep the bar intact until the elemental who maintained it with his magic came in for his shift, but the chill swirling through the room was nothing compared with the cold fury running through my veins.

Roslyn was sitting at a small round table that had been moved to the middle of the dance floor. In her teal-blue suit, she looked every inch the successful club owner she was. The bright color set off the dark luster of her black hair and the rich toffee color of her skin, while her understated makeup highlighted her toffee eyes and perfect features.

And she wasn't alone.

Beauregard Benson sat opposite her at the table. Long, gangly arms and legs, rumpled black hair, blue eyes behind silver glasses. He looked much the same as he had in the garage last night, wearing white pants and sneakers, with a pale pink button-up shirt and matching bow tie. I didn't see his white lab coat anywhere, but adding to the geeky-scientist illusion were the plastic protector and the notepad and pens once again lined up inside it in a neat row in his shirt pocket. He had one ankle crossed on top of the opposite knee, his pant leg pulled up enough to expose his sock, white with a pink argyle pattern in the center.

Benson's posture was easy and relaxed, but another guard stood a few feet behind the vamp, his arms crossed over his chest and his hard stare fixed on Roslyn, as if he expected her to cause trouble at any second.

That was *my* job.

At the sound of Silvio's footsteps, Benson looked in our direction. "Ah, Silvio. There you are. I was wondering what was taking you so long—"

Benson's mouth puckered at the sight of me and the knife I had at his minion's throat, but the expression quickly melted into a smile as he got to his feet. His figure was lean again, instead of having the bulked-up look it had last night after he'd drained Troy of his emotions. I wondered what he'd done to expend all that stolen life and energy so quickly. Probably best not to know.

"Ah, Ms. Blanco," he said. "So glad you could join us. And ahead of schedule too."

"Well, I got your invitation and hurried over here as fast as I could," I drawled, my voice as calm and even as his was.

His smile widened. "I don't think that we've been properly introduced. My name is Benson. Beauregard Benson."

✵ 12 ✵

Beauregard Benson bowed to me, as low, gallant, and charming as any old-fashioned Southern gentleman. But his blue eyes were as empty as mirrors, despite his veneer of manners and civility.

The third man cursed and started to reach under his jacket for his gun, but Benson snapped his fingers, as though he were calling off a junkyard dog. The other man froze at the sharp sound.

"There's no need for that," Benson purred again, although his high, nasal voice ruined his smooth words. "Is there, Ms. Blanco?"

Instead of answering him, my gaze went to my friend. "Roslyn?"

She slowly got up from the table and stepped back, removing herself from the line of fire, should it come to that. "I'm okay, Gin."

Benson gestured at the table. "Please, Ms. Blanco. Let's sit and talk."

"If you wanted to talk, you could have just called," I said in a sweet tone.

"Call me old-fashioned, but I prefer face-to-face conversations." His voice was as fake and syrupy as mine was.

He might as well have substituted *confrontations* for *conversations*, but I decided to play along—for now. Roslyn was unharmed, and I wanted to keep her that way. Going along with Benson was the easiest way to ensure her safety. Besides, part of me was curious about what the vampire possibly thought he had to say to me. Ah, that damned old curiosity. Going to get me stabbed in the back one day.

Maybe even right now.

"All right, then," I said. "Let's chat."

I dropped my knife from Silvio's throat and shoved him away. He stumbled forward a few steps before he managed to right himself. Silvio's hand crept up to the cut on his neck, and then he pulled his hand away and stared at the blood glistening on his fingertips. I thought he might shoot me a dirty look for ruining his clothes, but instead, he sighed, pulled a gray silk handkerchief out of his pants pocket, and wiped the blood off his fingers and neck. Silvio went to stand with the third man.

Benson gave his minion another curious look, as though he were interested in Silvio's wound, before resuming his seat at the table and gesturing at the empty chair across from him.

Keeping one eye on the vamps, I stalked across the bamboo floor to where Roslyn was standing. I touched her arm, and she nodded.

"I'm fine," she said in a voice loud enough for everyone to hear. "Really."

She turned away from Benson and made a show of smoothing her black hair back over her ears. Then she whispered out of the corner of her mouth, "Whatever you do, don't let him touch you."

Still looking at the three vamps, I kept my face blank, as though she hadn't said anything, although I was wondering at that strange piece of advice. Did Roslyn know that Benson liked to feed on people's emotions? I was going to heed her warning. After seeing what Benson had done to Troy last night, I had no intention of letting the vamp put his hands anywhere on me—ever.

"Roslyn, my dear," Benson called out. "Why don't you fix us a drink? You know what I like. And I assume you know what Ms. Blanco likes too."

His words indicated that she did know him. I wondered exactly how well they were acquainted.

Roslyn nodded at no one in particular. "Of course."

"Stay behind the bar," I murmured to her.

She nodded at me this time, then went around the elemental Ice bar and out of my line of sight, since I was still focusing on Benson, Silvio, and the third man. The sharp *tink-tink-tink* of ice filling glasses sounded, along with the soft, steady *splash* of liquid and the *rattle-rattle* of bottles and shakers, as Roslyn mixed our drinks.

I slid my knife back up my sleeve, went over to the table, and took the empty chair across from Benson, being sure to keep out of arm's reach of him. The vamp leaned back in his seat and crossed his right ankle over his left leg, once again giving me a view of his white-and-pink sock.

"So, Beauregard," I said. "Why the elaborate ruse? I would have been happy to talk to you somewhere other than here."

He smiled, the pearly glint of his fangs reminding me of a piranha's toothy grin. "Please, call me Benson. I find *Beauregard* to be a bit of a mouthful. Makes me feel like I ought to be an old, white-haired gentleman in a seersucker suit drinking mint juleps out on the veranda. As for the location, I thought that it would be prudent to meet in . . . neutral territory, which is why I chose Northern Aggression. Well, that and the fact that I hadn't seen my old friend Roslyn in quite some time."

I raised my eyebrows. "Really?"

"Really," he replied. "I used to be Roslyn's representative. Her business manager, of sorts."

So he'd known her back when she'd been working the Southtown streets. It must have been years ago, because I'd never heard of Benson being involved with hookers before. I wondered how Roslyn had managed to get out from under his thumb. He didn't strike me as the kind of guy to let anyone leave his organization, except in pieces.

Roslyn finished our drinks, and the bamboo floor creaked under her feet as she walked over and deposited two glasses on the table. A gin on the rocks with a fat wedge of lime for me and a Bloody Mary for Benson, complete with a tall, leafy stalk of celery. Roslyn stared at me, worry shimming in her toffee gaze, but I tipped my head, telling her that I could handle things. Then I casually dropped my hand down by my side, my thumb pointing back toward the bar.

Roslyn nodded at me, then at Benson, before heading back behind the bar. She moved far enough to my left so that I could see her out of the corner of my eye, and she made a show out of putting away the bottles of liquor, the lime, and the celery, although she kept one hand out of sight below the frosty surface at all times. She was ready to reach for the shotgun that Xavier kept under there if things went bad between me and Benson.

"Don't worry," Benson said, dragging his drink over to his side of the table. "There's no actual blood in this."

"It wouldn't bother me if there were."

"I assumed as much, given your reputation. But I must admit that I'm not like most vampires," he said. "I find drinking blood to be a bit . . . messy. And it's not nearly as interesting as other . . . pursuits."

I didn't give him the satisfaction of asking about his *other pursuits*. I was guessing that they involved a lot of screaming, violence, and death. Benson took a sip of his Bloody Mary and grinned at me. The tomato juice stained his fangs a pale pink. The color matched his shirt and argyle socks.

I took a sip of my own gin. Normally, I would have enjoyed the cool slide of the alcohol down my throat before it started its sweet, slow burn in the pit of my stomach. But not today. Not when faced with a monster like Benson. Not when Roslyn had been frightened and could still get hurt because of me.

"May I call you Gin?" Benson asked.

"Sure," I said, raising my glass to him. "Like the liquor."

He let out a pleased laugh. "Yes, that's what I hear you tell people. How quaint."

We sat there and sipped our drinks for the better part of three minutes. I didn't mind the silence, as it let me speculate about what he could possibly want. Sure, Benson had sent some men to kill me over the past several months, like most of the underworld bosses had, but we'd never had any direct contact. So why the meeting? Why now? The obvious answer was that it must have something to do with Catalina. But Benson hadn't seen her or me last night, and I couldn't puzzle out why he would want to have a conversation, instead of just sending some of his men to kill me, and her too.

But the lengthy quiet also gave Benson time to study me, everything from Silvio's blood staining my hand to the hard set of my mouth to the cold chill glinting in my wintry-gray eyes. But there was no lust in his gaze, only mild curiosity, as though I were a germ he was examining through the microscopic lenses of his glasses.

After a minute of that, he cocked his head to the side. He kept his eyes on my face, but I got the sense that he wasn't looking *at* me so much as he was looking *into* me, if that was even possible. Either way, his unfocused, dreamy expression reminded me of the far-off look that Jo-Jo sometimes got when she was getting a glimpse of the future with her Air magic. But it was much, much creepier on Benson.

Finally, he blinked and focused on me again. "You are exceptionally calm, Gin."

"Why shouldn't I be? After all, we're just having a friendly drink, right?"

A thin smile curved his lips. "Right." He leaned forward, putting his elbows on the table and clutching his Bloody Mary between his bony hands. "Well, then, let's get down to business. I do want to apologize for my actions regarding Roslyn, but as I said before, I thought it best to meet on neutral ground so my appearance would not be misconstrued and provoke an . . . unpleasant reaction. I have no desire to start a war with you, Gin."

"Why not? It seems to me like you've already begun, given all the men you've sent to my restaurant to try to kill me."

He shrugged. "It's just business. I had to try, the same as everyone else. I'm sorry if you found it . . . *upsetting.*"

He said the last word with obvious relish, then paused and stared at me, doing that weird looking-right-through-me thing again. Only this time, something also brushed up against my skin—that invisible sandpaper I'd noticed in the garage when Benson was sucking the emotions out of Troy.

But the sensation was much more intense now than it had been last night, so intense that it almost felt like . . . magic. I'd thought that Benson's emotional draining was some sort of special vampiric ability, but perhaps there was also an elemental component to it. If so, that would make him even stronger than I'd realized—and far more dangerous.

The phantom sandpaper rubbed and rubbed at my skin, as if trying to find a weak spot to bear down on and draw blood. I focused on remaining calm.

After several seconds, the uncomfortable sensation vanished, and Benson's mouth puckered with disappointment that I hadn't reacted whatever way he'd wanted me to.

"It takes a lot to crack that calm façade of yours, doesn't it?" he murmured.

"It's no façade."

"No," he murmured again. "It's not—not at all. How . . . disappointing."

I wouldn't say that it was disappointing. I wouldn't say that it was anything at all other than the way I was, but I had no idea what Benson was getting at. My gaze flicked past him to Silvio, searching for a clue to his boss's meaning, but Silvio's face remained as smooth as mine. The third man seemed a bit nervous, his arms crossed over his chest, his fingers tapping against his opposite elbows, but he wasn't the real danger here—Benson was. Off to my left, Roslyn held her position, one hand still below the bar, ready to draw her shotgun.

"Regardless, you can rest assured that none of my men will bother you again," Benson said.

"Oh, it's not me that I'm worried about," I drawled.

Benson frowned, but Silvio's lips twitched up with something that almost seemed like amusement. I blinked, and the expression vanished.

"Of course not," Benson said. "Your reputation does precede you."

"What can I say? It's the price of being famous. Or, rather, infamous in my case."

Silvio's lips twitched again, but Benson didn't seem to get my dry, dark humor. Instead, he leaned forward.

"Well, then, let's turn to the matter at hand."

"Oh?" I asked. "And what would that be?"

"Your sister. Detective Bria Coolidge."

Benson's nasal voice echoed through the club before the red velvet curtains on the walls soaked up the sound, if not the danger that accompanied his words.

My fingers curled around my glass of gin, my jaw tightened, and my spine straightened. Small motions, but Benson's eyes sharpened with interest behind his glasses.

"Finally, a reaction," he said. "I was beginning to think that you were made out of the stone that you are rumored to be able to control."

"Mild surprise is hardly a reaction," I drawled again.

"Why surprise?"

I shrugged. "I would have thought that a cop, any cop, would be beneath your notice. Well, except for the ones you bribe to keep your drugs flowing into Southtown. But even then, Silvio handles all of those dirty details, doesn't he?"

Benson shrugged back. "Of course he does. But your sister has come to my attention for her recent . . . interest in my activities."

"You mean because you tortured and killed her informant, stuffed a rat into his mouth, and then drew Bria's rune on his forehead with one of those pens in your pocket protector," I said in a flat voice. "Hard to imagine why she'd be upset about *that*."

He smiled. "I don't often indulge in such . . . showmanship, but your sister has been quite persistent. I thought I had finally warned her off with that boy's death, but then I heard a disturbing rumor this morning. That she has some witness who says that I murdered someone last night and that she's actually going to get this person to testify against me."

"How upsetting for you," I deadpanned.

So this was about Catalina after all. Bria had told the higher-ups in the police department that someone had seen Benson kill Troy, and someone in the po-po who was on Benson's payroll had given him a heads-up.

I stared at him, wondering if this was all some sort of twisted game, a feint to lure me away from the restaurant so he could send his men after Catalina. No, I decided. If he knew Catalina's identity, he wouldn't have bothered with all of this, and he would have already dispatched some men to kill her. But Silvio had seen her in the garage last night, so why hadn't he told his boss that he could ID the witness? He hadn't seemed interested when I'd mentioned blackmail before, which meant that money wasn't his motivation. So why in the world would Silvio protect someone like Catalina?

I glanced at Silvio, but his face was as calm and composed as ever. He had to know what I was thinking, but his features were a perfect mask for whatever his true thoughts might be. Impressive. Then again, since Benson liked to feast on emotions, it would be best to keep one's in check around the vamp, and Silvio had had years of practice.

Benson leaned back in his seat and crossed his arms over his skinny chest. "As I said, I have no interest in starting a war with you, Gin, and I've heard how very . . . protective you are of your sister. That's why I'm here. A business associate suggested that it might be better to contact you directly to avoid any unpleasantness."

Business associate? I wondered who that could be, but I didn't give him the satisfaction of asking.

"My terms are quite simple. Make this witness vanish, stay out of my way, and get your sister to do the same, and I will make sure that no one in my organization ever comes within a three-block radius of your restaurant ever again. How does that sound?"

I had to ask the question. "And if I don't?"

A faint smile crinkled his lips. "I might not want to start a war, but I know how to finish one. You're not the only one here with a reputation."

No, I wasn't. Benson hadn't become the king of Southtown and held on to all that territory for all these years by asking nicely.

Maybe it was a moment of weakness, but I didn't automatically sneer at and dismiss his offer. All things considered, it wasn't the worst proposal I'd ever heard. Get Catalina to keep quiet, stay out of his business, get Bria to do the same, and he'd leave all of us alone.

But the most shocking thing was that part of me actually wanted to take his deal.

Maybe it was selfish of me, since I knew what a monster he was, but part of me still wanted to say yes, just so there would be one fewer underworld boss I had to worry about, just so I wouldn't have to look over my shoulder and wonder when his men would come after me next. Or, worse, Bria, Roslyn, and everyone else I cared about.

But part of me bristled at his smug tone. I'd never liked bullies, and Benson was trying to strong-arm me into backing down.

And then there was Bria. She would never, ever go for such a deal. The cop in her wouldn't let her, especially not with her guilt over her informant's murder still fresh and raw in her mind and heart.

But mostly, though, I thought about Catalina and how she was determined to do the right thing because she felt like she owed it to an old friend, the ghost of the sweet boy she had loved once upon a time.

And I knew what my answer would be, what it should have been all along: no fucking way.

But before I could tell Benson what he could do with his offer, one of the doors at the front of the club banged open, and a man rushed inside. It was the vamp who'd been stationed by the main entrance, the one who'd been keeping such a careful watch out for me.

"Boss!" he called out, hurrying over to the dance floor, his gun in his hand. "Boss! I just found Johnny by the back of the club. He's dead—" The vamp skidded to a halt at the sight of me sitting with Benson. "She's—she's here!"

"Yes, Derrick, she's here," Benson said. "And you were supposed to warn me the second you saw her. Not let her kill Johnny and enter the club undetected. I am most disappointed with you."

His voice was calm, but Derrick swallowed, his face suddenly pale. Benson got to his feet and straightened his glasses. Behind the bar, Roslyn tensed, as if she knew what was coming. So did the third man, who'd been standing behind Benson, but he lifted his gun, clearly ready to shoot anyone who dared to interfere with his boss. Silvio remained as stoic as ever, although a muscle ticked in his jaw and his eyes glittered with some emotion I couldn't quite identify. It almost seemed as though

Silvio were dreading what his boss was about to do next, even though he knew that he couldn't stop it. I stayed in my seat, but I palmed a knife under the table.

Benson faced Derrick. He smiled again, showing off his fangs.

"Oh, shit," Derrick whispered.

Apparently, he'd seen the horror show before, and he wanted no part of it. Unlike Troy, he actually tried to get away. Derrick raised his gun and fired off a few shots, even as he started backpedaling. But his aim was lousy, and the bullets zipped up toward the ceiling instead of thunking into Benson's chest. I doubted they would have made a difference anyway.

Derrick didn't get three steps before Benson was on him.

One second, the vamp was standing beside the table. The next, he'd leaped halfway across the dance floor, some forty feet, to where his victim was. Drinking blood gave most vamps enhanced strength and speed, but Benson's long jump was truly spectacular. I wondered if the emotions he'd siphoned off Troy last night gave him even more power than drinking blood did. If so, that made Benson doubly dangerous.

Benson didn't waste any time trying to soothe Derrick like he had with Troy. Instead, he latched onto Derrick's arm, dragged the other man up against him, and buried his fangs in his minion's neck. The poor bastard didn't even have time to scream.

One, two, three slurps later, Benson let Derrick drop to the dance floor—dead.

I'd seen vamps drink before, and I'd had a particular

nasty one take more than a few bites out of me, but Benson's strike was supremely surgical—quick, brutal, effective.

And surprisingly neat. Somehow he had managed to avoid getting so much as a single drop of blood on his pink shirt and white pants. But his eyes now gleamed an electric blue behind his glasses, as his body absorbed the blood, the life, he'd just taken. I waited, wondering if his body, his muscles, would expand the way they had in the garage last night, but his figure remained lean and gangly. Perhaps that only happened when Benson ripped out someone's emotions, instead of just his blood.

Benson stepped over Derrick's body and strolled back to the table. Silvio held out his chair, and the vamp dropped into the seat again. Silvio stepped back, and Benson picked up his Bloody Mary and drained the rest of the drink.

"Refreshing," he murmured, setting the glass back down on the table.

I wasn't sure if he was talking about the liquor or the blood. I didn't really want to know.

Benson plucked the celery stalk out of the glass. The sound of his teeth tearing into the crisp vegetable was even louder than Derrick's gunshots had been. Benson took two more big bites of the celery before he dropped the leafy remains back into his glass.

Once again, he eyed me intently, that faraway look glazing his face, even as that invisible sandpaper scraped up against my skin. But I ignored the horrid sensation, pushed my anger down, and concentrated on remaining calm.

Benson blinked, his features cleared, and the blue glow in his eyes dimmed, as though he were disappointed by my lack of shock, surprise, and disgust.

"Please think about my terms, Gin. I would hate for your sister to share Derrick's fate—or, worse, that of her informant."

Behind the bar, Roslyn let out a strangled gasp. She knew exactly what happened to people who threatened my family. They ended up exactly like Derrick—or worse.

Usually worse.

Still, Roslyn was my family too, and I wasn't about to risk her safety to try to take out Benson. Not while he was riding high on all the blood he'd ingested. Not when he was purposefully trying to bait me into attacking him. Not when he wanted me to make a move against him, probably so he could use his magic to suck out my emotions and complete his afternoon feast.

If there was one thing I was good at, it was waiting, and there would be plenty of time to kill Beauregard Benson later.

"I don't speak for my sister," I said. "Although I can imagine what she would say to your offer. Starts with *F*, ends with *you*. You're a smart guy. I'm sure you can fill in the blanks."

Benson gave me a thin smile, his teeth rimmed with pink from his drink and Derrick's blood. "Perhaps you should have a chat with her, then. Consider it a suggestion between colleagues."

"We are *not* colleagues," I snarled.

He waved his hand. "Whatever label you want to put on it, then. Anyway, I'm afraid I must be going. I have another appointment to keep. But do think about what I said, Gin."

Benson got to his feet and snapped his fingers. Silvio stepped forward and reached into his gray suit jacket. I tensed, but he only produced a business card, which he placed on the table between me and his boss.

"If you need to reach me, Silvio can pass along any message," Benson said, bowing low to me again. "Good day, Gin. It was such a pleasure to meet you. And let me be the first to say that the legend of the Spider doesn't disappoint in person."

With a final, bland, polite nod, Benson strode off the dance floor, stepped over his own man's dead body, and left Northern Aggression.

Silvio and the third man stopped long enough to grab Derrick's arms, then dragged his corpse out of the club, following along behind their boss and the death he'd left in his wake.

❊ 13 ❊

I waited until the front doors banged shut behind Benson and his men before I got to my feet and hurried over to Roslyn, who was still standing behind the Ice bar.

"You okay?" I asked, setting my knife down on top of the frosty surface. "What happened?"

Instead of answering me, Roslyn reached under the bar, grabbed a bottle of whiskey, and fixed herself a double shot. She threw back the liquor like it was water, then made herself another double, which she also downed. It took her a third double before she finally met my gaze. Even then, the alcohol had done little to dull the fear straining her face or the faint tremors that shook her body.

"There was a knock on the back door," Roslyn said. "I was expecting a delivery, so I opened it without looking. They stormed into the club, guns drawn, and Benson made me sit down with him."

It was more or less what I'd expected, and her soft words only made me angrier. "Then what?"

"Benson told me to call and get you to come over here. I'm so sorry, Gin, but I didn't have a choice."

I waved away her apology. "I know you didn't. Thank you for warning me that something was wrong."

She stared at the spot on the dance floor where Derrick had died. Not so much as a speck of blood marred the surface, but Roslyn still shuddered. "I'd forgotten how cruel he can be."

"You know Benson?"

She shuddered again. "From back when I was still on the streets."

I frowned. "But I thought he was just into drugs."

"He is now," Roslyn said. "But back then, twenty years ago, when he was first starting out, he ran girls, guys too. I didn't work for him, but I still paid him protection money not to hurt me. That's how vicious he was. Eventually, he took over most of the other gangs. He was powerful enough that even Mab left him alone, as long as he stayed in Southtown and out of her way."

"How did you get away from him? Benson doesn't seem like the type to let anyone go."

A wry smile curved Roslyn's lips, chasing away some of her fear. "He isn't—or wasn't. But I scrimped and scrounged and saved up every penny I could get my hands on, and I made him an offer—a hundred thousand dollars to let me strike out on my own."

I let out a low whistle. "And he agreed to it?"

"He thought of it as an experiment of sorts. He's big on that, you know. Putting people in certain situations, seeing how they react and whether they can keep their promises to him." Her voice dropped to a whisper again. "He likes it when people fail."

I thought of Troy and Derrick. "Actions and consequences."

She nodded. "He thought that the club would fail and that I'd have to come crawling back to him. Then he would have had me and my money." She lifted her chin. "But that didn't happen, and it never, ever will."

Roslyn was a smart, savvy businesswoman. In her own way, she was more ruthless about her club than I was with my knives. Because not only was Northern Aggression Roslyn's pride and joy, but it also supported her sister, Lisa, and her young niece, Catherine.

"Has Xavier said anything to you about Bria? Or what happened at the parking garage?"

"He told me everything." She shook her head. "Poor Catalina. That girl has no idea what she's gotten herself into. Doesn't she know that no one talks in Southtown?"

Last night, I would have agreed with Roslyn. But now, after Benson had threatened her and Bria, my perspective had changed, and I saw how truly brave Catalina was being.

Even if it would most likely be the death of her.

Roslyn poured herself another drink, although she only cupped the glass between her hands, instead of throwing back the whiskey like she had before. "You need to watch out for Bria. I know she's faced down a lot of bad guys, but Benson is worse than most. You saw what he did to Derrick." Another tremor swept through her body. "And he wasn't even using his magic."

"Magic? What magic? What's his deal? Benson said that he didn't like to drink blood, but he seemed happy enough to sink his fangs into Derrick."

"Oh, he still drinks blood," Roslyn said. "We all have to do that. But Benson really gets his kicks by feeding on people's emotions. It's a rare vampiric ability. Xavier told me that's what he did to Bria's informant and the guy in the parking garage. That he pulled the fear and terror right out of them and left nothing behind but the empty husks of their bodies. Anger, lust, rage, sorrow, heartache—he can yank the smallest bit of feeling out of anyone. And when he digs out your emotions, he digs out the power that's inside you too, whether it's a giant's strength or an elemental's magic."

I thought of the way Benson had kept staring at me and the feel of that invisible sandpaper scraping against my skin. So I'd been right, and he'd been trying to sense my emotions, trying to rile me up so he could tear the anger out of me, along with my Ice and Stone magic.

I tapped my fingers against the cold bar. "He must have some special form of Air magic, maybe one that only vampires have and that they can only use in this one particular way, for him to be able to rip out people's emotions with just a touch of his hand. I'll have to ask Jo-Jo about it—"

The *beep* of a car horn outside the club, along with the *screech* of tires on the pavement, cut off my words. Roslyn and I looked at each other. Someone wanted to get in here in a hurry.

"Get down!" I hissed. "Behind the bar!"

Roslyn stopped long enough to yank her shotgun out

of its slot, then disappeared behind the thick, glittering sheet of elemental Ice. I grabbed my knife off the bar and raced toward the front of the club, plastering myself up against the wall inside the entrance.

I'd barely gotten into position when the doors burst open, and three figures rushed inside, all with guns in their hands.

Two men and a woman raced by me, and I let them go, instead of stepping out of the shadows and confronting them. I didn't want to get shot by accident. The three figures were so focused on what was up ahead in the club that they never even noticed me lurking behind them. I slid my knife back up my sleeve and followed them at a more sedate pace.

Xavier, Bria, and Finn skidded to a halt and took up a position so that they were back-to-back-to-back in the middle of the dance floor, their guns up, their eyes cutting left and right, looking for enemies.

"Roslyn!" Xavier called out.

"Here! I'm here!" Roslyn replied, standing up behind the Ice bar.

Xavier went over and grabbed her in a fierce hug, lifting her off her feet with one arm before he set her back down. He holstered his gun, cradled her face in his hands, and started whispering to her. Roslyn kept nodding, trying to convince him that she was fine.

"Where's Gin?" Finn asked.

"On your blind side," I drawled. "Just like always."

I stepped out onto the dance floor where he could see me. Finn lowered his gun and raised his eyebrows at me in a silent question. I nodded back, letting him know that I was okay.

"What about Benson?" Bria demanded. "Where is he?"

She snapped her gun from one side of the club to the other, as if she thought that Benson was still here and going to leap out from behind the red velvet curtains so she could shoot him.

"Glad to know that you're so concerned about my safety," I drawled again. "Roslyn's too."

Bria dropped her gun to her side and let out an exasperated breath. "Of course I'm glad that you guys are okay. It's just that when Finn called, I thought . . ."

"That this was your big chance to finally nail Benson," I finished. "Yeah, I think we all got that message loud and clear."

A guilty blush stained Bria's cheeks. The pale pink tint of her skin reminded me of Benson's teeth. But she didn't deny my accusation as she holstered her weapon. "So what happened?"

I had opened my mouth to tell her when Finn held up his index finger.

"Uh-uh," he said. "No way am I settling in for some bloody, gory, long-winded story involving Gin and a bunch of drug-dealing vamps unless I have a drink in one hand and many more already arrayed on the bar in front of me."

I rolled my eyes, while Bria gave Finn a sour look, but, as always, he was oblivious to our dirty glances. He wandered behind the bar and started perusing the bottles of liquor.

I took a seat at the corner of the bar, with Bria, Xavier, and Roslyn sitting close to me. Finn decided to play the role of bartender, shrugging out of his navy suit jacket and rolling up the sleeves of his white shirt. Then he went to work, pulling bottle after bottle off the shelves, flipping them around in his hands, spinning them behind his back, and showing off his cocktail-making skills. A few minutes later, he set our drinks on the bar, including another gin and tonic for me and mojitos for Bria and Roslyn. He poured himself and Xavier each a generous amount of Scotch.

"Manly drinks for manly men," Finn said, winking at Xavier.

Roslyn snorted, leaned across the bar, grabbed Finn's Scotch, and downed it.

"Hey!" Finn cried out. "I was going to drink that."

Roslyn gave him a sweet smile and pushed the mojito over to him. "Trust me. I need it more than you do. You can have the girlie drink instead."

Finn stared at the drink, then shrugged, picked it up, and started sipping it. "I do make a fine mojito."

"Enough already," Bria snapped.

She pulled a pad out of her back pocket, along with a pen she *click*ed on, ready to take notes. Her movements reminded me of Benson's when he'd recorded the aftermath of Troy's murder.

"What happened with Benson?" she growled. "I want all the details. Don't leave anything out, no matter how small."

I raised my eyebrows, but Bria kept staring at me. She wasn't going to give any ground, not when it came to this.

So I told her, Xavier, and Finn everything that had happened, with Roslyn chiming in too. When Roslyn and I finished, everyone was silent.

Finally, Bria turned her gaze to me, her blue eyes bright and accusing. "And you just let Benson walk out of here? And his men take the body with them?"

"What was I supposed to do?"

She slid off her stool and threw her hands out wide. "What you usually do. What you *always* do. Slice him open with your knives and wait for me and Xavier to come clean up the mess."

Her snarky words stung, but they were all too true. Bria and Xavier had taken care of more than one sticky situation I'd left behind as the Spider. I tried to rein in my temper, since I knew that she was hurting, but I found myself sliding off my own stool, crossing my arms over my chest, and staring her down.

"I never thought you minded doing that before," I said.

Roslyn, Xavier, and Finn looked back and forth between Bria and me. None of them moved, and none of them said a word.

Bria snorted. "Yeah, because it's so *easy* to explain away multiple bodies, two or three or even four a week, all of them not-so-shockingly clustered around the Pork Pit."

Finn winced at that. Yeah. Me too.

"I still don't understand, though," she continued. "Benson threatened you and me too. You've killed people for less. So why didn't you take him out?"

"Because Roslyn was here," I said, struggling to keep my voice level. "It was bad enough that Benson held her hostage. I didn't want her to get hurt in any fight I might have with him and his men. Besides, Benson's magic is a bit . . . troubling."

Bria snorted again, the sound louder and more derisive this time. "You mean his vampiric emotional mining of his victims? Yeah, I know all about that. I've seen it twice now, remember? But you're an assassin, you're the Spider, you're the biggest, baddest bitch in all of Ashland. You've said it yourself, more than once. You aren't supposed to be scared of things like that, and especially not of thugs like Benson."

I didn't respond, and I didn't let any of my emotions show on my face, especially not the anger and hurt that pinched my heart at her words. I'd thought that we were past our issues with my being an assassin and Bria being a cop, but apparently, that wasn't the case. At least not when it came to Benson.

Xavier slowly stood up, scraping his stool away from the bar. "Bria, calm down."

She scowled at him. "*Calm down?* You know what Benson did, you know what kind of monster he is, you know how long and hard we've been working to try to take him down. And Gin just lets him walk out of here and take a dead body with him. Don't tell me that you aren't pissed about that."

"I'd be more pissed if Roslyn and Gin were hurt—or worse," Xavier countered. "Wouldn't you?"

Bria blushed again, the expression darker, angrier, and guiltier than before, but she quickly regained her composure. "You're my partner; you're supposed to have my back. So why are you taking *her* side?" She stabbed her finger at me.

Xavier crossed his arms over his massive chest. "I've had your back for weeks now, and all you've done is bitch and moan about how we can't find enough evidence to arrest Benson. And now you're blaming Gin for being smart, for protecting herself and Roslyn, instead of trying to take him out for you."

Bria shook her head. "That's not true."

"Yes, it is," he replied, his voice much quieter and more ominous than before. "For as many times as you've complained about Gin being the Spider, right now, you're just pissed that she didn't whip out her knives and carve up Benson. That would have solved a lot of your problems, wouldn't it?"

Bria's mouth opened and closed, and opened and closed again, but she couldn't deny his words. More and more guilt stained her cheeks, turning them an ugly, mottled red.

"It's bad enough you've dragged Catalina into this. That poor girl doesn't know any better, but *you* do. You need to rein in this obsession you have with Benson," Xavier warned. "You keep going after him this way, all reckless, angry, and crazy, not caring who you piss off, step on, or hurt, and you'll walk right into some trap that he sets for you. Then *you'll* be the one we find in an alley somewhere, dead, drained, with a rat stuffed in your mouth and Benson's rune inked on your forehead."

Bria shook her head again, making her blond hair fly around her face, the strands dancing like angry bees. "I can't do that. You know I can't. Not after what happened to Max."

Her lips pinched together, and her hand crept up to the

primrose rune hanging around her neck, her fingers squeezing the pendant. Bria noticed me staring at her clutching her rune, and she loosened her grip on it. But the pain and guilt of Max's murder continued to shimmer in her eyes.

She turned away from me and stretched out a hand, pleading with the giant. "You saw what Benson did to Max. You *saw* it, Xavier. Don't tell me you can forget that. Don't tell me you can let it go."

"No, I can't forget it, and I can't let it go," he admitted, sadness rumbling through his words. "But we need to be smart and take the time to properly build our case the way we always do. That's how we'll get Benson, and that's how you can get justice for Max. Not by charging after him with no sort of plan in mind. That will only get you killed."

"What are you saying?" Bria asked.

Xavier straightened up to his full, towering height. "I'm saying that we should both take a break, at least for a few days, then come back at this with fresh eyes and calmer hearts. Starting right now. Call me when you're ready to go after Benson—the right way."

Xavier held out his hand. Roslyn took it, and the two of them left the bar and walked over to the door at the back of the club, the one I'd left open when I forced Silvio out onto the dance floor.

Roslyn didn't look back at us as she stepped through the opening. Neither did Xavier as he followed her and slammed the door shut behind them.

Bria, Finn, and I stared at the closed door, the hard bang slowly fading away.

"Well," Finn drawled. "That went well, so well, in fact, that I need another drink. Or three. Who's with me?"

He waggled a lime at Bria and me, then started cutting it up with a small paring knife, his movements quick and efficient. The tangy citrus scent drifted over to me, followed by the sharp smell of the mint he crushed and added to the drink. He pushed the finished product over to Bria, who shoved it right back at him, so hard that some of the liquid sloshed out of the top and spattered against the Ice bar.

"I don't want a damn drink," she growled.

"Well, I think you need one," he said. "Might help you relax some. Xavier's right. You have been a little obsessed with Benson lately. Even when you're with me."

Bria scowled at him. "And how is that different from anybody Gin's had in her crosshairs these past few months? Huh? Someone makes a move against her, but when she goes after them, knives first, none of you ever says a word about it—not a single *word*. So why the double standard, Finn?"

"Because you're better than me," I said in a quiet voice.

Bria turned her hot glare to me. "And what do you mean by that?"

I gestured at the gold badge clipped to her black leather belt. "I mean you're a cop, a good cop, and I'm an assassin. You're right. When someone comes after me, I retaliate, with no questions asked and no mercy given. But you're supposed to be better than that. You're supposed to follow the law. You're supposed to *use* the law to take down people like Benson."

Bria pressed her lips together, and anger sparked in her

eyes—more anger than I'd ever seen her show before. "I *have* been using the law, and it's gotten me nowhere. Every time I get the slightest bit of evidence on Benson, either it disappears, or he manages to tap-dance his way around it. I feel like Sisyphus pushing a rock up a hill, just to have it roll down and flatten me time and time again. I'm tired of it."

She shook her head. "Maybe I should just give up on the law. Do things the way *you* always do them. At least I'd get some results then, even if I'd rather see Benson rotting in prison than in the ground."

"You say that now, but you don't really mean it. I know you don't."

Bria let out a bitter laugh. "Yeah. Because Gin always knows best, right?"

"What do you mean by that?"

"Forget it," she muttered. "You wouldn't understand anyway."

But I could read between the lines and hear exactly what she wasn't saying. Bria was pissed at me, Xavier, Finn, and everyone else who wasn't helping her in her vendetta against Benson. I knew all about vendettas. Knew how they could pull you down a rabbit hole that you could have a very hard time clawing your way out of again. Knew how they could consume you. Knew how they could eat you up inside until there was nothing left but your need for revenge and then the hollow ache that remained behind should you ever actually achieve your goal. I didn't want Bria to end up like that.

I didn't want her to end up like *me*.

But I didn't know how to help her either. Not with this. Not without coming across like a complete hypocrite.

"Look," I said. "Be calm, be smart, and keep working on Benson, just like Xavier said. You know that he's the one pushing Burn. Sooner or later, he'll make a mistake, and you'll find some way to nail him. I have faith in you."

"He already made a mistake when he killed Troy and Catalina saw him do it," she said. "I have her statement, which is *exactly* what I need to nail him."

"And he knows that you have a witness. The second he figures out it's Catalina, he'll kill her. You know he will."

Bria gave me a cold look, not even bothering to acknowledge my words with some of her own. I'd always thought that my sister had the flat cop stare down pat, but she'd never used it to its full effect on me—until now.

"Forget about Catalina for a second. I can't believe that you aren't foaming at the mouth to go after Benson yourself," she sniped. "Especially after what he did to Roslyn."

I sighed. "Did it ever occur to you that maybe I get tired too?"

"And what would you have to get tired about?"

"Oh, I don't know. The blood, the bodies, the sneak attacks, constantly looking over my shoulder, wondering when the next moron is going to try to kill me," I snapped back. "And do you know what the worst part is?"

She didn't bother to answer.

"Knowing that I *have* to be vigilant, that I have to be on my guard every single minute of every single day for the rest of my life," I snarled. "I have to be prepared. I have to be ready—*always*. But the people who want to kill me? They just have to get lucky *once*, for one measly *second*, and it's lights-out for me. So forgive me for trying to get out of one situation without some bloodshed today."

Bria looked at me, anger still pinching her face, before she glanced at Finn, who was making yet another mojito.

"You've been awfully quiet through all of this. Don't tell me that the great Finnegan Lane doesn't have something to say." Her voice took on a mocking note.

Finn looked back and forth between Bria and me. He shook his head, not wanting to take sides. I didn't blame him. No one was going to win this argument.

Bria snorted in disgust before turning her attention back to me. "Well, do you know what I'm tired of, Gin? The fact that you never trust me to do my job."

"You're a good cop. I've never said otherwise."

"No, but you don't think that I can protect Catalina from Benson," she accused. "You've definitely said *that*."

"Only because Benson won't fight fair. You know he has other cops on his payroll, cops who will sell you out to him in a heartbeat."

"And you don't think I can handle them or Benson. Not like you can."

"No," I said, my voice as soft as hers was loud. "Not like I can."

Bria gave me another disgusted look. She opened her mouth, but her phone started ringing, saving us both from whatever harsh thing she'd been about to say. She pulled it out of her jeans pocket and looked at the screen. Her mouth twisted.

"Well, duty calls," she said, holding the phone up to her ear. "Detective Coolidge."

Then my baby sister whirled around and stormed out of Northern Aggression without another word.

❖ 14 ❖

Finn drained the rest of his mojito, grabbed his jacket, and mumbled something about checking in with his contacts, since he was still digging into several things for me, including Catalina, where her money was coming from, and the two mystery women from the Pork Pit. I slugged down my own gin and tonic in response. Finn squeezed my shoulder, and then we both left the club. Neither one of us was in the mood for conversation right now.

I walked over to the alley where I'd parked my car, got in, and started driving, trying to clear my head.

I wound up in the mountains above Ashland, in a park that was part of the Bone Mountain Nature Preserve, sitting on top of a blue fiberglass picnic table and staring out at the sweeping view of the rocky slopes. And I wasn't alone. Several couples were picnicking at the other tables, while others stood behind the stone wall that cordoned off the grassy park from the steep drop, their cameras *click-click-click*ing away as they snapped shots of the glorious mix of red, orange, and yellow leaves that painted the mountainsides.

The last time I was here, the police had been using the park as a staging area so they could hike up to the camp where Harley Grimes, his sister, Hazel, and their gang of miscreants had lived before the Deveraux sisters and I had killed them. I thought about that day at Jo-Jo's salon, when Bria had said she wanted to talk to me about something right before Grimes and his men had stormed inside. I'd been so distracted by rescuing Sophia that I'd forgotten all about my own sister. I should have remembered that Bria had been trying to tell me something. I should have asked her about it after things had calmed down.

Maybe if I had, Bria wouldn't be hurting, and I wouldn't be so angry at her.

Yeah, she'd lost her informant, but that was no excuse to lash out at the rest of us. Bria was being all pissy with us when all we were trying to do was get her to take a breath and think about things. But she was so hell-bent on going after Benson that she couldn't see that. Well, if she wanted me to stay out of her way, then fine. I was out. Done. Finished. She could go after him however she saw fit, law or no law. I didn't care anymore.

At least that's what I kept telling myself.

Despite the lovely view of the mountains, I was too restless and too worried about too many things to sit still for long, so after about half an hour of brooding, I got into my car and headed home, hoping that a hot meal would improve my mood, if not my situation.

Thirty minutes later, I crested the ridge that led up

to Fletcher's house, expecting the driveway in front of the house to be empty, but a car was sitting in my usual spot—a black Audi.

My eyes narrowed, and I thought back to the Audi I'd seen on the street outside the parking garage last night. It took me a moment to realize that it wasn't the same car, since this one was actually a dark navy instead of a true black. Also, the windows weren't tinted, letting me glimpse something very familiar, distinctive, and slightly disturbing dangling from the rearview mirror: one of the sparkly blue and pink pins shaped like the Pork Pit's pig logo that Sophia had ordered for the waitstaff to wear.

But the most interesting thing wasn't the pin or the car but who they belonged to. At the sound of my vehicle rumbling up the driveway, a figure got up out of the rocking chair he'd been perched in. His hand went to his gray tie, smoothing it down as he stepped to the edge of the porch.

Silvio Sanchez.

I was so surprised that I lifted my foot off the gas, and the car stalled in a thick patch of gravel. I let the tires churn, my gaze snapping from the woods to the left of the house, across the yard, and over to the ridge at the far right side of the clearing. But I didn't see any other vamps lurking in the trees, waiting in the Audi, or peeking around the corners of the house. If Benson had ordered his men to take me out, there would have been at least a dozen of them here, too many for all of them to hide, but I didn't spot so much as a shiver of movement. Silvio appeared to have come alone, which only made me more curious—and wary—about what he wanted.

So I put my foot down on the gas again, breaking free

of the gravel pit, and parked. I palmed a knife and got out of my car.

I approached him slowly, my eyes sweeping over the porch where he'd been sitting, wondering if he might have planted a bomb there, if this was in fact some sort of half-assed assassination attempt. But the chairs and tables were exactly as I had left them, except for the one Silvio had gotten out of, which was still rocking—a chair that now had a fat manila file folder lying on the seat. He must have brought that with him, although I couldn't imagine what sort of information it might contain.

I stopped a few feet away from the porch and stared at the vampire. He lifted his chin and returned my gaze with an unreadable expression of his own. I had a good poker face, but Silvio's was even better than mine. Then again, it wouldn't be smart to let your emotions show around Benson, lest he rip them right out of you.

Since Silvio wasn't giving anything away, I stepped even closer to him, turning my knife so that light glinted off the blade and flashed into his eyes, to see if that would crack his calm façade. He squinted, his lips puckered, and his gaze fell to my weapon. I started rubbing my thumb over the hilt of my knife, still trying to rattle him. But instead of looking concerned, he simply sighed and squared his shoulders, as if my carving him up was inevitable.

Maybe it was.

"Silvio."

"Ms. Blanco."

We stared at each other. In the woods in the distance, the *chirp-chirp-chirp* of birds hushed, and the rabbits rustling around in the underbrush stilled and burrowed down into the leaves. The animals could feel the tension in the air, and they didn't want any part of it.

Silvio cleared his throat, and his hand smoothed down his tie again, lingering on the pin glinting in the middle of the fabric, a *B* with two pointed fangs sticking out the ends of it. Benson's rune. I liked the Pork Pit pig logo far better.

"You're probably wondering what I'm doing here," he said.

"Not at all," I deadpanned. "I was expecting someone to show up to try to kill me today. Did you draw the short straw among Benson's men?"

Silvio sighed again and raised his eyes skyward, as if he found my comments childish. Didn't much matter to me. At this point, he was lucky that he was still breathing and not bleeding out all over the porch.

"Anyway," he continued, "I wanted to apologize for what happened at Northern Aggression. Roslyn is an acquaintance of mine, and I deeply regret scaring her."

"Oh, I don't think it was you so much as it was your boss."

A faint wince creased his middle-aged features. "I tried to persuade him to approach you some other way, but Beau enjoys the little dramas he creates."

"Like what he did to Derrick? Because that was certainly quite the floor show."

For the first time, true emotion flickered in Silvio's eyes. And unless I was mistaken, it almost looked like . . . grief. His nostrils flared, his lip curled up, and his jaw clenched tight, indicating that there was more than a little anger and disgust mixed in with his pain. And I suddenly realized why Silvio had been so tense at the club when Benson killed Derrick.

Silvio realized that I'd seen the chink in his armor. He blinked, and his face became perfectly blank once more.

"As I said before, Beau enjoys drama," he said, his voice tight.

"You cared about him—Derrick."

"We went out a few times. He was nice. Anyway, that's all over with now."

Silvio shrugged, as if to dismiss their relationship as nothing special, but his entire body stayed stiff and rigid. I sensed that there was a lot more to his feelings for Derrick than his casual words, but Silvio wasn't about to share that with me. I doubted that he shared much of anything with anyone. He'd been around Benson too long and was too used to keeping everything he was really feeling buried deep down inside where the vamp wouldn't sense it.

"It's only over because Benson wanted to show off to me," I said. "I'm sorry for your loss."

And I truly was. Sure, Derrick had screwed up by letting me slip past him, but Benson had to have known the chance of that happening was high. Like he'd said, I didn't have my reputation as the Spider for nothing. No, Benson had killed his own man simply because he'd wanted to. He'd wanted to rattle me, wanted to make me worry about what he might do to Bria, and me too, and Derrick had been unfortunate enough to be his demonstration, with Silvio being forced to witness the death of someone he cared about.

"Yes, well, you know quite a bit about loss yourself, don't you?" Silvio murmured. "Murdered family, murdered mentor, and then, of course, all the people you've killed yourself. Death seems to follow you around, Ms. Blanco."

I grinned, but the expression was sharper than the knife in my hand. "Maybe because he knows that I'll be leaving behind a lot of folks for him to escort over to the other side."

Silvio's mouth quirked in thought. "I wouldn't take you for a believer in such mythology."

"I read a lot."

He studied me again, but I kept my face smooth and easy, waiting him out. I didn't know what kind of game Silvio was playing, but I was determined to beat him at it.

One minute ticked by, then two, then three . . . and still, neither one of us moved, spoke, or did anything other than breathe. Finally, Silvio blinked.

"I wanted to warn you not to trust Beau," he said. "He may have offered you a truce today, but he won't live up to his end of the deal tomorrow. He'll keep sending men after you, trying to kill you."

"No, really?" I deadpanned again. "Because he struck me as being *so* trustworthy when he murdered his own man right in front of me."

Silvio's lips twitched with something that might have been genuine amusement. I leaned against the porch railing and stabbed my knife at him.

"As scintillating as our conversation has been, it's been a long day, and I would like to go inside my house and wash off the lingering stench of my encounter with your boss," I said. "So the next words out of your mouth had better be the real reason you came here, or I'll be sending Death someone else to collect tonight."

Silvio's amusement iced over and cracked away, leaving his features as cold as mine. "Very well. You asked me earlier why I didn't alert Beau to your presence in the parking garage last night. I didn't want to say anything at the club. Too many ears listening."

"Including Benson's, you mean. He wouldn't be very happy if he realized that you were the reason he had to worry about leaving a witness behind."

Silvio nodded. "Catalina is actually what I want to talk to you about."

My fingers curled around my knife. How the hell did he know her name? "What about her?"

Silvio squared his shoulders again. "She's my niece."

Of all the things he might have said, that was about the last one I was expecting. No, scratch that. His confession had never even entered my realm of possibilities. I had wondered why Silvio hadn't said anything to Benson about spotting Catalina and me in the garage. I had assumed it was because he had blackmail in mind, or even some nebulous dream of taking over Benson's operation himself, and Benson going down for Troy's murder would help him with that. But this . . . this changed *everything*.

"Catalina Vasquez is your niece?" I asked, my mind churning. "My Catalina? The student who works as a waitress at the Pork Pit?"

"One and the same."

My gaze flicked over to his car and the sparkly pig rune dangling from his rearview mirror. Well, now I knew where he'd gotten that from.

"I can see that you're surprised, but I assure you that

I'm telling the truth. Catalina's mother, Laura, was my sister. I brought some photos, in case you need further convincing." He gestured at the folder on the seat of the rocking chair. "May I?"

"Slowly."

Silvio opened the file and grabbed a slip of paper out of it, before crossing the porch and holding it out to me. I took it from him, and he quickly stepped back out of knife's reach.

It was a photo of Silvio standing next to a shorter woman with similar features—who was cradling a young Catalina in her arms. The picture had to be at least fifteen years old, but I could still tell that it was Catalina. Same eyes, same nose, same happy smile. And now that I saw Silvio and her in the same space, I could see the familial resemblance. Faint, but it was there in the shape of their faces, the arch of their eyebrows, and the curve of their lips.

"I came here because I care about Catalina very much," Silvio said, his voice tight with more emotion than he'd shown the whole time we'd been talking.

I placed the photo on the porch railing. I knew what he was going to say next.

"I came here, Ms. Blanco, because I want you to protect Catalina."

I let out a soft laugh and shook my head. "No, that's not what you're asking. That's not what you want me to do. Not really. At least have the guts to say it out loud."

His hand crept up to Benson's rune stabbed into the middle of his tie. He rubbed it a moment before dropping his fingers from the pin. "Very well. I came here because I want to hire you as the Spider. I want you to kill Beau."

✷ 15 ✷

His voice was as soft as my laugh had been, and his meaning was just as dark. But the determined pinch of his mouth, the slight flare of his nostrils, and the icy chill in his gray eyes told me that he meant every word.

"Name your price," he continued. "Whatever you want, I will gladly pay it."

For the first time, I saw Silvio Sanchez as more than an anonymous bad guy and disposable hired hand. I saw him for what he truly was in that moment: a man desperately trying to protect his family.

In a way, his actions eerily mirrored my own. Except that I had wanted Catalina to disappear and Bria to let go of her vendetta against Benson, whereas Silvio was taking a much more direct approach to the situation. I admired him for that, for doing what he thought was necessary, for having the courage to come here, knowing that I might kill him anyway simply because of what Benson had done to Roslyn.

But I'd told Bria the truth when I said that I was tired of all the blood, battles, and bodies. If I did what Silvio wanted, then I'd be in the thick of things with Benson, fighting him until one of us was dead. Did I really want to risk myself like that for Catalina? Until two days ago, she'd just been a girl who worked for me. Nothing more, nothing less. Did that really make her my responsibility? Was it my duty to protect all my employees from every bad, dangerous thing that life threw at them? What about their friends and families? Doing pro bono work, helping folks who couldn't help themselves, was all well and good. Fletcher had taught me that. But where did it *end*?

I supposed the answer to that last question was whether I could live with myself if I let Benson kill Catalina just for trying to do the right thing.

And the answer was a resounding *no*.

But the irony of the situation didn't escape me either. Silvio was doing what *I* usually did—getting to the point of the matter—while I stood on the sidelines, trying to keep everyone safe, including myself. I'd never considered myself to be a coward, but that's what I was being when it came to Benson. Cowardly—or at least too concerned with my own problems to help the person who needed it the most, Catalina.

"Well, Ms. Blanco?" Silvio asked. "Do we have a deal?"

Instead of answering his question, I asked a few of my own. "Why come to me at all? Why not persuade Catalina not to testify? Surely, that would be the easier option. Cheaper too."

"Believe me, I've tried." Silvio huffed. "I've spent all damn *day* trying, ever since Benson got the call this morning that there was a witness. The second I heard that, I knew it was Catalina. Like you said, I'd seen the two of you there, and *you* certainly weren't going to testify."

I raised my knife to my heart. "Oh, Silvio, you wound me with your lack of faith. I actually do like to do my public duty from time to time."

He barked out a laugh. "I just bet you do. Probably about as much as I do." He laughed again, the sound even more caustic than before. "And now Troy has gotten her in trouble again. I never did like that little punk."

"That's a bit harsh, isn't it? Considering who you work for and all the nasty things you've done for him."

"Bah." Silvio waved his hand, shooing away my words, and started pacing back and forth across the porch. "Even if it wasn't Troy, Catalina would still want to testify. Her mother raised her to be a good kid that way. Laura never liked what I did and who I worked for, just like you said."

"So why do it? Why stay with Benson?"

He shrugged. "Because there weren't any other options when Benson took over Southtown. It was join him or die. So I did what I had to do." He stopped pacing to stare at me. "You should understand that, if nothing else."

I looked down at my knife. Maybe it was the way the sun was gleaming off the blade, but for a moment, I was back in Southtown, back in that alley with Coral, clutching a broken beer bottle and staring at a man's blood on my hand.

"Ms. Blanco?"

I shook off the memory and concentrated on Silvio again. Oh, I did understand it, more than he realized.

More than I wanted to.

"So you think asking me to kill Benson will make up for all the bad things you've done?"

He laughed again. "Of course not. I'll pay for my sins, just like we all will in the end. But Catalina doesn't deserve to die for being in the wrong place at the wrong time. And she especially doesn't deserve what Benson will do to her. You saw what he did to Troy."

"Hard to forget."

"And he wasn't even using the full extent of his Air magic last night." A faint wince of concern creased Silvio's face.

Air magic? So my theory was right, and Benson did have that elemental power mixed in with his own vampiric ability.

Silvio stared at me, the ice in his eyes melting into a desperate plea. "Please. *Please* kill Benson. Whatever your current asking price is, I'll double it, triple it. And that's not all. I'll even help you, if you want. I've already started. See?" He gestured at the folder still on the rocking chair.

"Help? What sort of help?"

Silvio picked up the file, pulled a fat wad of papers and pictures out of it, and started showing them to me one by one. "Benson's daily and weekly schedules, blueprints of his Southtown mansion, photos of the exterior grounds and every room inside the structure, the routes he takes to meet with his drug suppliers." He hesitated. "I wasn't sure exactly how you go about doing . . . what you do, so I thought it pertinent to include a wide range of material about all aspects of Benson's life."

"You could always do the job yourself," I pointed out. "You're his right-hand man. You're close enough to kill him anytime you want to."

"Believe me, I've dreamed of it many times," Silvio murmured, slipping the papers and pictures back into the folder. "And if I thought that I could do it, then I would already be loading the gun. But Beau can sniff out the faintest hint of insurrection. It's his Air magic, you see, it—"

"Gives him a bit of precognition," I finished. "Yeah. I know."

Silvio pinched the bridge of his nose the way that I'd seen his niece do at the restaurant after a particularly stressful shift. "Then you can see my predicament, Ms. Blanco. I can't let him hurt Catalina, and I can't kill him myself."

"And maybe we should both trust my sister to do her job. Bria will do her best to protect Catalina. I can promise you that. She wants to take Benson down too badly not to."

Silvio gave me a sad smile. "Catalina has told me many good things about your sister. How dedicated she is, how honest, how brave. But I think we both know that it won't be enough. Not against someone like Benson."

The image of Troy's desiccated body filled my mind. The thought of Benson doing the same thing to Catalina, to Bria, turned my stomach. And I finally admitted to myself that my actions of the last two days had been nothing but stall tactics. I *was* tired of constantly fighting for my life—of all the blood and battles and bodies that just never seemed to end.

But I would never, *ever* get tired of protecting the people I loved.

So I stared into Silvio's eyes and held out my hand,

letting him see the poison promise glinting in my icy gray gaze.

He handed me the file without another word.

I hefted the folder in my hand. It felt even thicker and heavier than the ones in Fletcher's office. Silvio appeared to have done his homework. I hoped his information would be as useful as the old man's always was.

Silvio sucked in a breath and opened his mouth as if to thank me, but he thought better of it, and the air slowly hissed out between his teeth. Instead, he put his hand over his heart and bowed low to me—even lower than Benson had at Northern Aggression. But what surprised me the most was that there was no mockery in the gesture.

Then he straightened back up, nodded at me, stepped off the porch, and headed over to his car. He walked quickly, his shoulders high and tight, as if he expected me to dart forward and plunge my knife into his back at any second.

I seriously considered it.

I had the intel on Benson, which was all I needed to do the job. And it wasn't like Silvio was blameless in all of this. He'd stood by and watched Benson kill Troy, Derrick, and countless others before them. In a way, that made Silvio's hands even bloodier than his boss's. Besides, if what Silvio had said was true, and Benson could sense others' ill intentions toward him, then I was better off cutting Silvio's throat here and now, rather than letting him go back to Benson and risking that the drug kingpin would realize that his right-hand man was plotting against him—with me.

I looked at the photo of Silvio, Laura, and Catalina. His expression was somber, but he had his arm around his sister's shoulder in a protective way, and Catalina was grinning up at him, like he'd hung the moon.

I let Silvio walk.

He stopped at his car, slowly turning his head in my direction, as though he expected to find me right behind him, raising my knife high for the killing strike. But when he realized that I was letting him go, he didn't waste any time getting gone.

Silvio slid inside the vehicle, cranked the engine, and steered down the driveway, with the Pork Pit pig rune dangling from his rearview mirror winking at me all the while.

* 16 *

"I can't *believe* that you agreed to kill Benson for him."

I sighed, crossed my arms over my chest, and leaned back against the kitchen counter. "Really? Why not?"

"Isn't it obvious?" Finn said, his green eyes wide and accusing. "Because you didn't even talk price!"

Owen chuckled, far more amused by Finn than I was. The two of them were sitting at the table in the breakfast nook off the kitchen. As soon as Silvio had left, I'd called and asked them to come over to Fletcher's house for a powwow. Now I almost wished that I hadn't, given Finn's incessant whining about the fact that I hadn't negotiated payment for the job.

I hadn't called Bria at all—for obvious reasons.

"I mean, *really*, Gin," he muttered. "You can't just keep killing people for *free*. *Pro bono* is not a phrase that is in the Finnegan Lane vocabulary."

"Oh, no," I drawled. "But *greedy, shameless hustler* certainly is."

"Damn skippy."

Owen chuckled again. There was no use arguing with Finn, so I grabbed a spoon off the counter and went back to the pan on the stove. I'd already been through Silvio's file while I was waiting for them to show up, and I'd decided to make us all some dinner while Finn and Owen reviewed the info. After the emotional roller coaster of the day, I needed some serious comfort food, and I'd decided on good, old-fashioned sloppy joes.

I'd melted a little butter in the bottom of the pan, before browning up some ground sirloin, adding ketchup, and letting everything bubble away together. I leaned over the pan and breathed in, enjoying the spicy tickle of chili powder and black pepper steaming up from the simmering mixture. I gave my sloppy joe filling a final stir, then turned off the stove.

While Finn and Owen flipped through the papers and photos, I sliced up a loaf of Sophia's sourdough bread and started making sandwiches. I covered one piece of bread with a bit of mayonnaise, along with a thick layer of my spicy sloppy joe mix, then topped that off with some shredded sharp cheddar cheese and another piece of bread. I made six sandwiches, two for each of us, then grabbed the parmesan-dill potatoes I'd been roasting in the oven, along with parfait glasses filled with dark chocolate mousse I'd made earlier in the week. I put everything on a tray and carried it over to the table.

My stomach gurgled with happiness as we all dug into

the food. The warm, hearty potatoes pleasantly offset the slow burn of the spices in the sloppy joes, while the mousse was a rich cocoa concoction. I washed everything down with tart, crisp lemonade.

Owen and Finn must have been as hungry as I was, because we all finished our food in record time. Owen cleared the dishes away, while Finn and I stayed at the table.

"We should get started. No rest for the wicked and all that," Finn said in a cheery voice.

"Or the weary," I muttered, but he didn't hear me.

Finn grabbed the file, dragged it over in front of him, flipped it open, and started perusing the contents. "I have to hand it to Silvio. He knows what he's doing. There's thorough, and then there is what is in this folder. Photos, blueprints, dates, times, routes, contacts. It's all in here, along with every corner, alley, and parked car where Benson's dealers set up. Silvio even included what Benson's favorite meal is at Underwood's. The veal cutlets, in case you were wondering." He shook his head. "This is as good as any file in Dad's office—and better than some."

I'd thought the same thing, although I would never say so out loud. It felt . . . disloyal.

"Yeah," Owen called out, washing the dishes in the sink. "But is the information accurate? Or is he setting Gin up for some kind of fall?"

"It's accurate," I said, pointing to another folder on the table. "I dug out Fletcher's file on Benson. All of Silvio's info matches up with the old man's."

Some of Fletcher's information was out of date, since it was more than a year old, given his death last fall. But the important things he had noted about Benson corresponded with Silvio's file.

Finn let out a low whistle. "Well, it certainly seems like Silvio is serious about wanting Benson dead."

"Wouldn't you be, if Catalina was your niece?" Owen asked. "And how did you miss the fact that Silvio was her uncle?"

Finn shook his head. "I did a background check on Catalina, like I do with all the employees at the Pork Pit, but she started working there last year, well before—"

"Before I outed myself as the Spider by killing Mab," I finished.

He nodded. "So I didn't dig as deep as I should have. But Silvio is the one who paid for Catalina's car, her apartment, all of it. He actually set everything up through my bank, if you can believe that. On paper, it looks like a monthly life insurance payout, but it's actually a trust that he established in Catalina's name when she was born. She's had access to it since she was eighteen, but she didn't touch a penny of the money—"

"Until after her mom died." I finished his thought again.

"Well, you can't blame her for that, can you?" Owen murmured. "Wanting to get away from Southtown and all the memories there, good and bad."

"No, I can't."

We all fell silent, and the only sound was the hissing of the water as Owen kept washing and rinsing off the dishes.

Finn shook his head again. "And I still can't believe that Silvio just up and gave you all of this information on

Benson. It's better than a Christmas present. Why can't people ever make things this easy for me?"

"What can I say? I'm special," I quipped. "People throw things at me wherever I go."

He snorted. "You mean they pull out guns and try to shoot you with them. Knives, rune bombs, and the like."

"Well, I suppose that people wanting me dead is its own form of flattery. At least it makes me popular." I put my elbows on the table and leaned forward. "So how does it look to you?"

Finn shuffled through the information again. "Doing it up close and personal is out of the question. There's a lot of open space around the mansion, and his guards would be all over you the second you set foot on the grounds. But let's say that you managed to slip inside his mansion. Guess what? There are more guards on every single floor. Even if you got Benson, I don't think you could get out again. At least not without making a whole lot of noise and alerting the exterior guards."

"Providing that I could even get Benson in the first place," I muttered.

Something I wasn't so sure about, given his Air magic. Sneaking up on people was one of the things I did best, but if Benson knew I was coming, if his magic whispered to him that I was there, then I would lose the element of surprise. And I had a feeling that I would need every single advantage I could get to take him down.

Owen didn't hear me over the rush of the water, but Finn did, and he raised his eyebrows in obvious concern. I ignored his worry and waved my hand, telling him to continue.

"Sniping him from a distance is the best option," Finn said. "There are a couple of buildings close to his mansion that have good sight lines. If I were you, I'd wait until he goes out to his Bentley and put a bullet through his head."

He tapped his finger on a photo that showed Benson's baby-blue Bentley parked by itself on the street outside his mansion. "He never rides in anything else, and the car is always parked right there, according to Silvio's file."

"It's a wonder somebody doesn't steal it, if it's just sitting out there in the open," Owen said.

"No one would dare to steal Benson's car, because everyone in Southtown knows exactly who it belongs to and what he would do to them once he caught them," I said. "And he *would* catch them. A car like that would be hard to fence without word getting back to Benson."

"Yeah," Finn said in a dreamy tone. "But ain't she a beauty?"

He stroked his fingers over the photo, as if he could actually feel the perfect paint and polished chrome.

Owen finished with the dishes, slung a towel over his shoulder, and leaned against the counter. "But are you going to do it, Gin? That's the real question."

Benson had certainly given me reason enough by taking Roslyn hostage and menacing Bria. I'd killed people for less—*far* less—and anybody who threatened my friends or my family was fair game, as far as I was concerned. Not to mention my guilt that Roslyn had been targeted in the first place solely because of her friendship with me. I felt like I'd failed her, even though there was no way I could have predicted that Benson would use her to get to me.

"Well, Gin?" Finn asked. "What do you say?"

They both looked at me, Owen's face calm and accepting, Finn's bright and eager. Owen didn't have a stake in whether Benson lived or died, but Finn certainly did: Bria.

Benson couldn't hurt her if he was dead, and if I didn't kill him, I wouldn't put it past Finn to attempt the deed himself. But my killing the vamp—or even Finn doing the job—wouldn't satisfy Bria. Not really. Not with her burning need for revenge for her informant's death. That was the kind of poison promise that you had to fulfill yourself—by twisting a knife into your enemy's heart, feeling his warm blood coat your hands, and watching the fire flare out of his eyes.

"Gin?" This time, Owen asked the question.

Instead of answering, I dropped my gaze back down to the table, locking on a particular photo, the one of Silvio, Laura, and Catalina.

I reached out and traced my index finger over Silvio's arm as it curved around his sister's shoulder, his hand resting close to Catalina's smiling face. I thought of everything Catalina had already gone through with her mother's death, then witnessing Troy's murder. And everything that Silvio had endured over the years, all the bits and pieces of himself that had been sanded down and sucked away, not because of Benson's vampiric Air magic but just by Silvio working for him. The two of them didn't deserve to lose anything else. Not to the likes of Benson.

I picked up the photo and set it over on the far side

of the table where it would be out of the way. Then I grabbed the pictures that showed the exterior of Benson's mansion, before looking up at Owen and Finn in turn.

"Yeah," I said. "I'm going to do it. I'm going to kill Benson."

We finished our powwow. Before leaving, Finn promised to come by the restaurant tomorrow to help me start scouting out the best location to snipe Benson from. Owen offered to stay the night, but I sent him home too. It had been a long day, and the next few would be longer still, at least until Benson was dead, and I was determined to get every bit of rest I could.

For once, I didn't fall into my dreams and memories of the past, and I woke up feeling refreshed. Or perhaps my good mood was because I'd finally made the choice to take out the vampire. I'd been indecisive the past few days, wimpy, wishy-washy, and just plain whiny. I always felt better when I had a plan of attack.

But before I killed Benson, I had to get through another day at the Pork Pit.

I opened the restaurant right on time, keeping an eye out in case Benson had posted any of his men around the restaurant to watch me, but the street out front was clear, and so was the alley out back. And none of the customers who came and went was interested in anything but how much barbecue they could stuff themselves with. I savored the quiet. It wouldn't last.

At around three o'clock, I had enough time to take a break, so I sat on my stool, pulled the file of information on Benson out from a slot in the counter below the cash register, and read through it. I'd already reviewed it once last night before going to bed, but I was hoping that a fresh look today would help me figure things out.

Finn was right. Trying to get anywhere near Benson on his home turf would be suicide, but I didn't trust that I could take him out with a sniper rifle either. With his Air magic and the precognition that went along with it, he might be able to dodge a bullet at the last second.

No, I was going to do the hit face-to-face, with one of my knives, so I could be sure that he died. So I'd have to figure out another place to approach Benson, like maybe outside Underwood's when he went there for his usual Sunday-night dinner of veal cutlets. He liked them rare and bloody, according to Silvio—

My cell phone rang, cutting into my murderous musings. I pulled it out of my jeans pocket and stared at the caller ID. I frowned. I wouldn't have expected him to call. Not after what had happened at the club yesterday. Not when he was supposed to be taking some time off.

"Hello?"

"Gin?" Xavier's voice rumbled in my ear.

"Hey, man, what's up? How are you?"

After Owen and Finn had left the night before, I'd phoned Roslyn to check on her. She'd sounded okay, and Xavier had been at her house, but I hadn't spoken to him. Xavier needed some space from Bria and everything related to Benson right now—including me.

"I just heard from a buddy of mine on the force," he said. "He gave me a heads-up about something."

The dark note of worry in his voice made me sit up straighter. "What?"

He let out a breath. "Bria told the higher-ups that she would be bringing in the witness to Troy's murder this afternoon. She's supposed to be at the station with Catalina by five o'clock."

I let out a curse so loud that an old woman sitting in one of the booths sniffed and shook her finger at me in disapproval.

"Bria actually told them when she was showing up with Catalina?" I asked in a much lower voice. "She knows how dangerous that is, right? Benson is sure to hear about it. He'll try to stop them before they get to the station."

"I'm sure she stalled as long as she could, but she had to tell them." Xavier paused. "And I don't think she cares at this point, Gin. About anything other than getting Benson."

I cursed again, because he was right. The old lady gave me another disapproving sniff, but a cold glare from me had her ducking her head and examining the ketchup smears on her plate.

I'd hoped that Bria would spend a few more days dotting her i's and crossing her t's before she went ahead with her plan to use Catalina's testimony against Benson. Or at least until I could kill him and make everything else moot. But I should have known better. My sister could be as stubborn as I was when it came to people who hurt the folks she cared about. Bria had promised Max, her informant, that she would have his back, that she would watch out for him, that she would protect him, so I could understand her need to avenge him, even if that meant putting herself and Catalina in danger instead.

Bria and I might be pissed at each other right now, but I wasn't going to let my sister die.

"Do you know what route Bria is going to take to the station?" I asked. "I'll get ahead of her, go over there, and check it out. Make sure that everything's on the up-and-up."

"We talked about it yesterday," Xavier said. "Before we got the call about Roslyn. I'll text you the info as soon as we hang up. But there's only one potential ambush spot. That's why we decided on this particular route."

He rattled off a location I was familiar with, then paused again. "I'll meet you there, if that's okay."

"Are you sure? You and Bria didn't exactly part on good terms yesterday. I understand if you want to sit this one out."

"Bria's my partner," he said. "She's had my back dozens of times. I owe it to her to do the same, even if we're not getting along right now. What Benson did to Roslyn yesterday . . . it shook me up pretty bad. But the more I think about it, the angrier I get. Bria might be obsessed with taking Benson down, but she's not wrong about wanting to get him off the streets."

"I know. But getting herself and Catalina killed won't solve anything, so let's make sure that doesn't happen. What do you say?"

"I'd say that I wouldn't mind getting a little payback on Benson myself." I could hear the grin in Xavier's voice.

"I'm on my way. See you there."

"Will do."

Xavier and I hung up. A second later, my phone beeped with info on the route he and Bria had worked out—

A shadow fell over me, and someone cleared her throat.

The old woman I'd annoyed earlier with my cursing was standing in front of the cash register. She held out a twenty-dollar bill and her order ticket, even as she started tapping her high heel against the floor. I didn't want to waste a second in getting to Bria and Catalina, but I couldn't exactly run out the door when she was right in front of me.

So I gave her a bland smile and quickly cashed her out.

"You should watch yourself, young lady," she said in a snippy tone as I handed over her change. "Some of us don't appreciate such salty language."

My smile sharpened. "Sorry, ma'am," I drawled. "But I can assure you that cursing is going to be the least of my sins today."

* 17 *

I told Sophia what was happening and asked her to watch over the restaurant. She didn't like staying behind, but she grunted and said that she'd call Jo-Jo and let her sister know what was going on, before she went back to slicing tomatoes.

I called Owen and Finn, but neither one of them answered, so I left them both messages. Then I dialed Bria.

As expected, my call went to her voice mail. *Hi, you've reached Detective Bria Coolidge with the Ashland Police Department . . .*

"Bria," I snapped. "Pick up your damn phone. Benson knows that you're on your way to the police station with Catalina. He's going to set up roadblocks to try to catch you. Turn around. Go somewhere else, anywhere else. And call me back the second you get this."

But I couldn't afford to wait for anyone to return my calls, so I grabbed Silvio's file, went into the back of the restaurant, and grabbed the same duffel bag from behind the same freezer that I had yesterday when Benson was holding Roslyn hostage. Déjà vu all over again.

I hefted my bag onto my shoulder, opened the back door, and strode outside, scanning my surroundings as I hurried toward the far end of the alley. But no one was crouched down behind a trash can or lurking behind a Dumpster. Normally, I would have been happy that no one was lying in wait to try to kill me, but right now, the lack of assailants worried me.

Because if Benson didn't have any vamps watching me, then that meant he'd most likely sent them all after Bria instead.

Dread filled me at the thought, making me walk faster and faster, until my boots were *snap-snap-snapp*ing against the pavement. A few folks on the street shot me curious or even aggravated looks as I rushed past them, but I didn't care. Even if one of them had come up with a gun or a knife, I would have knocked them down and kept right on going.

But of course, today of all days, I'd decided to park my Aston Martin five long blocks from the restaurant, so it took me several minutes to reach the vehicle. I wanted to jump inside the car and peel away from the curb, but I made myself slow down and do my usual check for bombs and rune traps. I couldn't help anyone if I was blown to bits.

But the car was clean, so I slung the duffel bag on top of the hood, unzipped it, and reached inside, pulling out a black vest covered with all sorts of zippered pockets—and, more important, lined with silverstone. I didn't know how much of Benson's vampiric Air power the magical metal would absorb, should it come to that, but the silverstone would at least stop any bullets zipping in my direction and keep them from blasting through my chest.

I patted down the pockets on the vest, making sure that I had all of my usual supplies, including some extra knives. Satisfied, I zipped up all the pockets, then the vest itself over my chest. I grabbed the duffel bag again, opened the car door, and threw it into the passenger seat. Then I slid behind the wheel, cranked the engine, and pulled my phone out of my jeans pocket.

I called everyone again—Owen, Finn, and Bria—but no one answered. I cursed, even longer and louder than I had in the restaurant, but I forced myself to rein in my temper. If I couldn't warn Bria, then maybe I could stop her before Benson and his men did. So I checked the info Xavier had sent me.

It was a map of directions from Catalina's Northtown apartment to the main police station, which was downtown. But instead of taking the quickest, easiest route, Xavier's map showed a series of side streets that curled around and came at the station from the opposite end of town—straight through Southtown and the heart of Benson's territory.

Bria probably thought that she'd be better off taking the least expected route, and she would have been if she'd been dealing with anyone else. But Benson had more than enough vamps to cover every road around the station, not to mention all the dealers who worked for him and the regular folks who'd be too frightened not to do what he ordered them to do. No doubt, Benson had spread the word to watch out for a cop car cruising through Southtown and to let him know the second it was spotted. Then all he would have to do was close the jaws on his trap, and Bria and Catalina would be his for the taking.

That's what I would do.

More dread twisted my heart, wringing it out like a wet dish rag, but I kept studying the map, and I realized that Xavier was right. There was only one spot that would work for an ambush: a bridge that arched over the Aneirin River about three miles away from the station. That's where I would set up if I were Benson.

I threw the car into gear, slammed down on the gas, and zoomed away from the curb.

As I drove, I tried Bria a third time. No answer. I cursed again and had started to toss my phone aside in disgust when I realized that there was one person I hadn't called yet. So I scrolled through my contacts until I found her number. The phone rang . . . and rang . . . and rang . . .

"Hello?" Catalina's voice filled my ear.

"It's Gin," I snapped. "I know you're with Bria, and I know what you're doing and where you're going. Where are you right now?"

Her phone beeped. "Can you hold on a second?" she asked. "Silvio just texted me."

"No, I can't *hold on*. Tell me where you are."

Silence. I thought that she wasn't going to answer me— or, worse, that she'd hang up—but she finally sighed.

"We're driving through Southtown. We're almost to the police station." She hesitated. "Why?"

"Tell Bria to stop and turn around right *now*. Benson knows that she's bringing you in. He's sure to have men waiting for you. And whatever you do, don't get on the Carver Street Bridge."

"But we just pulled onto the bridge—"

Catalina's voice was lost in the sudden *screech-screech-screech* of tires. But the noise stopped as suddenly as it had started. For a moment, everything was eerily quiet. Then—

Crack!
Crack! Crack!
Crack!

The sounds of gunfire shot through the phone and echoed in my ear.

"Get down!" I heard Bria yell. "Get down!"

Catalina screamed. Something thumped, like she'd dropped her phone.

Then the line went dead.

I clutched the phone to my ear, hoping that Catalina would come back on the line.

But she didn't.

And she wouldn't, unless I got to Bria and her in time.

So I tossed my phone aside, grabbed the wheel with both hands, and zipped around a corner, driving faster than ever. For the first time, I was glad that Finn had badgered me into buying the Aston, because the car purred into high gear with no visible effort and hugged the road better than a creepy old cousin at Christmas not wanting to let go of his pretty young relatives.

I took another corner even faster, and the Carver Street

Bridge popped into view about a quarter-mile ahead. The bridge was one of the most interesting structures in Ashland, made of jagged pieces of gray river rock that had been fitted together, so that the whole thing resembled a life-size jigsaw puzzle. Walkways on either side of the two lanes let folks meander along the span and snap photos of the Aneirin River snaking by fifty feet below, while iron streetlamps curlicued up into the air, lining both sides of the bridge like soldiers snapped to attention.

I was on a road that ran parallel to the river, with brick storefronts off to my left and a narrow strip of grass off to my right before the slope plummeted down to the gray, gleaming surface of the water. Normally, at this time in the afternoon, the sidewalk would be full of people wandering in and out of the shops, with cars cruising by. But right now, everything was strangely still, the shops shuttered, the street deserted. No lights, no people, nobody open for business. I didn't even see any other vehicles.

Except for the ones at the bridge.

Two black cars were stopped at my end of the bridge, sitting nose-to-nose and creating a crude roadblock. Two more black cars were positioned the same way at the far end of the bridge, with one lone vehicle sitting sideways by itself in the center of the span—Bria's sedan.

Benson and his vamps must have been waiting on the side streets. Then, once they got word of Bria's location, they'd set up here. As soon as Bria had driven her car onto the bridge, they'd roared up and blocked both exits. That was bad enough, but even worse were the three vamps on my side of the bridge, standing behind their cars, all with guns out and firing at Bria's vehicle.

Crack!
Crack! Crack!
Crack!

I could hear the shots even above the smooth hum of the Aston's engine. The vamps kept up a steady assault with their weapons. They'd only been firing at the sedan a minute, two tops, but they'd made it count. The front tires were flat, the windshield had been completely busted out, and the engine block was smoking from all the bullets that had *ping-ping-ping*ed into it.

The vamps stopped to reload. I didn't even realize that I was holding my breath until a hand holding a gun reached out the shattered passenger's-side window of the sedan and fired back, making the vamps duck down behind their own cars.

I exhaled. Bria was alive, which meant that I still had a chance to save her and Catalina.

I was driving so fast that I couldn't tell which side of the bridge Benson was on, but I was sure that he was here somewhere. I would have been. But it didn't much matter. I was killing everyone who stood between Bria and Catalina and me. If I got Benson here at the bridge, all the better. But if I had to come back for him later, that was fine too.

I was fifty feet away from the bridge and closing fast.
Forty feet . . . thirty . . .
I reached up, tightening the seat belt over my chest.
Twenty feet . . . ten . . .
I grabbed hold of my Stone magic and used it to harden my body into an impenetrable shell. The crash would be brutal, and I couldn't afford to get knocked unconscious.
Seven feet . . . five . . . three . . . two . . . one—

My car rammed into the roadblock.

The air bag exploded in my face, momentarily obscuring my vision before finally deflating. The vamps had been so focused on killing Bria and Catalina that they didn't realize what was happening until it was too late. Two of them dived out of the way, but the third man wasn't so lucky. He rolled up and over my windshield, cracking the glass with his head, before vanishing from view. Even if he wasn't dead, he wouldn't be getting up from that anytime soon.

I'd built up so much speed that the force of the crash was hard and violent enough to slam the vamps' first vehicle into the second one, forcing it up and back over a curb and then careening across the thin strip of grass, down the briar-covered bank, and into the river fifty feet below. One of the men had ducked behind that second car for cover, and a scream tore through the air as it slammed into him, knocking him out into the open air. A loud *splat* sounded as he belly-flopped into the surface of the river. A second later, the water grabbed hold of the car and sucked it under too.

I grinned. Well, that was one way to break up a roadblock.

But I wasn't done yet. I threw my car into reverse, backing up about twenty feet, then shoved it into drive and rammed forward into the first car again, sending it up and over the curb too. But this impact wasn't as hard as the initial one, so I kept my foot on the gas, engine whining, tires screeching, the acrid scents of burning rubber and exhaust flooding the air. Finally, gravity took over, and that first car started sliding down the riverbank and crashed through the tangle of briars to join the second one already in the water. This end of the bridge was now clear.

I threw my vehicle into park. Then I grabbed a couple of guns out of my bag, unsnapped my seat belt, and kicked open the driver's-side door. I got to my feet and had started to run around the front of my car when I spotted a movement out of the corner of my eye. I pivoted in that direction—

Crack!

A bullet *thunk*ed into my chest, but my silverstone vest caught the projectile. Even if it hadn't, I was still holding on to my Stone magic to protect myself. My gaze snapped over to the third vamp, who had somehow survived the crashes and careening cars. With one hand, he clutched the bridge railing for support. With the other, he raised his gun at me again, his finger squeezing back the trigger.

Click.

Click. Click.

Click.

He kept pulling and pulling the trigger, with the same empty result every time. I smiled, raised one of my own guns, and shot him three times in the chest. He was dead before he hit the ground.

But I was already moving, running toward the sedan in the middle of the bridge, my boots crunching through the glass, bullet casings, and smoking, twisted bits of metal that littered the asphalt.

"Bria! Catalina!" I screamed.

"Gin!" Bria yelled back. "We're here!"

I reached the driver's side of the sedan and glanced in through the busted-out window. Catalina was crouched on the floor of the passenger's side of the car, with Bria draped over her, shielding the younger woman as best she could. My gaze flicked over them. Bloody cuts had sliced across their hands, arms, and faces from all the flying glass, but neither one of them seemed to be seriously injured—

Crack!

Crack! Crack!

Crack!

I ducked down beside the car as more bullets came zipping in my direction, my head snapping to the right.

The men on the far side of the bridge had gotten over their surprise, had pulled out their own guns, and were now firing at the sedan, trying to kill me, along with Bria and Catalina. I raised one of my own guns and returned fire, but I spotted at least eight men on that side of the bridge, all armed.

And Benson was there too.

The vampire kingpin stood about twenty feet behind his men, off to the left. He wore his usual white pants and sneakers, with a mint-green shirt and matching bow tie, his pen and notepad in his hands, as though he had been writing down details about the firefight. I didn't see Silvio anywhere. I wondered if he'd known about his boss's ambush plans. Maybe that's what he'd been texting Catalina about, warning her not to let Bria drive onto the bridge.

Benson's gaze met mine. But instead of seeming concerned that I was here, he tapped his pen against his lips before scribbling down another note.

"Gin!" Bria yelled.

"We have to get out of here!" I yelled back, pushing all thoughts of Benson's odd quirks out of my mind. "Now! Crawl out the windshield! I'll cover you!"

I raised my guns and fired again, as Bria slithered out the front windshield and onto the hood of the car, then reached back inside to help pull Catalina out. The two of them had just slid down in front of the hood when my guns *click-click-click*ed empty. Disgusted, I threw them aside.

The vamps realized that I was out of ammo, and they rose from behind their cars and took aim at me again—

Crack!

Crack! Crack!

Crack!

I tensed, expecting to feel more bullets slamming against my body, but this time, the vamps weren't the ones shooting.

Xavier was.

The giant had finally arrived, zooming up the street and turning his car at an angle on the road. I saw him lean out the driver's-side window and start firing at the vamps. One of them went down, then another one.

But it wasn't going to be enough.

Xavier was on the wrong side of the bridge, and there was no way we could get to the giant without going through Benson and all of his men. Some of the vamps whirled around to fire at Xavier, but the others eased out from behind their cars, guns in their hands, and started creeping in this direction.

"They're coming!" I yelled, backing up. "We have to get off the bridge! Now!"

Bria nodded. She grabbed Catalina's hand, pulled the younger woman to her feet, and started running.

I turned and followed them.

* 18 *

Bria, Catalina, and I raced toward my smashed-up car at this end of the bridge.

Crack!

Crack! Crack!

Crack! Crack! Crack!

The vampires kept firing, and bullets zipped through the air all around us. I kept my hold on my Stone magic, running directly behind Bria and Catalina and trying to use my body to screen them from the bullets as best I could.

Crack!

A bullet punched into the middle of my back. My vest caught it, but the hard, direct impact still made me stagger forward. My boots skidded through a patch of broken glass, and I had to windmill my arms to keep from falling flat on my ass. But I managed to regain my balance and keep going.

Catalina tried the passenger door of my car, but it wouldn't budge, so she wrenched open the back door and threw herself inside. Bria followed her. I ran around and jumped into the driver's seat. I'd left the engine running, so all I had to do was throw the car into gear, stomp down on the gas, and wrench the steering wheel.

The Aston fishtailed wildly at the sudden, sharp turn, with metal, glass, and more crunching under the tires, but I forced the wheel and the car in the direction I wanted to go—as far away from the vamps as I could get.

The street ahead was still deserted, probably on Benson's orders, but that was actually going to help us now. The car straightened out, and the engine started humming as we picked up speed.

For a moment, I thought that we were actually going to make it.

Crack!

But then a bullet sliced through one of the rear tires, the air escaping with a sad sigh. Still, I put my foot down on the gas, trying to make it as far as I could on the deflating rubber. The car *thump-thump-thump*ed along for about a block, before white sparks started flying up from the undercarriage. I steered the car over to the curb, stopped, and jammed the gearshift into park.

"Out, out, out!" I yelled.

I grabbed my duffel bag with its supplies from the front passenger seat, then kicked open the driver's-side door again and got out. Bria and Catalina were already waiting on the street. Catalina was holding her hand to her forehead, blood trickling out between her fingers from a nasty cut. Blood covered Bria's face, hands, and arms, but she had her gun out and pointed at the street behind us, watching our backs.

And with good reason.

Four vamps had made it to the end of the bridge and were running in our direction. They must have all had a pint or two of blood recently, because they were closing faster than Olympic sprinters racing toward the finish line.

But the charging men didn't worry me as much as the SUVs did.

In the distance, at the far end of the bridge, I could see the remaining vamps opening doors and climbing into the vehicles. One of the SUVs lurched forward and rammed into Bria's sedan, trying to push it out of the way and cross the bridge. The tires *screech-screech-screech*ed as the other SUVs whipped into U-turns, probably heading to the next bridge over so they could zoom across it and come at us from that direction too. If they got ahead of us, they could cut us off, then wait for the vamps to come up from the rear and box us in. We needed to be out of here before that happened, or we were dead.

"Now what?" Catalina asked, her panicked gaze flicking back and forth from the vamps to Bria to me.

I hefted my duffel bag a little higher on my shoulder. "We run."

I darted onto the sidewalk, with Catalina and Bria beside me, and raced toward the closest alley. Catalina glanced back over her shoulder, shoving her hair out of her face so she could see the men still chasing us. But she wasn't watching where she was going, so she banged into a mailbox and stumbled forward several feet before she regained her balance.

"Don't look back!" I yelled. "Just follow me!"

Catalina swiped some more blood off her face and gave me a quick, frightened nod.

I veered into the alley and zoomed over the cracked asphalt, darting around the overflowing Dumpsters, my boots sending crushed soda cans and crumpled paper bags skittering off in every direction. Behind me, I could hear Catalina's and Bria's footsteps smacking against the jagged pavement. I sucked in a breath and almost choked on the overwhelming stench of old take-out and other rotting garbage.

I reached the end of that alley and slowed down long enough to make sure that Benson and his SUVs full of vamps hadn't reached this area yet. But the street was clear, so I darted across it and turned into the next alley we came to in order to lose the men chasing us on foot. Catalina followed me, with Bria watching our backs.

We ran out the far side of that second alley, and the landscape shifted, as though we'd stepped into a completely different world. Gone were the brick storefronts and smooth sidewalks that lined the street near the river. In their places stood dilapidated row houses, potholes big enough to blow out your tires, and yards covered with more trash than grass. Many of the houses had been tagged with rune graffiti that flowed across the cinder-block walls, down the cracked concrete steps, and out onto the sidewalks and the street beyond. The red and black smears of spray paint ringed the potholes like crooked streaks of lipstick.

At first glance, the area seemed deserted. No one was strolling down the sidewalks. No kids were playing with toys in the yards. No old folks were sitting on their front stoops, shooting the breeze and sipping glasses of iced tea. But all around me, the stone of everything from the street to the sidewalks to the houses whispered of the danger, despair, and desperation of the people who called this place home.

This was the heart of Southtown.

It was also the worst possible place for us to be right now, since it was deep in Benson's territory.

My footsteps slowed as I glanced around, my head snapping left, then right, then back again. Thick brown sheets of cardboard held up with duct tape stretched across the windows of many of the houses, since the glass had been busted out long ago by bullets, fists, and rocks. Small holes had been cut here and there in the cardboard, and flashes of light and shadow appeared as folks peered out their peepholes at us, then scurried away. No doubt, someone was already dialing into Benson's network, and word would soon reach him about our location. We needed to move.

"Gin?" Bria asked, stopping beside me, her breath coming in soft gasps as she put her hands on her knees. "Where to now?"

That was the question—and the answer would determine whether we lived or died.

I glanced at first one end of the block, then the other. Going south would take us back toward the river, which was no good, since Benson could always order more of his vamps to guard the bridges. The police station was about two miles north of here, but I doubted we could make it on foot without running into some of Benson's men.

Killing my way through the vamp's goons didn't bother me. I could take care of myself. So could Bria. But blood was still oozing out of that gash on Catalina's forehead, and her face was white with fear, adrenaline, and the strain of running so far so fast. I unzipped my duffel bag long enough to grab a tin of Jo-Jo's healing ointment. The salve would take care of the ugly cut, but it wouldn't be long before her body shut down completely and she went into shock, if she wasn't already there.

"Here," I said, shoving the tin into Catalina's trembling hand. "Put that on your forehead."

Catalina took the container, but instead of popping off the top, she hunched over between Bria and me, her hands on her knees, her breath coming in ragged puffs, her hazel gaze locked on a beer bottle sitting upright on the curb, one that wasn't broken like all the others we'd waded through in the alleys.

Catalina stared and stared at that bottle, although I knew that she wasn't really seeing it. I started to look away but found myself strangely hypnotized by the glint of the afternoon sun on the glass, making it flare with an inner amber fire. A faint breeze gusted down the street, tickling my nose with a hint of stale, sour beer.

The color, the smell, the fingers of wind tangling my sweaty hair . . . For a second, I was in another place, another time, another street where I was clutching a beer bottle, getting ready to cut that man to save Coral—

"Gin?" Bria asked again.

I snapped back to this place, this time, this street. I knew where to go now.

"This way."

I hurried across the street, shoved through a gate in a chain-link fence, and jogged around the side of a house in the middle of the block. Classic jazz music purred out from behind the walls, and the whiff of fried meat seeped out of the cardboard-covered windows. I headed into the backyard, ducked under a clothesline filled with white undershirts and blue boxers that were snapping back and forth in the wind, and hopped over the waist-high fence at the edge of the yard.

Again and again, I repeated the process, cutting through yard after yard, taking a zigzag route, with Catalina and Bria behind me. Finally, we reached the last of the houses, but I didn't slow my pace until we'd crossed another street and ducked into an alley. Even then, I kept going until I reached the apartment building in the center of the block.

I stopped in front of the back door of the building. It was still red, although the color had long ago faded from that bright, glossy crimson I remembered to a dull, flat rust. More memories rose up in my mind about all the terrible things that had happened the day I'd followed Coral through that door, but I forced them back into the bottom of my brain. More terrible things were going to happen if I didn't get Bria and Catalina out of here.

"Gin?" Bria asked, her gun still clutched in her hand, her head swiveling back and forth from one end of the alley to the other. "Why are we stopping?"

Instead of answering her, I dropped my bag onto the

pavement and then crouched down in front of the door so that I was eye-level with the lock. Catalina slumped against the brick wall next to me, trying to get her breath back, her face even paler and bloodier than before. She still had that tin of Jo-Jo's ointment clutched in her hands, and she started fumbling with the top, her bloody fingers slipping off the smooth surface.

"You still have your phone?" I asked Bria.

"Yeah. Why?"

"Text Xavier. See if he got away from Benson's men and if his car is in one piece. Ask if he can pick you up at this address." I rattled off a location.

Bria frowned, but she pulled out her phone and did as I asked. Meanwhile, I reached for my Ice magic, pulling the cool power up out of the deepest part of me and letting it flow out through my hand. A silver light flared in my right palm, centered in my spider rune scar. A second later, I was holding two slender Ice picks, which I inserted into the lock.

Bria's phone beeped, and she read the message. "Yeah, Xavier's fine. He'll be at that location in five minutes."

"Good."

The tumblers clicked into place. I threw down my Ice picks, twisted the knob, and opened the door. The inside of the building was dim and murky, although I could see light spilling from the door at the far end of the hallway.

"Come on, Catalina," I called out. "Just a little farther now. Go inside and wait for us. Bria will be there in a second."

She'd quit trying to open the tin of salve, and she was

just standing there, swaying from side to side. Her hazel eyes were a bit unfocused, but she finally sighed and shuffled forward into the building with all the lifeless enthusiasm of a zombie. She stopped a few feet away and leaned against the interior wall.

I turned to Bria. "You need to go inside. Follow this hallway all the way to the end. It opens up into a courtyard. You can cut across there and into the building directly across from this one. Go straight through that building, and you'll come out on the street where Xavier will be waiting."

Bria nodded, then frowned. "How do you know all that?"

"Because I've been here before."

She opened her mouth, but after a moment, she swallowed down her many questions and asked the only one that mattered. "What about you?"

"I'll meet you there. I'm going to go down to the end of the alley and then jog around the block to make sure that none of Benson's vamps come up on you from behind. We only have one chance to get out of here, and this is it."

Bria nodded again. She bit her lip, looked up and down the alley to make sure that we were still alone, then reached out and hugged me tight with one arm.

"I'm so sorry," she whispered. "For everything. I just . . . I wanted to nail that bastard so damn *bad*."

Even though a dozen shallow cuts dotted my hand, I reached up and smoothed down her hair, leaving streaks of blood behind in her tangled golden locks. "I know."

Bria shuddered in a breath. I hugged her even tighter,

but when she dropped her arm and pulled back, her face was as calm and composed as mine.

"See you on the other side—"

The *screech-screech-screech* of tires cut her off. A black SUV stopped at the end of the alley. The doors opened, and vamps started pouring out, all with guns, all racing in our direction. They'd finally found us, and they were out for blood—ours.

Bria's mouth flattened into a determined line, and she raised her gun to fire at them. But I grabbed her shoulder, spun her around, and shoved her through the open door and into the building. She staggered forward, almost plowing into Catalina. While she struggled to right herself, I grabbed the duffel bag full of guns, ammo, and other supplies and tossed it inside too. Bria whipped around, but I reached through the opening, grabbed the door, and pulled it shut. Then I wrapped my hand around the knob and let loose with a burst of Ice magic. The intense silver light of my power pulsed for a moment, searing my eyes, before it faded away. By the time I blinked again, three inches of my elemental Ice coated the knob, the door, and a good chunk of the surrounding walls. A crude but effective lock. Nobody would be getting through that right now without an axe or some serious elemental Fire power.

"Gin!" I heard Bria's muffled yell through the door. "What are you doing?"

She rattled the knob on her side, but she couldn't get through the thick layer of Ice I'd caked on it.

"Go!" I shouted back to her. "Just go!"

Crack!

Crack! Crack!

Crack!

The vamps raised their guns and started firing. I cursed, then grabbed hold of my Stone magic, using it to harden my skin. But instead of running away, I palmed one of the knives hidden up my sleeves and sprinted toward the gunmen. I still needed to buy Bria some time to get Catalina through the building and over to the street so Xavier could pick them up, and I couldn't think of a better way to do that than by killing a whole passel of Benson's men.

The vamps' mouths gaped open, revealing their fangs. Apparently, my charge had surprised them, but they recovered quickly enough to empty their guns at me.

Crack!
Crack! Crack!
Crack!

Bullets *ping*ed off the walls, the trash cans, the Dumpsters, and even me, and the burn of gunpowder filled the air, overpowering the pungent scent of the garbage. But I kept running, and the vamps quickly ran out of bullets.

Aw, I just hated that for them.

Two of them cursed and stopped to reload, but it was too late, because I was already there. I grabbed the first man I reached, pulling him close and slicing my knife across his stomach one, two, three times, before shoving him away. He went down screaming.

I moved to the left side of the alley. This vamp was quicker than his friend, and he landed a quick one-two combo to my chest. But his blows didn't hurt all that much, thanks to the protective shells of my silverstone vest and my Stone magic, and I buried my knife in his throat before he could strike again. He died with a bloody wheeze.

A third man stepped up and grabbed my hand, trying to bend my wrist back to get me to drop my knife. So I slammed my Stone-hardened head into his, making his nose crunch like a potato chip. He let go of my hand and staggered back, but I reached out, latched onto his tie, and yanked him toward me, even as I shoved my knife into his heart. He yelped once like a wounded animal.

I stood there, eyes flicking back and forth, body tense, blood dripping off the end of my knife, but there were no more attackers to cut down, and the only sound was my harsh, raspy breaths—

Screech-screech-screech.

Three more SUVs pulled up at the end of the alley, and more vamps spewed out of the vehicles, close to a dozen this time, which was more than I could easily handle. Besides, I still needed to get to Bria and Catalina, so I turned and ran toward the far end of the alley.

Crack! Crack! Crack!

More bullets zipped in my direction, but I was booking it, and the vamps had to step over their dead buddies to take aim at me. I focused on the exit up ahead and forced myself to sprint even faster. Bria and Catalina should almost be to Xavier by now. I needed to get there too, so I put on an extra burst of speed and hurtled out of the alley—

Once again, I heard the *screech* of tires, but I didn't see the vehicle until it was too late.

I whirled around to find a black SUV bearing down on me. The driver hit the gas, making the vehicle jump the curb and careen up onto the sidewalk where I was standing. I had just enough time to reach for my Stone magic, trying to harden my skin even more, before the SUV slammed into me.

I rolled up and over the hood, cracking the windshield with my head just like the vamp I'd plowed into with my car at the bridge. The brutal impact made me lose my grip on my magic for one precious second. But that was all it took for me to fly off the side of the car and hit the pavement.

Lights out.

✵ 19 ✵

I wasn't sure how long I was unconscious. Probably only a few seconds, since I woke up sprawled across the pavement, my arms trapped underneath my chest as though I'd tried to break the flying fall with my hands.

Every single bone in my body ached, and I could feel more blood trickling out of all my many cuts and scrapes, but I was still in one piece. I must have managed to grab hold of enough of my Stone magic to protect myself before I hit the asphalt and blacked out—

Squeak-squeak-squeak.

Squeak-squeak-squeak.

Footsteps sounded on the pavement. I blinked and found myself staring at a pair of white sneakers. He shifted to one side, and his pant leg rode up, revealing one of his socks, mint-green with a white argyle pattern. I craned my neck up, then wished that I hadn't, as that small motion spread the aches in my bones out to all the other nerve endings in my body. I felt like an egg that someone had dropped on the sidewalk, cracked and oozing everywhere.

Beauregard Benson towered over me. The vamp's blue eyes flicked over my body, his gaze cold but curious at the same time.

"Amazing that her brains aren't leaking all over the street, along with the rest of her," he said. "But that's Stone magic for you. I'll be interested to see her reaction in the lab."

"The lab, sir? Don't you want to finish her off here?"

I blinked again. That was Silvio's bland tone. He might have wanted me to kill Benson, but no doubt, he'd be all too happy to hand his boss a gun so Benson could shoot me now.

"And waste this rare research opportunity? Absolutely not," Benson purred. "I have something *far* more interesting in mind for her. Give her a sedative, and get her in the car."

Silvio crouched down beside me, a syringe in his hand. He gave me an almost apologetic look, but he followed his boss's orders and leaned forward. The needle pricked my arm.

Lights out again.

The world didn't go completely black this time. But a fog enveloped my mind that made it hard for me to do more than just slowly blink, much less fight back. And every time I opened my eyes, something different was happening.

Blink.

Two of the vamps rolled me over onto my back, and Silvio patted me down, slipping off the spider rune ring on my right index finger. He also removed all of my knives, including the extra ones in my vest, then went over and retrieved the weapon I'd been holding when I was roadkilled by the SUV.

Blink.

The two vamps scooped me up off the pavement and shoved me into the back of an SUV. My arms and legs flopped every which way, as though they were made out of gelatin instead of flesh and bone. Silvio slid in next to me, carefully propping me up, straightening my legs, and folding my hands in my lap, making me comfortable. He even took the time to buckle my seat belt. I snickered at the irony of that, although the sound was barely louder than a croak.

Blink.

The SUV stopped in the circular driveway that fronted Benson's mansion. The vamps undid my seat belt, grabbed hold of my arms, and dragged me out of the vehicle, up a set of stairs, and into the building. Benson strode along in front of us, his sneakers *squeak-squeak-squeak*ing like they had the hiccups. My own boots skidded along the floor, the toes catching on the rugs and smearing blood, dirt, and bits of garbage all over the fine fabrics and glossy hardwood that peeped out between them. Silvio brought up the rear, moving as silently as a ghost.

Blink.

The vamps dragged me down a set of steps and into a large basement, one filled with people.

Most of them were probably in their late teens and early twenties, but their dull, glazed eyes, slack, wrinkled features, and thin, almost emaciated bodies made them seem much, much older, as though they'd already used up most of the life inside them and were waiting for the rest to be slowly extinguished.

These were the faces of addicts.

People sprawled across couches, curled up on futons, and lay facedown on pillows that had been strewn across the floor, their knobby knees and bony elbows making them look like toy sticks that a child had scattered everywhere in a tantrum. Their clothes ranged from typical street rags and tattered T-shirts layered one on top of another to khakis and cargo pants to high-end silk business suits. Plastic bags full of tin cans, expensive backpacks bulging with books, and silverstone briefcases stuffed with paperwork lay at the feet of their respective owners. Bums, college kids, office workers. All brought here by their need for something to drown out the voices in their heads, give them a thrilling high, or take away the dull monotony of their lives. All laid low by that need, circling the drain toward that final, utter oblivion.

Drugs were truly a terrible equalizer.

Incense burned in thick bunches in the corners, while fat sachet bags of potpourri dangled from the ceiling like mirror balls between several swirling ceiling fans. But the heavy perfumes, swirls of sweet smoke, and constant rush of air couldn't hide the foul, bitter stench of the blood, vomit, and urine that had soaked into the couches, futons, and pillows. And absolutely nothing could drown out the sound of the cinder-block walls, as the stone alternately screamed, shrieked, and spewed out nonsensical dark dreams, darker demons, and other desperate, dangerous desires.

Blink.

It was the wail of the stone walls that finally penetrated my own sedative-induced fog, and I focused on that desperate, mournful noise, letting it pull me up out of the tunnel vision I'd been trapped in. Slowly, my mind cleared. I tried to summon up the energy to wrench free of the men holding on to me, or at least get my arms and legs to move of their own accord. But no matter how hard I concentrated, I couldn't get anything to work, not even my tongue, which was as thick and dry as a wad of cotton stuffed into the bottom of my mouth.

I also reached for my magic, for all that Ice and Stone power flowing through my veins. But just like my limbs, my magic lay numb and heavy inside me, as though it were a two-ton boulder I was trying to lift. Sweat beaded on my temples from heaving, straining, pushing, and clawing at my power, but whatever drug Silvio had given me kept me from getting a grip on my magic, much less creating an Ice knife with it.

The people stirred as Benson moved through the basement, lifting their heads up out of the cold cradles of their spindly arms, their gazes suddenly sharp, alert, and completely focused on him. One man stretched out a skeletal hand and clutched at the vampire kingpin's pant leg as he passed, a helpless, pleading note in his incoherent cries. Benson stopped, pulled out his pen and pad, and made a few notes about the man's condition. Then he patted the man on the head like a dog and walked on.

Benson snapped his fingers, and the vamps dragged me through the drug den, with Silvio still following along behind us. A mirror covered most of the back wall, giving me a glimpse of my own reflection—dirty, beaten, bloody.

But not broken. Never that.

Benson opened a door set into the wall next to the mirror, and the vamps dragged me through it. I was expecting another drug den, but where the basement had the thinnest veneer of opulence, this area had the clinical, sterile, in-your-face feel of a doctor's office. A faint tang of alcohol hung in the air, mixed with some lemony cleaner. Everything was white, from the tile floor and ceiling to several industrial-size refrigerators along the back wall. Even the cinder blocks had been painted white, although dull stains marred the slick finish in spots. A long metal table hugged another wall, the top bristling with mortars, pestles, beakers, burners, and wooden racks full of small glass vials filled with brightly colored powders.

But my eyes locked onto the centerpiece of the room: a large white padded dentist's chair outfitted with silver-stone arm, leg, and neck shackles.

And I realized that this wasn't anything like a doctor's office.

It was a lab, and I was the rat.

"Strip her," Benson ordered, going over to one of the sinks along the wall and washing his hands.

The two vamps grinned at me, showing off their fangs. One of them pulled out a switchblade, flicked it open, and cut off my clothes with it. My vest, my long-sleeved T-shirt, my jeans, my underwear. The bastard even sliced off my boots and socks.

I tried to move my arms and legs, so I could grab the knife and slice open the vamp's throat with it before turning the blade on his buddy. But the sedative was still working its way through my system, and I couldn't even muster so much as a snarl.

Silvio stood off to one side of the lab, calm and composed as ever. He stared at me, his face completely unreadable, then pulled out his phone and started texting on it. If I could have, I would have broken his thumbs, grabbed the device, and force-fed it to him through his fucking teeth.

Benson finished washing his hands, then stood by and watched the whole damn thing. He even pulled out his pen and pad and took notes, although I had no idea what he thought was so interesting about my pale, naked body.

When I'd been stripped, Silvio put his phone away, reached into one of the cabinets over the sinks, and drew out a white hospital gown. The two vamps held my hands out, sticking my arms through the holes, while Silvio wrapped the gown around my body and tied it together in the back. He also attached a series of electrodes to my head and chest, along with an oxygen monitor on my left index finger, then hooked everything up to a couple of machines standing next to the metal table and flipped them on.

"Put her in the chair," Benson ordered.

The two vamps picked me up and plopped my ass in the chair.

Clink. Clink. Clink. Clink. Clink.

They snapped the silverstone restraints around my arms and legs, shackling me to the chair, before cinching the final one around my neck. I felt like a dog wearing one of those damn cone collars.

After he snapped the restraint around my neck, the vamp with the switchblade, the one who'd cut off my clothes, pinched my cheek with his fingers.

"How does that feel, honey?" he crooned. "Not so tough now, are you?"

Instead of verbally responding to his taunt, I snapped out with my teeth and caught the tender web of his hand in my mouth.

He screamed and tried to pull away, but I ground my teeth together as hard as I could. Coppery spurts of blood filled my mouth, and the vamp slapped at my head and face, but I ignored the blows. When he realized that I wasn't going to let go without a fight, the second vamp stepped forward and punched me in the stomach. Despite my best intentions, I couldn't help but cough as all of the air was driven out of my lungs. The first vamp finally wrenched his hand out of my mouth and stumbled away, clutching his wounded appendage to his chest.

For a moment, everything was quiet, except for the vamp's and my own gasps for breath, along with the steady *beep-beep-beep* of the machines monitoring my heart rate.

Then I turned my head to the side as far as it would go and spat a wad of his blood out onto the floor, ruining the glossy shine of the white tile. I grinned, knowing that my teeth were as bloody as, well, a vampire's after a quick sip of O-negative.

"Not as bad as *that* feels," I drawled, answering his earlier question. "You should watch where you put your fucking fingers."

Benson regarded me with an almost amused expression, as though my injuring his minion was somehow entertaining. Maybe it was to him.

The wounded vamp screamed again and lunged at me, but Silvio stepped in front of him, thwarting his attack.

"Enough," Silvio said. "That's enough. You know the boss doesn't like it when you damage his . . . subjects."

The injured vamp kept glaring at me, but he didn't try to push past Silvio. He was too afraid of Benson to do that.

I puckered my mouth and made a kissy noise at him.

The vamp's face turned as red as the blood dribbling down his wounded hand, but the second man grabbed his shoulder, spun him around, and marched him out of the lab, closing the door behind them.

That left me alone with Benson and Silvio.

"Well, then, let's get started," Benson said, a high, excited note in his nasal voice.

Silvio went over to a wooden stand in the corner and plucked a long white coat off it. Benson held out his arms, and Silvio helped his boss into the jacket, just like he had the night Benson murdered Troy. Silvio even grabbed a stethoscope from the table and hung it around the vamp's neck, like Benson was a real doctor, instead of just a sadistic bastard.

When the vamp was properly attired, he reached into his shirt pocket, pulled out a pen and his pad, and started circling around me.

Squeak-squeak-squeak. Scribble-scribble-scribble.
Squeak-squeak-squeak. Scribble-scribble-scribble.

He moved behind me, so I couldn't see him, but the squealing of his sneakers on the floor mingled with the scratching of his pen on the paper.

"You know, most people would be crying and pleading for their lives at this point," Benson said.

I didn't respond.

Suddenly, Benson leaned forward. He must have drunk some blood recently to amp up his speed, because I never even saw him move. One second, he was behind me. The next, his face was so close to mine that he could have reached out and kissed my cheek if he wanted to. Instead, he buried his nose in my grimy hair and sucked in a deep, audible breath.

"Mmm . . . rage," he murmured. "One of my favorite snacks."

Benson's own scent filled my nostrils, the same alcohol-and-lemon stench that permeated the lab. I glared at him out of the corner of my eye. That was all I could do, given the cuffs and the fact that I still couldn't quite grab on to my magic. Even if I could have reached it, my Ice and Stone powers were useless in this situation. Sure, I could harden my skin, but I'd still be stuck in the chair, and since my hands were tied down, I had no hope of using a pair of Ice picks to open the locks on the restraints.

Right now, Benson could do anything he wanted to me—torture me any way he wanted to, for as long as he wanted to—and I was powerless to stop him.

Completely, utterly, absolutely powerless.

For once in my life, I couldn't fight back, and that hurt me more than anything else.

Benson bent down in front of me so that his face was level with mine. I met his gaze with a flat one of my own, even though I was mentally counting down the seconds to my own death. Because it would be all too easy for him to reach out, touch my cheek, and use his vampiric Air magic to drain my cold rage—and the rest of my emotions—from my body.

I wasn't particularly scared of dying. I'd been too close to the end too many times to worry about it much anymore. When it happened, it happened. But I'd always hoped that I'd at least go down fighting. Not like this. Not so trapped.

Not so damn *helpless*.

But instead of finishing me off, Benson gave me a pleased smile. "You know, Gin, I was rather disappointed when you showed up on the bridge and even more so when I realized that you'd managed to get your sister and her witness to safety after all."

I kept my face blank, even as my heart lifted at his words. His men hadn't found Bria and Catalina. With any luck, they'd made it to Xavier, and the giant had driven them far, far away.

"But then I realized that this small setback didn't matter," Benson continued. "Not really. After all, I can always find and kill them later. They won't be able to hide for long. Not in Ashland, not from me."

That was all too true, and it was one of the many reasons that I needed to figure some way to get out of this chair. Or at least make sure that Benson was bleeding out before I took my last breath. Too bad I had no idea how to make either one of those things happen.

"But then, when my men captured you, I realized what a unique opportunity I had been presented with," he continued.

"Oh, really?" I drawled. "And what would that be?"

"To further my studies."

A chill slithered up my spine. "Studies? What studies?"

Benson straightened back up and swept his hand out to the side. "My observations on human nature, life, and especially death."

For the first time, I realized that my chair was facing the wall in the front of the room—a wall made out of one-way glass.

People sprawled on couches and pillows. Smoke spiraling up into the air. The ceiling fans spinning around and around. I could see into the drug den next door as clearly as if I were in the other room, although I couldn't hear any noise coming from that area. This room, maybe both of them, must be soundproof.

"Is that why you have all these people down here in your dungeon?" I asked. "So you can drug them up and experiment on them?"

"Of course." Benson beamed. "Like any good businessman, I have to keep on top of current market trends to meet customer demand. Have to keep growing, changing, and . . . innovating. I wouldn't want my products to get stale. That's when sales start to dip, and well, we just can't have that. Not these days, when there's such a nasty power struggle going on in Ashland."

I gave him another disgusted look. "You mean you have to keep coming up with new poisons to push on people to keep the cash rolling in."

He chuckled. "Ah, Gin. That's where you're wrong. I don't push anything on anyone. The first hit is always free."

"Yeah," I snarked. "It's all the others they pay the price for."

He shrugged. It didn't matter to him what his drugs did to people—only that he profited as much as he could from their pain and suffering.

"Tell me, how many of those folks are on your newest recreational hit? What's it called? Oh, yeah. Burn."

"Quite a few," he said in a cheerful tone. "It's been quite popular, more popular than I thought it would be, actually. I've made a tidy little sum on it, although not as much as I would have liked, since I've had to import it from out of town."

He gestured at the metal table. The glass vials with their cheery red, orange, and yellow powders reminded me of sugar sticks that kids might eat.

"But I'm reverse-engineering the formula, and I've almost got it, except for one small component. It's always more profitable to make products in-house, rather than contracting them out."

Benson kept staring at me, and I focused on him again. Maybe he thought that he could intimidate me with his steady gaze and faint smile. Please. If I got upset every time someone looked at me that way, I'd never get out of bed in the morning.

"You are amazingly calm," he said. "Your heartbeat has barely spiked this whole time, not even while you were attacking my man. It's fascinating, really, considering the situation you're in."

"And what situation would that be?"

He grinned, showing me his fangs. "In my mansion. In my lab. At my mercy."

I matched his toothy smile with one of my own. "I

imagine that you're rather like me in that *mercy* isn't exactly a popular word in your vocabulary."

His grin widened, and we fell into our silent staring contest again. Silvio stood off to my right, his hands clasped in front of his body, watching Benson and me watch each other, patiently waiting for his boss's next order.

"I find it interesting that you can be so very calm," Benson said. "But your disposition is exactly what I've been looking for to conduct my latest experiment. It involves Burn. You're going to help me test out a theory I have about it."

My stomach twisted at the casual way he said *experiment*, but I forced my gaze to stay on his. "Really? What's that?"

Excitement flared in Benson's eyes, making them gleam an electric blue behind his glasses. "Burn is one of the most potent drugs I've ever come across. It gives everyone an incredible high—humans, vampires, giants, dwarves. But it seems to affect elementals the most, and the stronger they are, the harder and faster Burn works on them."

That was more or less what Bria and Xavier had told me the night Troy was murdered.

"Because elementals have such an unusual reaction to Burn, it's easier to hook them on it, and they crave it more than any drug I've ever seen before," Benson said. "I've made more money selling Burn than I have with any other product I've ever produced, including oxy and meth. We're talking millions, Gin. And that's just in the few months that it's been available."

"So that's why you want to reverse-engineer it," I said. "You want to cut out your supplier and make it yourself so you don't have to share any of the profits."

"That's part of it," he admitted. "But this drug? It's going to help me finally take my rightful place in this town."

"And what would that be?"

He scoffed. "Pushing pills to bums, hookers, and gangbangers in Southtown is one thing. But I want to move up to a higher level of clientele. Northtown is where the *real* money is. Why, just think how much cash I can make getting all those rich Northtown elementals hooked on Burn. I'll make more money in six months than I would in ten years with my normal products in Southtown. Mab kept me locked away down here for years. Well, now that she's gone, I plan to take what I've wanted all along."

"Her spot as the head of the Ashland underworld." I didn't have any problem sketching in the outlines of his dream.

He shrugged again. "It's just good business. I'm tired of being everyone's middleman, the dirty little secret they don't want anyone to know about. I learned a long time ago that you're either on top or you're nothing."

Well, I couldn't argue with that, since I was currently shackled to a chair.

"Although it's not just power that I'm after," Benson continued. "It's the elementals' reaction to Burn that truly fascinates me. Like I said, there's one small component that I'm missing from the formula, and I think it's the key to how the drug affects elementals."

"So how I am going to help you with your little theory?" I sniped.

"I've tested it on all sorts of elementals. Air, Fire, Ice, and Stone. But I haven't had the opportunity to test it on someone who is gifted in more than one element, like you're rumored to be, Gin."

Benson kept his gaze locked on my face, gauging my reaction to his words and the fact that he wanted to make me his own human guinea pig. A cold tendril of fear curled up in the bottom of my stomach. My face stayed frozen, but my heart gave me away.

Beep-beep-beep. Beep-beep-beep.

The machine monitoring my pulse picked up speed as my heart thumped in time to my growing worry.

Benson cocked his head to the side. His eyes were still on my face, but once again, I got the sense that he wasn't looking *at* me so much as he was peering *inside* me. The faintest sensation swept over my body, one of invisible sandpaper sliding across my skin. I knew what it really was: the phantom teeth of Benson's Air magic, ready to tear into my body and rip out my emotions for him to feast on one terrified breath at a time.

It disgusted me.

Not too long ago, a vampire named Randall Dekes had bitten me, sinking his fangs into my body over and over again. That had been a brutal, vicious attack, but at least it had been head-on. Benson's magic was far more sinister than that. The sort of sneak attack you wouldn't even realize had started until he'd sucked away half your soul and was licking his chops in anticipation of dining on the rest.

Beep-beep-beep. Beep-beep-beep.

My heart continued to pick up speed, but instead of giving into my fear, anger, and disgust, I forced myself to take slow, deep breaths and remain calm. No way was I giving Benson any more ammunition in his deranged game of doctor. I wondered how many other people he'd done this to. How many people he'd shackled to this chair. How many of their emotions he'd snacked on while conducting his twisted *experiments*. I made a silent promise to myself that I was going to be the last one, that I was going to find some way to end him—even if it killed me.

Benson's lips puckered, his eyes focused, and the horrid feeling of that invisible sandpaper sliding across my skin vanished. Apparently, I'd annoyed him by not giving into my fear. Well, too damn bad.

"Silvio," he said. "Please retrieve the latest sample for me."

Silvio walked out of my line of sight. The door on one of the refrigerators *snick*ed open, and I heard him rustling around inside. A few seconds later, he came back over to his boss and held out a plastic bag.

A single pill lay inside.

Benson took the bag from him, opened it, and carefully drew out the drug. "I just got this in this morning. It's a new and improved formula that my supplier came up with. One that is supposedly ten times more potent than what my men have been distributing."

He held it up between his fingers so that I could look at it.

Unlike the red ones that I'd seen before, this pill was a vivid green, although it still featured the same crown-and-flame rune as the others. It looked so innocent, almost like a breath mint he was about to pop into his mouth, though it was anything but. I'd seen Benson's drug den, and I had no doubt that taking even just that one small pill would fuck me up in the worst way possible.

"Drugs have always fascinated me," Benson said, staring at the pill, a dreamy expression on his pasty face. "No, that's not quite right. People's *reactions* to drugs have always fascinated me. You can give a dozen people the same drug, the exact same chemical formula in the exact same dosage, and you will most likely get a dozen different reactions. Oh, the majority of them will be more or less the same, but there are always one or two that surprise you."

He waited, as if he expected me to chime in. When I didn't, he continued with his musings.

"Some people have violent allergic reactions, of course, which cut short any sort of pleasure they might experience from the drug," he went on. "But what's most interesting to me are the people who are so controlled, so buttoned-up, so tightly wound. The ones who have such a clamp on their emotions and never seem to show what they are really thinking or feeling. Drugs always seem to impact them the most—and in the most interesting ways."

He tilted his head to the side again. "I'm most curious to know what losing control would do to you, Gin."

I still didn't respond, but apparently, Benson was tired of chatting. Before I could try to move, before I could bite his hand, before I could do anything, he leaned forward, pried open my mouth, and shoved the pill inside.

I tried to spit it out, but he clamped his hand over my nose and mouth, cutting off my air. I could see the silent promise in his eyes. Take the pill, or he'd suffocate me right here, right now, in this chair, his experiment be damned.

Die now, or hope that I could survive what trip Burn might take me on.

No choice, really.

I swallowed the drug.

✷20✷

The pill had started to dissolve the second it hit my tongue, and my weak struggles with Benson had only hastened the absorption process. He removed his hand from my nose and mouth, and I barely had time to suck down a breath before Burn was in my system.

Bria and Xavier had warned me about the drug's powerful effects, but it was quite another thing to experience them firsthand. The rest of the limp, languid fog from the sedative Silvio had given me immediately vanished. A foul, bitter, almost smoky taste filled my mouth, and I could almost *feel* the pill sliding down my throat, like I'd swallowed a glowing ember, one that grew hotter and hotter the farther it dropped down my throat.

Then it hit my stomach, and the world erupted into flames.

The fire exploded low in my belly, dozens of hot, hungry little tendrils crawling outward from the epicenter like spiders scurrying through my insides, dragging burning threads of silk along behind them and weaving together a tight, inescapable web of flaming destruction.

I stared down at my stomach, almost expecting the spiders to come surging up out of my belly button and rip through the thin fabric of the hospital gown, stringing their stinging silk over the outside of my body as well as the inside. Sweat streamed down my forehead, the salt of it irritating my eyes, but that pain was small compared with what the drug was doing to me.

Burning, burning me alive, from the inside out.

I bucked and heaved and thrashed in the chair, so hard that the restraints bruised my neck, wrists, and ankles, but I couldn't break free of the cuffs. Even if I could have, I still couldn't have escaped the drug and what it was doing to me. All too soon, I had exhausted what little strength I had, and I sagged against the chair, gasping for air, even though every breath I took only seemed to add more fuel to the fire roaring through my veins.

While I'd been thrashing around, Benson had pulled a chair right up beside mine, his pen and pad in hand, observing my pitiful struggles. He leaned forward, his excited breath brushing against my face, as hot and eager as the drug coursing through my system.

Benson's nostrils quivered as he sniffed my emotions again. "Finally," he murmured. "*Fear.*"

He looked at the watch on his wrist, scrawled something on his pad, and then raised his eyes to mine again. "Tell me, Gin," he cooed. "We're five minutes into our experiment. What does it feel like? All of those sweet, sweet chemicals pumping through your body. Shooting straight into your heart, circling through your brain, and cycling back out again. What do they feel like, interacting with your own magic, your own elemental power? Hmm?"

"It . . . burns . . ." That was all I could rasp out.

I don't know how long I sagged in the chair, just waiting and waiting for the horrible burning sensation to leave my body. But instead of lessening, it only intensified, and then—suddenly—from one blink to the next—

I was *flying*.

That was the only way to describe the feeling. My body felt completely weightless, and I was soaring through the sky, with thick white clouds all around me. The lab, Benson, Silvio, they all fell away, and all I could see, hear, and smell was the blue, blue sky—the one that always reminded me of fall, Fletcher, and my murdered family.

I was so delighted that I laughed.

I'd spent so much of my life learning how to control my emotions, always pushing aside my pain, fear, and anxiety, especially these past few months with everyone gunning for me. But right now, I didn't have any worries. No cares, no complaints, no concerns of any kind. It was just me and the clouds drifting through the sky.

And I *loved* it, every single second of it.

But even more than that, I felt so *strong* in that moment. Powerful. Invincible. Unstoppable. Like I could zoom up through the clouds into the heavens above, wrap my fist around a star, and snuff it out. Smash my way through the moon with my bare hands. Eliminate everything and everyone who dared to displease me.

I didn't need Bria or Finn or Owen or any of the rest of my friends and family. I was better than the whole lot of them, all weak, pitiful, and small. Especially Bria, always worrying about doing things the right way. Always nattering on and on and *on* about the law and justice, instead of just doing what needed to be done, like I always did.

I didn't need Bria and her rules and regulations and her guilt about my being an assassin. Not anymore. I didn't need her hanging around, the albatross she was around my neck, such a bothersome *burden*.

All I needed was *this*—this feeling, this power, this drug.

All I needed was Burn.

"Only fifteen minutes in, and she's in the euphoria stage already," I heard Benson murmur. "She's reacting quicker to the drug than anyone before. Amazing."

"Isn't it?" Silvio's tone was as dry as Benson's was excited.

Their voices penetrated my dizzying rush, making me frown and look at the clouds clustered around me. The longer I stared at them, the more I realized that something was wrong. The puffy white edges started to darken and smoke, their edges singed like marshmallows that had been held over a campfire too long. Melting, melting everywhere . . .

And I started to fall.

In an instant, I wasn't strong anymore. Not powerful, not unstoppable, and certainly not invincible. No, I was the one who was weak, pitiful, and small.

My body grew hotter and hotter, even as the ground rushed up to meet me. But right before my impact, the brown earth dissolved into a pit of roaring green flames. I screamed, even though there was nothing I could do to keep from plummeting straight into the heart of that raging fire.

I sucked down another breath to scream, and I snapped back to reality. To the lab and the chair and Benson watching me, the rat in his cage.

"Twenty-five minutes in, and out of the euphoria stage already. Most fascinating indeed."

He glanced at his watch and scribbled another note on that damn pad of his.

But my anger at the vamp and his sick torture of me was quickly replaced by more pain, as Burn continued to rage through my body. The poison pulsed through every single part of me. I stared down at my arms, and I swear that I could actually *see* those spiders crawling around underneath my skin, their fat bellies swollen with bubbling green lava and their eyes flashing the same wicked color as they drew their matching strings of silk along behind them. The burning threads scorched every single part of me that they touched, wrapping around me tighter and tighter until I thought my whole body would spontaneously combust.

I started screaming then, and I didn't stop.

I *couldn't* stop.

Beep-beep-beep-beep-beep-beep.

Mixed in with my screams, the monitors continued to chirp out my heartbeat, the sound and tempo accelerating like a car engine.

"Silvio," Benson said, his voice seeming small and far away. "Check her vitals. I'm going to get some adrenaline. At the rate the drug is cycling through her body, the crash might kill her. And I'd hate to lose such an interesting test subject."

Test subject? I snarled at the idea that he wanted to do this to me again and again, although the sound was lost amid my screams and the high-pitched squealing of the monitors.

I was dimly aware of Benson sliding his chair away from mine, getting to his feet, and hurrying into the back of the lab. Then Silvio was leaning over me, pressing his fingers into the pulse point on my right wrist. The cool, soft touch of his hand made me sigh, although my relief was short-lived, as another wave of fire roared through my veins.

"Gin," Silvio whispered in my ear. "You're reacting badly to the drug. I think it has some sort of elemental magic in it. That's the ingredient that I think Benson is missing. If that's true, then whatever kind of magic it is, your own power doesn't like it. So you have to fight it. You have to fight the magic, or it will kill you. Do you understand?"

Silvio's face swam in front of my eyes, his bronze skin melting at the edges, just like the marshmallow clouds had. But I sucked in a breath and forced myself to concentrate, to focus, until his features solidified.

"Gin?" he whispered again, his tone more urgent than before. "Do you understand?"

I stared into his eyes, his gray eyes that were almost the same color as mine, as my power, as my magic.

Elemental magic . . .

Silvio's words swirled around and around my mind. Burn contained some sort of elemental magic? His shocking statement cut through some of my confusion. Well, that would explain why Benson hadn't been able to reverse-engineer the formula yet and also why the drug affected elementals the most, like Benson and Bria had both told me. I didn't like the feel of other elementals' magic, much less it actually being absorbed into my system. Silvio was right. If I didn't figure out what kind of power it was, or at least how to counteract it, the drug would kill me.

So for the first time, instead of trying to push it away or dampen it down or ignore it, I actually *concentrated* on the feel of the drug. But it wasn't enough. Even as I tried to focus on it, my own natural defenses rose up, trying to smother the heat with my own cold rage.

"Fight it, Gin!" Silvio gave me one more urgent whisper before moving away.

Benson stepped back into view, holding a large needle full of pale yellow liquid. Somehow I knew that if he stabbed me with that, if he pumped adrenaline into my veins, it wouldn't help me—it would kill me outright instead.

So I forced myself to relax. I let my legs go slack against the chair, unclenched my hands, and tilted my head back so that it rested on the cushion. Toe by toe, finger by finger, muscle by muscle, I relaxed every single part of my body as much as I could. I shuddered in a breath.

And then I let go completely.

My pain, my anger, my fear. I just . . . let go. I'd already eased the tension in my body, and without my emotions locked up tight behind their usual wall, the drug raged through my system unchecked.

It was brutal, like being boiled alive, but I swallowed down my screams and concentrated on the horrible, agonizing sensations sweeping through me, comparing them with all the other kinds of magic that had been used against me over the years.

Burn didn't contain my own Ice or Stone power, for I would welcome those cold and solid sensations, even when they were killing me. And it wasn't Air either, or pins and needles would have been stabbing into my body. Whatever magic was in the drug seemed the closest to Fire and the bright, hot burn I'd always associated with that power.

But it wasn't Fire.

Not really, not *exactly*.

So what the hell was it, then?

I forced myself to focus on the sensations and the fire that wasn't Fire that was still surging through me. The lab melted away, and suddenly, I was back in the Pork Pit, picking up that fork from the floor, the one the auburn-haired woman had been using.

Understanding flashed through me like lightning.

Maybe it was the drug and the hallucinations that went along with it, but in that instant, everything clicked into place, including Burn and exactly what kind of magic was in it.

And I knew what I had to do to save myself.

I lolled my head to one side and tilted it forward, so that I could see my right wrist shackled to the chair. I couldn't move my arm all that much, but I managed to curl my hand around so that I could see the silverstone symbol branded into my palm—that small circle surrounded by eight thin rays that represented patience.

The Burn drug might have sent threads of acidic fire

spinning through my veins, but I had spiders of my own.

Two of them, one in either hand.

I looked at my rune, and I thought of it as a real spider, sitting there in the palm of my hand, ready to do my bidding. And I pictured the same thing happening to my other rune on my left hand. Then I reached for my Ice magic. More of that damn acidic green fire covered the cold crystal spring of my power, trying to burn it to ash, but I ripped and clawed and tore off those stinging threads of silk, slicing through the sticky cobwebs of heat, until I could feel *my* magic—cold, hard, unstoppable.

Just like me.

I grabbed hold of that power and imagined pouring it into those spiders in my palms, until their bellies were as fat and swollen with my silvery Ice magic as the ones under my skin had been with their bright green chemical heat and pain and suffering.

Then I let my spiders loose.

They zipped through my body, carrying their own Icy strings of silk along behind them, weaving their own cold, crystalline webs in delicate but deadly patterns. Slowly, very, very slowly, a numb feeling began to spread through my body as my imaginary spiders froze me from the inside out.

And slowly, very, very slowly, things started to change.

My vision cleared, my breathing came more easily, and the sweat covering my body cooled. The agony from the drug lessened, although I could still feel the fiery combination of the chemicals and the elemental power licking at the strings of my Ice magic, trying to scorch right through them. So I focused on my own cold power that much more, using it to maintain and spread the numbness in my body. Anything else was too much for me right now.

But it was enough.

The longer I held on to my Ice magic, the more I could feel it freezing out the Burn drug in my body. I wasn't a hundred percent—not even close to that—but I knew that the danger had passed.

This danger, at least.

"What's happening? Why is her heart rate dropping?" Benson muttered, staring at the monitors. "She should be crashing hard right now, not stabilizing."

"Perhaps that batch of pills was not as strong as the supplier promised," Silvio murmured, his voice as bland as ever. "It did seem to flare out of her rather quickly."

Benson stared at the monitors *chirp-chirp-chirp*ing out my vitals, his face completely crestfallen, as though someone had just taken away his favorite toy. He set the needle full of adrenaline down on the table, then started flipping through his pad, reading back through his scribbles.

It was the first time I'd seen him show any real emotion, other than twisted pleasure, so I decided to lash out with the only thing I could: words.

"What's wrong, Beau?" I croaked, my voice hoarse and raspy from all my screams. "Did you not get the results you wanted? Aw, it's too bad that your little science project failed. But really, you should have known better."

He stiffened and gave me a withering glance. "And why is that?"

"Oh, c'mon, Dr. Frankenstein. Don't you know that the monster never reacts how you think she will?"

His black eyebrows drew together in confusion. Maybe it was the drug still working its way through my system or simply my relief at being alive, but his puzzled expression made me giddy, so giddy that I started snickering, which soon erupted into long, loud laughter, until tears were streaming down my face and my ribs ached.

But I couldn't stop laughing—I didn't *want* to stop.

Benson stared at me, even more confused than before. But my delighted peals soon made his uncertainty melt into anger. Red roses of embarrassment bloomed in his pale cheeks, and his blue eyes glittered with rage behind his silver glasses. He got to his feet, threw his pen and pad down onto the table, and ripped off his white lab coat.

"Clean her up," he snarled, slapping his coat down onto the back of his chair. "I want her ready to go for round two as soon as possible. I'm going to check with the supplier and get a fresh batch of pills to use on her."

Silvio nodded. Benson gave me one more disgusted look before stomping out of the lab and slamming the door behind him to cut off the sound of my merry, mercurial, maniacal chuckles.

Silvio spent a few minutes unhooking me from the monitors and other contraptions. He didn't say a word as my crazy laughter finally slowed, sputtered, and then stopped. When he had finished putting the machines away, Silvio pulled out his phone and sent a quick text. Then he moved behind me, out of my line of sight, before coming back into view and setting a thick white plastic garbage bag on top of the table.

Clink-clink-clink.

I cocked my head to the side. I knew that sound—it was the clatter of silverstone blades scraping together. My knives were in that bag. Too bad I couldn't get to them. Too bad I couldn't do anything but sit in this damn chair.

I thought Silvio would grab my knives again and leave the lab, but he hesitated, then came over to stand beside me. And then he did the strangest thing of all.

He reached out and unlocked the silverstone restraint around my neck.

I blinked, wondering if maybe I was still flying high on Burn and hallucinating, but Silvio quickly opened the shackles around my wrists, then the ones around my ankles. We stared at each other, him as calm as ever, me completely confused. This had to be some sort of trap, some sort of trick on Benson's part. No doubt, he had ordered Silvio to unshackle me just so he could watch me try to escape in my weakened state and take some more stupid notes for his so-called scientific observations.

But I didn't care, and if there was one thing that I was good at, it was surviving impossible situations and leaving the bodies of my enemies strewn behind in my wake. Starting here and now with Silvio.

"Here," Silvio said, leaning over the chair and stretching his hand out to me. "Let me help you up—"

I reached up, wrapped my right hand tightly around his neck, and used my left hand to push myself out of the chair. We tumbled to the floor. Silvio tried to slither out from under me, but I reached for what little magic I had left—my Stone power this time—and hardened my hand with it. I used my viselike grip to put even more pressure on his throat, squeezing, squeezing tight.

"You make a sound or a move that I don't like, and I will crush your windpipe," I hissed. "What is this? Why did you free me? What game is Benson playing now? Is this all part of his experiment?"

"No . . . game . . ." Silvio croaked. "Trying . . . to . . . help you."

I lay on top of the vamp, waiting for him to start clawing at my hand or punching me in the face. If he really wanted to, he could throw me off him. My arms and legs were about as steady as a bowl of soup right now, and the only reason I was holding him down was that my body was complete dead weight.

But instead of fighting, Silvio stayed still. "You held up . . . your end of the . . . bargain," he rasped. "You saved . . . Catalina . . . from him. Just trying . . . to return . . . the favor."

His gray gaze locked with my much frostier one, but I didn't see anything in his eyes except cool, calm clarity. Silvio had already accepted his own death, whether it was here at my hand or later on at his boss's.

"Benson will kill you for this," I said, trying to rattle him, trying to see if he really meant what he said. "You know he will."

Silvio nodded as much as my Stone-hardened hand would let him. "I am . . . well aware of that."

I stared into his eyes, but his calm expression didn't flicker or waver, not even for a second. He was either sincere in his desire to help me, or he was one of the best actors I'd ever seen. Either way, I made my decision. No choice, really. As much as I hated to admit it, I wasn't getting out of here on my own. Not when I was weak, still partially drugged, and running low on magic and had my bare ass hanging out of the back of a hospital gown.

"All right, then," I said, releasing my grip on my Stone magic and Silvio's throat. "If you're so determined to betray your boss, then help me up. And find me some damn clothes."

❈ 21 ❈

Silvio rolled me off him. He grabbed Benson's white lab coat and tossed it at me before going over to a large metal safe in the back corner of the room.

Still lying on the floor, I stretched out my hand, dug my fingers into the fabric, and pulled the coat over to me. Even that tiny effort made sweat trickle down the small of my exposed back, and sitting up against the side of the torture chair made me pant for breath.

Silvio ignored my slow progress, spun the dial around on the front of the safe, and yanked the door open. He drew a black leather-bound book out of the dark depths of the safe before shutting and locking it again. He hurried back over to me. The vamp sighed, shook his head, and hoisted me up. It was all that I could do to stand upright, while he yanked my arms and body this way and that, maneuvering me around like a doll he was dressing.

I gritted my teeth to hold back my frustrated snarls. I

hated being so weak, so dependent, so damn *helpless*, but time was the most important thing right now, and if I had to be humiliated to escape, well, so be it.

Anything would be better than being strapped down in that fucking chair again.

Silvio buttoned the coat over my chest. Then he grabbed the plastic garbage bag full of my knives off the table and handed me one of the weapons, before sliding the book from the safe inside the plastic and tying the bag tight around my wrist.

"What's that?" I asked. "That book."

"Insurance."

Before I could ask him what he meant, Silvio reached out, scooped me up into his arms, and headed toward the door. The bag of knives hanging off my wrist smacked against his hip, but he didn't seem to notice.

"Turn the knob for me, then relax, like you're still riding high on the drug," he said. "We'll get a lot farther a lot faster that way."

I tucked the knife in my hand up the sleeve of the coat, then did as he asked and went slack in his arms. Silvio put his back into the door, pushed it open, and left the lab.

He stepped back out into the drug den. Some of the addicts perked up as Silvio walked past them, but when they realized that he wasn't Benson with a fresh hit for them, they sank back down onto their pillows and slid deeper into their despair. Two guards had been posted at the bottom of the stairs, and they frowned as Silvio stopped in front of them.

"Where you are going with her?" one of the vamps asked.

"Upstairs to get her cleaned up. She threw up all over the lab," Silvio said in a bland tone. "Boss's orders. He has special plans for this one."

Both of the men winced at the words *special plans*, but they stepped aside so we could pass. Silvio climbed the stairs, still holding me in his arms.

"I hope you had a nice, tall glass of blood for breakfast," I said. "You'll need the energy, what with all this lying and backstabbing you're doing."

"Giant's blood, actually," he replied. "Two big glasses. I like to plan ahead. I thought that I might need a bit of extra strength today."

"Are you saying that my ass is heavy?" I drawled. "Why, Silvio, I think I'm insulted."

He huffed, although it sounded suspiciously like a laugh.

Silvio reached the top of the stairs, turned right, and started moving down a long hallway. We passed room after room, all of them furnished with white couches, chrome lamps, and glass tables. Everything was sleek, chic, and polished to a high gloss, but no photos, books, magazines, or knickknacks of any kind adorned the furniture. I'd been too drugged earlier to pay much attention to my surroundings, but the inside of Benson's mansion was very much a reflection of his lab and his own personality—cold, clinical, sterile.

The drug den and the lab were in the center of the mansion, and shadows cloaked the interior like demons about to break free from the walls. Or maybe that was just more hallucinations brought on by Burn.

But the guards were very real.

Vampires were stationed at the end of every hallway, all of them armed with guns and cell phones. A few of them stopped Silvio long enough to ask where he was taking me, but he gave them the same cleanup answer as before, and they let us pass. But the farther Silvio walked and the more guards he spoke to, the faster his steps became, until his wing tips were *bang-bang-bang*ing like a drum on the floor.

"Slow down," I hissed. "You're practically running, and running makes people suspicious."

"We're on a tight timetable, Ms. Blanco," Silvio snapped back. "In case you haven't guessed."

We glared at each other, but he did slow his steps enough to keep me from griping at him anymore.

Silvio turned into another hallway, and I spotted a set of patio doors at the far end that weren't being guarded. Through the glass, I could see the green expanse of the lawn outside. My heart lifted.

Silvio let out a relieved sigh. "Almost there—"

"Hey, Silvio!" a high feminine voice called out behind us. "Wait up!"

His steps faltered. His mouth pinched into a frustrated frown even as his eyes locked on the doors up ahead, and he debated whether to make a run for them. But he knew as well as I did that that would send all the guards racing in our direction, so he stopped and turned around.

A vamp came jogging up the hallway to us.

"Yes, Joan?" Silvio asked.

Joan stopped and waved her phone in the air. "I just got a text message from the boss asking where *she* is." She jerked her head at me. "Benson wants to know why the two of you aren't in the lab. What are you doing all the way over here?"

Silvio stiffened. "Beau wanted me to get her cleaned up."

"Yeah, but why didn't you just dump her in one of the tubs in the bathroom close to the lab like usual?" Joan frowned. "What are you doing, Silvio? You're not . . . actually . . . *helping* her—"

Before she could finish her thought, I palmed the knife hidden up the sleeve of my stolen lab coat and lashed out with it. I'd been hoping to catch the vamp in the throat, but she saw the glint of the weapon and jerked back at the last second. My knife only sliced across her breastbone, but that was more than enough to get her to stop asking questions.

Joan screamed and staggered back, clutching at the wound I'd opened up on her chest. Her head cracked against the wall, and she dropped to the floor, unconscious.

"Now you've done it," Silvio muttered.

"What?" I sniped. "She was a second away from figuring it out anyway—"

Thump-thump-thump-thump.
Thump-thump-thump-thump.

Joan's scream must have been louder than I thought, or the vamps had better hearing, because footsteps started pounding in our direction. Silvio cursed, turned, and ran toward the doors.

But he wasn't quite fast enough.

A vamp stepped out of one of the rooms at the end of the hallway, his gun already drawn. When he realized what Silvio was doing, he snapped the weapon up and took aim. I reached for my Stone magic, even though I didn't have enough of it to harden my body, much less protect Silvio and me from the bullets that were going to start flying in our direction—

Pfft. Pfft.

The vampire dropped to the floor, blood leaking out of the two holes in the back of his skull. Silvio skidded to a stop.

Outside on the patio, a hand smashed through the rest of the glass on the door, then reached through, unlocked, and opened it. A second later, a familiar figure appeared—one that could have almost been . . . me.

I blinked, but it wasn't another hallucination.

She was dressed all in black, from her boots to her jeans to the long-sleeved T-shirt that she wore underneath her vest. Even her gun was black. So was the silencer attached to the barrel. She wasn't wearing her detective's badge, and the only bit of color on her was the silverstone primrose rune that glinted in the hollow of her throat.

Bria lowered her gun and smiled at me. "Hey, there, big sister."

For a moment, I was stunned into silence. Then I found my voice again. "Bria? What are you doing here?"

Her grin dimmed. "Saving you. If it's not already too late—"

Crack! Crack!

A vamp appeared at the opposite end of the hall. Silvio hunkered down, but the bullets went wild. Bria stepped forward and raised her own gun.

Pfft. Pfft.

She dropped the vamp with two shots to the chest, but shouts rose up from deeper in the mansion, growing louder and louder as more and more guards headed in our direction.

Bria looked at Silvio. "Can she walk?"

"She's going to have to," he said.

He set me down on my feet and passed me over to Bria, who grabbed onto my waist with her left hand. I sagged against her, but I managed to stay upright, even though the bag of knives still dangling from my wrist swung and rattled every which way, making it hard to keep my balance. Bria started dragging me toward the doors, but Silvio didn't move to follow us.

"What are you doing?" I asked. "You have to come with us—or you're dead."

He shook his head. "There are too many guards. You need someone to lead them away from your location if you have any chance of escaping."

His mouth pinched, his shoulders slumped, and sorrow sparked in his gray eyes. "Take care of Catalina for me, okay?"

"Silvio!" I hissed. "Silvio!"

But he had already started running in the other direction, back into the heart of the mansion, toward Benson and the rest of his men.

"Come on, Gin," Bria said. "He made his choice. Let's make sure that it counts."

I nodded, and we headed toward the open patio door. I managed to stay upright, but my legs were weak, my steps slow and clumsy, so Bria ended up doing most of the work. She maneuvered herself outside through the opening, but my bare foot caught on the the dead vamp's leg, and I did a header through the door and onto the balcony. My skull cracked against the ground hard enough to cause white stars to flash before my eyes, while the knives in my bag *clank-clank-clank*ed together, sounding as loud as gongs to my aching brain. All I wanted to do was lie there and kiss the cool, smooth stones under my face, but Bria wasn't about to let me give up.

"Move!" my sister ordered, reaching forward and hoisting me to my feet again.

Crack! Crack!

Gunshots zinged outside after us, shattering the glass in the other door. I staggered to my left, out of sight of the hallway, and clutched a stone column for support. Bria threw herself down, then rolled over onto her back, aimed her gun, and waited—just waited.

A few seconds later, two vamps crashed through the doors. Bria shot them both in the chest, and they went down screaming. She scrambled to her feet, grabbed my arm, and pulled me toward the balcony steps.

"Move!" she ordered me again. "C'mon, Gin! You don't want to die here, do you? You know you want to come back later and kill every single one of these bastards!"

I grinned, despite the fact that my head was still spinning from my fall and my legs threatened to buckle with every step I took. She knew just what to say to motivate me.

I let Bria lead the way, while I focused on holding on to her hand and just putting one foot in front of the other without stumbling. If I fell again, the vamps would catch up to us and swarm all over us.

Bria yanked me down the steps, across another patio, and out onto the lawn. Behind us, more and more shouts rose up, as guards poured out of the mansion and gave chase. Staccato *crack-crack-crack*s of gunfire split the air, kicking up dirt and grass around us, but Bria didn't hesitate, and it was all that I could do to keep up with her. A stitch throbbed in my side, sweat streamed down my face, my legs wobbled like a newborn calf's, and my bag of knives *slap-slap-slapp*ed against my body, but I forced myself to stumble forward. If I stopped, we were done for, and I'd be damned if I was going to be the cause of Bria's death. Not when she'd risked herself to rescue me. So I sucked down as much air as I could, ignored all my aches and pains, and staggered on.

A vamp stepped out from a cluster of trees in front of us. He raised his gun and took aim, but instead of stopping and doing the same, Bria tightened her grip on my hand and kept running straight at him. The vamp's fingers curled around the trigger of his gun—

CRACK!

This gunshot was louder and sharper than all the rest, and the vamp went down without a sound, given the bullet that had just ripped through his neck. I grinned. Finn was working his own kind of magic with his sniper rifle.

More of those loud, booming *crack*s sounded, and the guards realized that someone besides Bria was shooting at them. They dived behind the benches, bushes, and trees that dotted the lawn, trying to see where the shots were coming from, but they wouldn't find the source of the commotion. Finnegan Lane was one of the best snipers around, and he would have picked a perfect perch, someplace where Benson's guards had no chance of shooting back at him.

While Finn took down as many of the guards as he could, Bria kept running, pulling me along behind her like a mother with a wayward child. All I could do was follow where she led me. But I didn't care where we were going, as long as it was away from Benson and all the drug-induced horrors inside his mansion—horrors that made me shudder even now, despite the fact that we were running for our lives.

We kept moving, and I realized that we weren't heading toward the street that fronted the mansion or to any sort of waiting vehicle. Instead, Bria was dragging me to the very back of Benson's estate, which butted up against the Aneirin River. But I didn't have the breath or energy to ask her where we were going.

Finally, we reached the river and the simple stone bridge that arced over it. Bria pulled me out into the middle of the span, then abruptly stopped. I stood there, swaying from side to side like a tree about to topple over, while Bria guarded our backs, taking the time to reload her gun. Above the faint *click-click-click*s of her checking her weapon, I heard something else. Something low and steady and quickly coming this way. I frowned, wondering at the rumbling sound.

Was that . . . a boat?

Bria finished with her gun, then turned back to me. "Here! You have to climb over the side!"

She helped me hoist one of my legs over the railing, then the other. She hopped over too, so that we were both standing on the edge. With one hand, Bria held on to the side of the bridge, and with the other, she gripped her gun. In the distance, more guards appeared on the lawn, all of them with weapons, all of them heading in this direction.

Crack! Crack! Crack! Crack!

Finn took out as many of the vamps as he could with his sniper rifle, but at this point, there were more of them than even he could shoot. Some of the guards broke off and headed away from the mansion, no doubt to try to find his sniper's nest. But I wasn't worried. Finn would be packed up and long gone before they ever found his location. So I focused my attention on staying upright and holding on to the side of the bridge with my weak, sweaty, trembling hands.

"Get ready!" Bria yelled at me, grinning a little. "Our ride's almost here!"

I nodded, but she didn't see me, since she was already turning back and firing at the guards who were racing toward our position.

That low rumbling grew louder and louder. I risked a glance back over my shoulder, looking for the source of the sound. I squinted, and something zoomed into view in the distance on the far side of the bridge, up the river, but closing fast.

A white speedboat with blue and red racing stripes.

I blinked, but the image didn't melt or vanish into thin air, so I knew that it was real. The speedboat zipped up the river as easy as you please, and I realized that this must be Bria's escape plan. Instead of risking getting caught on a Southtown street by Benson and his men, she'd chosen a less obvious but much quicker getaway route. I nodded in approval, even though the motion almost caused me to pitch off the bridge and fall into the water.

Bria heard the boat too, and she holstered her gun and grabbed my hand. More shouts rose up from the guards, who were sprinting toward us. And with the blood they drank and the extra speed it gave them, the vamps were closing *fast*. Another thirty seconds, and they'd be at the end of the bridge. They could easily shoot and kill us from there.

"Here we go," Bria said, her voice lost in the continued *crack*s of gunfire, as she eyed the rippling water below us. "One . . . two . . . three!"

She yanked me off the bridge with her.

❖ 22 ❖

For a moment, the sensation was the same as the Burn drug—that airy feeling of flying, flying high. I laughed at how good it felt to just be . . . free. My head snapped back, and all I could see was the blue, blue sky, dotted here and there with marshmallow clouds, just like in my hallucinations.

But then gravity took over, the way it always did, sucking me back down to earth and reality. My head dropped, along with my body, and the rush of air tore away the rest of my crazy, cackling laughter. Instead of a pit of imaginary fire, the dark and very real surface of the Aneirin River thirty feet below zoomed up to meet me, the water ready to close over me in its cold, deadly embrace.

And then the boat popped into view.

It was the same speedboat I'd seen before, and it slowed so that it was in sync with Bria and me and our downward plummet. This time, I didn't have to worry about falling, because someone was there to catch me—Owen.

He was standing at the back of the boat, along with Xavier. Bria's feet hit the ledge at the very rear of the vessel, her arms windmilling as she tried to find her balance, but Xavier reached out and grabbed her before she tumbled backward into the water. I actually landed square in the center of the boat, almost right on top of Owen, who reached out and took hold of me, keeping me from slamming face-first into one of the leather seats. The impact jarred me from my bare feet all the way up to my knees, before shooting up my legs and through my hips and back. Bones crunched together in my right ankle, making me yelp, and the bag of knives hanging off my wrist slammed into my side hard enough to bruise my ribs.

"We've got them!" Xavier yelled. "Go! Go! Go! Go!"

The engine roared, and the boat started picking up speed again, racing away from the bridge. But the vamps who'd been chasing Bria and me weren't ready to give up. They skidded to a stop on the span, took aim with their weapons, and started firing at us. The bullets *plop-plop-plopp*ed into the water all around us. Xavier pulled the gun from the holster on his belt and returned their fire. So did Bria.

But one vamp was a little quicker and braver than all the others. He hopped up onto the bridge railing, then leaped off, trying to launch himself far enough out to land in the boat with the rest of us. His legs pumped, like he was riding a bicycle in midair, and he reached out with one hand . . .

And landed in the river three feet behind us.

The resulting splash sprayed us all with water. I laughed again as the cool, wet drops trickled down my face.

"Get us out of here!" Owen yelled. "Now!"

The engine whined, louder and harder this time, and the boat picked up more and more speed as it zoomed away from the bridge.

The sounds of gunfire faded away, drowned out by the powerful motor, and I knew that we were finally safe. I laughed at that too.

Owen helped me sit up against the side of the boat, his hands stroking my sweaty, tangled mess of hair back away from my face. Worry darkened his violet gaze. "Gin! Are you okay?"

I finally managed to get my crazy chuckles under control enough to smile at him, although the expression was more of a grimace, given the shooting pains in my ankle. "Never better."

Owen smiled back at me, but the relieved expression quickly melted into a concerned frown. "What happened? What did Benson do to you?"

And just like that, the rest of my laughter dried up, and tears pricked my eyes instead. I told myself it was because of my broken ankle. Nothing else.

"Gin?" he asked again.

I shook my head. I couldn't talk about it. Not now, not yet. Maybe not ever. Because I could still remember all too clearly the horrible, horrible thoughts I'd had about Owen, Finn, and especially Bria while I was riding high on Burn. How I'd thought that I was better than them. How I didn't need them. How they were weak. How Bria was a burden.

Guilt and shame surged through me, burning even worse than the drug.

Owen opened his mouth to ask me another question, but I leaned to one side, looking past him at the person driving the speedboat—a tall, muscular man with blue eyes and golden hair pulled back into a ponytail.

"And here I thought that you only had the one really big boat," I said, trying to make my voice light and teasing, despite the pain that rasped through my words.

Phillip Kincaid looked over his shoulder and grinned at me, a few strands of hair flying around his face. "What can I say? I like to diversify."

I laughed again, even as the rest of my strength evaporated and my body slumped against the side of the boat. My arms and legs felt cold, numb, and nerveless, except for the throbbing pain in my ankle.

"Call Jo-Jo," Bria said, somewhere far over my head. "Benson really did a number on her."

Fear and panic pulsed through my body, sharper and more painful than all my injuries. Jo-Jo couldn't heal me. I was hanging on to my sanity by a thread. The feel of any more magic right now would snap that slender strand.

I clutched at Owen, panting for breath. "No healing. No magic. Too much . . . of it . . . in Burn."

He frowned. "Burn has magic in it?"

I nodded, trying not to hyperventilate.

"It's okay, Gin," Owen said, gently cradling me in his arms. "Calm down. Just breathe. You're safe now."

I turned my head so that my face was buried in his neck and did as he said, drawing his rich, metallic scent deep down into my lungs, trying to clear the lemony stench of the lab from my mouth and throat, if not my mind and heart.

"Safe," I replied, although my voice was so soft I doubted he heard me.

Then my eyes closed, and I let the blackness take me.

Coral's laughter echoed in my ears as I followed her into the Southtown apartment building. The door banged shut behind me, making me jump and yelp.

Coral laughed again, her voice sly with amusement. "Relax. It's just a door. It won't bite you. This way, kid."

Her heels clattered on the floor ahead of me, and I hurried to follow the noise. The inside of the building was almost pitch black, and I ran my hand along the wall so I wouldn't bump into anything. The smell of burnt popcorn, scorched coffee, and Chinese food filled my nose, while my shoes scuffed through old newspapers, empty cans, and wet, squishy blobs on the floor—some of which squeaked and skittered away at my touch. Most likely trash, vomit, and rats, all of which I was better off not seeing. I shuddered and walked on.

Coral pushed through a door at the end of the hallway, and we stepped outside into a large square courtyard surrounded by buildings on all sides. I blinked against the bright, sudden glare. The buildings were all four stories tall, each with a set of stairs climbing from one level to the next. Doors lined all of the levels, from the ground floor to the top story. No one stood on the balconies or perched on the stairs, but music drifted out from behind some of the doors, along with the blare of TVs.

"This courtyard connects all of these buildings," Coral said. "Here, I'll show you."

My stomach grumbled again, and I wondered when we were going to get to the food she'd promised me, but I kept quiet as she strolled around the square, opening some of the doors on the other buildings, leading me down hallways and back out again.

Several minutes later, we ended up back where we'd started in the center of the courtyard.

"Um, why are you showing me all of this?"

"Because it's always good to have an escape route," Coral said in a wise, knowing voice. "Trust me on that."

I sighed, and my stomach gurgled, the grinding noise rising to a plaintive wail.

She laughed again, then gave me a dazzling smile. "But enough with the grand tour. C'mon. Let's go to my place."

She looped her arm through mine and led me over to a set of stairs in the first building we'd walked through. We climbed all the way up to the fourth floor and went over to a door in the corner.

"Home, sweet home," Coral said, opening the door and stepping inside.

I followed her, and she closed the door behind us, throwing a series of locks.

Click. Click. Click.

The sounds seemed even louder than the banging door downstairs earlier, and I had to curl my hands into fists to keep from jumping in surprise again. To take my mind off the fact that I was locked in an apartment with a complete stranger, I focused on the scene before me.

The apartment was tiny, with the main area only about twenty-five feet square. A door to the right led to a small bedroom, with an even smaller bathroom attached to it. A stove splattered with grease stains stood along one wall, next to an old pea-green refrigerator with rusty dents in the sides. An orange plastic table with two mismatched lawn chairs was squeezed in between the fridge and a blue plaid couch covered with threadbare blankets and flat pancake pillows.

"So what do you think?" Coral asked.

"It's nice."

She snorted. "It's a dump is what it is. But it's mostly mine, and that's all that matters, right?"

"Why just mostly?"

She waved her hand. "I have a . . . landlord who drops by sometimes. But I can handle him."

I knew that she really meant her pimp, but I didn't say anything.

Coral bumped her skinny leg into the rickety coffee table, rattling several open, empty pill bottles sitting there and causing a bit of white powder to puff up from the wooden surface. She saw me staring at the bottles, and she stepped toward me, her eyes narrowing, her lips twisting into an angry snarl, her hands clenching into fists. It almost seemed like she thought I was going to try to steal something off the table, even though it was just junk.

"What's with all the bottles?" I asked, trying not to shrink away in fear. "Have you been sick?"

"Yeah. Something like that." She stepped back, her face smoothed out, and her fists loosened. "But enough about me. Let's talk about you."

Coral circled around me. I tried not to fidget as her hazel eyes swept over my body from head to toe.

"You're in pretty good shape, all things considered." She wrinkled her nose. "Well, except for how you smell. So what do you want first, kid? Food or a hot shower?"

The choice was easy. "Food."

"Smart girl."

She went over to the fridge, pulled open the door, and drew out a white paper bag. The top of the bag had been rolled down, but a pink figure was printed on the side. I squinted. Was that a . . . pig?

"You like barbecue?" Coral asked. "It's day-old leftovers, but they warm up good."

My stomach rumbled again, answering her.

Coral unwrapped half of a barbecued beef sandwich, slapped it on a paper plate, and shoved the whole thing into a microwave that perched precariously on top of the fridge. A minute later, she set the sandwich in front of me at the table.

"Enjoy."

She didn't have to tell me twice. I picked up the sandwich and started taking big bites out of it, chewing and swallowing as fast as I could, just in case she changed her mind and tried to take it away from me. The sandwich was hot, too hot to eat, really, but the sweet-and-spicy sauce and the smoky flavor of the meat were so good that I didn't care that it burned my tongue. I ate that sandwich, then used my fingers to scoop up the stray bits of meat and sauce that had fallen onto the paper plate and sucked them up too.

When I was done, I looked at Coral, a silent question in my eyes.

"Don't worry," she said. "I've got another sandwich you can eat—later. First, let's get you cleaned up."

I made a noise of protest, wanting the food right now,

since I was still so hungry, *but Coral grabbed my hand and pulled me into the bedroom. She opened the closet and started rifling through the clothes inside.*

"Here," she said. "You can put these on when you get done."

She held up a tank top and a pair of short-shorts, both in black satin. I didn't want to wear the clothes, since I would freeze in them, but they were clean, and she'd been so nice to me so far, so I just nodded and took them from her.

Coral jerked her thumb over her shoulder. "The bathroom's right there. Try not to use up all the hot water, okay?"

"Thank you," I whispered, clutching the skimpy clothes to my chest. "For everything."

Tears stung my eyes, but I blinked them back. Coral frowned, and a shadow passed over her face, but the dark expression quickly melted into her usual sunny smile.

"No problem, kid."

She winked at me again, then stepped back out into the main room, pulling the door to the bedroom closed behind her.

I went into the bathroom, stripped off my filthy clothes, and got into the shower. I moaned at how good the hot water felt cascading over my skin, and I used up the better part of a bar of soap scrubbing myself from head to toe, along with half a bottle of shampoo washing my nasty rat's nest of hair.

By the time I finished, I felt more like myself than I had in, well, since the night my family was murdered. Sure, this apartment wasn't much, not nearly as fancy as my bedroom had been, but the thought of leaving it behind and going back out onto the streets filled me with dread. Maybe Coral would be nice enough to let me stay with her for a few days. I could help her. Cook and clean and do whatever she wanted me to.

I'd do just about anything to keep from being cold and hungry and tired and scared again.

I wrapped a towel around my body and grabbed the black satin tank top and short-shorts from where I'd put them on the closed toilet lid. But instead of pulling them on, I hesitated. Maybe Coral would let me stay if I didn't use so many of her things, including her clothes. It couldn't hurt to ask, right?

So I turned the water in the shower back on, then stopped up the tub so I could wash my clothes in it, before leaving the bathroom and going back into the bedroom. The door had swung open a crack, letting me see out into the main part of the apartment. Coral was pacing back and forth in front of the couch, holding a phone up to her ear. I stayed in the bedroom, not wanting to disturb her.

"Yeah, tell Reggie that I've got a live one for him," she said. "A new girl. I haven't seen her around before, but she can't be more than thirteen, fourteen tops. She doesn't seem like she's been working, so we are talking fresh, new territory here. Know what I mean?"

She laughed, but her cheerful chuckle froze me to the bone. My breath stuck in my throat in surprise, and my damp fingers dug into the slick fabric in my hands.

"So how much will he give me for her?" Coral said, her voice as hard and brittle as her face. "I want some pills too. Double what he gave me for the last girl. Enough to last me at least a month this time."

Fear spiked through me, sweeping away the lingering warmth of the shower. She was . . . she wanted to . . . she was going to sell me to her pimp.

The person on the other end said something, and Coral smiled.

"Good. She's taking a shower right now, so tell him to come get her while she's clean." She paused, listening to the other person again. "He can be here in five minutes? Perfect. I'll be waiting."

I gasped. Her pimp was already on his way, and if he found me here, he'd beat me and rape me and then drug me up and make me work for him.

I had to get out of here—now.

I rushed back into the bathroom and started pulling on my clothes as fast as I could with my trembling hands. It was hard shoving the dirty layers of cloth on over my damp skin, but I managed it.

I didn't want to think about what would happen if I didn't.

I left the water in the bathroom running so Coral would think that I was still in the shower. I couldn't go out through the front of the apartment, not with her waiting for me out there, so I stepped around the bed and hurried over to the window.

Cardboard held up with duct tape covered the space, but I tore at the tape with my fingernails, ripping it and the heavy sheet of paper away from the frame and throwing them down. I stuck my head out through the open space, my heart lifting at the sight of the rusty fire escape clinging to the side of the building.

The door at the front of the apartment screeched open, and the murmur of voices sounded—Coral's, along with a much lower, deeper tone. Her pimp was already here.

More panic rippled through me, and I hoisted my leg out the window, ready to step out onto the fire escape. I glanced down and saw a man strolling around the side of the building, smoking a cigarette. I froze, half in and half out the window. I didn't know if the guy worked for Coral's pimp, but I couldn't risk him seeing me.

I was out of time and other options, so I ducked back into the apartment, hurried over to the closet in the corner, threw open the door, and crammed myself inside. The door wouldn't shut all the way, not with me and all the clothes and shoes stuffed inside, so I held on to the knob, peered out the crack, and concentrated on being as quiet as possible.

"Hey, kid," Coral called out, stepping into the bedroom. "I've got someone I want you to meet—"

Silence.

"Dammit!" she snarled.

Footsteps snapped against the floor, and I got a flash of her running across the tiny room before she was out of my line of sight.

"Dammit!" Coral snarled again. "She must have gone out through the window. That sly little bitch. Eating my food without paying for it."

Silence. Then another voice spoke, that same low, deep murmur I'd heard earlier.

"So what you're saying is that you called me over here for nothing?"

I assumed the voice belonged to Reggie, her pimp. His tone was stone-cold. He wasn't happy with Coral—not at all.

"I'm sure I can find her again," Coral said. "A girl like that? She'll never make it on the streets. She'll probably come back here in a few days, begging me to take her in."

She laughed again, but the sound was tinged with desperation.

"I told you before that this was your last chance, Coral," Reggie rumbled. "You promised to find me a new girl to cover your debts for all those pills I gave you."

"But I did! It's not my fault she bolted."

"Doesn't matter. She's gone." Reggie paused. "But you're still here, and I'm tired of your excuses."

"Reggie, wait. Please, man! I'm good for the money! I just need a few more days—"

Coral sucked in a breath, as if she were going to scream. A loud smack sounded. Coral let out a low moan of pain, then a strangled yelp, before I heard another sound.

Thwack. Thwack. Thwack.

Reggie was hitting her—over and over again—and I knew that he wouldn't stop until he beat her to death. I stood in the dark closet, frozen with fear, wondering what to do. Should I try to help Coral and risk Reggie turning his anger on me? Should I run out of the apartment while he was beating her? Or should I just stay quiet and hidden and wait until it was over?

No, I thought. That would make me no better than Coral. I had to try to help her, despite what she'd wanted to do to me. If nothing else, maybe Reggie would leave her alone long enough to chase me when I ran out of the apartment. So I squared my shoulders and sucked in a breath, hoping that I could take the pimp by surprise and then outrun him—

But it was too late.

Something slammed up against the closet door, then dropped down to the ground in front of it. Through the crack, I could see Coral's face, her hazel eyes frozen open wide in pain, terror, and fear. Blood pooled on the floor underneath her head and started oozing into the closet, further staining *my ratty stolen shoes. I clamped my hand over my mouth to keep from screaming.*

Dead—she was dead.

And I would be too if I didn't stay quiet.

So I swallowed down my screams, making myself stand absolutely still inside the closet, despite the skimpy satin clothes pushing at my back, wanting to shove me forward.

For a moment, the only sound was raspy breathing, although I couldn't tell if it was mine or Reggie's.

Then a floorboard creaked.

"Stupid bitch," Reggie rumbled. "You should have just paid me when you had the chance."

Coral's eyes stared straight ahead, even as more and more of her blood seeped into the closet.

Silence. Then footsteps moving away. A few seconds later, the front door opened, then slammed shut again.

I stood in the closet, staring at the growing blood on the floor, and counted off the seconds in my head. Ten . . . twenty . . . thirty . . . forty-five . . . sixty . . .

When three minutes had passed, I felt safe enough to slip out of the closet. The first thing I did was rush out to the main room and throw the locks on the door. Then I went back into the bedroom.

Coral lay sprawled on the floor, her head facing the closet, while the rest of her was twisted the other way. Bruises blackened her face, while her blood had already soaked into her hair, turning the bright crimson strands a dull rusty color.

I crouched down and stared at Coral's lifeless body. She'd tried to turn me into her, tried to sell me to her pimp, tried to use me the way so many other people had used her. But that's the way things were on the streets, especially in Southtown, and I couldn't help but feel sorry for her all the same—and guilty that I hadn't done something to try to save her.

Then my stomach rumbled again, and I thought about that other sandwich Coral had said was in the fridge. I closed my eyes, hating myself for what I was about to do, but I was still so hungry. So I stepped over Coral's body and went into the kitchen, trying to come up with some sort of plan about what to do next. When I was done eating, I would take whatever food was left, then go through her clothes to see if there was a warm coat I could swipe to stave off the chill of the nights, if not the growing coldness in my own heart . . .

The rocking woke me.

It was a gentle, steady, soothing motion, almost like I was in a swing someone was pushing, even though I was lying in a bed. A loud *splash* sounded, before giving way to a regular, rhythmic *slosh-slosh-slosh* of water, and I felt myself slipping back down into the darkness . . .

Wait a second. Why was there a splash? Why was there water here? Wasn't I at Jo-Jo's house? And if not . . . where *was* I?

I cracked my eyes open, but instead of an airy fresco of a cloud-covered sky like I would have seen at Jo-Jo's, the ceiling was low and made out of golden wood. Worry curled in my stomach, and I propped myself up on my elbows and looked around.

I was in some sort of guest bedroom. Well, really, it was more like a spacious stateroom. The four-poster bed I was lying on took up one corner of the area, the pale blue silk sheets that covered my body providing a nice contrast with the glossy, golden wood of the frame. The other furniture was made of the same wood, all of it trimmed with polished brass accents. A living-room suite took up the front half of the stateroom, complete with two pale blue couches that faced each other and a flat-screen TV mounted on the wall between them. A door off to my left led into a large bathroom decked out in blue tile.

It was definitely a room I'd never been in before, and my head snapped over to the windows, as I wondered what I might see through them. But the glass panes were round instead of square, and the white lace curtains had been drawn back, revealing an unexpected sight: the sun setting over the river.

Understanding flashed through me. I wasn't in any sort of house. Oh, no.

I was on a boat.

✳ 23 ✳

Instead of bolting out of bed, I wedged a couple of pillows between my back and the frame and propped myself up against the soft cushions. The sight of the strange room didn't bother me anymore, because I had a sneaking suspicion of exactly where I was.

On board the *Delta Queen*, Phillip Kincaid's riverboat casino.

I wondered why Owen and the others would bring me here, though, instead of taking me to Jo-Jo's salon. Maybe they figured that this would be safer, since Jo-Jo's would be one place Benson and his men would be sure to look for me.

I sat up a little higher on the bed. The motion made a dull ache roar to life in the back of my skull, one that quickly intensified and spread through the rest of my body. I was still wearing the white hospital gown Benson's men had put on me. Cuts and scrapes dotted my hands and arms, and the side of my face throbbed from where I'd fallen onto the stone balcony. But worst of all was my busted ankle, which sent out shooting stabs of pain with every beat of my heart.

Jo-Jo must have been waiting for the final dregs of the Burn pill to leave my system so she could heal me. No doubt, Owen had told her about the elemental magic in the drug, and Jo-Jo wouldn't have wanted to risk using her Air power on me and making things worse. But the aches and pains that flooded my body were a small price to pay for escaping from Benson. So I would be patient and endure the discomfort while I waited for Jo-Jo to come finish the job.

And when that was done and I was well, I would get on with the business of killing Beauregard Benson.

I should have started planning the hit that very first night after he'd murdered Troy and Xavier had told me how obsessed Bria was with bringing Benson down. I should have laid his throat open with my knives the second I saw him at Northern Aggression. I should have found a way to kill him on the bridge when his men were shooting at Bria and Catalina. But I'd been tired and troubled and too damn slow, and Benson had captured and almost killed me as a result, all in the name of his fucking drug empire and his so-called science experiments.

He wasn't going to get away with that. He wasn't going to get away with any of it.

Not one damn *thing*.

The stateroom door *creak*ed open, and Bria appeared, as if she'd been standing right outside, waiting for me to wake up. Maybe she had been.

Some of the tension in her face eased when she realized that I was awake, and she walked over and sat down in a chair next to the bed. She was still wearing the same black clothes she had on when she'd rescued me, although she'd taken off the vest, and the holster attached to her belt was empty. She clasped her hands together, staring at her interlaced fingers instead of at me. Specks of blood marred the pale skin of her hands. More of it had spattered up onto her face and neck, with a few drops staining her primrose rune an ugly crimson.

In a weird way, she looked just like me after a long day of killing. Then again, that's what this had been for Bria, first at the bridge firing at Benson's men, then at the mansion shooting everyone who came close to us so she could rescue me. It was an odd bit of role reversal, and I wasn't sure how I felt about that—or how it would affect Bria.

"Catalina?" I asked.

"She's fine," Bria said. "She's here on the boat too. We were able to go through that courtyard and those buildings and meet up with Xavier, just like you said. He drove us over here. Xavier thought that the riverboat would be a good place to hide out. There's room enough for all of us, and it will be an easy position to defend if Benson decides to attack."

I nodded. That was smart of Xavier, and he was right. This way, we'd at least be able to see Benson and his men coming. And they would be coming. The vamp still needed Catalina dead, and he'd want revenge on Bria for rescuing me.

As for me, no doubt, the vampire kingpin would want to drag me back down to his lab to conduct some more experiments on me, since I was such a *fascinating* test subject. I couldn't hold back the cold shiver of fear that swept through me. I'd been tortured before, more times than I cared to remember, actually, by some seriously nasty folks. But being strapped down to that chair in Benson's lab, knowing that he could do anything to me that he wanted, knowing how absolutely helpless I was to stop him . . . it would take me a while to get over that.

If I ever truly could.

Bria drew in a breath, squared her shoulders, and finally looked me in the eye. "I'm sorry," she said in a soft voice. "For all of this. I should have done things differently. I should have let you know what was going on from the very beginning, when Benson killed Max. I shouldn't have pushed Catalina to testify, and I shouldn't have said all those terrible things to you and everyone else at Northern Aggression."

"You did what you thought was right."

Guilt pinched her lips. "But you're my sister, and you know just as much about this world as I do. More, really, because you've lived in it longer. I should have listened to you. I *wanted* to listen to you. I hope you know that. It's just that every time I thought about Max and what Benson did to him . . ." She trailed off. "I couldn't let it go. I couldn't let him get away with it. Not when I'd promised Max that I would protect him, that I'd keep him safe, and he died because I didn't keep my word."

"Max didn't die because you didn't keep your word. He died because he got in too deep."

She shook her head, her blond hair flying around her shoulders. "That's not how it feels to me."

I didn't say anything. Nothing I could say would lessen her guilt. Not about this. Not now, maybe not ever.

She let out a bitter laugh. "And do you know what the worst part is? I almost did the exact same thing to Catalina. I told her that I could protect her too, and look what happened. Benson and his men almost killed us on that bridge. They *would* have killed us, if not for you."

Bria stared down at her hands again, which were clasped together so tightly that her fingers were white from the strain. The tension made the drops of blood on her skin stand out that much more. "And then I would have had an innocent girl's blood on my hands, just like Max's is already."

I leaned over and took her hands in mine. "You're a cop, Bria. You were just doing your job. You were trying to bring a bad guy to justice. There's nothing wrong with that."

Her lips twisted into a grimace. "There is when you lose focus, when you lose control. And that's exactly what I did with Benson. Xavier was right. I was so desperate to take Benson down that I lost track of everything else, and it has cost me so much. Roslyn was held hostage, and I pushed Finn away. Xavier and I are on shaky ground, Catalina is still in shock, and you . . ." Bria's voice dropped to a raspy whisper. "I don't even want to *think* about what Benson did to you."

"It wasn't that bad," I quipped. "At least the chair was comfortable."

A laugh escaped from her lips before she could stop it. But the faint chuckle didn't keep two tears from streaking down her face.

"I almost got you killed. I'll never forgive myself for that, Gin. Or for the things I said to you at Northern Aggression. And I know that you won't either."

I remembered all the terrible thoughts I'd had about her while I was flying high on Burn. More guilt and shame rippled through me. Bria wasn't the only one who'd never forgive herself. But as much as I hated to admit it, being force-fed that drug had given me a better understanding of my sister. She'd been hurt and helpless over Max's murder, and she'd lost control and lashed out as a result—just like I had when I was tripping on Burn.

"Gin?" Bria asked.

I shook my head. "We had a fight. It's what sisters do. It sucks, and we both hurt each other, but we'll get through it—together. The important thing is not to let it linger, not to let it fester. If I were in your position and Benson had killed one of my informants, I would have reacted in the exact same way. Actually, I would have been worse. I probably would have marched over to his mansion, knocked on his front door, and buried my knife in his heart the second he said hello."

Bria laughed again. "And that is exactly what makes you *you*. No matter what, you always protect the people you love. And I didn't do that. Not today. Not for a long time now."

More tears trickled down her cheeks. The salty drops slid off her chin and spattered onto her primrose rune, smearing the bloodstains on the silverstone.

I stared at her rune, the symbol for beauty. "You know, a wise old man once told me that everyone makes mistakes from time to time."

"Fletcher?"

I nodded. "And he was right. You made some mistakes. We all have, by not listening to each other. But you're lucky—*we're* lucky—in that you still have a chance to fix them."

She gave me a wry smile. "And how do I do that?"

"You find a way to take down Benson and keep Catalina safe. With some help from me, of course."

Bria threaded her fingers through mine. "I wouldn't have it any other way."

I squeezed her hand tightly. "And neither would I."

❊24❊

Bria and I were still holding hands, enjoying the easy quiet between us, when another person opened the door and entered the stateroom—a dwarf wearing a string of pearls and a pink dress patterned with large white roses.

Jolene "Jo-Jo" Deveraux marched over to the bed, planted her hands on her hips, and stared at me with a critical gaze, her clear eyes almost devoid of color except for her black pupils. She clucked her tongue at my sorry state and shook her head, although the motion didn't so much as ruffle a single one of her perfect, white-blond curls.

"Sorry I haven't been in to see you before now, darling," she said. "But I had to wait until that nasty drug was completely out of your system."

"No worries. It only hurts when I breathe."

Jo-Jo let out a hearty laugh, then went into the bathroom to wash her hands. Bria got up, and Jo-Jo came back out and took her seat next to the bed, scooting the chair even closer to me. The dwarf's eyes began to glow a pale, milky white, as did the palm of her hand, as she brought her Air magic to bear. She leaned forward, and a series of invisible pins and needles began to stab their way up and down my body. Air elementals like Jo-Jo used oxygen and all the other natural gases in the air to clean out infected wounds, mend broken bones, and stitch up ripped skin.

Feeling myself being put back together again was never pleasant, especially since Jo-Jo's Air magic was the opposite of my own Ice and Stone power. The dwarf using her magic on me in any way would never seem right, just as being around my power when I was actively using it would never sit well with her.

But what made it worse today was how much it reminded me of Benson.

The pins-and-needles sensation made me think of the phantom sandpaper I'd noticed when Benson murdered Troy and then again when he was reaching out, trying to feel my emotions in Northern Aggression and in his lab. Even though Jo-Jo would never use her magic like that, would never, ever hurt me, a low warning snarl rumbled out of my throat.

"Gin?" Bria asked. "Are you okay?"

"I'll be fine," I said through gritted teeth, my fingers twisting in the silk sheets. "Do me a favor and distract me. Tell me about Silvio. How did he help you?"

"It was all his idea," she said. "After Catalina and I made it to Xavier's car, I didn't want to leave you behind, but some vamps rolled up in an SUV, and Xavier had to floor it to get away from them. Xavier and I had just gotten to the riverboat with Catalina when Silvio texted me. I had no idea how he had my number, but he told me that Benson had captured you and that he had a plan to help you escape. I didn't believe him, but Catalina told me that he was her uncle and that he was telling the truth. Silvio told me how to get past the guards to make it to that patio and said that he would be there waiting with you. He said that jumping off the bridge into a boat would be the quickest way to get you away from Benson, and he was right."

She sighed. "I wish he would have come with us. Benson's probably killed him by now."

I had my doubts about that, but another uncomfortable wave of Jo-Jo's magic sweeping through my body kept me from answering. It took the dwarf another five minutes before she leaned back and released her hold on her magic. The white glow faded from her hand and her eyes.

"There, darling," Jo-Jo said. "Good as new."

I flopped back against the pillows, panting for breath, sweat streaming down my face. But slowly, the memory of Jo-Jo's magic faded away, and I moved my arms and legs. Just like she said, everything felt brand-new, including my previously shattered ankle.

I could have lain there and drifted off to sleep, but I forced myself to sit upright. "I need that bag, the one that was tied to my arm when you rescued me."

Bria frowned, but she went over, grabbed the bag from where it had been sitting on a coffee table, and brought it over to me. I ripped through the plastic. My knives lay inside, along with my spider rune ring, but I was more concerned about what was in the very bottom of the bag: the black leather-bound book that Silvio had slipped inside.

I pulled the book out and started flipping through it. And I realized that it wasn't a book so much as it was a ledger, one that chronicled Benson's entire drug operation.

The first half of the ledger was gibberish, at least to me. Chemical compounds, formulas, and equations for Benson's drug cocktails. I quickly flipped past those sections.

The back half of the book was *much* more interesting, featuring rows of columns, numbers, and, most important of all, names—names of everyone who bought drugs from or sold them to Benson. They were even ranked, in terms of how much money they made or cost the vampire.

I recognized many of the names, including some of the other underworld bosses like Lorelei Parker and Ron Donaldson. The ledger was practically a who's who of bad folks in Ashland. I flipped to the very back and the most recent entries. I scanned down the rows of names of Benson's drug suppliers until I found the one I was looking for.

"What's that?" Jo-Jo asked.

"Insurance." I repeated what Silvio had said to me in the lab, and I finally realized why he'd given me the ledger. "Benson won't kill Silvio. Not yet. By now, he will have realized that Silvio slipped me this. He'll want to know what I plan to do with his little black book before he kills Silvio."

I snapped the ledger shut, then looked at Bria. "What

do you say we mount another rescue mission? You and me together this time."

Her smile matched the one on my face.

We worked out the rough outlines of our plan, although Bria insisted that we wait until the morning to implement it. I didn't want Silvio to be tortured like I had been, but it was already too late for that. I just had to hope that he could hold on until we could save him. Besides, I wanted to be at full strength when I faced Benson again, and my body still needed time to recover from all the trauma it had been through today.

My mind and heart too.

Jo-Jo and Bria left so I could relax, but I was too restless to drift off to sleep, so I threw back the covers, padded into the bathroom, and took a long, hot shower to wash the lemony stench of Benson's lab off me, if not the memories from my mind.

Unfortunately, those would linger for a long, long time to come.

I wrapped a towel around my body and stepped back out into the stateroom to find Owen sprawled across one of the couches, staring at a muted football game on the TV. He straightened up and turned off the TV.

"Hey," he said. "Jo-Jo sent me on in. I've been waiting out here. I didn't want to disturb you."

He'd been giving me some quiet time to myself, time to process all the horrible things that had happened and bury them deep down where no one would ever see them. My heart swelled with love for him. Owen was so good about giving me the space I needed. But I was tired of being hurt and heartsick and reliving the horrors that Benson had visited upon me. Right now, I wanted— I *needed*—to feel something good, something strong, something real and more powerful than anything Benson could ever do to me.

Owen.

"Gin?" he asked, getting to his feet. "Are you all right? Do you want me to get Jo-Jo?"

Instead of answering him, I went over to the door and threw the lock. I didn't want anyone interrupting this. I sashayed back over to Owen, stopping in front of him. I kept my gray gaze on his violet one as I loosened the towel and let it drop to the floor.

Appreciation and desire sparked in his eyes, but Owen hesitated. "Are you sure?"

"I'm sure," I replied in a husky whisper. "I don't want to think about Benson or anything else but you for the rest of the night."

Owen reached for me, but I put my hand on his chest and backed him over to the bed. He reached for me again, but I kept him at arm's length as I unbuttoned his shirt and unzipped his pants. He stepped back long enough to shed his clothes and grab a condom from his wallet. I took my little white pills, but we always used extra protection. He reached for me a third time, and I finally let his arms encircle me.

For a while, we just stood there, our foreheads touching, our breath mingling together, my hands resting on his broad shoulders, even as his fingers stroked up and down my back in light nonsense patterns. Then I stepped forward, and we both eased down onto the bed together.

Sensing my need for control, Owen lay back and let me explore his body. I kissed him gently, teasing my tongue against his, stoking the fire that always burned between us.

For a long time, that's all I did. But then my kisses grew bolder, harder, and longer, and my hands began to wander. I lifted my lips from Owen's and kissed my way down his body, starting with the crooked tilt to his nose before moving to the scar that slashed across his chin and then down to his muscled chest. Eventually, my lips, tongue, and hands slid even farther down, exploring his hard length.

Owen groaned. "You drive me crazy."

I grinned and took him in my mouth.

He groaned again, his muscles bunching and twitching with every hot flick of my tongue and gentle nibble of my teeth. Just before he went over the edge, I backed off and kissed my way back up to his mouth.

We broke apart, and he stroked my hair. "Gin?"

I knew what he was really asking. I nodded, lay back, and finally let him touch me, *really* touch me, his hands exploring my body just as mine had explored his, from the sensitive curve of my neck to my breasts and then down to the tangle of curls between my legs. Owen slipped a finger inside me, even as his tongue danced around one of my nipples, then the other one. The low, languid fire that had been flickering inside me erupted into something much hotter and far more intense.

Suddenly, it was all too much and not enough at the same time.

"Condom," I rasped. "Now."

Owen ripped open the packet and covered himself with it. The second he was finished, I plastered myself on top of him, kissing him hard and deep, my hands touching every single part of him. Then I rose up and slid down onto his hard length, making us both cry out.

Owen put his hands on my hips, steadying me, anchoring me, grounding me, as I rode him hot, hard, and fast. The pleasure and pressure between us built and built, until we both exploded, finding our release together.

Then, when it was over, I slumped down over his body. Owen's arms went around me, and he drew me even closer to him, cradling me against his chest and murmuring how much he loved me over and over again. I buried my face in his neck.

And it was only then that I truly let go and drowned in all the horrible emotions and memories of the day.

My feeling of frenzy slowly dissipated, and I shuddered out a breath, going limp and boneless in Owen's warm, solid embrace. His murmurs slowly faded away, but he kept stroking my hair, arms, and back, as if trying to reassure me with every soft skim of his fingers that this was real, that he was here, and that neither one of us was going anywhere.

Maybe he was trying to prove that to himself too.

For the first time since Benson had shoved that Burn pill into my mouth, I felt truly safe, like the vampire would never be able to hurt me again. Of course, that wasn't true, and it wouldn't be true, not until I killed him. But as I listened to Owen's heart drumming in his chest, I let myself have the illusion of safety, at least for the rest of this night.

Because tomorrow would be even more dangerous than today. Tomorrow I would face down my enemy—and only one of us would live through the confrontation.

* 25 *

I drifted off to sleep and woke up sometime before dawn. Owen was still holding me close with one arm, while the other was thrown up over his head. He must have grabbed the sheets sometime during the night and flipped them up onto us, because we were cocooned together in a warm web of silk. Not wanting to disturb him, I slid out of his embrace and out of bed.

I went into the bathroom, stepped into the shower, and turned it on as hot as I could stand it, letting the water beat against my body. Jo-Jo had healed my injuries last night, but my muscles still felt stiff and sore from all the fights of yesterday, so I stood under the scalding spray until everything felt loose and warm. A white, fluffy robe was hanging on the back of the door, so I grabbed it and put it on before going back out into the stateroom.

Owen was still asleep, soft snores rumbling out of his mouth, but I was too restless to lie back down, so I unlocked the door and went out into the hallway. The only sound was the soft, steady *slosh-slosh-slosh* of water against the riverboat. Jo-Jo had said that Phillip had everyone, except for a few of his most trusted workers, cleared off the boat when Owen and the others brought me on board. I climbed a set of stairs, which took me to the third level, then opened a door and stepped outside onto the main deck.

It was a beautiful September morning, cool and crisp, and I shivered with a delicious chill as a faint breeze danced over my face and gusted through my wet hair. The sun was just rising over the tops of the eastern mountains, streaking the sky with layers of red, orange, and yellow. The warm, vibrant colors reminded me of those in the heart-and-arrow sign outside Northern Aggression.

Despite the early hour, I wasn't the only one out and about. Sophia was here too, sitting in a white cushioned deck chair next to the gangplank that led to the ground and watching a movie on her tablet. Probably one of those old westerns she loved so much, judging from the faint *toot-toot* of a train whistle and the soft *crack-crack-crack*s of gunfire that drifted out of the device. An open metal thermos sat on the deck next to her chair, the wisps of steam curling up out of the container bringing the rich scent of chicory coffee along with them. A shotgun lay next to the thermos on the deck, and a second, matching weapon was propped up against the railing.

Judging from the blanket that was draped over her shoulders like a serape, Sophia had been out here all night, screening movies, drinking coffee, and keeping a watch in case Benson and his men found us and decided to attack.

Her devotion touched me, and more tears pricked my eyes. I told myself they were just there because the sun was already so bright.

Sophia glanced over at the sound of the door opening, then smiled and waved at me. I waved back. But she didn't get up out of her chair and approach me, and I didn't walk over and talk to her. I still needed a little more quiet time to think about things, and Sophia respected that. I went over to the far side of the deck, leaned my forearms on the railing, and watched the last bit of night give up its ghost to the dawn.

I hadn't been at the railing long, maybe ten minutes, when one of the doors creaked open, and soft footsteps sounded. I glanced over my shoulder. Catalina stood in the middle of the deck, wrapped in a white robe, a hesitant look on her face, as if she wasn't sure if she would be welcome. I waved her over, and she joined me. She mimicked my pose, and we stood there staring out at the rippling surface of the river.

"It's so beautiful," she said, skimming her hand along the brass railing. "Everything here is. I drive by the *Delta Queen* every day on my way to work at the Pork Pit, but I never thought that I'd get a chance to come on board, much less see the inside. It's nice."

I nodded, although *nice* was a bit of an understatement, since the *Delta Queen* was six levels of gleaming whitewashed wood trimmed with blue and red paint. A paddle wheel at the very back loomed up over the rest of the riverboat, casting a large shadow that cloaked Catalina and me, despite the early hour.

"I wanted to thank you," she said. "For helping Bria

and me. For saving us. What you did . . . how you got us off that bridge and away from Benson and his men . . . it was *amazing*. It was everything I've ever heard about you and more."

I gave her a questioning, sidelong look, and a bit of a blush stained her bronze cheeks.

"I had heard all the rumors about you being an assassin, about you being the Spider."

"But?"

Catalina drew in a breath. "But . . . I never really thought they were *true*. At least, not until I saw you handle Troy and those two vamps at the college. You seemed so nice, so . . . normal. I thought it was just some crazy story people were making up. An urban legend or something."

"But weren't you ever curious before then?" I asked, facing her. "About everything that happens at the restaurant? Especially about me and why I'm always so . . . disheveled?"

That was a nice way of saying bruised, beaten, and bloody.

She shrugged. "I was, but you were always so nice to me I figured that there was no way you could do what people said you did, that you could be what everyone said you were. Besides, even if I'd realized sooner that all the rumors were true, I wouldn't have cared anyway."

"Why not? Working for an assassin isn't the sort of thing most people can overlook."

She shrugged again. "With the way my life has been the past year, coming to the Pork Pit, working there, waiting tables, it was like a relief, you know? Because no matter how angry I was over my mom's death, no matter how much I missed her, I knew that I could come to the restaurant and forget all about it, at least for a little while. During my shifts, I could just hang out, do my job, and pretend I wasn't falling apart on the inside."

"But you don't need to work in the restaurant. Not with that trust fund Silvio set up for you."

She nodded. "I know, and I've thought about quitting. But working at the restaurant, it was . . . an escape for me, you know? A place where I could feel like I was actually *normal*. Just a girl, just a waitress, just a college student. Instead of someone with a dead mom, an uncle who works for the biggest drug dealer in town, and a trust fund full of money made from other people's misery."

She closed her eyes, and her hands tightened around the railing, as if she were bracing herself for something. After a moment, she opened her eyes and looked at me again.

"I'm sorry about what happened yesterday," she said, her voice dropping to a low, raspy, guilty whisper. "About what Benson . . . did to you. I heard Bria and the others talking about it. It's horrible, and it's all my fault. You were right. I never should have agreed to testify. I almost got you and Bria killed."

I shook my head. "No, you were right, and I was wrong. You were just trying to get justice for Troy the best way you knew how. Don't ever apologize for that. Not to me, not to anyone. What happened, what Benson did to me, it's not your fault. I knew that you and Bria were in trouble, and I made the choice to help you, no matter the consequences. I would make the same choice again—and again."

She nodded, then stared off into the distance, chewing her lip in worry. "What about Silvio? Bria told me that he helped rescue you, and that he went back into the mansion to lead the guards away. Do you think that he's still . . . alive?"

"I don't know, but I'm going to find out. I promise you this: if he is still alive, then I will do everything in my power to save him, the same as he did for me. Will that work for you?"

Catalina nodded, and some of the tension drained out of her body. "So what happens now?"

"You're going to stay here and stay safe," I said. "Don't worry. I'll handle the rest."

Catalina and I both went back to our staterooms to try to get some more shut-eye. I crawled back into bed next to Owen, snuggling up against his warm, muscled body, and drifted off to sleep with no trouble.

Then again, I was never particularly troubled when I decided to kill someone.

I slept another two hours and woke up feeling refreshed and ready to get on with my inevitable confrontation with Benson. Owen had slipped out of bed while I was sleeping, although he'd left me a note propped up on the nightstand.

Buffet. Main deck. Phillip's treat.

Well, that sounded promising. So I put on some clothes that Jo-Jo had brought to the riverboat for me and headed out to find the others.

At dawn, the main deck had been empty, except for Sophia and her shotguns, but now two tables had been set up in her place, each one covered with an impressive spread of food. Bacon, scrambled eggs, biscuits with sausage gravy, country-fried ham, stacks of toast with different kinds of fruit preserves. My stomach rumbled, and I realized how long it had been since I had eaten. I fixed myself a heaping plate of food, grabbed a tall glass of orange juice, and took everything over to a third table that had been positioned at the bow of the boat, close to the railing, so that the diners would have a view of the river.

Phillip was sitting at the table, his plate already clean, a mimosa in his hand, and a pitcher full of the same perched at his elbow. Owen was there too, talking softly to his best friend. So was Finn, who had not one, not two, but three plates of food in front of him, all of which he was eating from at the same time, taking first a bite of scrambled eggs and then one of biscuits and gravy and following that up with a *crunch-crunch-crunch* of bacon and toast slathered with strawberry preserves.

I sat down next to Finn, not so gently nudging his plethora of plates out of my way. "Where are the others?"

"Sophia, Jo-Jo, and Catalina are still sleeping below deck," Owen rumbled, reaching across the table and squeezing my hand. "Xavier went to check on Roslyn. She still had to run things at Northern Aggression last night, so she got a hotel room under a different name instead of driving over here. Bria went with him."

"And how is that going?" I asked. "Xavier and Bria?"

Owen shrugged. "As well as can be expected."

I squeezed his hand back, then leaned over and kissed him.

Finn made a gagging noise. "Please. Some of us are eating."

"I have to agree with Lane," Phillip said, waggling his champagne flute at me. "It is far too early in the day for *that* sort of thing."

I gave Owen another kiss, just to annoy them, then sat back in my chair and started eating. The biscuits were light, fluffy, and baked to golden perfection, while the sausage gravy was thick and creamy, with a nice, peppery bite. I cut my stack of toast into triangles, sampling the strawberry, blackberry, and apricot preserves in turn, enjoying the bright burst of sweet, sticky fruit that tickled my tongue.

Everything was good, and I didn't mind eating someone else's food, but it had become a tradition for me to fix the postbattle meal, and I was a little put out that I hadn't been able to do that here. Maybe it was petty of me, but I wanted everyone to be oohing and aahing over the meal that I had fixed. Not some stranger's.

"So what's the verdict on the buffet?" Owen asked, his violet eyes twinkling a bit, knowing exactly what I was going to say.

"Serviceable." I sniffed. "But I could do better."

Phillip rolled his eyes. "I'll be sure to give your regards to my chef, with all his many years in culinary school and time working in some of the finest restaurants on the East Coast."

"Better watch out, Gin," Owen said, teasing Phillip and me. "Gustav doesn't take insults to his food too kindly, and he's almost as good with knives as you are."

"Oh," I drawled. "I doubt that."

Owen snickered, but Phillip rolled his eyes again and drained the rest of his mimosa in exaggerated annoyance.

I polished off two plates of food. So did Owen, and Finn was still going strong and well into his fourth one. While he finished eating, we sat there in companionable silence, listening to the rush of the river. A faint breeze ruffled my hair, bringing a rich, earthy smell along with it. I breathed in deeply, letting the taste of fall come in through my mouth and roll over my tongue before trickling down into my throat and lungs. Perhaps it was my imagination, but the air seemed tangier than ever before, with an almost metallic, coppery taste to it.

Or maybe that was just my anticipation of making Beauregard Benson bleed later on today.

"So what's the plan?" Finn asked, shoving another strip of bacon into his mouth.

I shrugged. "I figured that we would have a nice, leisurely morning here on the riverboat, and then I would suit up, go over to Southtown, knock on Benson's front door, and kill him when he answers. With y'all backing me up, of course. After that, who knows? Drinks at Northern Aggression all around?"

The three guys looked at one another, then at me.

"You're not going to be a little more . . . circumspect about things?" Phillip asked. "You know, slip into his mansion late at night, kill him under the cover of darkness, and leave his bloody body for his men to find the next morning?"

Instead of answering him, I stared up into the sky. A bit of cloud cover had formed, making it seem as though rays were streaming out of the sun. The bloody streaks reminded me of Coral's hair. Thanks to my dreams, I'd been thinking a lot about my time with her, especially how I'd hidden in the closet while her pimp beat her to death. And I'd realized that I'd been doing the same exact thing these past several months, hiding at the Pork Pit and waiting for the underworld bosses to try to take me out, when I should have been the one on the offensive, on the attack, instead.

It was time to do something about that, all of it, starting with Benson.

"Gin?" Owen asked.

"No," I growled, answering them. "No sneak attacks. Not today. I'm tired of skulking around in the shadows, and there's no point in it. Not anymore, when everyone in the underworld knows who I am. They've been messing with me for months now. Well, I think it's finally time I showed them exactly who they are dealing with, starting with Benson."

Owen, Finn, and Phillip exchanged glances at the cold violence echoing through my words, but they didn't try to talk me out of my plan.

"Besides," I said in a more normal voice, "Benson has to realize that I'll be coming for Silvio, if nothing else."

"And?" Owen asked.

I let out a breath. "And it's personal too. I won't deny it. That bastard strapped me down to a chair, pumped me full of drugs, and sat there and took notes like I was his own private lab rat. I can't let that stand. Not as Gin, and definitely not as the Spider. I can already imagine what folks are saying about me."

Finn winced. "Nothing good. The rumors are already

flying around. Basically, most of them boil down to Benson making you scream like a girl."

I stabbed my finger at him. "Exactly. Everyone knows that he got the upper hand on me and that you guys had to come and bust me out of his mansion. If I don't take care of him now, it'll only get worse. It'll renew everyone's interest in killing me."

"Did that ever really wane?" Phillip asked in a snide voice.

I shot him a dirty look, but he merely arched a golden eyebrow in return before pouring himself another mimosa from the pitcher on the table.

"As I was saying, Benson's probably been crowing all over town about how he so thoroughly humbled me," I said. "Well, I plan to return the favor. Benson thinks that he's the king of Southtown, and he's put all his rivals in the ground for years now. I say it's time to knock the king off his throne."

Finn sighed, grabbed a final strip of bacon off his plate, and crunched down on it. "Why do I get the feeling that this is going to be some grand operation that will most likely involve me schlepping to some disgusting rooftop and getting my clothes dirty yet again?"

I grinned. "Funny you should mention that. I've already worked out some of the details with Bria. Here's what we're going to do."

✷ 26 ✷

Just before noon, I strolled down the street that led up to Beauregard Benson's mansion.

Forget the sidewalks. I walked right down the center of the street between the two faded double yellow lines, just like I had been doing for the last several blocks.

I'd started my journey at the community college, where the whole shebang had begun a few days ago. It seemed ironic and rather fitting. I'd parked my car in the lot there, gotten out, and headed into Southtown on foot. I'd been walking ever since.

At first, everything had been normal. People moved on the streets, flowing in and out of restaurants, grocery stores, and other businesses. Conversation floated through the air, along with the rumble of cars and the smells of exhaust and fried foods. But the deeper I headed into Southtown, the more storefronts were boarded up, the more rune graffiti covered the buildings, and the more people ducked their heads and scurried away from one another as fast as they could.

It wasn't all that far from the college to Benson's mansion, maybe ten blocks, but eyes had been on me the whole time.

Gangbangers had already gathered on the street corners, smoking, drinking, and selling their daily allotment of weed, pills, and other drugs. A few vampire hookers had already started trolling for clients, slowly sashaying back and forth on the sidewalks, while their pimps dozed on the stoops or in their cars, knowing that the real action wouldn't start until sunset. The bums had begun their daily trash rounds, digging in the Dumpsters for whatever they could salvage, while the working-class folks hurried along the sidewalks or zoomed by in their cars. But everyone peered at me, wondering what the crazy chick was doing and how many more blocks I would make it before someone started hassling me.

Good. For once, I wanted everyone to notice me. I wanted everyone to see the Spider and exactly what she was capable of.

That wasn't to say that there weren't a few problems with my march. There was still traffic on the street, and drivers beeped their horns as they approached me, wondering what I was doing strolling down the pavement like I owned it.

I was wearing my usual ensemble of dark jeans, black boots, a long-sleeved black T-shirt, and my black silverstone vest. With my hair pulled back into a ponytail, I looked like some college student who'd gotten lost in the bad part of town. I didn't seem particularly threatening, but one look at my hard face and cold eyes had most drivers putting their feet on the gas and steering away from me as fast as they could. A few of the gangbangers whistled and catcalled in my direction, but I gave them the same flat stares that I gave the drivers, and their jeers and laughter soon quieted down. Given the mood I was in, I was killing anyone who got between me and Benson, stepping over their bodies, and walking on. The folks on the street didn't have his Air power and the precognition that went along with it, but it was easy to tell that I was up to no good.

As I walked, I whistled out a cheery tune. I was actually looking forward to what was coming. For months now, my anger and frustration about everyone targeting me had been slowly building. All I'd wanted was to be left alone, but the underworld bosses hadn't gotten the message. Well, Benson was going to be the perfect outlet for all my rage, and he was going to help me drive my point home—right before I shoved my knife through his heart and out the other side.

But something curious and most unexpected happened: the farther I went, the more people appeared on the sidewalks. The gangbangers, the hookers, the pimps, even some of the homeless bums, started following me. Someone must have recognized me, because it wasn't long before the whispers began.

"Hey, isn't that the Spider?"

"You mean the assassin chick?"

"I thought she was dead, that Benson killed her."

"Apparently not. Looks like she's here for payback."

I grinned. And then some.

The whispers continued, and the crowd followed me block after block, until I finally reached my destination.

The street I was on led straight into the one that fronted Benson's estate, which spread out before me like the palace of a king. I'd been too woozy from the sedative yesterday to really appreciate the beauty of the prewar gray stone mansion with its elegant crenellation and soaring columns. It used to be an apartment building, from the information that Silvio had given me, before Benson had it converted into his own private residence and drug-cooking factory. The mansion butted right up against the street, and I'd seen the lush green grounds and the river beyond it for myself yesterday, when Bria rescued me.

To my left, a familiar sedan rolled down the street and stopped at the corner. Bria and Xavier got out of the car, along with Owen. The three of them stayed next to the sedan and drew their guns, just like we'd planned.

I walked right up to the low stone wall that cordoned off the mansion from the street, raised my fingers to my lips, and let out a loud, ear-splitting whistle, the way Sophia had taught me years ago. The sharp *shriek* caught the attention of the guards patrolling the lawn between the wall and the mansion, and their heads snapped around in my direction. One of them yanked his phone out of his jacket pocket and started texting frantically on it, no doubt alerting his boss that I was here, out in the open for everyone to see.

When I was sure that I had the guards' attention, I turned to face the people who had gathered on the sidewalks behind me. A few of them ducked down behind mailboxes or pressed their backs up against the sides of buildings. Nobody liked the wide, crazy smile on my face but me.

"I'm glad that y'all could make it," I called out in a loud, booming voice. "Because the show's about to begin."

I swept my hand out to the side and gave them all a low, gallant bow, something I'd seen Finn do more than once. Then I straightened up and focused on my first target: Benson's baby-blue Bentley.

It was parked by itself on the street in its usual spot, to the right of the open gate that led to the mansion. The pale blue paint gleamed under the noon sun, the silver trim and accents shimmered, and the glass in the windshield was so clear and perfect that it looked like it wasn't even really there. It truly was a beautiful machine, a work of art in its own mechanical right. I paused a moment, admiring the sleek lines, gleaming glass, and flawless paint.

Then I grinned and stepped over to the car.

As I walked, I casually swung the tool in my right hand back and forth, like the pendulum of doom that it was. I'd come into Southtown with my usual assortment of knives, but I'd also brought along one more weapon for this particular purpose: one of Owen's blacksmith hammers. A long, hard length of silverstone that had been blackened from the countless hours he'd used it in his forge. The perfect weapon for caving in lots of things. Giant skulls, dwarven kneecaps, elemental rib cages.

Fancy cars.

I approached the Bentley and started twirling the hammer around and around, moving it from one of my hands to the other and back again, limbering up my shoulders, the way I'd seen Owen do in fights. I liked the solid, substantial weight of the hammer in my hands, although I would always prefer the sharp, slender sheaths of my knives.

The crowd behind me pressed forward a little, tiptoeing to the edges of the sidewalks, although all the folks made sure to stay on the opposite side of the street, well away from me and my insanity. Everyone sucked in a collective breath as I walked around and around the car, looking for the best place to make my first strike.

"Don't do it, lady," someone in the crowd called out.

"Doesn't she know whose car that is?"

"Crazy assassin bitch must have a suicide wish."

I grinned at that last muttered comment. If they only knew.

I stopped next to the driver's-side door, hoisting the hammer up and over my shoulder. Everyone behind me sucked in another breath. Then I brought the weapon down as hard as I could onto the front windshield.

The hammer punched into the glass with a loud, satisfying *crack*, the jagged tears zigzagging out like the silken strings of a spider's web—my web of destruction.

That first swing got me going, and I smashed the hammer into the car over and over again. Each *crack* of glass and *crunch* of metal satisfied the primal need I had deep down inside to hurt Benson as badly as he had wounded me, to take something away from him just like he had taken from me, to destroy a part of him the way he had done to me.

Oh, yes. All the rage, all the frustration, all the fear and helplessness I'd felt when Benson had drugged me. I took it all out on his car. I slammed the hammer into all of the windows, the roof, the sides. I even palmed one of my knives and slashed all four tires. I let it all out, using the car as a substitute for Benson. Because I would need to keep my emotions in check when I faced the vampire, lest he try to feed on my feelings, and I was working all the rage out of my system now, leaving nothing behind but the cold determination to end him.

Bria, Xavier, and Owen kept their eyes and guns on the guards, but none of them made a move toward me. Neither did anyone in the crowd. They were all too shocked by my actions.

Finally, after about three minutes of whaling on the car, I lowered the hammer and stepped back, breathing hard, although I felt much calmer, my earlier tension wiped away by the energizing exertion.

"Oh, man," Finn groaned through the receiver hidden in my ear. "Really, Gin, did you have to smash up the car? I'm starting to think that's some sort of fetish of yours."

"Maybe," I agreed in a cheery voice. "I do quite enjoy it."

I twirled the hammer around again and slammed it into the hood, adding another dent to the dozen already there.

"Great," someone muttered in the crowd. "Crazy assassin bitch is talking to herself now."

"Is it my imagination, or are your admirers making snide comments about your sanity?" This time, Phillip's voice sounded in my ear.

I couldn't see him, but Phillip was ensconced with Finn on the rooftop closest to Benson's mansion. He, Finn, Bria, Xavier, Owen, and I were all wearing earpieces so that we could communicate with one another.

"Apparently, you agree with them," I murmured back.

"If the hammer fits . . ." Phillip trailed off.

"Says the man who likes to throw people off his riverboat," Owen cut in.

"You've been holding out on me, Philly," I chimed in again, using Eva's nickname for him. "That sounds like fun."

"See?" Phillip said in a smug voice. "Your crazy woman agrees with me, Owen."

"Whatever," Owen rumbled back.

"Enough talk," Bria cut in.

"Yeah." Xavier joined the conversation. "You've finally got some guards headed your way, Gin—a lot of them."

I glanced toward the mansion. Sure enough, about a dozen vamps were marching in my direction, all of them clutching guns. Several were murmuring into their phones, trying to coordinate with one another, but I looked past them. Waiting—just waiting for the king himself to make his appearance.

A few seconds later, the front doors opened, and Beauregard Benson came striding out of the mansion, wearing his usual white pants and sneakers, along with a baby-blue bow tie and a matching button-up shirt, complete with his pocket protector full of pens. And he wasn't alone. Silvio shuffled along behind his former boss, two vamps holding on to his arms.

The last knot of tension in my chest loosened. I was glad to see that Benson hadn't killed Silvio outright for his betrayal. As long as he was still breathing, Jo-Jo could heal the damage that had been done to him—on the outside anyway. As for the inside, well, Silvio would have to deal with that in his own way and his own time, just like the rest of us did.

"All right, guys," I murmured. "It's go time. Just keep the guards off my back, and I'll handle Benson."

"Are you sure?" Finn asked. "I'd be happy to put a couple of bullets in his skull."

"And he might send them spinning away into the crowd with his vampiric Air magic," I countered. "No, Benson's *mine*."

Nobody said anything. They all knew why that was so important to me.

Benson was still about two hundred feet away from me, so I leaned down and propped Owen's hammer up against the side of the smashed-up Bentley. Then I looked over my shoulder at the crowd milling around behind me.

"Anybody who steals that hammer will have to answer to me," I called out.

Mutters rippled through the crowd, and everyone scuttled back a few steps.

"No way, man."

"Not me."

"Uh-uh. I ain't touching that stupid hammer."

I stepped away from the hammer and the car and backed up so that I was standing in the middle of the street, just behind the center lines. Through my earpiece, I could hear the others murmuring as they checked everything a final time. Finn and Phillip readied their rifles, taking aim at the guards, while Bria, Xavier, and Owen remained clustered around her sedan, weapons in hand, ready to support me however they could. I didn't anticipate needing them to help me kill Benson, though. I wanted to do it myself.

I *needed* to do it myself.

Benson pushed through his guards, snarling at them to get out of his way, before storming through the open gate, crossing the sidewalk, and stepping out into the street in front of me. His cold blue gaze flicked over to his smashed car, and a spark of anger flashed in his eyes before he was able to hide it. Looked like I'd finally gotten under his skin. The vamp might feed on other people's emotions, but he had some of his own too, mixed in with the cruelty pumping through his veins. Still, he kept his features calm as he faced me.

"Gin," he said. "What a pleasant surprise. I wasn't expecting to see you again so soon. And looking so well. Why, your recovery is quite remarkable, considering how much you were screaming only yesterday."

Snide snickers rippled through the ranks of the guards, but I shut out the sound of their mockery. Benson was trying to make me angry so that he could more easily feed on my emotions and make himself stronger. Well, that wasn't going to happen. I'd spent most of my life pushing aside my feelings, hardening my emotions, and letting ice run through my veins instead of anything else, and I saw no reason to stop now.

Not until after I'd stopped *him*—for good.

"I am feeling much more like myself today," I drawled right back at him. "It's a wonder what a good night's sleep will do for you. Well, that and not being strapped down to a chair and force-fed your nasty drugs. Kind of cowardly of you, Beau. Filling me full of sedatives and that Burn pill instead of facing me head-on, villain to villain. Mab Monroe certainly never would have done anything like that. Say want you want to about her, Mab had style and power to spare. You? All you have are your sick little experiments and the emotions you rip out of other people."

Murmurs swept through the crowd behind me, and even a few of Benson's own guards nodded their heads in agreement. The vampire kingpin's smile tightened, as though he were grinding his teeth together to hold the expression in place.

"Yes, well, Mab had her way of doing things, and I have mine," he said, straightening his silver glasses a tiny bit. "I'd say that it's been working out pretty well for me so far. Since I have all of this."

He swept his hand out wide, as if to encompass his mansion, his men, and all of Southtown.

"You're right. Pushing your poison on people has worked out pretty well for you, if not for your car."

This time, the laughter was on my side of the street, as one person and then another in the crowd snorted in agreement. Benson's lips puckered with displeasure. That spark of anger shimmered in his gaze again, and a muscle ticked in his jaw before he was able to smooth out his features.

"Why are you here, Gin?" he asked in a voice that was as mocking as mine. "Desperate for another hit of Burn already?"

"Sorry to disappoint, but once was more than enough for me."

"Too bad," he purred. "Your reaction to the drug was quite . . . interesting."

Benson peered at me through his glasses, but I kept my gaze steady and level with his. The vamp puckered his mouth again, disappointed that he hadn't gotten a rise out of me.

"Well, then, let me guess," he said. "You're here to get your traitor back."

He snapped his fingers, and the guards holding on to Silvio dragged him forward, stopping on the sidewalk behind Benson.

Silvio wasn't a pretty sight. He was wearing the same gray suit he'd had on yesterday, but now it was rumpled, ripped, torn, and dirty, with the ends of his filthy white shirt hanging down like two broken, jagged teeth. Blood dotted the sleeves of his jacket, with larger crimson smears and spatter streaked down his pant legs. His head was bowed, letting me see the crazy cowlicks that marred his normally smooth gray locks.

Benson snapped his fingers again, and one of the guards dug his hands into Silvio's hair, jerking his head up.

And I finally saw the full extent of how Benson had tortured him.

Silvio's face was a smushed shell. His nose had been broken repeatedly, judging from all the odd bits of bone jutting out against his skin. Bruises blackened the rest of his features, and puncture marks dotted his neck, several sets of them, as red and angry as wasp stings. Someone had been feeding on Silvio. Benson, most likely.

But the more I stared at Silvio, the more I realized that the physical injuries were nothing compared with the other trauma he'd experienced.

Sunken cheeks, waxy skin, dull gray eyes with barely

a flicker of light left in them. Silvio looked pale and extremely, pitifully, painfully thin, as if his naturally slender body had been reduced to the point of starvation overnight. I wondered if Benson had fed him some Burn pills or if he'd just used his Air magic to suck out Silvio's emotions and most of his life along with them. Either way, the vamp was a beaten, brittle, broken husk of a man. I'd never seen someone look that close to death and still be standing upright, although the two guards propping him up were helping Silvio with that.

I was a bad guy, I was an assassin, and I killed people, but at least I didn't torture them before I sent them off this mortal coil.

I might make an exception for Benson, though.

Through my earpiece, I heard Xavier let out a low whistle. "They worked him over good, didn't they?"

I gave no indication that I'd heard him. Instead, I focused my attention on Benson again.

"Actually, you're right," I said, finally answering his question. "I am here to get Silvio back. So if you will be so kind as to send him over to my friends."

I pointed at the two guards holding Silvio, then over at Bria, Xavier, and Owen. The men shifted on their feet, their eyes flicking back and forth between me and their boss. They didn't want to disobey Benson, but they didn't want to tangle with me either.

When it became apparent that they weren't going to release Silvio, I grinned at them. "Or I can always come get him myself," I said, flexing my hands into fists. "I haven't killed anyone yet today, and it's almost noon. Time to rectify that, don't you think?"

Benson laughed. "Oh, I'm not giving you Silvio. He's going to die for betraying me. But I will offer you a deal."

"And what would that be?"

"Silvio has already admitted that he gave you something of mine. A ledger. Give it back to me, and I'll make the rest of his death quick and painless. I'll also let you and your friends leave here alive."

"Oh?" I said. "You mean that ledger?"

I pointed at Bria, who reached through the open window of her sedan and pulled out the black leather-bound book.

Benson blinked like an owl, but he didn't say anything.

"Fascinating stuff you have in that little recipe book of yours," I said. "Although I have to admit that I skimmed over all the drug formulas. Science isn't really my thing. What I found the most interesting were the names of all your dealers, suppliers, and top-tier clients. Kind of sloppy of you to write all that info down in one place. I imagine your clients would be plenty pissed if all those damning details got out about them."

"What are you proposing?" Benson snapped, a sharp edge to his voice that hadn't been there before.

"It's simple. You turn yourself over to my sister, Detective Coolidge. I'm sure you remember her."

Bria gave Benson a toothy smile, then tossed the ledger back through the open window and into the sedan.

"You go along with Bria peacefully, since she has more than enough evidence to arrest you now. And when she drags your sorry ass into the police station, you admit to everything—and I do mean *everything*—

involving your drug empire, including Troy's murder. Max's too."

He arched his black eyebrows. "You don't really expect that to happen, do you?"

I let out a pleased laugh. "Of course not. But I had to give you the chance, which is more than you gave Catalina."

Benson swept his hand out again. "And why would I agree to any such deal when I can just order my men to kill you where you stand and take what I want?"

The vamps raised their guns. Half of them aimed their weapons at me, while the other half targeted Bria, Xavier, and Owen, still standing by the sedan. Instead of taking cover, I held my hand up and snapped my fingers.

Crack!

A bullet punched through the front windshield of the Bentley and sent the rearview mirror flying. Benson flinched before he could stop himself, while his guards and the crowd ducked and screamed.

"Show-off," I muttered.

Finn laughed in my ear.

"I wouldn't suggest a firefight, unless you want your brains painting the street," I said in a pleasant tone. "I have two very good snipers just itching to kill as many of your men as they can. Before they put a bullet through your skull too."

All of the guards snapped up their weapons and scanned the surrounding rooftops, but I knew that they wouldn't spot Finn or Phillip in their snipers' nest.

After several seconds, Benson made another sweeping motion with his hand, and his men slowly lowered their guns.

"What's your proposal?" he finally asked.

"Why, Beau, isn't it obvious? The Grim Reaper has come knocking on your door, and I'm here to make sure that he doesn't go away disappointed."

* 27 *

Benson eyed me, and I could almost see the wheels turning in his mind about how he could wiggle out of this. He was more than happy to strap me down to a chair and pump me full of drugs, but fighting me on equal footing was something else—something that all his calculations, observations, and experiments hadn't prepared him for. I'd changed the rules of the game by coming here, by openly challenging him, and he didn't like it—not one little bit.

Too damn bad.

After a few seconds of silent contemplation, Benson threw back his head and laughed, as if my challenge was some great joke. His dark, evil chuckles rang out through the street, and mutters of unease rippled through the crowd. They knew what Benson was capable of, and they didn't want any part of it. Couldn't blame them for that.

But I was ready to end this—and him.

"Ah, come on, Beau," I said, when his laughter finally died down. "I'm here, you're here. We've even got a crowd to see our heavyweight title bout. Don't tell me that you're going to be too chicken-shit to take me up on my offer."

Instead of waiting for him to laugh at me again, I turned to the people behind me. More of them had gathered while I'd been jawing with Benson, with others walking this way and more cars cruising in this direction.

I threw my hands out wide. "C'mon," I called out. "Don't y'all want to see a show?"

Whistles, claps, and screams of approval roared back to me. I faced Benson again, my grin even wider and more predatory than before.

"You wouldn't want to rob all these folks of a little blood sport, now, would you?" I said. "It would be a shame if they and I walked all the way down here for nothing. Then again, it would prove you to be the coward that you really are."

"I am not a coward," he snarled. "I am a *scientist*."

I clucked my tongue at him. "Could have fooled me. Here I am, offering you the biggest, baddest prize in all of Ashland. Me, the assassin, the Spider. So why are you hesitating, Beau? Unless you think that you're not up to the task of taking me on."

Everyone sucked in a collective breath at me so openly, so boldly, identifying myself as the Spider.

Silence.

And then the crowd *roared*.

It was so loud for a moment that I couldn't hear anything, not even Finn, Owen, and the others murmuring to one another through my earpiece. But the explosion of emotion quickly died down to a series of taunting jeers and harsh, accusing shouts rising up from the crowd, egging me on. Some of Benson's own guards started looking at him sideways, wondering why their boss wasn't salivating at the idea of killing me. But Benson was too busy staring at the people behind me to pay attention to his own men. His eyes glowed a faint blue as he reached for his vampiric Air magic and used it to feel all the emotions surging off the crowd—the same mix of excitement, anticipation, and derision that I could hear in their catcalls, shouts, and jeers.

Benson frowned, realizing the same thing I did: that the people on the street, the ones he'd lorded over for so long, were very close to openly sneering at him. And that if he didn't do something soon, the crowd would turn against him completely, thinking that he was weak. And so would his men.

"Come on, Beau," I called out, mocking him one final time. "I'm here, and I'm ready to go. So why don't you man up and face me? Winner take all."

Benson stared at me, his face calm, but more and more of that anger sizzled in his eyes, even hotter than the blue burn of his magic. He didn't like being so openly and directly challenged, especially not on his home turf.

"Oh, very well," he huffed, as if I were a mere fly that was annoying him. "If you insist."

"Oh, but I do."

Benson snapped his fingers.

Nothing happened.

He snapped them again.

And still, nothing happened.

After a few seconds, when he realized that no one was obeying his command, probably to bring him a white lab coat, Benson turned his head and glared at his guards. They swallowed, but none of them scurried forward.

Benson gave them all another cold look, then started unbuttoning his shirtsleeves. He rolled up the fabric, revealing his pale, skinny forearms. His movements were slow, deliberate, and meant to intimidate me. Didn't work. Never did.

I looked at Bria and rolled my eyes. She grinned back at me.

Finally, when he deemed himself appropriately ready for the fight, Benson glanced over his shoulder at his men clustered behind him. "If anyone interferes before I kill her, shoot them."

Concerned whispers shot through the crowd at the thought of a firefight, but the large majority of people crept even closer, wanting to have the best view possible.

Benson stepped forward so that he was standing about ten feet away from me, directly on the other side of the center lines. He let out a loud, put-upon sigh and started swinging his arms back and forth, loosening up for the fight. He flexed his fingers, rolled his shoulders, and even cracked his neck a couple of times, the dry *snap-snap-snap*s almost as loud as gunshots in the eerie, absolute silence that had descended over the street.

I arched an eyebrow, more than a little bored by his show, but I kept my gaze on him the whole time. Because I wouldn't put it past him to try to lull me to sleep with his exaggerated stretching routine.

As if he could hear my thoughts, Benson smiled, an evil light flaring in his eyes, then stepped forward and launched himself through the air at me.

I'd been expecting some sort of sneak attack, and I immediately reached for my Stone magic and used it to harden my body.

Still, for a split second, everything slowed down but was somehow magnified at the same time, almost as if I had the enhanced senses that so many vampires did.

The pearl-white gleam of Benson's fangs in his mouth. The smell of car exhaust mixed with that metallic tang of autumn and the vamp's own lemony scent. The rush of air flowing over my face as he leaped toward me. His looming shadow blotting out the sun and sky overhead.

It was that last small sensation, that cold touch of darkness on my face, that snapped me back to the here and now. I spun around, whirling out of the way of Benson's first attack.

I didn't know how many other folks' blood and emotions Benson had been snacking on besides Silvio's, but they gave him enough strength to leap the ten feet that separated us like he was stepping over a crack in the sidewalk. And it made him fast too, so fast that he was able to pivot back in my direction and slam his open palm into the center of my chest like he was some sort of kung-fu master.

The force of the blow knocked me back ten feet and sent me careening down the street like a ball of tumbleweed. I rolled to a stop facedown on the pavement, trying to shake off the jarring impact. Benson wasn't playing around, and he would have caved in my rib cage with that one crushing blow if I hadn't been using my Stone magic to protect myself. My power also saved me from splitting my skull wide open on the asphalt, but I still felt the hard *smack* of the landing, and it took me a few seconds to stop my eyes from spinning around in their sockets.

"Dude, is she down already?"

"Stay back!"

"Watch out!"

The crowd's excited chatter was all the warning I had, and I heaved my body to the side just in time to avoid his feet landing where my head had been a moment ago. I shook off the rest of my daze and got back into the fight.

Before Benson could leap at me a third time, I scrambled up onto my hands and knees and lashed out with my foot, kicking him in the side of his left knee. Benson staggered forward, and to my surprise, some enthusiastic cheers rose up from the crowd.

"That's it!"

"Get that bastard!"

"Kill him!"

Apparently, home-court advantage wasn't all it was cracked up to be, and Benson wasn't nearly as beloved in his little kingdom as he thought he was. I grinned. I was starting to like these people cheering me on.

I palmed a knife and threw myself at Benson, hoping to slam the weapon into his back and end him, but he used his enhanced speed to snap back up onto his feet and slide out of range of my weapon. I was too committed to the blow to stop, so I staggered past him, although I managed to right myself and regain my balance. Knife in hand, I whipped around. Benson did the same, and we faced each other in the middle of the street.

His hands clenched into fists, and he cracked his knuckles a few times in anticipation of hitting me again. I twirled my knife around in my hand, in hopes of doing the same to him. I *would* do the same to him.

Or I'd die trying.

The people pressed forward, forming a loose ring around us, hooting, hollering, and cheering at the tops of their lungs. Bria, Xavier, and Owen held their position by the sedan, alternating between keeping an eye on Benson's guards and shooting worried looks at me. Through my earpiece, I could hear Owen murmuring. I didn't focus on his words, but the sound of his voice was more than enough encouragement for me.

Meanwhile, Benson's guards had formed a line on the sidewalk in front of his mansion, their guns out but down by their sides—for now. They still thought that their boss was going to kill me, so they weren't going to interfere. They couldn't, not if Benson was going to continue to be the king that he'd portrayed himself as for so long.

Benson might be a villain, but I was one too, and I was eager to show him that I could be more ruthless than he ever dreamed of being.

"You should give up now, Gin," Benson called out as we circled each other. "Who knows? Instead of killing you, I might take you back down to my lab for a while. Test some of my new drugs on you. I'd love to see your reactions to them. I know that you'd grow to love it too. Quicker than you think. Everyone does."

My hand tightened around my knife, so hard that I

could feel the spider rune in the hilt pressing into the larger, matching scar embedded in my palm. "I'd rather gut myself like a fish than be your damn science experiment again."

Benson grinned, showing off his fangs, the tips of his teeth as sharp as the knife in my hand. "Well, then, I guess it's a good thing that I don't have a problem with that scenario either. Only I'm afraid that I'll be the one doing the gutting, not you."

He let out a loud roar and charged at me. I let him come.

Benson swung at me, this time using his enhanced vampire strength to put even more force behind his blows. But I still had my Stone magic, so I used it to harden my skin, head, hair, and eyes into an impenetrable shell. Oh, Benson's punches still hurt, each one as hard and brutal as me slamming Owen's hammer into the vamp's car, and the blows knocked me this way and that, like I was a bit of gravel flying across the road after a semi roared by. But the brutal assaults didn't crack my ribs and break all the bones in my face the way he wanted them to.

While Benson concentrated on pummeling me, I lashed out with my knife at him.

Punch.

Slash-slash.

Punch.

Slash.

Punch-punch-punch.

We traded blow after blow after blow, his fists pounding into my chest and face over and over again. I got in a few glancing swipes with my knife, but every time the blade would start to sink deep enough into Benson's body to do some real damage, he would use his enhanced speed to dart back out of range of the edge of the blade. It was a small, subtle movement but extremely hard to do, and I found myself being impressed with his technique. We were playing a game of inches, and he was winning.

"You're going to lose," Benson taunted me when we broke apart after another furious exchange. "Face it, Gin. You're going to run out of magic long before I run out of strength."

"Oh, I don't know," I snapped back at him. "Considering that you've already started sucking wind, I'm willing to put my belief in my magic—in myself."

Benson frowned as he realized how true my words were. His breath was coming in sharp gasps, sweat was sliding down his forehead, and the rims of his glasses had fogged up from his exertions.

He growled, stepped forward, and shoved me in the chest with both hands. His strength sent me flying again, this time right into the side of his smashed-up Bentley. My back slammed into the driver's-side door, adding another dent there, while my legs slid out from under me, and my ass hit the pavement. I raised my knife, expecting Benson to do another one of his soaring leaps on top of me, but instead, he snapped his fingers. One of the guards hurried over to his boss's side and raised his gun, pointing it at my head. I tensed, wondering if Finn could take him out before he pulled the trigger.

But Benson had something else in mind.

Even as his man turned toward me, Benson came up behind him. Then he casually reached out with one hand, jerked the other man back up against his body, and plunged his fangs into his own guard's neck. Benson took several long pulls of blood out of the vamp, who screamed and thrashed against his boss's body, even as his gun slipped from his fingers and clattered onto the pavement. But Benson wasn't content to just take the man's blood and his strength along with it.

Oh, no.

Even as the guard's screams grew louder and his thrashes weaker, Benson clamped his hand onto the side of the man's head, a blue glow pulsing out from between his fingers like the bright flare of a star. The bastard was sucking the fear, pain, and terror out of his own man just to make himself stronger—just so he could beat me.

It disgusted me, how casually Benson would disregard his own man's loyalty, how he would betray it in this most ultimate, intimate way in front of everyone, but it didn't surprise me.

Because that was exactly the kind of scum he was.

Well, not for much longer, not if I could help it.

I scrambled to my feet and started forward. But it was already too late for the guard. Benson ripped his fangs out of the other man's neck, dropped his hand from his head, and let him go. The guard flopped to the ground, dead.

Benson let out a loud, satisfied sigh that had everyone in the crowd screaming, ducking down, and hurrying to put as much distance as they could between themselves and the vamp and still be able to see our death match.

Benson turned to face me. I'd never seen him look anything but cold, clinical, and detached, but right now, he was a fucking mess. His clothes were torn, ripped, and dirty from our fight, his black hair stuck out from his head at odd, spiky angles, and patches of sweat darkened his baby-blue shirt. Even worse, his body had swelled up, his muscles filling out and bulging with all the life, blood, and emotions he'd just sucked out of his guard.

But it was his face that was truly gruesome.

The dead guard's blood was smeared all over Benson's mouth, the most garish sort of lipstick imaginable, while more blood had run down his chin and spattered all over his shirt. Crimson specks even dotted the lenses of his silver glasses like dead bugs splattered all over a car windshield.

But it was his eyes that worried me the most. They pulsed a bright blue from the terrified emotions he'd sucked out of his dying guard, burning hotter than the noon sun overhead. Benson was stronger now than ever before.

And I wasn't.

I'd already used up a good chunk of my magic just keeping him from breaking every single bone in my body. I needed to finish this, I needed to kill him, before my own magic ran out entirely, just like he said. Or I'd be the one dying in the street today.

Benson grinned, showing off his fangs, stained red with blood. "What were you saying about my winding down? I can do this all day long, Gin. But you can't."

I tightened my grip on my knife. "I don't have to do it all day long. It shouldn't take me more than another minute, two tops, to finish off the likes of you."

Benson growled and launched himself at me again. But I was expecting the move, so I was able to sidestep at the last possible second, and he slammed into his own car instead of me, putting a bigger dent in the metal with the force of his own body than I had with Owen's hammer.

But it didn't slow him down for an instant. Benson let out a loud, guttural growl, reached down, hooked his hands on the bottom of his car, and flipped it over onto its side, causing the people gathered on the sidewalks to scream in surprise and terror. Benson grinned, whirled around, and took a menacing step forward, as though he were going to plunge into the crowd and do to them what he had done to his own guard. He would too, the second he felt like he needed another hit of power.

In his own way, Benson was just as much of an addict as all the people he'd gotten hooked on his drugs over the years.

He chuckled at the crowd's fear, his eyes burning brighter than ever before. He might not be able to feed on their emotions without touching them, but he could sense their fear, and it was adding to his own twisted high. I had to distract Benson from the crowd before he attacked someone else and became too strong for me to kill, so I darted over, grabbed Owen's hammer from where it had landed, and hurled it in his direction.

But Benson was truly hopped up on adrenaline, emotion, and blood now, and he whirled around almost too fast for me to follow. One second, he was doing his best bogeyman impression with the crowd. The next, he'd snatched Owen's hammer out of midair. He let out an amused chuckle, then turned and hurled the weapon as hard as he could. It sailed away as free and easy as a kite, as if Benson had the strength of some Olympic god, and it didn't stop until it clattered against the side of his mansion, knocking a chunk of stone off the side before falling to the ground.

Benson grinned at me again, his fangs seeming even bloodier than before. "And now, Gin, I think it's time for you to die."

Before I could move, before I could react, before I could even think about ducking, Benson was on me. I lashed out with my knife, but he let out a mocking laugh and slapped the weapon out of my hand. I palmed another knife, but Benson slapped that one away too, sending it flying through the air. It came to a stop right beside my first knife. I started to reach for the third knife against the small of my back, but Benson stepped forward, grabbed my shoulders, and slammed his head into mine.

With all of that fresh blood and emotion pumping through his veins, this blow was harder and sharper than all the others he'd landed so far. I felt like my skull had gotten run over by a Mack truck, and I lost my grip on my Stone magic.

Benson used the opening to head-butt me again.

I managed to bring enough of my magic back to bear to keep the blow from killing me outright, but my brain rattled around in my skull like a coin tumbling through a slot machine. White, gray, and black stars winked on and off in my vision, and I was flat on my back on the pavement before I realized what was happening.

I lay there, trying to *blink-blink-blink* the dangerous spots away and come up with some sort of plan that would let me kill Benson without getting dead myself. In my earpiece, I could hear Bria, Xavier, Owen, Finn, and Phillip all screaming at me to *getup-getup-getup!*, but scrambled brains aren't great for comprehension or action.

I blinked again, and Benson was kneeling on the pavement beside me, his hand wrapped around my throat. He easily hoisted me off the ground and lifted me up into the air, so that my feet were kicking in the breeze and my gaze was level with his.

Out of the corner of my eye, I could see Bria, Owen, and Xavier start forward, only to draw up short as Benson's men moved in front of them, cutting them off from me.

"I don't have the angle," Finn yelled in my ear. "I don't have a shot!"

"Neither do I!" Phillip yelled back.

Things had not gone my way, and my friends were still trying to save me. But they were going to be too late.

So I'd just have to save myself.

I pushed all the noise away. Finn and Phillip still screaming in my ear. Bria, Xavier, and Owen shouting from behind the guards. The excited whispers of the crowd. I ignored it all and focused on Benson. The sweaty warmth of his hand wrapped around my throat. The strength in his arm as he held me up. The hot blue glow of magic in his eyes. The bloody flecks painting his glasses. The lemony scent wafting up from his body.

It was that last one, his smell, that made me flash back to my time in his lab. Different day, same situation. Because right now, I was just as helpless as I'd been in his chair, when Benson shoved that Burn pill down my throat and then made me swallow it—

Malevolent understanding burned through me like

acid, making me grin. Because I wasn't helpless. Not here, not now, not *ever*.

And I knew how I could beat Benson: the exact same way he'd beaten me.

All around us, the crowd gasped, pressing forward in anticipation of the end. They knew that this was the moment when the vamp could snap my neck with a thought, if he so chose.

Benson knew it too, because he started laughing. He turned this way and that, lifting me up higher and higher into the air for the crowd's and his own inspection and amusement, as if I were some sort of trophy he'd won and was hoisting skyward.

But what the bastard didn't realize was that he hadn't won—not yet—and that I wasn't about to let him be the end of me.

Finally, Benson quit waving my body through the air and brought me back down so that my eyes were level with his again. He stared at me, his happy face creasing into a thoughtful frown. Once again, he did that weird, tilting thing with his head, staring at me like a bird about to gobble up a worm, as if he were surprised by something I'd said, even though he had such a tight grip on my throat that I could have barely done more than croak out a few words, even if I'd wanted to crow about how I was going to kill him.

"Fascinating," he said. "Truly fascinating."

Benson loosened his hold on my neck and waved his free hand in front of my face. The rough, sandpaper feel of his Air magic sloughed against my body, trying to pinpoint the emotions under the surface of my skin and tear them out of me. But I didn't let them. Instead, I reached for my Ice magic and let the cold power center me the way it had done so many times in the past.

Benson gave me a little shake, as if trying to rattle the emotions out of me, like pennies stuck to the bottom of a glass jar. I gritted my teeth as my brain sloshed around inside my skull again, but I didn't give him the satisfaction of hissing in pain. Instead, I focused on my magic, letting it make me as cold as ice—literally—from the inside out.

But my lack of response, my lack of emotion, my lack of fear, made him go from curious to enraged in a heartbeat.

"How can you be so damn *calm*?" he hissed. "Don't you know that I'm seconds away from killing you? Where's your fear? Your panic? I want your terror, Gin. Give it to me. Give it to me *now*."

I rasped out a low chuckle. "Oh, sugar, do you really think that you're the only nasty thing that's ever had his hand around my throat? Please. This isn't my first heavy-weight bout, but it's going to be your last."

He shook me again, then brought his face even closer to mine, so close that I could smell the coppery stink of blood on his breath, mixed with his lemony scent, both as bitter and foul as any poison. "You should be scared, you stupid fool."

"No," I countered. "*You* should be scared. You like get-ting people hooked on your drugs because it makes it that much easier for you to feed on their emotions. You're so proud of your power, of your formulas and experiments, and you think that they make you so smart, so *superior* to everyone else. But you're just as much of an addict as all those poor people in your basement. You've been the undisputed king of Southtown for so long that you've forgotten one important thing—the *only* thing that matters right now. Kind of sad, since you so painfully reminded me of it yesterday down in your lab."

"And what would that be?" he hissed again.

I smiled, my features even more predatory than his. "That no matter who you are—addict, assassin, or vampire—everybody needs air to breathe, even you."

I shoved my hand out so that I was touching his right cheek, cupping it almost the way a lover might.

Then I unleashed my Ice magic on the bastard.

A silver light flared between us, leaking out from the spider rune scar branded in the center of my palm. For a moment, the light was so intense that I couldn't even see Benson standing in front of me. But I didn't need to see him, because I could feel my magic, and I directed it at him with all the force of an arctic blizzard.

In an instant, his skin was severely frostbitten and even bluer than his eyes. He drew in a breath, and the air crystallized and froze deep in his lungs, killing all of that precious tissue. And then, for the coup de resistance, I coated his entire face with three inches of elemental Ice, a trick I'd learned from Bria.

By the time I dropped my hand, Benson looked like he was wearing a bubble of bluish glass over his face. His hand slipped from my throat, and he staggered back, beating and clawing at the elemental Ice on his face. I dropped to the ground, gasping for breath, but I was already pushing the pain away and coming back up onto my hands and knees. I lashed out with my foot, driving it into the side of Benson's knee, and then I sent out a burst of Stone magic, cracking the pavement under his feet.

This time, he was the one who landed flat on his back. Using his enhanced strength, Benson finally broke through the Ice on his face and started sucking down some much-needed oxygen, his breath coming in painful rasps, given how much of his lungs I'd just destroyed. While he was busy wheezing, I flattened my hands against the asphalt and reached for my power.

I didn't have a fancy chair to help me subdue the vampire, but I didn't need one. Benson might be the king of Southtown, but the foundation of everything around us was made of stone—*my* element, the one that I was queen of.

Like the street he was lying on.

So I pressed my palms into the pavement and sent my Stone magic racing through it, causing more and more of the asphalt to *crack-crack-crack-crack*. And then I poured even more of my power into the pavement, causing all those broken bits of stone to rise up and come together again, until they formed five specific shapes.

Shackles.

Using my magic, I clamped a Stone shackle around each of Benson's arms and legs and his neck, then sank them down deep into the asphalt, as though they were about to pull him down into the center of the earth along with them. For extra insurance, I coated each shackle with three inches of elemental Ice, so that even if Benson could use his strength to break through the restraints, he'd still have to expend even more energy to get through the Ice too.

He must have already used up a good portion of the dead guard's blood and emotions, because he heaved and bucked and thrashed against my improvised restraints, but he couldn't break free of them.

Just like I hadn't been able to break free of the ones in his lab.

Desperate, Benson looked at me, his fingers crawling across the broken stone, trying to touch me so he could siphon off enough of my emotions to escape. Well, he was finally going to get his wish, since I was more than ready to open up about my *feelings*.

I went down on one knee beside the vamp, staring at him as dispassionately as he had stared at me in his lab. Then I slowly drew the knife from against the small of my back and tapped the point of it on my cheek, as if I were considering all the secrets of the universe.

"Tell me, Beau," I drawled. "How does it feel to be completely helpless? What sort of emotions are *you* feeling right now? Hmm? Why, I think it would make for a fascinating scientific study, don't you?"

He opened his mouth to scream or perhaps yell at his men to shoot me, but before he could, I raised my knife and slammed it into his heart.

"Why, I do believe that's agonizing discomfort you're experiencing," I murmured. "Every nerve ending in your body probably feels like it's on fire right now. Sort of how I felt when you pumped me full of Burn."

Benson screamed, but I clamped my hand over his bloody mouth, cutting off the sound.

"Now, what was it you told Troy the night you murdered him? Oh, yeah. *Don't be frightened. It'll only hurt for a minute.* Well, you're right about that. Because I'm not like you. I don't torture people. I've already killed you with that one blow."

I leaned forward so that he could see my eyes—eyes that were a lot colder than the elemental Ice that I'd encased him with. Benson's panicked blue gaze locked with my calm gray one.

"You wanted me to share my emotions with you. Well, do you know what I'm feeling right now?" I purred. "I'm sure you can sense it with your magic. There's only one word for it, really: *satisfaction.*"

I removed my hand from his mouth and ripped the knife out of his chest. The vamp arched his back, but he couldn't break free of my Ice and Stone shackles, and he didn't even have the energy left to scream. Instead, he sputtered and sputtered, as if he couldn't believe that the same thing was being done to him that he'd done to me and countless others.

Slowly, his body grew still, and his breath came in ragged gasps, flecks of foamy blood spewing out of his lips and coating his glasses.

"And now your body is shutting down from the massive trauma that I just inflicted on it—and you. And that chill you're feeling? That's not my Ice magic. It's my *emotions*—and your own death, taking hold of you breath by breath."

Benson almost seemed to nod his head in agreement. Then his body relaxed, his head lolled to the side, and his gaze fixed on something that only he could see.

The bastard was dead.

Good riddance.

❊ 28 ❊

I watched the blood dribble off Benson's chest and start pooling in the spiderweb cracks in the pavement. All around me, the stone of the street, sidewalks, and buildings chattered with the violence that the vampire and I had just dished out to each other. But I didn't mind the shocked sounds. They told me that I'd made it through another battle and had killed another enemy who had threatened me and mine.

But as I got to my feet and turned around, I wondered how much more trouble I'd just caused for myself.

Because folks stood two and three deep on the sidewalks in places, and everyone was staring at me—the curious gawkers, Benson's guards, Silvio, my friends.

The silence grew and grew, and my gaze swept from one face in the crowd to another. People whispered to one another, their low muttering sounding remarkably like that of the blood-spattered stone under my feet.

"Um, Gin?" Finn said in my ear. "This might be a good time for you to say something."

"You think?" I murmured back.

I stepped forward. Several folks in the crowd gasped and backed away from me, probably thinking that I was going to do the same thing to them with my knife that I had done to Benson. Some of them probably deserved it. The pimps who beat their hookers just because they felt like it. The dealers who sold drugs to kids just to make a few extra bucks. The gangbangers who hurt innocent people just because they'd had the misfortune to get in the way of their turf wars. These were not nice people gathered around me.

Then again, I wasn't particularly nice either.

Still, for the most part, I had a live-and-let-live policy. As long as you didn't come after me, I wasn't going to go after you. So I decided to make that clear to everyone within spitting distance.

I stabbed my bloody knife toward Benson's body. "The so-called king of Southtown is dead."

"Long live the queen!" someone shouted in a voice that sounded suspiciously like Finn's.

"I'm not the damn queen of anything," I growled.

My angry glare was enough to get the crowd to shut up again, so I continued with my impromptu speech.

"Benson terrorized everyone who came into contact with him. Not because he needed to but because he wanted to. Because he *liked* it."

Several people nodded in agreement, including many of Benson's own guards.

"But I'm not Benson. I'm the Spider."

Once again, the crowd gasped.

"I'm the Spider," I repeated. "And despite the rumors you might have heard, I don't treat people like shit just because I can. I don't hurt or torture or kill them just because it amuses me."

"So what are you saying, lady?" another voice called out.

"I'm saying that y'all are free to do as you please after I leave." I stabbed my finger at Benson's mansion. "I'm going in there, but when I come back out, it's yours. Loot it. Cover it with graffiti. Burn it to the ground for all I care."

A couple of folks in the back of the crowd starting high-fiving each other, already thinking about all of the shiny things they could spirit away from the mansion.

"I don't want Benson's mansion, and I sure as hell don't want to take his place."

"You're just going to leave us alone?" someone else called out. "Really?"

I shrugged. "Sure."

I started to walk away, but then I looked back over my shoulder, causing the crowd to tense up again. They were as used to double-crosses as I was.

I stabbed my bloody knife in their direction. "One word of warning. You cross me or you mess with me and mine in any way, and you'll be like Benson there. You won't know what hit you until you're bleeding out on the pavement. Do we understand each other?"

Silence.

"Do we *understand* each other?"

I sent a little surge of Stone magic into the pavement at

my feet, making the blacktop ripple, crack, and splinter in several places.

"Yes!"

"Oh, yeah!"

"Loud and clear, lady!"

"Good," I said. "Don't make this crazy assassin bitch come back down here and tell you again."

Then I turned and walked away, leaving Benson's bloody body shackled in the middle of the street for all to see.

I grabbed the knives I'd dropped earlier, then walked over to the two guards who still had Silvio propped up between them. The guards looked at me, then at each other, as if they were thinking about dropping Silvio in order to attack me.

"Really?" I asked. "Did you not just see what I did to your boss?"

They winced, knowing that I had an excellent point.

"Put Silvio down gently, then leave. Tell the rest of the men to do the same, if they want to live."

This time, the two men didn't hesitate. They eased Silvio to the ground, propping him up against the stone wall that marked the edge of Benson's property, then scurried away as fast as they could to deliver my message. I stared down the other guards, but one by one, they all tucked their guns under their jackets, tiptoed past me, and disappeared into the still milling crowd.

Bria, Xavier, and Owen rushed over to me, each one hugging me in turn. A minute later, Finn and Phillip appeared at the end of the block and headed in our direction.

"Aw, man," Finn said, coming up to stand beside me, a black duffel bag dangling from his hand. "I didn't even get to shoot anybody."

"Well, look on the bright side," I drawled. "Your clothes didn't get messed up. Neither did your hair."

Finn perked up at my reasoning.

I crouched down next to Silvio, who was still slumped against the wall. His dull gray eyes slowly fixed on me.

"Catalina?" he croaked.

"She's fine," I said. "And you will be too. There's an Air elemental healer we know. We'll get you over to her lickety-split. But I need to ask you something first."

"Anything."

"Where did Benson keep his notes? The ones on his experiments?"

"Most of it was in the ledger I gave you," Silvio rasped. "But there's more. In the safe. In the lab."

I grimaced, but I listened as he told me the combination to the safe. I got to my feet and stepped back, while Xavier bent down and gently picked up Silvio, cradling the vampire in his massive arms as if he weighed no more than a child. He probably didn't, given all the blood and emotions Benson had drained out of his body.

Owen touched my arm. "We'll be back soon."

"Okay."

He hugged me again, pressing a soft kiss to my forehead, and then he, Xavier, and Phillip got into the sedan and left with Silvio.

Finn rubbed his hands together in unrestrained glee. "Oh, boy. It's looting time."

I rolled my eyes. "Go on in if you want to. Go see what else Benson had in his safe."

Finn jerked his head at Bria, who was standing over the vampire's body. "What about you guys?"

"We'll be there in a minute."

Finn nodded, hopped over the wall, and crossed the lawn, heading for the mansion. I went over to Bria.

My sister stared down at Benson, her gaze moving from his frostbitten face to the crude shackles on his arms and legs to the blood that had filled in all the cracks around him. Her features were blank, but she kept rubbing her fingers over the gold detective's badge on her black belt.

"Are you sorry that it went down like this?" I asked. "That you weren't able to arrest him?"

She chewed her lip a moment. "Yes and no. Part of me wanted to bring him in, to do things my way."

"But?"

"But after seeing what he did to you, knowing how he tortured you . . ." She sighed. "Part of me just wanted him dead. And now he is, thanks to you."

Bria fixed her gaze on me. "But most of all, I'm glad that you're okay, Gin. I hope that you can forgive me for dragging you into my war with Benson."

"There's nothing to forgive. It was my war too. It has been for months now, ever since the underworld bosses started trying to kill me. I just finally decided to do something about it."

She nodded, then reached out and hugged me, so tightly that I felt the primrose rune around her neck press into my collarbone. I hugged her back even tighter, telling myself that the cold, hard touch of the silverstone symbol against my skin was what was making me blink back tears. Yeah. Right.

"C'mon," I said, pulling back. "Let's go see what's in the safe before Finn steals it all for himself."

Bria nodded and linked her arm through mine. Together, we turned and walked away, leaving Beauregard Benson behind for good.

Bria and I entered the mansion, which was eerily quiet, and headed down to the basement. The drug den was empty of the addicts I'd seen before, although those thick wads of incense still burned in the corners of the room. I didn't know where all the people had gone, if Benson had gotten rid of them or if they'd left on their own. But wherever they were, I hoped they'd get some help.

Bria and I walked through the basement and into the lab. Everything looked the same as I remembered it—the refrigerators in the back, the metal table with its vials of powders and scientific instruments, the chair sitting in the middle of it all like a giant white spider.

Sweat beaded on my forehead as I stared at the chair with its shackles, and I could have sworn that I could hear my own screams echoing through the room. But those were just my memories. I'd survived the chair, I'd survived Benson, and I'd survive my memories too, along with the nightmares they were sure to bring with them.

But I had to move forward, because things weren't over yet—not between me and the person who had supplied Benson with his Burn pills.

So I moved past the chair and went over to Finn and Bria, who were standing in front of the safe. Finn ran his hands over the metal and let out a low whistle of appreciation.

"Benson wasn't messing around when it came to this," he said. "I'm glad you got the combination from Silvio, or we'd be here the rest of the afternoon trying to crack this sucker."

I rattled off the numbers, and Finn spun the dial, opening the safe. The first thing he pulled out was a brick of cash. He let out another whistle, this one more cheerful than before.

"Nice," Finn purred, and he tossed the cash into his open duffel bag on the floor.

I looked at Bria. "See what I mean?"

She laughed.

Money, guns, drugs. We found all that and more in the safe, along with dozens of notepads. Only these didn't contain Benson's formulas, the names of his clients, or the money he had coming in and going out. They were records of all his twisted experiments on people, including elementals like me.

Finn let out another low whistle, then showed me the entry that Benson had made in his notepad yesterday, after he'd forced that Burn pill down my throat.

Shows immediate, violent reaction to drug. Indicative of subject's own extreme elemental power, Benson had written in an elegant script. *Subject experiencing effects of drug in rapid, accelerated succession. Further tests are definitely needed to test limits of subject's tolerance and endurance of this and other formulas.*

My stomach twisted as I thought of all the pain I'd experienced because of the drug. Once again, my own screams echoed in my ears, but I squashed the phantom sounds. This was the reason I'd asked Silvio where Benson's notes were. I hadn't wanted anyone to find the vamp's observations about me. I didn't want anyone to know my weaknesses.

And especially not my fears.

So I ripped those pages out of the notepad and handed it back to Finn. He took it without a word and put it with the others he'd collected.

We finished cleaning out the safe, stuffing all the contents into Finn's duffel bag. Then the two of us headed over to Bria, who had opened all of the refrigerators in the back of the lab. My sister had her hands on her hips and a pensive look on her face as she stared at the racks full of pills, powders, and other illegal substances.

"You know, there are millions of dollars' worth of drugs in these right now," I said. "It would be a big win for you, Bria, turning all this stuff over to the police."

"Oh, yeah," Finn said. "You'd totally get a promotion out of it. Maybe two."

Bria smiled at his efforts to cheer her up, but the expression quickly slipped from her face.

"Benson cared more about all of this than he did about anything else," she murmured, reaching out and snagging a plastic bag of red Burn pills from inside one of the refrigerators. "He murdered Max and Troy and was willing to do whatever was necessary to kill Catalina. And for what? *This?*"

She shook the bag, making the pills rattle around inside, before tossing it back into the refrigerator. "No matter how long I'm a cop, and all the bad things that I see, sometimes I think that I will never truly understand people."

I shrugged. "Benson was a monster. No one is arguing that."

Bria looked at me, her eyes dark and haunted. "But I was a monster too. Because I was willing to risk Catalina to get to all of *this*. No matter how dangerous it was to her or anyone else. And I did risk you, and I almost lost you. I won't make that mistake again, Gin. I promise you that."

She held out her hand, and I took it and squeezed it.

"I know," I said, my voice rough with emotion.

Finn cleared his throat. "I hate to interrupt the sister-bonding moment, but we need to do something with all of this. If we don't, this place will be looted and picked clean. Not that I blame the folks outside. I'd be eager to come in here and get my fair share of loot too, after Benson had put the squeeze on me for so many years. So what do you want to do with it?"

"Let's burn it all," Bria said. "I know it goes against procedure, but these drugs are dangerous, and I want them all destroyed, right here, right now. Not locked up in evidence where some dirty cops can and probably will get their hands on them and put them right back out on the streets. What do you say, Gin?"

"Burning it is fine with me." I pointed to the chair in the middle of the lab. "As long as we start with that."

✳ 29 ✳

After taking Silvio over to the riverboat so he could be reunited with Catalina and healed by Jo-Jo, Xavier, Phillip, and Owen returned to the mansion. They appeared just in time to help me, Finn, and Bria carry Benson's stash of drugs outside and throw them onto the front lawn.

Most of the crowd from earlier had drifted away, although a few folks hung out on the corners across the street, checking their phones and waiting for us to leave so they could enter Benson's mansion. A brutal fight, a bloody death, and an afternoon of looting and larceny. Just another day in Southtown.

I dumped the last bags of Burn pills out of a cardboard box I'd grabbed from the lab, then stepped back to admire our handiwork.

The torture chair sat in the middle of the pile, although you could hardly see the white cushions now for all the plastic bags we'd piled on top of it. Phillip had nosed around in the mansion and found a can of gasoline, which he sloshed all over everything. I'd grabbed a box of matches out of the supplies in Finn's duffel bag, and I handed it to Bria.

"Why don't you do the honors?"

"With pleasure," she murmured.

Bria plucked a match out of the box and struck it against the side. She stared at the flickering fire a moment.

"For Max," she whispered, then tossed the match into the center of the pile.

WHOOSH!

And just like that, what was left of Beauregard Benson's empire went up in flames.

The guys went back into the mansion to check and make sure we'd found all the drugs, but Bria and I stayed on the lawn. We'd been watching the drugs burn for about ten minutes when I noticed the vehicle—a black Audi with tinted windows.

I was really starting to hate the sight of that car.

It was parked on the street about fifty feet away from the entrance to the mansion, giving the occupants a clear view of me, Bria, and our bonfire of drugs. I knew exactly who was inside. I had known ever since I saw the name of Benson's Burn supplier in his ledger last night on the riverboat.

I also knew that my enemy would come find me soon enough. She'd be too curious not to.

So I stood by Bria's side and kept an eye on the car

until the occupants got bored and drove off. I waited a few minutes, but they didn't circle back around, and I realized that my friends and family were safe.

At least for today.

But my relief was short-lived. About five minutes after the Audi left, sirens started wailing in the distance. I looked out over the river and spotted a couple of cop cars headed in this direction, their blue and white lights flashing as they crossed the closest bridge.

The others heard the noise too, and we all gathered around the bonfire, which was still going strong.

Finn picked up his duffel bag of loot and slung it over his shoulder. "Well, I would say that's our official cue to leave. I'll go get the car. Fellas?"

Owen and Phillip moved off with him. That left me standing with Bria and Xavier.

"How are you going to explain things this time around?" I asked.

Bria and Xavier exchanged a look, and then my sister shrugged.

"Probably that we got a tip about a drug war gone wrong between Benson and some unknown assailant. We were first on the scene and found Benson dead in the street and all his merchandise going up in flames."

"You think that will work? You don't think someone in the crowd will rat me out?"

Bria and Xavier exchanged another look.

"Nobody talks in Southtown," they said in unison.

They both laughed a little, and then my sister turned to me.

"Nobody's going to testify against you, Gin," she said. "Not after what they saw you do to Benson."

I grimaced, but she was right. And I realized that in a way, I'd become just like the drug kingpin. I didn't know how I felt about that—or what the consequences of my actions here today would be.

Finn pulled his Aston Martin up to the entrance and beeped the horn. The wail of the sirens grew louder as the cop cars crossed the bridge.

"Go," Xavier rumbled. "We've got your back."

"Always," Bria added.

I flashed them both a grateful smile, then jogged over to Finn, Phillip, Owen, and our getaway car.

News of Beauregard Benson's death consumed the newspapers and airwaves for the next few days. Story after story was reported about the vampire's death and the destruction of his mansion, which was looted and burned to the ground the night I killed him.

The police spun it as a drug war gone wrong, but Bria was right. No one who'd witnessed my fight to the death with Benson stepped forward to contradict the cops' theory, although Finn told me that word of what I'd done to the vampire had already spread like wildfire through the underworld. Apparently, all the other crime bosses were on high alert, thinking that I was going to come after them next. Which meant that they would no doubt be sending more and more people to try to kill me first. So I'd solved one problem and created about a dozen more for myself, the way I always did.

But I wasn't worried about the criminals as much as

I was curious about how Benson's Burn supplier was handling the news of his death. I imagined that she was rather pleased with it. Not that I would normally do anything that would ever please *her*, but Benson hadn't given me a choice. Still, I couldn't help but feel like my strings had been pulled and that I would have been forced into some sort of confrontation with the vampire sooner or later, even if Catalina hadn't witnessed Troy's murder. But all I could do was wait and see if my theory would turn out to be correct.

So life slowly went back to normal, and I returned to my regular duties at the Pork Pit.

Three days after I'd killed Benson, I was wiping down the counter next to the cash register when the bell over the front door chimed, and a familiar figure strolled inside: Silvio.

I hadn't seen or talked to him since Xavier, Owen, and Phillip whisked him away to the *Delta Queen* to be healed by Jo-Jo, although I'd heard from Phillip that Silvio had been staying on board the riverboat the past few days, getting his strength back. But he looked as cool and collected as ever, in an elegant gray suit and matching shirt and tie. His hair was slicked back into its usual style, and his face and body had filled out again, thanks to all the food I'd been sending over to the riverboat, much to the consternation of Phillip's chef, Gustav.

Silvio looked around the restaurant, staring at the other customers, before smoothing down his tie and heading over to me. He gestured at the stool closest to the cash register.

"May I?" he asked.

"Sure," I replied. "Knock yourself out."

He took a seat. Catalina pushed through the double doors, coming out of the back of the restaurant after taking a break. This was her first day back working her regular shift. When she'd come in at noon, I'd told her that she could take as much time off as she needed, but Catalina had insisted on staying. She said returning to her routine would help her deal with things. I couldn't argue with that, since I was doing the same thing myself. Trying to lose myself in the rhythms of cooking and running the restaurant instead of thinking about what Benson had done to me.

I just hoped that Catalina's recovery wouldn't be as slow as mine.

Catalina's face lit up at the sight of her uncle. She came around the counter and kissed his cheek. Silvio gave her a light, affectionate pat on the shoulder. Catalina grinned at him before moving around the restaurant, seeing to the needs of the other customers. Silvio watched her seat a couple and hand them a pair of menus before turning back to face me. His gray gaze swept over me, lingering on my blue work apron and the sparkly pig pin that I'd hooked on to it.

"You are looking quite well, Gin," he said. "All things considered."

"So are you, Silvio."

He smoothed down his tie again, which no longer had Benson's rune tacked into the middle of it.

"Yes, well, your friend Ms. Deveraux took excellent care of me."

I nodded. "She always does that."

"I want you to know that I offered to compensate her for her services, but she wouldn't take my money," he said, frowning a little, as though the thought distressed him.

Jo-Jo had told me all about Silvio's repeated attempts to pay her for healing him. Even I had been impressed by the dollar amount he'd quoted her. It seemed that Silvio had been saving up for a rainy day, to have that kind of cash stashed away. Then again, he'd worked for Benson. I would have been saving up for a long time too.

I waved my hand. "Don't worry about Jo-Jo. She actually likes patching people up. Besides, she's on my payroll. It's all been taken care of."

He nodded. "I thought as much."

Catalina came back over, and Silvio stopped her and ordered some food. I'd thought that perhaps he'd simply come to check up on his niece, but it looked like he was actually going to eat. Or perhaps he was just biding his time and working up to whatever he really wanted to talk to me about. Either way, I decided to let him stay. He could still use a few more pounds on his lean figure, and one of the Pork Pit's triple chocolate milkshakes was a great way to get started on that.

Sophia fixed Silvio's food, and Catalina set the plates in front of him, which included a grilled cheese sandwich and side orders of onion rings, potato salad, and fried green tomatoes. He washed it all down with the milkshake I made him, and then I gave him a piece of cherry pie topped with vanilla-bean ice cream for dessert, but he merely nibbled on that, claiming that he was full.

In between waiting on the other customers, Catalina chatted with her uncle, laughing and joking with him and me too. With Benson no longer a threat, she seemed to be back to her usual cheerful self, although the darkness in her eyes told me that she was still haunted by what happened to Troy.

Just like I was haunted by what happened to Coral all those years ago. But I'd learned to live with my pain, memories, and regrets, and I hoped that Catalina would too.

Eventually, though, Catalina's shift ended, and she packed up her things to go to class. She kissed Silvio's cheek, waved good-bye to me, and left the restaurant, making the bell on the front door chime on her way out.

"She always told me how much she enjoyed working here," Silvio murmured. "But I never really believed her."

"Why not?"

He shrugged. "I wanted better things for her than working in some greasy dive."

I arched my eyebrows. "No offense taken."

"I meant none."

"And now?"

He shrugged again. "I can see the charm of your establishment."

"Thanks," I drawled. "But don't go overboard with the compliments. They might go to my head or something."

Silvio arched an eyebrow back at me, then carefully, politely, thoughtfully stacked his dirty dishes on top of each other and moved them off to the side on the counter.

He'd brought a silverstone briefcase into the restaurant, which he'd set on the stool next to him. He popped open the top and pulled out an electronic tablet.

"So," he said, staring up at me expectantly, his finger

poised over the screen. "Where shall we begin in organizing your schedule?"

I blinked. "My schedule? What schedule?"

He tapped at something on the tablet, then turned it around where I could see it. The image on the screen looked suspiciously like . . . a calendar. The sort that a businessman might use to keep track of meetings, lunches, and whatnot.

I stared at his suit, then at his briefcase, then at the tablet he was still holding out to me. And I finally got an inkling of why Silvio was really here.

I laughed. "Sorry, Silvio, but I'm not the type who needs or wants an assistant."

He waved his hand, pooh-poohing my objections. "A business owner such as yourself, not to mention a prominent elemental, needs a professional assistant. Trust me on that."

I shook my head. "I'm sorry, but I really don't. Besides, you worked for Benson for years. Don't you want to take a break? Rest and relax and all of that?"

Silvio's index finger *tap-tap-tapp*ed on the tablet, making image after image flash by on the screen. "What do you think I've been doing? I've been sitting on that riverboat for the past few days, and I'm already bored out of my mind. I'm one of those people who need to keep working, Gin."

"And you've decided that you want to work for me?" I shook my head again. "Some folks would say that you had a death wish, Silvio. In case you haven't noticed, I'm not exactly the safest person to be around. And it's only going to get worse, given what I did to Benson. No doubt, the other underworld bosses will see it as the opening salvo in some sort of war against them."

He nodded. "Of course they'll see it that way."

"And here I thought that I was just doing a bit of pest extermination."

Silvio gave me a patronizing look, apparently not getting my joke. Admittedly, it was a bit lame.

"By killing Benson in the manner that you did, you declared yourself to be a major power player in Ashland and worthy of being Mab Monroe's successor. You've thrown your hat into the ring, Gin. There's no taking it back now."

I sighed. "I know. But it had to be done. I couldn't let things keep going on the way they were."

He nodded. "And I believe it was precisely the right action to take. Whatever you think of Beau, everyone knew that he was strong and not someone to be trifled with. Now they'll think the same of you. Trust me. People won't just come here to kill you anymore. They'll want to do business with you too. Perhaps even hire you as the Spider. All that means meetings and a calendar and a schedule to keep."

I groaned.

"And that's why you need me," Silvio continued. "To keep everything organized, but mostly, to be your eyes and ears and keep you apprised of any threats."

"You want to spy on the other underworld bosses for me?"

"I wouldn't call it *spying*. Not exactly. But you'd be surprised how much you can learn by just being someone's assistant, hanging around outside of meetings, chatting with other assistants, and the like."

The truth was that I could use a middleman of sorts, if only to try to warn would-be assassins away from me and the restaurant. But I wasn't about to take advantage of Silvio that way. That would make me no better than Benson, always expecting him to fetch my coat for me.

I shook my head again. "I appreciate the offer, Silvio. Really, I do. But I don't need an assistant. So take this time for yourself. Do the things that you've always wanted to do. You don't owe me anything for saving you, if that's what this is about."

Silvio straightened up, his face as indignant and insulted as if I'd slapped him with a black glove. "Of course I don't owe you anything. Frankly, I didn't expect you to come back for me. It was rather stupid of you to do so, especially for me, a complete stranger. And you should have just let Mr. Lane put a couple of bullets into Beau's head, instead of facing him down yourself. In the future, I hope that you will refrain from taking such foolish risks. I would hate to have to search for another employer."

The chiding note in his voice reminded me of Fletcher. I raised my eyebrows at him, and Silvio calmed down.

"But I do owe you for Catalina," he said. "I told Laura that I would watch out for her, and I haven't exactly done a terrific job of it. But you saved Catalina from Benson, you protected her when I could not, and I am more grateful for that than you will ever realize. I always pay my debts, Gin. You should know that about me."

"I would have helped Catalina regardless of you or anything else."

He smiled a little. "I know that too. It's why I'm going to work for you instead of just paying you off."

"Lucky me," I murmured.

But Silvio wasn't about to be denied. He gestured down at his tablet again. "Now that that's all settled, why don't we get started?"

⁕ 30 ⁕

I protested again that I didn't need an assistant, or whatever Silvio saw himself as, but he remained stubbornly steadfast in his insistence that I did. Luckily, some new customers came into the restaurant to take me away from him. I thought that would be the end of things, but he didn't leave. Instead, he picked up his stuff and settled himself in an out-of-the-way booth next to the restrooms, alternately texting on his phone and tapping on his tablet.

I had no idea what he was so furiously typing, but I didn't have the heart to send him away. If he truly was trying to organize my schedule, it would probably go something like this.

Eat breakfast. Come to work. Check for booby traps. Open restaurant. Ask Sophia to dispose of the latest bodies in the cooler. Kill would-be assassins during afternoon trash run.

And so on and so forth.

But Silvio seemed happy enough doing whatever he

was doing, so I left him alone. Besides, I had other things to worry about—like the black Audi.

I'd been keeping an eye out for it, wondering when the occupants would make an appearance at the Pork Pit. And when it pulled up to the curb and sat there idling, it seemed as though its occupants were debating whether they really wanted to come inside. Oh, she wanted to come inside, all right. And I wanted her to.

I wanted to confront my new enemy and my oldest problem face-to-face.

I was mildly surprised that it had taken her this long to make an appearance, but I was grateful for the last few days of solitude. I finished wiping down the table I'd been working on, then wandered over behind the counter to where Sophia was chopping up some onions.

"Two women are going to come into the restaurant," I said. "An elemental and a giant. Just keep cooking. Don't pay any attention to them, no matter what happens."

"Who are they?" Sophia rasped.

"They're connected to this whole Benson mess. I can handle them. Nobody you need to worry about today. Okay?"

She nodded and kept chopping onions.

As if on cue, the bell over the front door chimed, and two women walked into the restaurant: the giant and the auburn-haired woman.

One of the waitresses went over to seat them and take their order. The waitress handed me the ticket for their burgers, potato salads, onion rings, and sweet iced teas, and I spent the next few minutes fixing their food. Once again, the giant stared around the restaurant, her cold, flat eyes assessing everyone inside. Her gaze lingered on Silvio, who was seated three booths away, but he kept fiddling with his tablet as though he were totally engrossed in it, and her eyes moved past him.

The auburn-haired woman kept glancing at me, not being nearly as subtle as she was the first time she'd eaten in my joint, but I paid no attention to her, as though I didn't notice her stares. When I was finished with their food, I handed the plates off to the waitress, who served them. Then I sat down on my stool behind the cash register, reading my way toward the conclusion of *You Only Live Twice*, as if they were just another pair of customers.

They weren't, of course, especially since I was certain that both of the women wanted me dead. Well, the feeling was definitely mutual. But this was their chess game, and I would play along—for now.

I stayed by the cash register and read my book while the two women ate. Eventually, they began talking to each other in low voices. Silvio started typing and tapping even more furiously on his tablet. I had no idea what he was doing, and I was too concerned about this new threat to care.

The women finished their food, but they dawdled over their dirty dishes, chatting as though they were having the grandest time in the world. Maybe they were. Or maybe they were just waiting for me to notice them. Well, they'd waited long enough.

I was about to get off my stool, go over, and formally introduce myself when the giant slid out of the booth and came over to the cash register, the order ticket in her hand. She handed me some bills, telling me to keep the change. I thought that she would walk away, but instead, she jerked her thumb over her shoulder.

"She'd like a word with you," the giant said.

"I just bet she would."

The giant blinked, apparently surprised by my snide tone, but I decided to oblige her. The giant stayed by the cash register, so I walked around the counter, went over, and slid into the booth across from the auburn-haired woman. She looked at me, and I stared back at her.

Silence.

All around us, the other diners kept eating, talking, and laughing, but the auburn-haired woman and I sat in quiet contemplation, studying each other the way enemies do.

Heart-shaped mouth. Perfect cheekbones. Vivid green eyes with large black pupils. Just the right amount of understated makeup to bring out her pale, milky complexion.

Up close, she was even more stunning than I remembered, easily one of the most beautiful women I'd ever seen, right up there with Roslyn. She was dressed in an expensive white business suit that showed off the toned, sleek lines of her body, but my gaze locked onto her most important feature.

Her rune necklace.

She hadn't been wearing it the first time she was in here, but a thick silverstone chain ringed her neck now, with a large pendant nestled in the hollow of her throat, a crown with a flame in the center of it. The rune for raw, destructive power, the same symbol that had been stamped into the Burn pills. The crown was also crafted out of silverstone, but it was the flame in the center of the design that caught my eye, since it was made out of a single large emerald.

But the more I looked at the rune, the more I stared at her, the more I saw another rune, another face, another woman. One who was all too familiar to me. I imagined that this new version was going to be just as much trouble for me as the last one was—maybe even more so.

"It's so lovely to finally meet you in person, Ms. Blanco," the woman purred, her voice low, smooth, and silky, just like her mother's had been. "I've heard so much about you and your restaurant. I was delighted to find that the food was as good as people have claimed it was."

It was a backhanded compliment, if that, the sort of zinger that high-class society folks deliver with pomp and panache, as if life is a game they can win by putting people down to score the most points.

Then she smiled, as if she'd thought of that half-assed insult especially for me, and I flashed back to the last time and place I'd seen that soft, sly expression on her crimson lips: Mab Monroe's funeral.

Back then, she'd been wearing a black veil to partially obscure her face, and I hadn't had a clue to her identity, but I knew exactly who she was now. I'd had my suspicions the second I'd picked up her fork the first time she'd come into the Pork Pit, although reading through Benson's ledger had confirmed many of my theories, in addition to finally giving me her full name.

"I'm sure you're wondering who I am and why I wanted to talk to you," she said.

"Not particularly. Lots of folks like to come in and

chitchat with me about all sorts of things. The weather, sports, books I'm reading, all their best-laid plans to kill me. Some of them are more entertaining than others. You haven't really impressed me so far, either with your wit or with the lousy tip you told your bodyguard to leave."

Her smile melted a little at my snarky sarcasm, but she quickly turned the wattage back up on it. This was her moment, her time to shine, her grand entrance, and she wasn't going to let me ruin it.

She really should have known better—just like her mother before her.

She drew in a breath. "I'm—"

"There's no need for introductions. I know *exactly* who you are," I said, cutting her off.

Her face crinkled a faint bit in displeasure. I was ruining her shocking reveal. "You do?"

"Oh, yeah," I drawled. "It's not every day that you meet someone with the same three initials. M.M.M. Quite distinctive."

Her eyes glittered. "Yes, but do you know what those initials stand for?"

"Of course," I replied. "It was written down in Beauregard Benson's little black book, so to speak. He might have been a sick son of a bitch, but he was an excellent records keeper, especially when it came to his drug empire and all of his buyers and suppliers. You were the focus of his most recent entries. Benson made several pages of notes, speculating on how you had perfected your Burn formula and wondering if you had ever tested it on yourself or your giant friend there. I have to admit that I'm a mite curious about that myself."

She didn't respond, so I gave her a winning smile and held out my hand to her to shake.

"But you're right. It *is* so very nice to finally meet you in person," I said. "Madeline Magda Monroe."

* 31 *

M.M. Monroe didn't like having her thunder stolen, not at all, but she recovered quickly. She leaned back, crossed her arms over her chest, and gave me a cool, assessing look.

"I'm sure that you know my name too," I said, dropping my hand down to the table and mimicking her posture. "It's Gin, like the liquor. I don't think that we should stand on formality, do you? Not after all our families have been through together over the years."

She smiled again. "Like the fact that you killed my mother?"

Mab's was the face I saw when I looked at Madeline. She had the same cheekbones, the same nose, and the same curve to her lips as the Fire elemental, if not Mab's coppery red hair and absolute black eyes. Finn and I had long thought that M.M. Monroe had to be some sort of relative of Mab's, if only given the last name, and we'd considered the possibility that Mab might have had a child, even though Finn hadn't been able to find any birth records. But it was easy for me to tell that Madeline was Mab's daughter, one who looked to be about my age, perhaps a year or two older.

I shrugged. "It was no less than she deserved, since she killed my mother and my older sister and almost succeeded in doing the same to me and my baby sister when we were kids. Besides, you didn't seem too broken up about your mama's death at her funeral. From what I remember, you weren't weeping and wailing. I can't be sure because of that veil you were wearing, but I sort of imagine that you were smiling the whole time."

This time, Madeline shrugged. "My mother and I didn't see eye-to-eye on much. Things would have soon gotten . . . difficult between us, if you hadn't killed her when you did."

In other words, the two of them would have come to blows and most likely engaged in an elemental duel to see who maintained control of Mab's empire. Yeah, I could see that happening. And I had to wonder who would have been left standing in the end. Mab had been extremely powerful, but Madeline seemed to have plenty of elemental juice in her own right.

"Either way, it hardly matters now, does it?" Madeline said, waving her hand and making a silverstone-and-emerald ring sparkle on her right hand. It too was shaped like her crown-and-flame rune. "My mother is dead."

"And you've finally come to Ashland to lay claim to your inheritance."

She smiled again, leaned forward, and steepled her

hands together on the tabletop. "Something that I have *you* to thank for, Gin. My inheritance might have been tied up in the courts for years if you hadn't uncovered my mother's will during that whole nasty situation at the Briartop museum. For that, you have my thanks."

I didn't want her damn thanks. I didn't want anything from her. But this was another part of the chess game between us, so I decided to match her move for move.

"What can I say?" I drawled. "I'm all for the truth coming out."

Her smile widened, revealing a hint of teeth that were as white as her suit.

"Well, now that we know each other, why don't you introduce me to your friend?"

I gestured at the giant, who was leaning against the counter by the cash register and keeping an eye on Sophia. Apparently, she knew how dangerous the Goth dwarf could be, although Sophia was completely ignoring her and still chopping onions.

Madeline gestured at the giant, who strolled over toward us. "As you noted before, this is my personal bodyguard, Emery Slater."

Surprise surged through me. Slater? This just kept getting better and better.

"As in Elliot Slater, I presume," I murmured.

The giant's eyes were cold and empty as she stared me down. "He was my uncle."

"And Gin killed him too," Madeline said, clasping her hands together again. "Isn't it funny how much family history there is among the three of us?"

"Oh, it's just a laugh riot," I drawled.

Madeline and Emery stared at me, but I focused on Madeline. She was the real threat.

"Well, I hope that you've enjoyed your time in Ashland so far. I've given you quite the tour of the city these past few days, what with y'all following me around in your car."

Madeline blinked. Apparently, she hadn't thought that I'd connected them with the black Audi.

"How long have you been in town? I know that you've been supplying Benson with his Burn pills for several weeks now. He was trying to reverse-engineer your formula, you know. But he couldn't quite figure out what your secret ingredient is."

She let out a pleased laugh. "Sounds like you've been investigating me, Gin."

"Nothing so intense as that. You give me too much credit."

"Oh, no. I haven't given you nearly *enough* credit. You see, I had hopes that you would kill Beauregard, but I admit that I was doubtful about whether you could actually do it."

So I'd been right about my strings being pulled and there being another player in this game between Benson and me. I thought back to the night that Troy was murdered and how I'd seen the Audi outside the parking garage. And I realized exactly who Madeline and Emery had been following then.

My eyes narrowed. "You knew that Bria had her sights set on Benson. That's why you were following her around the night I spotted you outside the parking garage. You wanted to see what she was up to regarding Benson."

Madeline beamed at me. "Clever too. People really do underestimate you, Gin. But yes, you're exactly right. Your sister is quite formidable. Benson was rather worried about her and what she might dig up on him. He expressed his concerns to me more than once, so I suggested that he be more . . . proactive about the situation. Really send your sister a message."

My stomach twisted. "You're the one who told him to kill her informant Max."

Madeline gave a delicate shrug of her shoulders. "I merely suggested that he take action. Nothing more, nothing less."

A sick, sick feeling filled my stomach at the thought that I'd been indirectly responsible for Max's gruesome murder. That Madeline had used him—and Bria—as a way to get to me.

"Of course, given the number of men Benson had sent after you these past several months, I was hoping that you would take the initiative and kill him yourself, thus solving both of our problems. But that didn't look like it was going to happen. So I decided to . . . accelerate things." Madeline favored me with a thin smile.

"By having Benson kill a low-level informant? What did you think that would get you?"

"Why, it made your sister, the good detective, become even more determined to bring him down," she replied, as if the answer should have been obvious. "I knew that Benson would never allow himself to be arrested and that your sister equally wouldn't give up until she'd nabbed him. Something would have to give, and I knew that something would be *you*, Gin. That you would get involved somewhere along the way. Although I have to admit that having your waitress witness one of Benson's executions was just the icing on the cake."

I didn't respond, my mind whirling at her subtle, skillful machinations—and how effective they'd turned out to be.

Madeline leaned forward, her green gaze fixed on my gray one, as though we were two conspirators discussing our secret, hush-hush plans. "You see, Gin, I've been studying you these last several months, ever since I spotted you at my mother's funeral. You really are something of a reluctant assassin, aren't you? You never kill people anymore unless they target you first . . . or go after your family."

I had to work very hard to keep from showing any sort of emotion. This bitch had set up Max and even Bria to be killed just so that I would get involved and take care of Benson for her. I thought that I was playing chess with her, but Madeline had really been toying with me this whole fucking time.

I'd always thought that Mab was the most dangerous person I'd ever known, but I was beginning to realize that Madeline was just as deadly, because she was even more devious than her mother. Mab had taken control of Ashland and kept it by ruling with an iron, flaming fist. Everyone knew that crossing Mab would lead to a quick, painful, Fire-filled death.

But Madeline . . . Oh, she would kill people outright, just like her mother had, but I got the impression that what she really enjoyed was playing games—whispering a few words into the ears of the wrong people at the right time and then standing back and watching as the poison promise of her web took shape, trapping everyone in its deadly threads.

One I hadn't even realized I was stuck in until this very moment.

But I couldn't help but ask some of the many questions on my mind. "And what does my killing Benson get you? How do you benefit?"

She gave another delicate shrug of her shoulders. "Not having to go through a middleman, for starters. Benson gave me far less than what my drugs were worth, and I knew that he was trying to reverse-engineer my formula for Burn, even going so far as to insist that I share my ingredients list with him. It was becoming most annoying. So I decided to cut him out and take control of the drug trade in Ashland for myself. And you made it all possible."

My stomach twisted again at how easily she'd played me, but all I could do now was try to figure out what her endgame was and how to keep her from using or hurting anyone else I cared about.

"Benson forced me to take one of your Burn pills, you know," I said, trying another tactic. "As one of his so-called experiments. He wanted to record its effect on me. I was quite surprised to feel elemental magic running through my veins, along with whatever chemicals are in the drug."

"Oh, that's thanks to me," Madeline said in an airy tone. "I put a few drops of my own blood into every batch of the drug. I knew it was the one ingredient that Benson couldn't figure out and the one that he could never replicate. My magic is what gives the drug its special . . . kick."

"Your acid magic," I said in a blunt tone.

It had taken me a while to figure out exactly what kind of magic she had, but acid was an offshoot of Fire, Mab's power, so it made sense that Mab's daughter could be gifted in acid magic. And it would certainly explain the unending burning sensation I'd felt when Benson forced me to swallow that Burn pill. I'd never met anyone with acid magic before, though. It was a rare ability, as rare as me being gifted in two elemental areas.

Madeline smiled even wider. "Very clever of you to figure that out, Gin. Would you like a demonstration too? Here. Let me show you."

I tensed, but Madeline only reached for the mug she'd been drinking her coffee out of, dragging it closer. It was a sturdy cup, made of solid ceramic that would survive being dropped on the floor. Madeline held her finger up over it. Her eyes flashed a bright, wicked green, and I felt a gust of magic roll off her, the same powerful, burning sensation that had coated her fork that first day she came into the restaurant.

Pale green drops of liquid oozed out of Madeline's index finger, *drip-drip-dripp*ing onto the surface of the cup. One drop was enough to cause acrid green smoke to rise from the white ceramic surface. Two drops made it start to bubble, and three drops made it start to melt. A minute later, the handle of the mug collapsed down into the rest of the ceramic puddle, and her acid was also starting to eat into the actual surface of the table.

"Anyway, I'm so glad that we were able to have this little chat and clear the air," Madeline purred. "But I'm afraid that I really must be going. I'm finally moving into the Monroe family mansion, and I want to be there to oversee everything. Plus, there just always seems to be some sort of paperwork to sign, per my new lawyer."

A horrible, horrible thought occurred to me. "Your new lawyer?"

"Well, I suppose that's not quite right, since he's someone we're all quite familiar with."

Madeline waved her hand at the window. I looked through the glass. One of the back doors of the Audi opened, and a man got out of the car. He wore a suit and was clutching a silverstone briefcase, like any other sixty-something businessman. But his most distinctive feature was the elegant mane of silver hair that swirled around his head, seeming at odds with his smooth, unlined face.

Jonah McAllister, Mab's old lawyer and my personal nemesis.

McAllister saw me staring at him and gave me a mock salute before bowing low. Malice glimmered in his cold brown eyes, and I knew that he was enjoying my absolute shock and surprise at this little bombshell that Madeline had just dropped in my lap.

"I have big plans for Jonah," Madeline said. "No one knows more about my mother's business dealings than he does. He's been helping me get up to speed on all *sorts* of things in Ashland."

I didn't respond. I couldn't. Not at that moment. Instead, I looked at the three of them in turn.

Madeline Monroe. Emery Slater. Jonah McAllister.

My worst nightmare come back to life.

I stayed rooted in my seat, but Madeline gracefully slid out of the booth and got to her feet.

"As I said before, it was so lovely to meet you in person, Gin. I'm sure that we'll be seeing more of each other very soon."

She gave me one more smile, then headed for the door, which Emery was already opening for her. My two newest enemies strolled out into the fall night to greet my oldest one. As the door shut behind them, the bell attached to it chimed merrily, as if announcing the start of a new boxing round.

Ding-ding-ding.

Madeline had definitely landed the first punch. All I could do was hope that I could withstand the rest of the fight—and the knockout blow that was coming sooner rather than later.

32

Their business concluded, Madeline, Emery, and Jonah got into the Audi and drove away.

I sat in the booth for several minutes after they left, thinking about my conversation with Madeline and all the not-so-veiled threats on both sides. Silvio cleared his throat, then got up, walked over, and slid into the opposite side of the booth from me. He watched what was left of the ceramic mug continue to bubble as the green acid burned through it and the tabletop.

"I couldn't help but overhear your conversation with Ms. Monroe," he murmured. "As well as her earlier one with Ms. Slater."

"You couldn't help it?"

He shrugged. "Vampiric hearing has its uses."

I didn't respond. Silvio cleared his throat again.

"Obviously, she wants to kill you," he said. "But she also wants to wipe out everyone and everything that you care about to send a message to everyone else in Ashland. She wants to hurt you in the worst way possible. So does the giant. They were talking about their plans for you during dinner. Monroe wants to make an example out of you to the entire underworld, so that she can more easily take control of things. She's not going to kill you immediately. She wants to make you suffer first. She wants to eat away at you a little bit at a time, much like the acid on that cup, until there's nothing left but a brittle shell that she can easily smash and destroy at her leisure."

"I would expect nothing less from the daughter of Mab Monroe."

Silvio shifted in his seat. "Not just Mab Monroe."

My eyes narrowed. "What do you mean by that?"

He looked around the restaurant, making sure that no one was listening to us, then leaned forward. I did the same.

"I heard her talking to Beau the first time she came to the mansion to do business with him," Silvio said in a low voice. "He knew that she was Mab's daughter, but she was really trying to impress him, so she told him about her father: Elliot Slater."

I couldn't keep my mouth from gaping open at the revelation. "Elliot Slater was Madeline's *father*?"

Silvio shrugged again. "Well, I gather it was in genetic material only. Apparently, he and Mab had a victory celebration one night when he was drunk, and she was thinking about what sort of man might give her a strong, worthy heir to the Monroe family name. So she decided on him. That's the story that Madeline told Beau. She made it sound like it was a rather spur-of-the-moment sort of thing on Mab's part. But here Madeline is, all the same."

So not only did Madeline have magic, but she also had giant blood running through her veins, which meant that she was even stronger than I'd feared.

Silvio didn't say anything else, although he kept his gray gaze focused on me. He knew what Madeline's coming to town meant for me. No doubt, he knew some other little tidbits about the acid elemental too, since he'd watched Benson deal with her over the past several weeks. Maybe Silvio was right. Maybe I did need an assistant after all.

I roused myself from my troubled musings and stared at him. "That file of information that you gave me on Benson. Is that something you'd like to do again?"

"What do you mean?"

"I mean that I want to know everything there is to know about Madeline Magda fucking Monroe," I growled.

I didn't add that I would need the information if I had any hopes of figuring out what her next move was—and how I could kill the bitch.

Silvio nodded. "I did something similar for Beau. He was insistent on my compiling very thorough dossiers on all his enemies. He wanted to know just as much about them as he did about his drugs and experiments. It was actually one of the few parts of my work that I liked. I've always enjoyed research. In another life, I might have become a librarian, if you can imagine that, maybe even worked in Cypress Mountain or somewhere like that."

Oh, I could more than imagine it. Silvio had the kind

of sharp, orderly, analytical mind that I'd associate with a librarian or a researcher. Well, I was going to put that big brain of his to good use.

"You still want a job with me?"

He nodded.

"Well, you've got one," I said. "Start digging. I want to know all about her, Emery Slater, McAllister, and everyone they have working for or with them. Coordinate with Finn. He'll help you. I want a preliminary report by the end of the week. I will pay you, of course, and reimburse you for any bribes or other expenses that you have."

I quoted him a figure that made Silvio blink in surprise. Apparently, Benson had never paid him that much, but I knew that any info he could find for me on Madeline, Emery, Jonah, and what they were planning would be worth more than a briefcase full of diamonds.

Silvio nodded, typing down some notes on his tablet. "It will be my pleasure."

I let out a bitter laugh. "Oh, I doubt that there will be anything pleasurable about this, when it's all said and done."

Silvio left, with a promise to return when I opened back up in the morning. He seemed almost giddy at the prospect of working for me. Well, what passed for giddy for him, which was a mild smile and a bit of spring in his step. I supposed that his enthusiasm was good, since I couldn't muster a single scrap of it right now.

My other customers finished their meals, paid, and left, so I sent Sophia and the waitstaff home and closed down the Pork Pit for the night.

I wasn't supposed to be over at Owen's for dinner for another hour, so I spent that time driving aimlessly, my mind still on my disturbing conversation with Madeline Magda Monroe.

Silvio was right. She wanted to kill me, and so did Emery Slater. In a way, I couldn't blame them for it. I had killed members of both of their families, after all, even if Mab was the one who'd started things, by murdering my mother and my older sister all those years ago.

As for Jonah McAllister, well, teaming up with them would be a chance to save his own miserable hide from the underworld bosses who wanted him dead, and it would give him another shot at taking me down. Win-win for the slimy lawyer.

But the more I thought about the three of them, the more a sinking sense of déjà vu washed over me. This time last year, I was slowly being drawn into a battle with Elliot and Mab. I'd eliminated them, although I'd barely managed to survive the deadly confrontations myself. And now the next generation of Monroes and Slaters had stepped up to take their place and continue their blood feud with the Snow family. I'd have to be on my guard now more than ever before. So would the rest of my friends and family.

But brooding about what Madeline might be up to wouldn't do me any good, and it was time for me to show up at Owen's, so I put aside my worries as best I could and steered in that direction.

It was almost nine when I stopped my car in front of Owen's mansion. The house was dark, except for a light burning in the kitchen. Owen had said that Eva was spending the night at Violet's, which meant that we'd have the place to ourselves. He was probably in the kitchen, fixing a late supper for us.

I let myself into the house and headed for the kitchen, but the area was empty, with only the small light over the stove turned on.

"Owen?" I called out.

No answer.

He must be waiting in his bedroom for me, reading a book, watching TV, or maybe taking a shower. So I headed down the hallway in that direction, my thoughts turning back to Madeline and her acid magic—

As I passed the downstairs living room, the lights suddenly snapped on, making me freeze in my tracks. What happened next also took me by surprise, although it really shouldn't have, considering that I had been expecting it for days now.

"Happy birthday, Gin!"

My friends and family screamed out the words, blowing horns to punctuate their jubilation as they popped up from their hiding places behind the couches and chairs. A large banner bearing the words they'd just yelled was draped over the TV, while clusters of colorful balloons had been tied to the lamps on the end tables.

All I could do was just stand there in the doorway, blinking at them all with my mouth hanging wide open, like the surprised, clueless idiot I was.

Owen, Finn, Bria, Xavier, Roslyn, Phillip, Eva, Sophia, Jo-Jo and her gentleman friend, Cooper Stills, Violet and her grandfather, Warren T. Fox. They were all there, along with Catalina and Silvio, all of them wearing goofy birthday hats and giving me happy grins. Well, everyone except for Silvio. He looked a little chagrined by the red-and-white polka-dot hat perched on top of his head and the matching horn clutched in his hand. Yeah. I would have been too.

Owen grabbed my hand and tugged me into the living room. One by one, my friends came over, hugged me, and wished me a happy birthday. I grinned and smiled and made the appropriate oohing and aahing noises at the pile of presents on the coffee table in front of the TV and the tiers of frosted chocolate cupcakes on another table.

Finn gave me a smug, satisfied grin. "Did we surprise you? C'mon. You can admit it. You didn't think that I would throw the party on your *actual* birthday, did you?"

I blinked. I hadn't realized that today was actually the day until right now, but I turned up the wattage on my forced smile so he wouldn't see that I'd forgotten my own birthday.

"Yeah, you got me good this year."

Owen came over and slung his arm around my shoulder, pulling me close. "I thought you would figure it out as soon as I called you this morning and asked you to come over tonight. But Finn was right. You looked totally surprised."

"I was," I admitted, slipping my arm around his waist. "I told you that Finn *always* manages to surprise me. And he's not the only one these days."

Owen gave me a quizzical look, wondering who else I was referring to, but I didn't feel like talking about Madeline tonight, so I stood on my tiptoes and kissed his cheek instead. Owen smiled back at me, and then we were caught up in a conversation with Bria, Roslyn, Xavier, and Phillip. Then one with Jo-Jo and Cooper. And so on.

Finally, my friends made me sit down on the couch in front of the table full of presents.

"Here," Owen said. "Open mine first."

He handed me a square, flat white box. I untied the violet ribbon and pulled the top off to find a black velvet box nestled inside the first one. I cracked open that box, expecting some sort of jewelry, given the shape. It was jewelry, all right.

A necklace—a spider rune necklace.

My breath caught in my throat at the sight of the silverstone pendant lying on top of the black velvet. Somehow, some way, Owen had made a perfect replica of the spider rune pendant that I'd worn when I was a kid, the one that Mab had melted into my hands all those years ago. Not only that, but each one of the tiny links in the delicate silverstone chain was also shaped like my spider rune, although they were much, much smaller than the main pendant.

"Well?" Owen asked, a hesitant note in his voice. "Do you like it? I've been working on it for a while now, and I thought tonight would be the right time to finally give it to you."

"It's perfect," I whispered, stroking my hand over the rune, my fingers trembling just a bit. "Absolutely perfect."

Owen gently took the box from me. "Here. Let's put it on and see how it looks."

My hair was pulled back into a ponytail, so he was able to easily drape the necklace around my throat and hook it together in the back. A moment later, the spider rune slid into the hollow of my throat, the slight weight feeling odd after so many years of not wearing it. I got to my feet and went over to the mirror on one of the walls.

The silverstone gleamed against my skin, the spider rune winking at me like an old friend. It was a little disconcerting, seeing my rune as an actual object after all the years of it being branded into my hands. But it was also a welcome feeling.

"What do you think?" Owen asked.

"It's perfect," I repeated in a much stronger voice. "Absolutely perfect."

I loved the necklace, truly, I did, and it was one of the most thoughtful presents that anyone had ever given me. No doubt, Owen thought that he'd been giving me a cherished piece of my past by crafting the necklace. He had, but he'd also given me something even more important for my future: a weapon to use against Madeline Monroe.

Because the entire necklace was made of silverstone, which meant that it would absorb my magic, just like my spider rune ring, and I planned on stuffing the metal with as much power as it would hold. I had a feeling that I'd need the extra reservoir of magic in the coming days.

Behind me, Finn let out a long, loud, put-upon sigh. "Way to overachieve, Grayson," he muttered. "You totally ruined the new toaster I got her."

I laughed, then turned, wrapped my arms around Owen's neck, and kissed him for all I was worth.

"Enough of *that*," Phillip called out. "You can thank him in private later."

Owen and I broke apart, laughing.

My friends gathered around me, oohing and aahing over the necklace. The only one who didn't join in the revelry was Silvio. He sipped a glass of ginger ale and stood in the corner, as calm and stoic as ever. Every once in a while, he would give me a measured look. He knew what was coming as well as I did: Madeline Magda Monroe wanting to burn my world to a crisp before she killed me. But for tonight, he was willing to ignore it.

And so was I.

So I laughed and smiled and ate birthday cupcakes and opened the gag gifts that everyone had gotten for me, including Finn, who had somehow found a toaster that featured a giant black spider perched in a web on the side. I promised him that I'd use it at the Pork Pit. I pushed all thoughts of Madeline from my mind and savored this time with my friends and family.

Because I had a sinking feeling that this would be the last birthday I ever celebrated with them.

But there would be time enough to worry about Madeline, Emery, Jonah, and their schemes tomorrow. Tonight I would enjoy my birthday and remember that this was what was important—my friends, my family, and the memories we made together.

They were what mattered, they were the ones I was determined to protect, and they were what I would be fighting for in the days and weeks to come.

Happy birthday to me.

Turn the page for a sneak peek at the
next book in the Elemental Assassin series

by Jennifer Estep

Coming soon from Pocket Books

�֍ 1 �֍

It was torture.

Watching your mortal enemy get everything she'd ever wanted was torture, pure and simple.

Madeline Magda Monroe stood off to one side of a wooden podium, her hands clasped in front of her strong, slender body and a serious, thoughtful expression on her beautiful face. Next to her, a city official sporting a brown plaid jacket and a gray handlebar mustache droned on and on and *on* about all the good things that her mother, Mab Monroe, had done for Ashland.

Please. The only good thing Mab had ever done in her entire life was die. Something that I'd been all too happy to help her with.

Then again, that's what assassins did, and I was the Spider, one of the best.

Madeline's crimson lips quirked, revealing a hint of her dazzling white teeth, as though she found the same irony in the speaker's words that I did. She knew precisely what a sadistic bitch her mother had been, especially since she was cut from the exact same bloodstained cloth.

Still, even I had to admit that Madeline made an angelic figure, standing there so calmly, so serenely, in her tailored white pantsuit, as though she were truly enjoying listening to all of the prattle about Mab's supposed charitable works. It was high noon, and the bright sun brought out the coppery streaks in Madeline's thick auburn hair, making it seem as if her long, flowing locks were strings of glowing embers about to burst into flames. But Madeline didn't have her mama's famed elemental Fire power. She had something much rarer and far more dangerous: acid magic.

Madeline shifted on her white stilettos, making the sun shimmer on the silverstone necklace circling her delicate throat—a crown with a flame-shaped emerald set in the center of it. A ring on her right hand featured the same design. Madeline's personal rune, the symbol for raw, destructive power, eerily similar to the ruby sunburst necklace that Mab had worn before I'd destroyed it—and her.

Just staring at Madeline's rune was enough to make my hands curl into tight fists, my fingers digging into the scars embedded deep in my palms—each a small circle surrounded by eight thin rays. A spider rune, the symbol for patience.

Mab had given me the scars years ago, when she melted my spider rune necklace into my palms, forever marking me. I just wondered how many more scars her daughter would add to my collection before our family feud was settled.

"I'd say that she looks like the cat who ate the canary, but we both know that she'd just use her acid magic to obliterate the poor thing." The suave, drawling voice somehow made the words that much snarkier.

I looked to my left at the man who was leaning against the maple tree that shaded us both, his shoulders relaxed, his hands stuck in his pants pockets, his long legs crossed at the ankles. His hair was a dark walnut, blending into the trunk of the tree behind him, but amusement glinted in his green eyes, making them stand out despite the dappled shadows that danced over his handsome face. His ash-gray Fiona Fine suit draped perfectly over his muscular figure, giving him a casual elegance that was the complete opposite of my tense, rigid, watchful stance.

Then again, Finnegan Lane, my foster brother, always looked as cool as an ice-cream sundae, whether he was out for a seemingly simple stroll in the park, wheeling and dealing as an investment banker, or peering through a sniper's scope, ready to put a bullet through someone's skull.

Finn arched an eyebrow at me. "Well, Gin? What do you say?"

I snorted. "Oh, Madeline wouldn't use her acid magic herself. She'd manipulate someone else into killing the bird *and* the cat for her—and have the poor fool convinced that it had been his idea all the while."

He let out a low chuckle. "Well, you have to admire that about her."

I snorted again. "That she's a master manipulator who likes to make people dance to the strings that she so gleefully wraps around them before they even realize what's happening? Please. The only thing I admire about her is that she's managed to keep a mostly straight face through this entire farce of a dedication."

Finn and I were standing at the back of a crowd that had gathered in a park in Northtown, the rich, fancy, highfalutin part of Ashland that was home to the wealthy, powerful, and extremely dangerous. The park was exactly what you'd expect to find in this part of Northtown: lots of perfectly landscaped green lawns and towering trees with thick tangles of branches, along with an enormous playground that featured sandboxes, seesaws, swing sets, and a merry-go-round. It was a picturesque scene, especially given the beautiful, blue-sky October afternoon and the rich, deep, earthy scent of autumn that swirled through the air on the faint breeze. But the pleasantly warm temperature and cheery rays streaming through the burnt-orange leaves over my head did absolutely nothing to improve my mood.

At my harsh words, a couple of people in the crowd turned to give me annoyed looks, but a cold glare from me had them easing away and facing the podium again.

Finn let out another low chuckle. "You and your people skills never cease to amaze me."

"Shut up," I muttered.

As the speaker droned on, my wintry gray gaze swept over the park, and I thought about the last time I'd been here—and the men I'd killed. A vampire and a couple of giants, some of Mab's minions, who were torturing and about to murder an innocent bartender before I'd intervened. The seesaws, the swing sets, the merry-go-round, the lawn. Men had died all over this park, and I'd even drawn my rune in one of the sandboxes in a dare to Mab to come find me, the Spider, the elusive assassin who was causing her such consternation.

And now here I was again, months later, confronted with the next Monroe who wanted to do me in.

Sometimes I wondered if I could ever really escape the past and all the consequences of it. Mab murdering my mother and my older sister, then trying to kill me and my younger sister, Bria, leaving me alone, injured, and homeless. Fletcher Lane, Finn's dad, taking me in and training me to be an assassin. My finally killing Mab earlier this year. All the underworld bosses who'd been trying to murder me ever since then.

The city official finally wrapped up his tediously long speech and gestured at Madeline. She stepped forward, reached up, and took hold of a long black rope attached to an enormous white cloth that had been draped over the wrought-iron gate that arched over the park entrance. Madeline smiled at the crowd, pausing just a moment for dramatic effect, before she yanked on the rope, ripping away the cloth, while giving an elaborate flourish with her free hand.

Fancy, curlicued letters spelled out the new name in the black metal arch: *Monroe Memorial Park*.

I glared up at the sign, wishing I had one of the blacksmith hammers that my lover, Owen Grayson, used in his forge, so I could kneecap the gate, send it crashing to the ground, and then knock out each and every one of those damn letters in the toothy smile of the arch. Especially the ones in *Monroe*.

But of course, I couldn't do that. Not now. Maybe late

tonight, when the park was nice and deserted, and there was no one around to see me vent my pent-up rage on an innocent sign.

This wasn't the first dedication I'd attended in the past few weeks. After finally making her grand appearance in Ashland back in September, Madeline had wasted no time in claiming her millions in inheritance as M.M. Monroe, moving into Mab's mansion, and letting everyone know that she intended to pick up all of her mother's business interests, legitimate and otherwise.

I didn't know exactly what her master plan was, but Madeline had set about ingratiating herself with all sorts of civic, charitable, and municipal groups, saying she wanted to continue all of the good works her mother had funded while she was alive. Of course, she was lying through her perfect teeth, since Madeline was no more charitable than her mama had been. But if there was one thing that folks in Ashland responded to, it was cold, hard cash—or at least the promise of it.

And so the dedications had begun. A wing at the Briartop art museum, the new train station, several bridges, a good chunk of the interstate that wrapped around the downtown loop, and now this park. Every few days, it seemed like someone was engraving, chiseling, painting, broadcasting, or proclaiming something else in Mab's name at dear, dutiful daughter Madeline's teary and oh-so-grateful requests.

And I'd been to every single breakfast, luncheon, dinner, tea party, cocktail hour, coffee klatch, barbecue, and fish fry, trying to figure out what my new enemy was up to. But Madeline was an excellent actress; all she did was smile and make small talk and preen for the cameras. Every once in a while, I would catch her staring at me, a small smile playing across her lips, as though my obvious stakeouts were amusing her. Well, that made one of us.

Of course, I had Finn digging into Madeline, trying to find out everything he could about her past, her personal life, and her finances, in hopes that there might be a clue somewhere to what she was planning for me and the rest of the Ashland underworld. But so far, Finn hadn't been able to find anything out of the ordinary. Neither had Silvio Sanchez, my new self-proclaimed personal assistant.

She had no criminal history. No massive debt load. No large cash withdrawals from her bank accounts. No sudden, hostile takeovers of any businesses—legal and otherwise—that Mab had once owned. And perhaps most telling of all, no late-night hush-hush meetings with the underworld bosses.

Yet.

Still, I knew that Madeline had some sort of scheme in mind for me. Impending evil always made my spider rune scars itch in warning—and anticipation of turning the tables on my enemies.

Usually, Madeline ignored me at the dedications, but apparently, she wanted to chitchat today, because she shook hands with the official, then strolled in my direction. And she wasn't alone.

Two people followed Madeline. One of them was a giant bodyguard dressed in a white silk shirt and a black pantsuit, around seven feet tall, with light hazel eyes and a sleek bob of golden hair that curled under at the ends. The sun had reddened her milky cheeks, giving her skin a bit of hot, ruddy color and darkening the faint freckles that dotted her face. The other was a much shorter man, clutching a silverstone briefcase in front of him and dressed in a light gray suit that was even slicker and more expensive than Finn's. A lion's mane of hair wrapped around his head, the arches, dips, and waves as pretty and perfect as icing decorating a cake. His elegant silver coif hinted at his sixty-something age, despite the tight, tan, unlined skin of his face.

Emery Slater and Jonah McAllister. Emery was the niece of Elliot Slater, who'd been Mab's number one giant enforcer before I'd taken credit for killing him, while Jonah had been Mab's personal lawyer and someone whose many crimes I'd taken great pleasure in exposing back during the summer. Needless to say, there was plenty of hate to go around among the three of us.

"Incoming," Finn murmured, straightening up, pushing away from the tree, and moving to stand beside me.

Madeline stopped in front of me, with Emery and Jonah flanking her. The giant and the lawyer both shot me icy glares, but Madeline's features were warm and welcoming as she sidled a little closer to me, a serene smile stretched across her face.

"Why, Gin Blanco," she purred. "How good of you to come out to my little dedication today. And looking so . . . spiffy."

I wore what I always wore: black boots, dark jeans, and a long-sleeved black T-shirt. Next to Madeline and her crisp white suit, I resembled one of the hobos who sometimes slept in this park. Madeline might seem all sweetness and light on the outside, but on the inside, I knew that her heart was as full of venom and as vicious as mine.

"Why, Madeline," I drawled right back at her. "You know that I wouldn't have missed it for the world."

"Yes," she murmured. "You do seem rather fond of popping up everywhere I go."

"Well, you can hardly blame me for that. It's always so very lovely to see someone of Mab's stature honored in such small but touching ways."

Madeline's lips quirked again, as if she were having trouble holding back her laughter at my blatant lie. Yeah. Me too.

"Funny thing, though," I said. "You know what I've noticed? That Mab's name isn't actually *on* anything. It's always just 'Monroe Memorial this' and 'Monroe Memorial that.' Why, if I didn't know better, I'd almost think that *you* were going around town putting *your* name on everything. Instead of your dearly departed mama's."

Finn chuckled. Emery and Jonah shifted their cold stares to him, but Finn kept laughing, completely immune to their dirty looks. He was rather incorrigible that way.

Madeline's green eyes crinkled a bit at the corners, as if she were having to work to maintain her sunny smile. "I think that you're mistaken, Gin. I'm honoring my mother exactly the way that she would have wanted me to."

"And I think that you have as little love for your dead mama as I do," I said. "You couldn't care less about what she would have wanted."

Anger flashed in Madeline's eyes, making them flare an even brighter, more vibrant green, the same intense, wicked color as the acid that she could summon with just a wave of her French-manicured hand. She didn't like me calling her out on her true feelings for her mother, and she especially didn't like the fact that I'd pointed out that the dedications were all about her ego, not Mab's.

Good. I wanted to make her angry. I wanted to piss her off. I wanted to rile her up so much that she couldn't even see straight, much less think straight, especially when it came to me. Because that's when she would make a mistake, and I could finally figure out what her endgame was and how I could stop it before she destroyed everything and everyone I cared about.

"But who am I to judge?" I drawled on. "I wouldn't care either, not if she had been my mother. I guess it's one of those little things that we'll just have to agree to disagree on."

Madeline blinked, and she forced her crimson lips to lift a little higher. "You know, I think that you're right. We are just destined to agree to disagree—about a great many things."

We stared each other down, our stances casual and our features perfectly pleasant but with a deadly, dangerous coldness lurking just below the smooth surfaces.

"Anyway, I'm afraid I must be going," Madeline said, breaking the silence. "I have another dedication to prepare for tomorrow. This one's at the library downtown."

"I'll be there with bells on."

"No," she said in a pleased voice. "I don't think you will. But I do thank you for coming out here today, Gin. As you said, it's always so very lovely to see you."

Madeline smirked at me, then pivoted on her stiletto and moved back toward the podium, shaking hands and thanking everyone for their support and well wishes. Emery and Jonah each gave me one more hostile glare before they trailed after her. Soon the three of them were in the heart of the crowd, with Finn and me standing by ourselves underneath the maple.

"She really is something," Finn said in an admiring tone, his eyes locked onto Madeline's lithe, gorgeous figure.

Despite the fact that he was involved with Bria, Finn was still a shameless flirt who loved to charm every woman who crossed his path. He would never do that with Madeline, for obvious reasons, but that didn't keep him from ogling her for all he was worth. I scoffed and rolled my eyes.

"What?" he protested. "She's like a black widow spider. I can admire the beauty of such a creature, even if I know exactly how deadly it is."

"Only you would think that being eaten during your postcoital bliss would be worth it."

Finn shrugged, then flashed me a mischievous grin. "But what a way to go."

He stared at Madeline another moment before looking over the rest of the crowd. He must have spotted someone he knew, perhaps one of the clients at his bank, because he waved, murmured an excuse to me, and headed in the direction of a wizened old dwarf who was wearing a large pink sun hat and an even larger diamond solitaire that could have had its own zip code. Finn never missed an opportunity to mix business with pleasure, and a moment later, he was attached to the dwarf's side, having winked and wiggled his way past the female giant serving as her bodyguard. Finn gave the elderly woman a charming smile as he bent down and pressed a dainty kiss to her brown, wrinkled hand. Well, at least he was an equal opportunity flirt.

But I continued to watch Madeline, who was still shaking hands and was now standing directly below the arch that bore her family's name. Maybe it was the way the sun was hitting the metal, but the word *Monroe* seemed to flicker and gleam with a particularly intense, sinister light, as though it were made out of some sort of black fire, instead of just sturdy old iron.

Madeline noticed me staring at her and gave me another haughty, pleased smirk before turning her back and ignoring me completely. Emery and Jonah did the same, moving to flank their boss again.

All I could do was stand there and watch my enemy have a grand old time, basking in the warm glow of everyone's collective, attentive goodwill.

Maybe I was wrong when I told Finn that being eaten was the worst part.

Maybe waiting for the black widow to kill you was the real torture.